CONDOR

Other titles by James Grady

MAD DOGS

CONDOR

OUR CONDOR SKY

★

SIX DAYS OF THE CONDOR

★

LAST DAYS OF THE CONDOR

JAMES GRADY

NO EXIT PRESS

OUR
CONDOR
SKY

JAMES GRADY

NO EXIT PRESS

Our Condor Sky

In 1975, generals in the KGB – the Soviet Union's chief spy agency – got their Russian hands on a new Robert Redford movie: *Three Days of The Condor.*

In that movie – produced by Dino De Laurentiis, directed by Sydney Pollack, also starring Faye Dunaway, Cliff Robertson, Max von Sydow, and Tina Chen – screenwriters Lorenzo Semple Jr, and David Rayfiel adapted a slim first novel by a 24-years-old unknown dreamer into a ticking-clock masterpiece propelled by Redford's character of a bookish intelligence analyst who comes back from lunch to the New York office of his obscure secret CIA research department and finds his co-workers murdered.

Redford's CIA codename was Condor.

As Redford/Condor insists to the Faye Dunaway character he kidnaps:

'Listen, I work for the CIA. I'm not a spy. I just read books. We read everything published in the world, and we… we feed the plots – dirty tricks, codes – into a computer, and the computer checks against actual CIA plans and operations. I look for leaks, I look for new ideas. We read adventures and novels and journals… I… I… who'd invent a job like that?'

In 2008, Pulitzer Prize nominated Pete Earley revealed that the movie stunned Russia's KGB generals and convinced them they had fallen behind their CIA foes in a critical espionage endeavor: the work they saw Redford/Condor doing.

So the KGB created their own top secret unit inspired by Condor.

Like in the movie and novel, the KGB headquartered their new secret division in a quiet neighborhood – Flotskaya Street in Moscow – and stuck a phony brass plaque by its front door proclaiming that place to be the 'All-Union Scientific Research Institute of Systems Analysis' – a nonsense name instead of the *real* title of the 'Scientific Research Institute of Intelligence Problems of the First Chief Directorate of the KGB' – known by its Russian initials of NIIRP.

Both the movie and the novel projected Condor's secret department as a small bureaucratic entity with fewer employees than the fingers of your two hands.

The KGB's Condor-inspired NIIRP employed 2,000 Soviet citizens.

Picture a snow-dusted January 2008 night inside Washington, D.C.'s Beltway.

Our dog Jack and, *not quite 60 me*, are shuffling downhill back toward my middle class, two kids launched suburban home and author's lair, when through the darkness, I hear my wife Bonnie Goldstein shouting: 'You've got a phone call!'

That call came from Jeff Stein, a former Vietnam war undercover spy, then a journalist for *Congressional Quarterly* covering espionage. Jeff had Earley's book, and barely contained his excitement as he interviewed me about Condor and the KGB.

I was blown away.

As crime author Mark Terry noted in his 2010 essay about *Condor* for THRILLERS: 100 MUST READS, master novelist John Le Carré says: 'If you write one book that, for whatever reason, becomes iconic, it's an extraordinary blessing.'

Call me blessed.

And come with me to that lucky blessing's beginning in Washington's blustery January of 1971, long before my Condor soared in a now – *so far* – 44 years' flight that's become three novels, a handful of novellas and short stories, a globally famous movie, a filmed TV series – and a template for a fundamentalist assassin and Russian spies.

In 1971, I was a senior at the University of Montana, a Congressional Journalism Intern, one of 20 *Woodstock* (generation) *warriors* brought from America's colleges to Washington to work on Congressional staffs and be night schooled by a scrappy genre of journalists called *investigative reporters*. I lived on A Street, Southeast, six blocks from the white icing Capitol dome in a rented third-floor garret.

Every weekday, I brushed my recently barbered hair, put on my only suit, struggled into a boxy tan overcoat, and walked through winter residential streets to my internship on the staff of a United States Senator.

And every workday, I walked past a white stucco townhouse set back from the corner of A and Fourth Street, Southeast. A short, black-iron fence marked the border between the public sidewalk and that building's domain. Shades obscured the windows. A bronze plaque by the solid black door proclaimed the building as the headquarters of the American Historical Association.

But I never saw anyone go in or out of that building.

Fiction creates alternative realities.

And most fiction is born from a *what-if* question.

Two history-altering *what-if* questions hit me as I walked past that townhouse:

What if it's a CIA front?

What if I came back to work from lunch and everybody in my office was dead?

Logical questions considering those times.

The Cold War ruled. Kim Philby haunted Britain while ghosts of JFK, RFK, MLK and Lee Harvey Oswald made America tremble. *Dr Strangelove* caressed Doomsday weapons. The Soviet Union sprawled as an evil Gulag wasteland behind an Iron Curtain, while Communist China coiled like an invisible dragon behind a Bamboo Wall. J Edgar Hoover's FBI knew everything about everybody. Israeli avengers stalked the globe: they got Eichmann, they could get anybody. Apartheid bedeviled South Africa. South American drug dealers were still 'small-time,' but America's Mafia had a French connection for heroin. 'Terrorists' were often called 'revolutionaries,' whether they wore KKK robes, counterfeit Black Panther berets, the PLO's *kufiah*, or the Weather Underground's long hair and love beads stolen from *the rainbow daze* of the Sixties. Cults like the murderous Manson family stalked our streets. Something enshrouding and protecting our globe called the ozone layer was in jeopardy because of deodorant we sprayed in our armpits. Not far from my rented garret, President Nixon's White House henchmen were formalizing 'dirty tricks' into thuggish crews called 'Plumbers' created for truth suppression, burglaries, and murder. In Vietnam, my generation was in that war's twelfth year of Americans killing and dying.

Only the ignorant weren't paranoid.

My what-if fantasy about a covert CIA office on Capitol Hill had a visible counterpart. A flat-faced, masked windowed, gray concrete building with an always-lowered garage door and an unlabeled slab of gray wood entrance crouched on Pennsylvania Avenue amidst restaurants, bookstores and bars just three blocks from the Capitol dome. Hill staffers shared the common knowledge 'secret' that the building belonged to the FBI, one of their 'translation centers.'

Sure, but what do they really do?

Within pistol range of that secretive FBI fortress sat the townhouse headquarters for Liberty Lobby, an ultra right wing political sect that in coming years would with impunity advertise and sell illegal drugs through the mail – Laetrile, a compound its salesmen claim cures cancer that the great actor Steve McQueen decamped to Mexico to use in the days before cancer killed him.

The last lecturer to my class of interns was Les Whitten, a novelist, translator of French poetry, and partner to Jack Anderson, whose syndicated investigative reporting column ran in almost a thousand newspapers. Unbeknownst to them, Jack and Les were under surveillance by the CIA. Les was the epitome of a muckraker – a term of honor.

I stayed after class that night in a Congressional office to persuade Les to tell me the 'great story' about the CIA he'd told the class he would break the next week.

Allen Ginsberg is *the* Beat poet. He'd seen the best minds of his generation destroyed by madness, dragging themselves through America's streets in search of an angry fix. The horrors of heroin screamed too loudly for the man inside the poet to ignore. Cherubic, bald, bearded, homosexual, *Om*-chanting Ginsberg, hated by conservative cheerleaders of 'law & order,' did what his critics didn't dare: he declared a personal war on heroin. Les's 'great story' concerned Ginsberg's investigations into the CIA's allies in our Southeast Asian war and their ties to the heroin business.

As Les stood in the nighttime halls of a Congressional office building and whispered his news to me, the world trembled.

But I was just a college kid headed back to my hometown of Shelby, Montana, sixty miles east of the Rocky Mountains, thirty miles south of Canada, and a million miles from 'real world' places like New York and London.

My grandfather'd been a cowboy and card shark for saloons, my grandmother was a polio-crippled midwife who'd seen eight of her own children survive, including my mother and her four sisters who all lived in our hometown and who helped raise me like a pack of fun-loving coyotes. My Sicilian uncle had a still-unclear-to-me management role in our local red stucco two story brothel that was protected by the cops and county health officials, a...*confusing* civic attitude toward law and morality that also manifested in our frontier doctor/former mayor performing often tragically botched illegal abortions in his office above Main Street, a reality that, judging from his steady stream of out of town patients, everyone West of the Mississippi River knew.

You know the kid I was.

Coke-bottle thick eyeglasses. Off in the clouds. The son

of loving, respectable middle class parents who did their best. My workaholic father managed movie theaters, which meant I grew up seeing thousands of Grade B movies. My mother was a county librarian, which meant I didn't need to worry about how long I kept the thousands of crime and adventure novels I devoured. I'd worked since grade school: theater ticket taker, motion picture projectionist, janitor, hay bale bucker, rock picker, tractor jockey, gravedigger. I put myself through my state university shoveling for the city road crew.

When I went to the University of Montana, I was so naïve I thought that the Journalism Department included my passion: writing fiction.

I'd started spinning fictional tales before I could write, dictating stories to my patient mother (she threw them away). By my high school graduation, I'd written my senior class play and had dozens of short stories rejected by magazines. I was seven weeks into my university studies before I realized that the Journalism major I'd chosen did not cover fiction. But the J School gave me scholarships the fiction writing department couldn't – though that department did have novelist professors James Lee Burke and James Crumley, plus poet Richard Hugo, the only one of that illustrious American literary trio whose classes I took. Yeah, *dumb me*. My journalism major trained me in tight prose, let me review movies for the student newspaper - coolest gig *ever* for a cinema and writing nut. I got to cover *the times a'changing* in the streets. And staying in journalism landed me the gig in Washington.

When I came back from my D.C. internship, I had no idea how to make my dreams work. All I wanted to do –

well, not *all* – was write fiction. In the autumn of 1971, I began an 'independent undergraduate studies' fifth year to give me what I thought was a necessary academic umbrella to write fiction…

…only to be saved – *dazzled*, actually – by another dose of great luck.

Montana was rewriting its outdated, robber-baron bred state constitution – Dashiell Hammett created *noir* fiction with *Red Harvest*, his debut novel of crime and corruption set in the old constitution's Montana. The staff of the new constitutional effort needed an emergency replacement who could write fast and had a resume involving government (*say*, interning for a U.S. Senator). They picked me.

After the convention, Spring of 1972, I disappeared on the road for a few months, came back to Helena, Montana and after a brief foray as a laborer/fire hydrant inspector, took a *feed-me* job in government bureaucracy.

The rage to write burned in me like a heroin addiction welded to sex.

I'd decided that the only way to learn how to write a novel…was to write a novel.

And that the only way to be a writer…was to write.

I lived in a second story apartment above a cottage not far from the state capitol building in Helena. For a while, my roommate was one of America's smartest Baby Boomers named Rick Applegate. Often, I stole my fictional characters' names from the spines of Rick's nonfiction books (*Condor*'s Heidegger). Our neighbors were a *so cool* couple: he was an affable whip-smart lawyer, she was that tawny haired artsy woman so many of us *Sixties soldiers* wanted to be or wed. I lived in that apartment long enough to meet their first born, a baby girl named Maile Meloy who grew up to be a major American author, but I moved out of town before they brought home their second child, a son Colin Meloy, leader and chief writer for the famous 21st Century indie folk rock band The Decemberists. I labored in a bureaucracy, jogged and studied Judo, saw my girlfriend when I could, soared in AM radio rock 'n' roll, read hundreds of novels, went to movies, saved my pennies and spent hours at the kitchen table hunkered over a battered green manual typewriter.

And felt two *what-if* questions from my Washington, D.C. days come to life.

In those days, James Bond, *super spy*, dominated espionage fiction. Despite fine movies having been made from their excellent books, John Le Carré and Len Deighton were overshadowed by 007. Eric Ambler, Joseph Conrad, and Graham Greene could be found on library shelves, but at bookstores, they were blanked out by the glitz of *Dr. No*, *Goldfinger*, and *From Russia With Love* (the best Bonds) – Sean Connery and Ursula Andress, sex and a Walther PPK.

As much as I love '*Bond, James Bond*,' I didn't want to write about a superhero. I wanted my imaginary hero to feel real, even though he worked for the CIA.

The Central Intelligence Agency, America's best-known spy shop. In that fearful post-Joe McCarthy era, when assassinated JFK had publicly loved James Bond and secretly been entangled in covert intrigues like assassination plots against Cuba's Fidel Castro outsourced to the Mafia by our spies, the CIA was invisible.

When I researched Condor, I found only three credible

books on the CIA, two by David Wise and Thomas Ross (*The Invisible Government* and *The Espionage Establishment*) and one by Andrew Tully (CIA: *The Inside Story*). I stumbled across a book by historian Alfred W McCoy, who braved the wrath of the U.S. government, French intelligence agencies, the Mafia, the *Union Corse* (the major French criminal syndicate), the Chinese Triads and our exiled *Kuomintang* Chinese allies to write The Politics of Heroin In Southeast Asia. McCoy tramped the mountains of Laos, air-conditioned government corridors of Saigon (now Ho Chi Minh City), and along the *klongs* of Bangkok to show how, in our crusade against communism, America's government had *in the least* embraced ignorance about the gangsterism of those we called our allies. Allen Ginsberg *redeemed*.

Those works plus a few columns by muckraker Jack Anderson constituted the only 'reporting' I did on the CIA.

My imagination was thus unencumbered by much reality.

Prose fiction in that era treated the CIA like a phantom. CIA agents made appearances in hundreds of novels, but they were inscrutable.

Three notable exceptions were *Richard Condon*, whose *The Manchurian Candidate* military intelligence nightmare blew me away in adolescence as both a novel and a movie; a cynical novel by *Noel Behn* and its John Huston-directed movie *The Kremlin Letter* ('off the books' spy groups, not the CIA); and great novels by *Charles McCarry*, who worked as a deep cover CIA operative.

Another CIA agent named *Victor Marchetti* – who post-*Condor* 1974 co-authored *The CIA And The Cult Of Intelligence*, an expose censored word-by-word – first wrote a 1971 novel that followed a then-common practice: he changed the name of the CIA, further distancing fiction from reality.

Hollywood treated the CIA with a Tinkerbell touch: the CIA meant fancy gadgets, trenchcoated knights in righteous pursuit of *truth, justice and the American way*.

An engrossing exception that few people saw was the 1972 movie *Scorpio*, starring Burt Lancaster as a CIA executive who may or may not deserve the French assassin the Agency forces to hunt him. During its Washington filming, the cast for that movie stayed in the same hotel that Nixon's Plumbers used as a base of operations to burgle the Watergate complex across the street. Nixon burglar and *former* CIA agent E. Howard Hunt even spy-trick 'coincidentally' rode the elevator with the movie's co-star Alain Delon and tried to impress the actor by speaking French.

I was a fan of my high school days TV show *I Spy* starring Bill Cosby and Robert Culp, but TV in the Sixties broadcast in the shackles of censorious 'standards,' and those two American agents too often came off like super spies. Over-the-top 'spy' TV shows like *Mission Impossible, The Avengers* and *The Man From Uncle* were addictively entertaining, but TV's most realistic 'spy show' was the Patrick McGoohan drama called *Secret Agent* in the U.S. (with a great Johnny Rivers rock 'n' roll theme song) and in Britain called *Danger Man*.

Of course, there was Alfred Hitchcock. *The King.* His movies often unfolded in worlds of espionage and international intrigue. But for Hitchcock, spies were merely agents of *the MacGuffin* – that force that throws often innocent characters together, the 'what it's about' for suspense and action.

For my novel, I 'invented' a CIA job I'd love if I couldn't be a writer: reading novels for espionage hints.

After my experiences in the U.S. Senate, working on Montana road crews and for a federally-funded state office, I decided that even a secret agency was still a government bureaucracy powered by the same forces and foibles I witnessed every day.

So, I thought, knowing all that, how would I organize the CIA?

And I 'projected' the answers to my questions in my fiction, including creating such (to me) obvious things as a 'panic line' for agents in trouble, because whatever my plot was, my hero had to panic and had to need all the help he could get. I chose his name to reflect what 21st slang refers to as 'a nerd.' No cool Hemingway 'Nick' or TV *Hawaii Five-O* 'Steve' for my guy: he became *Ronald Malcolm*. Like me, even his friends called him by his last name.

And like me, my hero had to be young, fresh out of college, a Sixties Citizen who was definitely *not* from the generations still in charge.

Hollywood had capitalized on youth's 'counter-culture' with movies like James Dean's *Rebel Without A Cause*, Arlo Guthrie's multi-media saga *Alice's Restaurant*, and *Easy Rider*'s motorcycle outlaws.

But Sixties souls were still rare in prose fiction, with wonderful exceptions like Evan Hunter's *Blackboard Jungle*, Charles Webb's *The Graduate*, Richard Farina's *Been Down So Long It Looks Like Up To Me*. Young protagonists were particularly rare in *noir thriller* fiction except for the sagas of hyper-cool British author Adam Diment, who'd scored a publishing deal at 23, launched his first novel in 1967 and then vanished in 1973 like a Tom Pynchon-Alfred Hitchcock hero.

Diment showed that a hero could be *talking 'bout my generation*, not some never-ages hero like Bond or some mysterious uncle like George Smiley.

Nights and weekends for four months, I sat in that yellow kitchen nook in Helena, Montana and let my imagination command my fingertips on that green typewriter. I had no idea what I was going to call the book until I finished it, realized I had a chronology that fit into six days: our culture already had a thriller titled '*seven* days' (IN MAY). I spent a Saturday lunch coming up with Malcolm's codename, settled on 'condor' because it connoted death and sounded cooler than 'vulture.'

Of course, I was a nobody living thousands of miles from the publishing world of New York. I had no one to advise me, make a phone call, write a letter, knock on a door.

I searched the library for publishers of fiction akin to my manuscript. Found 30. I used my work's 'high tech' IBM Selectric typewriter and Xerox machine, crafted a synopsis that did not reveal the novel's ending, a sample chapter, and a biography that while true, hinted at mystery in my life: *Could he be…?* Dropped 30 packets of hope in the U.S. mail. Of the 30 publishers, half responded in my pitch packet's self-addressed, stamped envelopes; of that half, six said they'd consider my book. I picked one at random, sent the manuscript off.

Four months later, still having heard nothing, I was

about to leave my job in Helena for a starving-author's life in Missoula, then a more 'cosmopolitan' Montana city. I called publisher number one, got through to the editor, who politely told me they were rejecting my novel. I waited until I had my new address and phone number in Missoula, then dropped the manuscript in the mail to W.W. Norton, and moved.

My parents and friends were terrified: nobody we knew made a living writing fiction. I didn't care. In 1973, I was 24 living in a shack in Missoula. Subsisting off my savings. Hustling less than a month's rent worth of freelance journalism. Sneaking showers in my *alma mater* University dorms. Spending only what I had to – I rationed Cokes I drank to nights my karate club practiced. Excitedly pounding out fiction on that green machine, including one 12+ hour marathon session that ended only when my typing fingers began to bleed – call that chapter of my life *Blood on The Keys*.

That period's output included a 'college awakening' novel hopefully no one else will ever read and one comic caper novel called *The Great Pebble Affair*, published under a pseudonym in America, under my name in Britain, France and Italy.

But before then, back in the real world, my bank account was dwindling. The news increasingly focused on scandals of crime and intrigue coming out of the Nixon White House. Washington sounded much more exciting than starvation row. My former boss Senator Lee Metcalf had a year-long Fellowship open to Montana applicants who were journalists – a stretch for me, but the Missoula paper had published my freelance work and the national magazine *Sport* was about to run my three paragraph story about a prairie dog (*aka* 'gopher') racing stunt back in my hometown. I applied for that Fellowship, started thinking about road crew jobs or white collar bureaucracy work that wouldn't sap my creativity for my *'real'* work.

When the phone rang.

The man on the call introduced himself as Starling Lawrence, an eventual novelist but then an editor from W.W. Norton, who said they wanted to publish Condor and would pay me $1,000 — more than 10 percent of the annual yearly salary I'd made as a bureaucrat. Of course I said *yes*, and he said: 'We think we can sell it as a movie, too.'

Doesn't he know that kind of thing only happens in movies? I thought, but said nothing, and refrained from laughing: he was going to publish my novel.

Two weeks later, as I stood in my empty bathtub, trying to use duct tape to rig a shower out of some stranger's discard plumbing parts, again the phone rang.

Starling Lawrence and a pack of Norton staffers were on the line, telling me that famed movie producer Dino De Laurentiis had read Condor in manuscript and wanted to make it a movie. Dino later told me he knew after reading the first four pages. He bought the book outright, and my share of the sale would be $81,000.

I stood there holding the spool of gray duct tape, listened while Starling excitedly rehashed what he'd told me, then I said: 'You'll have to excuse me, I need to go back to fixing my shower and I haven't heard a word you've said after $81,000.'

I could subsist writing fiction for *years* on that!

A week later, Senator Metcalf gave me a new Fellowship to work in Washington.

I was 24 years old.

Every novel is two books: the manuscript the author writes, and the product that publishers, editors, and the author carve out for readers. In the process of creating that second book, the author is both beef and butcher.

My manuscript Condor is as he's become in legend, but the novel published in 1974 is not quite the story I first created.

The manuscript is a *noir* spy story propelling Condor through my *what-ifs* with a plot about rogue CIA operatives smuggling heroin out of the Vietnam war. That MacGuffin races Condor through his six days of life changing peril during which the woman he dragoons into being his lover and co-target (Faye Dunaway) is killed by an assassin, an act that transforms Condor from *victim and prey* to *hunter and killer*.

A Prologue and Epilogue set in Vietnam bookend my D.C. spy-slaughtering saga. The manuscript also set the story in rock 'n' roll, from the silky Temptations singing '*Just My Imagination*' on the radio as we meet Condor 'girl watching' to the climax when I call it *assassination* or call it *justice*, Condor murders the villain in the Men's Room at National (now Reagan National) airport while the piped-in lavatory bland instrumental music plays four quoted lines from the Beatles: '*I Get By With A Little Help From My Friends.*'

Those Beatles lines were first to go: what I saw as literary journalism, the song rights holders saw as a necessary fee. I was too nervous about my economic future to risk that in-hindsight paltry sum. My editor thought the Temptations playing on the radio as Condor stole time from his work to sit at the window and watch for a certain unknown girl to walk by seemed too *obvious*. While the girl stayed – how often had I sat at that window, plus that girl is a diversionary red-herring for Faye Dunaway's character – the radio and song got red-lined.

But I was proud of how little editing the book seemed to need from Starling and the hardback publisher, though he did have me drop my Vietnam Prologue and Epilogue.

Then, after the Hollywood sale, the paperback publisher's editorial committee asked Norton if I would make two 'small' changes.

First, change heroin into something else: 'Could it be some kind of super drug?' With the movie *The French Connection* having been a hit, 'the feeling is, heroin's been done.'

Second, let the Faye Dunaway heroine live: 'Killing her is so dark.'

Losing the rock 'n' roll made me sad. Dropping the EPILOGUE and PROLOGUE in favor of faster, more immediate plot development made sense.

But changing heroin into 'some kind of super drug' was ludicrous.

And letting the heroine live meant Condor had no trigger to transform into the kind of assassin he'd been fleeing.

So I came up with Condor only *thinking* she'd been killed on the theory that was 'good enough' for his homicidal revenge motivation.

As for heroin, this rube from Montana ran a Trojan

horse past the 'sophisticated' New York City paperback editors: instead of heroin, have the bad guys smuggling bricks of morphine. 'Wonderful!' was the response. I realized those faceless gatekeepers knew next to nothing about our world's narcotics scourge. Nobody smuggles morphine bricks into America, it's not worth it. Morphine is an early manufactured stage of…heroin. But at least morphine was real, not some committee hallucinated 'super drug' that would have made Condor a parody of truth.

Still, I was only a 24-years-old first time novelist. I was lucky to get off with the light editing Condor received. Hell, I was lucky to be published at all.

Some lucky novels are three books: the author's original work, the edited published volume, and the story Hollywood projects onto the silver screen.

Casting for *Condor* locked up Robert Redford before I'd even met my editor in the *going up* elevator of his New York skyscraper.

And history exploding in our streets after the manuscript's acceptance inspired changes for the movie's creative team.

Already the plot had been shifted from Washington to New York because Redford had to shoot two movies that year: *Condor* and *All The President's Men*. His family lived in New York and he didn't want to move to Washington for a year. Of the two movies' plots, only *Condor* could be moved to New York.

More importantly came the MacGuffin.

Just after *Condor* sold, the United States got hit with its first oil embargo. Petroleum Politics suddenly ruled. That change was too powerful to ignore, so the MacGuffin went from *drugs* to *oil*. And instead of my *noir* dark ending, the brilliant screenwriters came up with a chilling, culturally impactful *Lady or The Tiger?* climax.

There's no way to describe what it's like for a novelist to walk onto a movie set created from a vision born in the writer's fevered dreams.

Director Sydney Pollack showed me around, letting me see the exacting detail with which he approached his art, right down to hand-selecting the assassins' never-filmed-before guns. I listened in awe as he described how to create tension in a scene by having nothing happen – except, of course, that the ruthless killer and his prey ride the same elevator surrounded by innocent witnesses. Sydney explained that in film, telling a chronological chase story meant he couldn't show an increasingly scruffy Redford on the run for six days and night, so everything compressed into…three days.

Redford went out of his way to be gracious, stood outside with me one wintry Manhattan morning on the front steps of the set's secret CIA office and talked about 'our' work while we ignored two mink-coated high society women who'd imperiously breezed through the police lines only to look up and see who was standing there. Those two *oh-so-sophisticated* Manhattan matrons… clutched each other like schoolgirls, hip-hopped past us in gasping glee.

I've often wondered if Redford has that effect on women, too.

Hollywood took my slim first novel, elevated and enhanced it into a cinematic masterpiece. My whole life has been blessed by the shadow of Condor.

But until the KGB story broke, who knew that shadow was so huge?

In the same year that the great American author of my generation Bruce Springsteen released his seminal *Born To Run* album, 'my' movie came out, Nixon had resigned, my Senate Fellowship had ended, I had two more novels about to be published, and I'd jumped at a chance to join Jack Anderson's muckrakers. After all, Nixon's thugs had plotted to murder Jack, and Les Whitten, the man who'd helped lead me to Condor, was one of my bosses.

And though I'd rushed a sequel into another bestseller, I realized that the quintet of Condor novels I envisioned would crash into the image created by Robert Redford.

I let Condor fly away.

Vanish.

Until 9/11.

As that smoke cleared, Condor flew back.

His return was influenced by a claim Watergate burglar Frank Sturgis made to me after 'my' movie hit theater screens. Sturgis claimed that the CIA rotated codenames, and that briefly, before my novel was even written, he'd been codenamed Condor. Frank was a crook, a liar, and a spy – charming though thuggish – but this may have been true.

I'd published a novel about spies and an attack on the World Trade Towers seven years before 9/11 (*Thunder*), but that infamy compelled me to write about our new world of spies. I realized that the best way to do so would be to bring back Condor.

Both practically and out of respect for readers and

movie-goers, I couldn't violate the legend or images Robert Redford gave the world. I had to merge Redford with my original – and on-going – vision of Condor.

The result was a 2005 novella called *condor.net*, where a young CIA cyber intelligence analyst with the recycled codename of Condor finds himself slammed into the same but post-9/11 slaughterhouse of intrigue and corruption as my first Condor.

Then I tried to shoo Condor from my literary sky.

Failed.

Four other Condor short fictions flew from me, two novellas and two short stories published in magazines and as stand-alones in the U.S., England and France – all of the stories dealing with my original, aged-with-our-times Condor as he survives where I'd slyly locked him up in my 2006 novel MAD DOGS: the CIA's secret insane asylum.

But then: *done*, right?

No.

One night I swirled awake with a novel that my wife Bonnie nailed with the perfect title over our morning coffee: *Last Days Of The Condor*.

I had to do it *true*.

Write a novel true to my original character fused with Redford. Write the story true to his literary history my short tales had created. Write a novel true to my belief that 'literary franchise' characters should age as they would in our reality. Write a novel as true to its times – our times now – as I could.

Plus, Condor had become a cultural force – including in 1980, inspiring a hired American assassin to disguise himself as a Washington, D.C. mailman to gun down the exiled diplomat target of his fundamentalist puppet masters in Iran.

Condor inspired parodies on the TV shows *Seinfeld*, *The Simpsons*, *Frasier*, *King of The Hill* and cultural chatter references on shows like NCIS. The avant-garde rock group Radiohead samples the movie's dialog on a song.

In his January 2000 *Washington Post* essay on films of the preceding century, Pulitzer Prize winning movie reviewer and renowned novelist Stephen Hunter picked *Three Days Of The Condor* as the movie most emblematic of the 1970s, the film typical of its paranoid times. Also, wrote Hunter: 'This marks the globalization of the cinema as Tinseltown has surrendered its own natural mantle of world centrality.'

And on that morning when my wife and I shared coffee and smiles over the *Last Days* title of my novel a-borning, Condor was back in the sky over our brave new world where spies target all of us – the secrets in our cell phones, the power in our elections, what happens when we sit on a park bench in Salisbury, England.

Now more than ever before, we all live in Condor's world.

Listen.

You can hear his wings.

James Grady, March 2018

SIX DAYS

OF THE

CONDOR

JAMES GRADY

NO EXIT PRESS

Six Days of the Condor was originally dedicated to Rick Applegate, Shirley Hodgson, and my parents – Tom and Donna Grady. Without their emotional support, the young man I was might never have created Condor. This volume merges past and present. Such a revision requires an addition to the original crew of dedicatees. Along with them, this one is for my wife Bonnie Goldstein, my children Rachel and Nathan.

Thanks for sharing my ride.

Preface

The events described in this novel are fictitious, at least to the author's best knowledge. Whether these events might take place is another question, for the structure and operations of the intelligence community are based on fact. Malcolm's branch of the CIA and the 54/12 Group do indeed exist, though perhaps no longer under the designations given to them here.

For the factual background to this story, the author is indebted to the following sources: Jack Anderson, *Washington Merry-Go-Round* (various dates); Alfred W. McCoy, *The Politics of Heroin in Southeast Asia* (1972); Andrew Tully, *CIA: The Inside Story* (1962); David Wise and Thomas B. Ross, *The Invisible Government* (1964) and *The Espionage Establishment* (1967).

James Grady, 1974

Wednesday

Four blocks behind the Library of Congress, just past Southeast A and Fourth Street (one door from the corner), is a white stucco three-story building. Nestled in among the other town houses, it would be unnoticeable if not for its color. The clean brightness stands out among the fading reds, grays, greens, and occasional off-whites. Then, too, the short black iron picket fence and the small, neatly trimmed lawn lend an aura of quiet dignity the other buildings lack. However, few people notice the building. Residents of the area have long since blended it into the familiar neighborhood. The dozens of Capitol Hill and Library of Congress workers who pass it each day don't have time to notice it, and probably wouldn't even if they had time. Located where it is, almost off 'the Hill', most of the tourist hordes never come close to it. The few who do are usually looking for a policeman to direct them out of the notoriously rough neighborhood to the safety of national monuments.

If a passerby (for some strange reason) is attracted to the building and takes a closer look, his investigation would reveal very little out of the ordinary. As he stood outside the picket fence, he would probably first note a raised bronze plaque, about three feet by two feet, which proclaims the building to be the national headquarters of the American Literary Historical Society. In Washington, D.C., a city of hundreds of landmarks and headquarters of a multitude of organisations, such a building is not extraordinary. Should the passerby have an eye for architecture and design, he would be pleasantly intrigued by the ornate black wooden door flawed by a curiously large peephole. If our passerby's curiosity is not hampered by shyness, he might open the gate. He probably will not notice the slight click as the magnetic hinge moves from its resting place and breaks an electric circuit. A few short paces later, our passerby mounts the black iron steps to the stoop and rings the bell.

If, as is usually the case, Walter is drinking coffee in the small kitchen, arranging crates of books, or sweeping the floor, then the myth of security is not even flaunted. The visitor hears Mrs. Russell's harsh voice bellow 'Come in!' just before she punches the buzzer on her desk releasing the electronic lock.

The first thing a visitor to the Society's headquarters notices is its extreme tidiness. As he stands in the stairwell, his eyes are probably level with the top of Walter's desk, a scant four inches from the edge of the well. There are never any papers on Walter's desk, but then, with a steel reinforced front, it was never meant for paper. When the visitor turns to his right and climbs out of the stairwell, he sees Mrs. Russell. Unlike Walter's work area, her desk spawns paper. It covers the top, protrudes from drawers, and hides her ancient typewriter. Behind the processed forest sits Mrs. Russell. Her gray hair is thin and usually disheveled. In any case, it is too short to be of much help to her face. A horseshoe-shaped brooch dated 1932 adorns what was once a left breast. She smokes constantly.

Strangers who get this far into the Society's headquarters (other than mailmen and delivery boys) are few in number. Those few, after being screened by Walter's stare (if he is there), deal with Mrs. Russell. If the stranger comes for business, she directs him to the proper person, provided she accepts his clearance. If the stranger is merely one of the brave and curious, she delivers a five-minute, inordinately dull lecture on the Society's background of foundation funding, its purpose of literary analysis, advancement, and achievement (referred to as 'the 3 A's'), shoves pamphlets into usually less-than-eager hands, states that there is no one present who can answer further questions, suggests writing to an unspecified address for further information, and then bids a brisk 'Good day'. Visitors are universally stunned by this onslaught and leave meekly, probably without noticing the box on Walter's desk which took their picture or the red light and buzzer above the door which announces the opening of the gate. The visitor's disappointment would dissolve into fantasy should he learn that he had just visited a section branch office of a department of the Central Intelligence Agency's Intelligence Division.

The National Security Act of 1947 created the Central Intelligence Agency, a result of the World War II experience of being caught flat-footed at Pearl Harbor. The Agency, or the Company, as many of its employees call it, is the largest and most active entity in the far-flung American intelligence network, a network composed of eleven major agencies, around two hundred thousand persons, and annually budgeted in the billions of dollars. The C.I.A.'s activities, like those of its major counterparts – Britain's M.I.6., Russia's K.G.B., and Red China's Social Affairs Department – range through a spectrum of covert espionage, technical research, the funding of loosely linked political action groups, support to friendly governments, and direct paramilitary operations. The wide variety of activities of these agencies, coupled with their basic mission of national security in a troubled world, has made the intelligence agency one of the most important branches of government. In America, former C.I.A. Director Allen Dulles once said, 'The National Security Act of 1947 ... has given Intelligence a more influential position in our government than Intelligence enjoys in any other government in the world.'

The main activity of the C.I.A. is simple, painstaking research. Hundreds of researchers daily scour technical journals, domestic and foreign periodicals of all kinds, speeches, and media broadcasts. This research is divided between two of the four divisions of the C.I.A. The Research Division (R.D.) is in charge of technical intelligence, and its experts provide detailed reports of the latest scientific advances in all countries, including the United States and its allies. The Intelligence Division (I.D.) engages in a highly specialized form of scholastic research. About 80 per cent of the information I.D. handles comes from 'open' sources: public magazines, broadcasts, journals, and books. I.D. digests its data and from this fare produces three major types of reports: one type makes long-range projections dealing with areas of interest, a second is a daily review of the current world situation, and the third tries to detect gaps in C.I.A. activities. The research gathered by both I.D. and R.D. is used by the other two divisions: Support (the administrative arm which deals with logistics, equipment, security, and communications) and Plans (all covert activities, the actual spying divisions).

The American Literary Historical Society, with headquarters in Washington and a small receiving office in Seattle, is a section branch of one of the smaller departments in the C.I.A. Because of the inexact nature of the data the department deals with, it is only loosely allied to I.D., and, indeed, to C.I.A. as a whole. The department (officially designated as Department 17, C.I.A.I.D.) reports are not consistently incorporated in any one of the three major research report areas. Indeed, Dr. Lappe, the very serious, very nervous head of the Society (officially titled Section 9, Department 17, C.I.A.I.D.), slaves over weekly, monthly, and annual reports which may not even make the corresponding report of mother Department 17. In turn, Department 17 reports often will not impress major group co-ordinators on the division level and thus will fail to be incorporated into any of the I.D. reports. *C'est la vie.*

The function of the Society and of Department 17 is to keep track of all espionage and related acts recorded in literature. In other words, the Department reads spy thrillers and murder mysteries. The antics and situations of thousands of volumes of mystery and mayhem are carefully detailed, and analysed in Department 17 files. Volumes dating as far back as James Fenimore Cooper have been scrutinised. Most of the company-owned volumes are kept at the Langley, Virginia, C.I.A. central complex, but the Society headquarters maintains a library of almost three thousand volumes. At one time the Department was housed in the Christian Heurich Brewery near the State Department, but in the fall of 1961, when C.I.A. moved to its Langley complex, the Department transferred to the Virginia suburbs. In 1970 the ever-increasing volume of pertinent literature began to create logistic and expense problems for the Department. Additionally, the Deputy Director of I.D. questioned the need for highly screened and, therefore, highly paid analysts. Consequently, the Department re-opened its branch section in metropolitan Washington, this time conveniently close to the Library of Congress. Because the employees were not in the central complex, they needed only to pass a cursory Secret clearance rather than the exacting Top Secret clearance required for employment at the complex. Naturally, their salaries paralleled their rating.

The analysts for the Department keep abreast of the literary field and divide their work basically by mutual consent. Each analyst has areas of expertise, areas usually defined by author. In addition to summarising plots and methods of all the books, the analysts daily receive a series of specially 'sanitised' reports from the Langley complex. The reports contain capsule descriptions of actual events with all names deleted and as few necessary details as possible. Fact and fiction are compared, and if major correlations occur, the analyst begins a further investigation with a more detailed but still sanitised report. If the correlation still appears strong, the information and reports are passed on for review to a higher classified section of the Department. Somewhere after that the decision is made as to whether the author was guessing and lucky or whether he knew more than he should. If the latter is the case, the author is definitely unlucky, for then a report is filed with the Plans Division for action. The analysts are also expected to compile lists of helpful tips for agents. These lists are forwarded to Plans Division instructors, who are always looking for new tricks.

Ronald Malcolm was supposed to be working on one of those lists that morning, but instead he sat reversed on a wooden chair, his chin resting on the scratched walnut back. It was fourteen minutes until nine o'clock, and he had been sitting there since he climbed the spiral staircase to his second-story office at 8.30, spilling hot coffee and swearing loudly all the way. The coffee was long gone and Malcolm badly wanted a second cup, but he didn't dare take his eyes off his window.

Barring illness, every morning between 8.40 and 9.00 an incredibly beautiful girl walked up Southeast A, past Malcolm's window, and into the Library of Congress. And every morning, barring illness or unavoidable work, Malcolm watched her for the brief interval it took her to pass out of view. It became a ritual, one that helped Malcolm rationalise getting out of a perfectly comfortable bed to shave and walk to work. At first lust dominated Malcolm's attitude, but this had gradually been replaced by a sense of awe that was beyond his definition. In February he gave up even trying to think about it, and now, two months later, he merely waited and watched.

It was the first real day of spring. Early in the year there had been intervals of sunshine scattered through generally rainy days, but no real spring. Today dawned bright and stayed bright. An aroma promising cherry blossoms crept through the morning smog. Out of the corner of his eye Malcolm saw her coming, and he tipped his chair closer to the window.

The girl didn't walk up the street, she strode, moving with purpose and the pride born of modest yet firm, knowledgeable confidence. Her shiny brown hair lay across her back, sweeping past her broad shoulders to fall halfway to her slender waist. She wore no make-up, and when she wasn't wearing sunglasses one could see how her eyes, large and well-spaced, perfectly matched her straight nose, her wide mouth, her full face, her square chin. The tight brown sweater hugged her large breasts and even without a bra there was no sag. The plaid skirt revealed full thighs, almost too muscular. Her calves flowed to her ankles. Three more firm steps and she vanished from sight.

Malcolm sighed and settled back in his chair. His typewriter had a half-used sheet of paper in the carriage. He rationalised that this represented an adequate start on his morning's work. He belched loudly, picked up his empty cup, and left his little red and blue room.

When he got to the stairs, Malcolm paused. There were two coffeepots in the building, one on the main floor in the little kitchen area behind Mrs. Russell's desk and one on the third floor on the wrapping table at the back of the open stacks. Each pot had its advantages and disadvantages. The first-floor pot was larger and served the most people.

Besides Mrs. Russell and ex-drill instructor Walter ('Sergeant Jennings, if you please!'), Dr. Lappe and the new accountant-librarian Heidegger had their offices downstairs, and thus in the great logistical scheme of things used that pot. The coffee was, of course, made by Mrs. Russell, whose many faults did not include poor cooking. There were two disadvantages to the first-floor pot. If Malcolm or Ray Thomas, the other analyst on the second floor, used that pot, they ran the risk of meeting Dr. Lappe. Those meetings were uncomfortable. The other disadvantage was Mrs. Russell and her smell, or, as Ray was wont to call her, Perfume Polly.

Use of the third-floor pot was minimal, as only Harold Martin and Tamatha Reynolds, the other two analysts, were permanently assigned that pot. Sometimes Ray or Malcolm exercised their option. As often as he dared, Walter wandered by for refreshments and a glance at Tamatha's frail form. Tamatha was a nice girl, but she hadn't a clue about making coffee. In addition to subjecting himself to a culinary atrocity by using the third-floor pot, Malcolm risked being cornered by Harold Martin and bombarded with the latest statistics, scores, and opinions from the world of sports, followed by nostalgic stories of high-school prowess. He decided to go downstairs.

Mrs. Russell greeted Malcolm with the usual disdainful grunt as he walked by her desk. Sometimes, just to see if she had changed, Malcolm stopped to 'chat' with her. She would shuffle papers, and no matter what Malcolm talked about she rambled through a disjointed monologue dealing with how hard she worked, how sick she was, and how little she was appreciated. This morning Malcolm went no further than a sardonic grin and an exaggerated nod.

Malcolm heard the click of an office door opening just as he started back upstairs with his cup of coffee, and braced himself for a lecture from Dr. Lappe.

'Oh, ah, Mr. Malcolm, may I ... may I talk to you for a moment?'

Relief. The speaker was Heidegger and not Dr. Lappe. With a smile and a sigh, Malcolm turned to face a slight man so florid that even his bald spot glowed. The inevitable tabcollar white shirt and narrow black tie squeezed the large head from the body.

'Hi, Rich,' said Malcolm, 'how are you?'

'I'm fine ... Ron. Fine.' Heidegger tittered. Despite six months of total abstinence and hard work, his nerves were still shot. Any inquiry into Heidegger's condition, however polite, brought back the days where he fearfully sneaked drinks in C.I.A. bathrooms, frantically chewing gum to hide the security risk on his breath. After he 'volunteered' for cold turkey, traveled through the hell of withdrawal, and began to pick up pieces of his sanity, the doctors told him he had been turned in by the security section in charge of monitoring the rest rooms. 'Would you, I mean, could you come in for a second?'

Any distraction was welcome. 'Sure, Rich.'

They entered the small office reserved for the accountant-librarian and sat, Heidegger behind his desk, Malcolm on the old stuffed chair left by the building's former tenant. For several seconds they sat silent.

Poor little man, thought Malcolm. Scared shitless, still hoping you can work your way back into favor. Still hoping for return to your Top Secret rating so you can move from this dusty green bureaucratic office to another dusty but more Secret office. Maybe, Malcolm thought, if you are lucky, your next office will be one of the other three colors intended to 'maximise an efficient office environment', maybe you'll get a nice blue room the same soothing shade as three of my walls and hundreds of other government offices.

'Right!' Heidegger's shout echoed through the room. Suddenly conscious of his volume, he leaned back in his chair and began again. 'I ... I hate to bother you like this ...'

'Oh, no trouble at all.'

'Right. Well, Ron – you don't mind if I call you Ron, do you? Well, as you know, I'm new to this section. I decided to go over the records for the last few years to acquaint myself with the operation.' He chuckled nervously. 'Dr. Lappe's briefing was, shall we say, less than complete.'

Malcolm joined in his chuckle. Anybody who laughed at Dr. Lappe had something on the ball. Malcolm decided he might like Heidegger after all.

He continued, 'Right. Well. You've been here two years, haven't you? Ever since the move from Langley?'

Right, thought Malcolm as he nodded. Two years, two months, and some odd days.

'Right. Well, I've found some ... discrepancies I think need clearing up, and I thought maybe you could help me.' Heidegger paused and received a willing but questioning shrug from Malcolm. 'Well, I found two funny things – or rather, funny things in two areas.

'The first one had to do with accounts, you know,

money payed in and out for expenses, salaries, what have you. You probably don't know anything about that, it's something I'll have to figure out. But the other thing has to do with the books, and I'm checking with you and the other research analysts to see if I can find out anything before I go to Dr. Lappe with my written report.' He paused for another encouraging nod. Malcolm didn't disappoint him.

'Have you ever, well, have you ever noticed any missing books? No, wait,' he said, seeing the confused look on Malcolm's face, 'let me say that again. Do you ever know of an instance where we haven't got books we ordered or books we should have?'

'No, not that I know of,' said Malcolm, beginning to get bored. 'If you could tell me which ones are missing, or might be missing …' He let his sentence trail off, and Heidegger took the cue.

'Well, that's just it, I don't really know. I mean, I'm not really sure if any are, and if they are, what they are or even why they are missing. It's all very confusing.' Silently, Malcolm agreed.

'You see,' Heidegger continued, 'some time in 1968 we received a shipment of books from our Seattle purchasing branch. We received all the volumes they sent, but just by chance I happened to notice that the receiving clerk signed for *five* crates of books. But the billing order – which, I might add, bears both the check marks and signatures of our agent in Seattle *and* the trucking firm – says there were *seven* crates. That means we're missing two crates of books without really missing any books. Do you understand what I mean?'

Lying slightly, Malcolm said, 'Yeah, I understand what you're saying, though I think it's probably just a mistake. Somebody, probably the clerk, couldn't count. Anyway, you say we're not missing any books. Why not just let it go?'

'You don't understand!' exclaimed Heidegger, leaning forward and shocking Malcolm with the intensity in his voice. 'I'm responsible for these records! When I take over I have to certify I receive everything true and proper. I did that, and this mistake is botching up the records! It looks bad, and if it's ever found I'll get the blame. Me!' By the time he finished, he was leaning across the desk and his volume was again causing echoes.

Malcolm was thoroughly bored. The prospect of listening to Heidegger ramble on about inventory discrepancies did not interest him in the least. Malcolm also didn't like the way Heidegger's eyes burned behind those thick glasses when he got excited. It was time to leave. He leaned toward Heidegger.

'Look, Rich,' he said, 'I know this mess causes problems for you, but I'm afraid I can't help you out. Maybe one of the other analysts knows something I don't, but I doubt it. If you want my advice, you'll forget the whole thing and cover it up. In case you haven't guessed, that's what your predecessor Johnson always did. If you want to press things, I suggest you don't go to Dr. Lappe. He'll get upset, muddy the whole mess beyond belief, blow it out of proportion, and everybody will be unhappy.'

Malcolm stood up and walked to the door. Looking back, he saw a small, trembling man sitting behind an open ledger and a draftsman's light.

Malcolm walked as far as Mrs. Russell's desk before he let

out a sigh of relief. He threw what was left of the cold coffee down the sink, and went upstairs to his room, sat down, put his feet up on his desk, farted, and closed his eyes.

When he opened them a minute later he was staring at his Picasso print of Don Quixote. The print appropriately hung on his half-painted red wall. Don Quixote was responsible for Ronald Leonard Malcolm's exciting position as a Central Intelligence agent. Two years.

In September of 1970, Malcolm took his long delayed Master's written examination. Everything went beautifully for the first two hours: he wrote a stirring explanation of Plato's allegory of the cave, analysed the condition of two of the travelers in Chaucer's *Canterbury Tales*, discussed the significance of rats in Carnus's *The Plague*, and faked his way through Holden Caulfield's struggle against homesexuality in *Catcher in the Rye*. Then he turned to the last page and ran into a brick wall that demanded, 'Discuss in depth at least three significant incidents in Cervantes' *Don Quixote*, including in the discussion the symbolic meaning of each incident, its relation to the other two incidents and the plot as a whole, and show how Cervantes used these incidents to characterise Don Quixote and Sancho Panza.'

Malcolm had never read *Don Quixote*. For five precious minutes he stared at the test. Then, very carefully, he opened a fresh examination book and began to write:

'I have never read *Don Quixote*, but I think he was defeated by a windmill. I am not sure what happened to Sancho Panza.

'The adventures of Don Quixote and Sancho Panza, a team generally regarded as seeking justice, can be compared to the adventures of Rex Stout's two most famous characters, Nero Wolfe and Archie Goodwin. For example, in the classic Wolfe adventure *The Black Mountain* ...'

After finishing a lengthy discussion of Nero Wolfe, using *The Black Mountain* as a focal point, Malcolm turned in his completed examination, went home to his apartment, and contemplated his bare feet.

Two days later he was called to the office of the professor of Spanish Literature. To his surprise, Malcolm was not chastised for his examination answer. Instead, the professor asked Malcolm if he was interested in 'murder mysteries'. Startled, Malcolm told the truth: reading such books helped him maintain some semblance of sanity in college. Smiling, the professor asked if he would like to 'so maintain your sanity for money?' Naturally, Malcolm said, he would. The professor made a phone call, and that day Malcolm lunched with his first C.I.A. agent.

It is not unusual for college professors, deans, and other academic personnel to act as C.I.A. recruiters. In the early 1950s a Yale coach recruited a student who was later caught infiltrating Red China.

Two months later Malcolm was finally 'cleared for limited employment', as are 17 per cent of all C.I.A. applicants. After a special, cursory training period, Malcolm walked up the short flight of iron stairs of the American Literary Historical Society to Mrs. Russell, Dr. Lappe, and his first day as a full-fledged intelligence agent.

Malcolm sighed at the wall, his calculated victory over Dr. Lappe. His third day at work, Malcolm quit wearing a suit and tie. One week of gentle hints passed before Dr. Lappe called him in for a little chat about etiquette. While the good Doctor agreed that bureaucracies tended to be a little stifling, he implied that one really should find a method other than 'unconventional' dress for letting in the sun. Malcolm said nothing, but the next day he showed up for work early, properly dressed in suit and tie and carrying a large box. By the time Walter reported to Dr Lappe at ten, Malcolm had almost finished painting one of his walls fire-engine red. Dr. Lappe sat in stunned silence while Malcolm innocently explained his newest method for letting in the sun. When two other analysts began to pop into the office to exclaim their approval, the good Doctor quietly stated that perhaps Malcolm had been right to brighten the individual rather than the institution. Malcolm sincerely and quickly agreed. The red paint and painting equipment moved to the third-floor storage room. Malcolm's suit and tie once more vanished. Dr. Lappe chose individual rebellion rather than inspired collective revolution against government property.

Malcolm sighed to nostalgia before he resumed describing a classic John Dickson Carr method for creating 'locked-door' situations.

Meanwhile Heidegger had been busy. He took Malcolm's advice concerning Dr. Lappe, but he was too frightened to try and hide a mistake from the Company. If they could catch you in the bathroom, no place was safe. He also knew that if he could pull a coup, rectify a malfunctioning situation, or at least show he could responsibly recognise problems, his chances of being reinstated in grace would greatly increase. So through ambition and paranoia (always a bad combination) Richard Heidegger made his fatal mistake.

He wrote a short memo to the chief of mother Department 17. In carefully chosen, obscure, but leading terms, he described what he had told Malcolm. All memos were usually cleared through Dr. Lappe, but exceptions were not unknown. Had Heidegger followed the normal course of procedure, everything would have been fine, for Dr. Lappe knew better than to let a memo critical of his section move up the chain of command. Heidegger guessed this, so he personally put the envelope in the delivery bag.

Twice a day, once in the morning and once in the evening, two cars of heavily armed men pick up and deliver intra-agency communications from all C.I.A. sub-stations in the Washington area. The communications are driven the eight miles to Langley, where they are sorted for distribution. Rich's memo went out in the afternoon pickup.

A strange, and unorthodox thing happened to Rich's memo. Like all communications to and from the Society, the memo disappeared from the delivery room before the sorting officially began. The memo appeared on the desk of a wheezing man in a spacious east-wing office. The man read it twice, once quickly, then again, very, very slowly. He left the room and arranged for all files pertaining to the Society to disappear and reappear at a Washington location. He then came back and telephoned to arrange a date at a current art exhibit. Next he reported in sick and caught a bus for the city. Within an hour he was engaged in earnest conversation with a distinguished-looking gentleman who might have been a banker. They talked as they strolled up Pennsylvania Avenue.

That night the distinguished-looking gentleman met yet another man, this time in Clyde's, a noisy, crowded Georgetown bar frequented by the Capitol Hill crowd. They too took a walk, stopping occasionally to gaze at reflections in the numerous shopwindows. The second man was also distinguished-looking. Striking is a more correct adjective. Something about his eyes told you he definitely was not a banker. He listened while the first man talked.

'I am afraid we have a slight problem.'

'Really?'

'Yes. Weatherby intercepted this today.' He handed the second man Heidegger's memo.

The second man had to read it only once. 'I see what you mean.'

'I knew you would. We really must take care of this, now.'

'I will see to it.'

'Of course.'

'You realise that there may be other complications besides this,' the second man said as he gestured with Heidegger's memo, 'which may have to be taken care of.'

'Yes. Well, that is regrettable, but unavoidable.' The second man nodded and waited for the first man to continue. 'We must be very sure, completely sure about those complications.' Again the second man nodded, waiting. 'And there is one other element. Speed. Time is of the absolute essence. Do what you must to follow that assumption.'

The second man thought for a moment and then said, 'Maximum speed may necessitate ... cumbersome and sloppy activity.'

The first man handed him a portfolio containing all the 'disappeared' files and said, 'Do what you must.'

The two men parted after a brief nod of farewell. The first man walked four blocks and turned the corner before he caught a taxi. He was glad the meeting was over. The second man watched him go, waited a few minutes scanning the passing crowds, then headed for a bar and a telephone.

That morning at 3.15 Heidegger unlocked his door to the knock of police officers. When he opened the door he found two men in ordinary clothes smiling at him. One was very tall and painfully thin. The other was quite distinguished, but if you looked in his eyes you could tell he wasn't a banker.

The two men shut the door behind them.

> 'These activities have their own rules and methods of concealment which seek to mislead and obscure.'

> — President Dwight D. Eisenhower, 1960

Thursday, Morning to Early Afternoon

The rain came back Thursday. Malcolm woke with the start of a cold — congested, tender throat and a slightly woozy feeling. In addition to waking up sick, he woke up late. He thought for several minutes before deciding to go to work. Why waste sick time on a cold? He cut himself shaving, couldn't make the hair over his ears stay down, had trouble putting in his right contact lens, and found that his raincoat had disappeared. As he ran the eight blocks to work it dawned on him that he might be too late to see The Girl. When he hit Southeast A, he looked up the block just in time to see her disappear into the Library of Congress. He watched her so intently he didn't look where he was going and he stepped in a deep puddle. He was more embarrassed than angry, but the man he saw in the blue sedan parked just up from the Society didn't seem to notice the blunder. Mrs. Russell greeted Malcolm with a curt 'Bout time'. On the way to his room, he spilled his coffee and burned his hand. Some days you just can't win.

Shortly after ten there was a soft knock on his door, and

Tamatha entered his room. She stared at him for a few seconds through her thick glasses, a timid smile on her lips. Her hair was so thin Malcolm thought he could see each individual strand.

'Ron,' she whispered, 'do you know if Rich is sick?'

'No!' Malcolm yelled, and then loudly blew his nose.

'Well, you don't need to bellow! I'm worried about him. He's not here and he hasn't called in.'

'That's too fuckin' bad.' Malcolm drew the words out, knowing that swearing made Tamatha nervous.

'What's eating *you*, for heaven's sake?' she said.

'I've got a cold.'

'I'll get you an aspirin.'

'Don't bother,' he said ungraciously. 'It wouldn't help.'

'Oh, you're impossible! Goodbye!' She left, closing the door smartly behind her.

Sweet Jesus, Malcolm thought, then went back to Agatha Christie.

At 11.15 the phone rang. Malcolm picked it up and heard the cool voice of Dr. Lappe.

'Malcolm, I have an errand for you, and it's your turn to go for lunch. I assume everyone will wish to stay in the building.' Malcolm looked out the window at the pouring rain and came to the same conclusion. Dr. Lappe continued. 'Consequently, you might as well kill two birds with one stone and pick up lunch on the way back from the errand. Walter is already taking food orders. Since you have to drop a package at the Old Senate Office Building, I suggest you pick up the food at Jimmy's. You may leave now.'

Five minutes later a sneezing Malcolm trudged through

the basement to the coalbin exit at the rear of the building. No one had known the coalbin exit existed, as it hadn't been shown on the original building plans. It stayed hidden until Walter moved a chest of drawers while chasing a rat and found the small, dusty door that opened behind the lilac bushes. The door can't be seen from the outside, but there is enough room to squeeze between the bushes and the wall. The door only opens from the inside.

Malcolm muttered to himself all the way to the Old Senate Office Building. He sniffled between mutters. The rain continued. By the time he reached the building, the rain had changed his suede jacket from a light tan to a black brown. The blond receptionist in the Senator's office took pity on him and gave him a cup of coffee while he dried out. She said he was 'officially' waiting for the Senator to confirm delivery of the package. She coincidentally finished counting the books just as Malcolm finished his coffee. The girl smiled nicely, and Malcolm decided delivering murder mysteries to a senator might not be a complete waste.

Normally, it's a five-minute walk from the Old Senate Office Building to Hap's on Pennsylvania Avenue, but the rain had become a torrent, so Malcolm made the trip in three minutes. Jimmy's is a favorite of Capitol Hill employees because it's quick, tasty, and has its own brand of class. The restaurant is run by ex-convicts. It is a cross between a small Jewish delicatessen and a Montana bar. Malcolm gave his carry-out list to a waitress, ordered a meatball sandwich and milk for himself, and engaged in his usual Jimmy's pursuit of matching crimes with restaurant employees.

While Malcolm had been sipping coffee in the Senator's office, a gentleman in a raincoat with his hat hiding much of his face turned the corner from First Street and walked up Southeast A to the blue sedan. The custom-cut raincoat matched the man's striking appearance, but there was no one on the street to notice. He casually but completely scanned the street and buildings, then gracefully climbed in the front seat of the sedan. As he firmly shut the door, he looked at the driver and said, 'Well?'

Without taking his eyes off the building, the driver wheezed, 'All present or accounted for, sir.'

'Excellent. I watch while you phone. Tell them to wait ten minutes, then hit it.'

'Yes, sir.' The driver began to climb out of the car, but a sharp voice stopped him.

'Weatherby,' the man said, pausing for effect, 'there will be no mistakes.'

Weatherby swallowed. 'Yes, sir.'

Weatherby walked to the open phone next to the grocery store on the corner of Southeast A and Sixth. In Mr. Henry's, a bar five blocks away on Pennsylvania Avenue, a tall, frightfully thin man answered the bartender's page for 'Mr. Wazburn'. The man called Wazburn listened to the curt instructions, nodding his assent into the phone. He hung up and returned to his table, where two friends waited. They paid the bill (three brandy coffees), and walked up First Street to an alley just behind Southeast A. At the street light they passed a young, long-haired man in a rain-soaked suede jacket hurrying in the opposite direction. An empty yellow van stood between the two buildings on the edge of the alley. The men climbed in the back and prepared for their morning's work.

Malcolm had just ordered his meatball sandwich when a mailman with his pouch slung in front of him turned the corner at First Street to walk down Southeast A. A stocky man in bulging raincoat walked stiffly a few paces behind the mailman. Five blocks farther up the street a tall, thin man walked toward the other two. He also wore a bulging raincoat, though on him the coat only reached his knees.

As soon as Weatherby saw the mailman turn on to Southeast A, he pulled out of his parking place and drove away. Neither the men in the car nor the men on the street acknowledged the others' presence. Weatherby sighed relief in between wheezes. He was overjoyed to be through with his part of the assignment. Tough as he was, when he looked at the silent man next to him he was thankful he had made no mistakes.

But Weatherby was wrong. He had made one small, commonplace mistake, a mistake he could have easily avoided. A mistake he should have avoided.

If anyone had been watching, he would have seen three men, two businessmen and a mailman, coincidentally arrive at the Society's gate at the same time. The two businessmen politely let the mailman lead the way to the door and push the button. As usual, Walter was away from his desk (though it probably wouldn't have made any difference if he had been there). Just as Malcolm finished his sandwich at Hap's, Mrs. Russell heard the buzzer and rasped, 'Come in.'

And with the mailman leading the way, they did.

★

Malcolm dawdled over his lunch, polishing off his meatball sandwich with the specialty of the house, chocolate rum cake. After his second cup of coffee, his conscience forced him back into the rain. The torrent had subsided into a drizzle. Lunch had improved Malcolm's spirits and his health. He took his time, both because he enjoyed the walk and because he didn't want to drop the three bags of sandwiches. In order to break the routine, he walked down Southeast A on the side opposite the Society. His decision gave him a better view of the building as he approached, and consequently he knew something was wrong much earlier than he normally would have.

It was a little thing that made Malcolm wonder. A small detail quite out of place yet so insignificant it appeared meaningless. But Malcolm noticed little things, like the open window on the third floor. The Society's windows are rolled out rather than pushed up, so the open window jutted out from the building. When Malcolm first saw the window the significance didn't register, but when he was a block and a half away it struck him and he stopped.

It is not unusual for windows in the capital to be open, even on a rainy day. Washington is usually warm, even during spring rains. But since the Society building is air-conditioned, the only reason to open a window is for fresh air. Malcolm knew the fresh-air explanation was absurd because of the particular window that stood open. Tamatha's window.

Tamatha – as everyone in the section knew – lived in terror of open windows. When she was nine, her two teenage brothers had fought over a picture the three of them had found while exploring the attic. The older brother had slipped on a rug and had plunged out the attic window to the street below, breaking his neck and becoming paralyzed for life. Tamatha had once confided in Malcolm that only a fire, rape, or murder would make her go near any open window. Yet her office window stood wide open.

Malcolm tried to quell his uneasiness. Your damn overactive imagination, he thought. It's probably open for a perfectly good reason. Maybe somebody is playing a joke on her. But no staff member played practical jokes, and he knew no one would tease Tamatha in that manner. He walked slowly down the street, past the building, and to the corner. Everything else seemed in order. He heard no noise in the building, but then they were all probably reading.

This is silly, he thought. He crossed the street and quickly walked to the gate, up the steps, and, after a moment's hesitation, rang the bell. Nothing. He heard the bell ring inside the building, but Mrs. Russell didn't answer. He rang again. Still nothing. Malcolm's spine began to tingle and his neck felt cold.

Walter is shifting books, he thought, and Perfume Polly is taking a shit. They must be. Slowly he reached in his pocket for the key. When anything is inserted in the keyhole during the day, buzzers ring and lights flash all over the building. At night they also ring in Washington police headquarters, the Langley complex, and a special security house in downtown Washington. Malcolm heard the soft buzz of the bells as he turned the lock. He swung the door open and quickly stepped inside.

From the bottom of the stairwell Malcolm could only

see that the room appeared to be empty. Mrs. Russell wasn't at her desk. Out of the corner of his eye he noticed that Dr. Lappe's door was partially open. There was a peculiar odor in the room. Malcolm tossed the sandwich bags on top of Walter's desk and slowly mounted the stairs.

He found the sources of the odor. As usual, Mrs. Russell had been standing behind her desk when they entered. The blast from the machine gun in the mailman's pouch had knocked her almost as far back as the coffee-pot. Her cigarette had dropped on her neck, singeing her flesh until the last millimeter of tobacco and paper had oxidized. A strange dullness came over Malcolm as he stared at the huddled flesh in the pool of blood. An automaton, he slowly turned and walked into Dr. Lappe's office.

Walter and Dr. Lappe had been going over invoices when they heard strange coughing noises and the thump of Mrs. Russell's body hitting the floor. Walter opened the door to help her pick up the dropped delivery (he heard the buzzer and Mrs. Russell say, 'What have you got for us today?'). The last thing he saw was a tall, thin man holding an L-shaped device. The postmortem revealed that Walter took a short burst, five rounds in the stomach. Dr. Lappe saw the whole thing, but there was nowhere to run. His body slumped against the far wall beneath a row of bloody diagonal holes.

Two of the men moved quietly upstairs, leaving the mailman to guard the door. None of the other staff had heard a thing. Otto Skorzeny, Hitler's chief commando, once demonstrated the effectiveness of a silenced British sten gun by firing a clip behind a batch of touring generals. The German officers never heard a thing, but they refused to copy the British weapon, as the Third Reich naturally made better devices. These men were satisfied with the sten. The tall man flung open Malcolm's door and found an empty office. Ray Thomas was behind his desk on his knees picking up a dropped pencil when the stocky man found him. Ray had time to scream, 'Oh, my God, no ...' before his brain exploded.

Tamatha and Harold Martin heard Ray scream, but they had no idea why. Almost simultaneously they opened their doors and ran to the head of the stairs. All was quiet for a moment; then they heard the soft shuffle of feet climbing the stairs. The steps stopped, then a very faint metallic *click*, *snap*, *twang* jarred them from their lethargy. They couldn't have known the exact source of the sound (a new ammunition clip being inserted and the weapon being armed), but they instinctively knew what it meant. They both ran into their rooms, slamming the doors behind them.

Harold showed the most presence of mind. He locked his door and dialed three digits before the stocky man kicked the door open and cut him down.

Tamatha reacted on a different instinct. For years she thought only a major emergency could get her to open a window. Now she knew such an emergency was on her. She frantically rolled the window open, looking for escape, looking for help, looking for anything. Dizzied by the height, she took her glasses off and laid them on her desk. She heard Harold's door splinter, a rattling cough, the thump, and fled again to the window. Her door slowly opened.

For a long time nothing happened, then slowly Tamatha turned to face the thin man. He hadn't fired for fear a slug would fly out the window, hit something, and draw attention to the building. He would risk that only if she screamed. She didn't. She saw only a blur, but she knew the blur was motioning her away from the window. She moved slowly toward her desk. If I'm going to die, she thought, I want to see. Her hand reached out for her glasses, and she raised them to her eyes. The tall man waited until they were in place and comprehension registered on her face. Then he squeezed the trigger, holding it tight until the last shell from the full clip exploded, ejecting the spent casing out of the side of the gun. The bullets kept Tamatha dancing, bouncing between the wall and the filing cabinet, knocking her glasses off, disheveling her hair. The thin man watched her riddled body slowly slide to the floor, then he turned to join his stocky companion, who had just finished checking the rest of the floor. They took their time going downstairs.

While the mailman maintained his vigil on the door, the stocky man searched the basement. He found the coalbin door but thought nothing of it. He should have, but then his error was partially due to Weatherby's mistake. The stocky man did find and destroy the telephone switchbox. An inoperative phone causes less alarm than a phone unanswered. The tall man searched Heidegger's desk. The material he sought should have been in the third drawer, left-hand side, and it was. He also took a manila envelope. He dumped a handful of shell casings in the envelope with a small piece of paper he took from his jacket pocket. He sealed the envelope and wrote on the outside. His gloves made writing difficult, but he wanted to disguise his handwriting anyway. The scrawl designated the envelope as a personal package for 'Lockenvar, Langley headquarters'. The stocky man opened the camera and exposed the film. The tall man contemptuously tossed the envelope on Mrs. Russell's desk. He and his companions hung their guns from the straps inside their coats, opened the door, and left as inconspicuously as they had come, just as Malcolm finished his piece of cake.

Malcolm moved slowly from office to office, floor to floor. Although his eyes saw, his mind didn't register. When he found the mangled body that had once been Tamatha, the knowledge hit him. He stared for minutes, trembling. Fear grabbed him, and he thought, I've got to get out of here. He started running. He went all the way to the first floor before his mind took over and brought him to a halt.

Obviously they've gone, he thought, or I'd be dead now. Who 'they' were never entered his mind. He suddenly realised his vulnerability. My God, he thought, I have no gun, I couldn't even fight them if they came back. Malcolm looked at Walter's body and the heavy automatic strapped to the dead man's belt. Blood covered the gun. Malcolm couldn't bring himself to touch it. He ran to Walter's desk. Walter kept a very special weapon clipped in the leg space of his desk, a sawed-off 20-gauge shotgun. The weapon held only one shell, but Walter often bragged how it saved his life at Chosen Reservoir. Malcolm grabbed it by its pistol-like butt. He kept it pointed at the closed door as he slowly sidestepped towards Mrs. Russsell's desk. Walter kept a revolver in her drawer, 'just in case'. Mrs. Russell, a widow, had called it her 'rape gun'. 'Not to fight them off,' she would say, 'but to encourage them.' Malcolm stuck the gun in his belt, then picked up the phone.

Dead. He punched all the lines. Nothing.

I have to leave, he thought, I have to get help. He tried to shove the shotgun under his jacket. Even sawed off, the gun was too long: the barrel stuck out through the collar and bumped his throat. Reluctantly, he put the shotgun back under Walter's desk, thinking he should try to leave everything as he found it. After a hard swallow, he went to the door and looked out the wide-angled peephole. The street was empty. The rain had stopped. Slowly, standing well behind the wall, he opened the door. Nothing happened. He stepped out on the stoop. Silence. With a bang he closed the door, quickly walked through the gate and down the street, his eyes darting, hunting for anything unusual. Nothing.

Malcolm headed straight for the phone corner. Each of the four divisions of the C.I.A. has an unlisted 'panic number', a phone number to be used only in the event of a major catastrophe, only if all other channels of communication are unavailable. Penalty for misuse of the number can be as stiff as expulsion from the service with loss of pay. Their panic number is the one top secret every C.I.A. employee from the highest cleared director to the lowest cleared janitor knows and remembers.

The Panic Line is always manned by highly experienced agents. They have to be sharp even though they seldom do anything. When a panic call comes through, decisions must be made, quickly and correctly.

Stephen Mitchell was officer of the day manning I.D.'s Panic phone when Malcolm's call came through. Mitchell had been one of the best traveling (as opposed to resident) agents in the C.I.A. For thirteen years he moved from trouble spot to trouble spot, mainly in South America. Then in 1967 a double agent in Buenos Aires planted a plastic bomb under the driver's seat in Mitchell's Simca. The double agent made an error: the explosion only blew off Mitchell's legs. The error caught the double agent in the form of a wire loop tightened in Rio. The Agency, not wanting to waste a good man, shifted Mitchell to the Panic Section.

Mitchell answered the phone after the first ring. When he picked up the receiver a tape recorder came on and a trace automatically began.

'493-7282.' All C.I.A. telephones are answered by their numbers.

'This is …' For a horrible second Malcolm forgot his code name. He knew he had to give his department and section number (to distinguish himself from other agents who might have the same code name), but he couldn't remember his code name. He knew better than to use his real name. Then he remembered. 'This is Condor, Section 9, Department 17. We've been hit.'

'Are you on an Agency line?'

'I'm calling from an open phone booth a little ways from … base. Our phones aren't working.'

Shit, thought Mitchell, we have to use double talk. With his free hand he punched the Alert button. At five different locations, three in Washington, two in Langley, heavily armed men scurried to cars, turned on their engines, and waited for instructions. 'How bad?'

'Maximum, total. I'm the only one who ...'

Mitchell cut him off. 'Right. Do any civilians in the area know?'

'I don't think so. Somehow it was done quietly.'

'Are you damaged?'

'No.'

'Are you armed?'

'Yes.'

'Are there any hostiles in the area?'

Malcolm looked around. He remembered how ordinary the morning had seemed. 'I don't think so, but I can't be sure.'

'Listen very closely. Leave the area, slowly, but get your ass away from there, someplace safe. Wait an hour. After you're sure you're clean, call again. That will be at 1.45. Do you understand?'

'Yes.'

'O.K., hang up now, and remember, don't lose your head.'

Mitchell broke the connection before Malcolm had taken the phone from his ear.

After Malcolm hung up, he stood on the corner for a few seconds, trying to formulate a plan. He knew he had to find someplace safe where he could hide unnoticed for an hour, someplace close. Slowly, very slowly, he turned and walked up the street. Fifteen minutes later he joined the Iowa City Jaycees on their tour of the nation's Capitol building.

Even as Malcolm spoke to Mitchell, one of the largest and most intricate government machines in the world began to grind. Assistants monitoring Malcolm's call dispatched four cars from Washington security posts and one car from Langley with a mobile medical team, all bound for Section 9, Department 17. The squad leaders were briefed and established procedure via radio as they homed in on the target. The proper Washington police precinct was alerted to the possibility of an assistance request by 'federal enforcement officials'. By the time Malcolm hung up, all D.C. area C.I.A. bases had received a hostile-action report. They activated special security plans. Within three minutes of the call all deputy directors were notified, and within six minutes the director, who had been in conference with the Vice-President, was personally briefed over a scrambled phone by Mitchell. Within eight minutes all the other main organs of America's intelligence community received news of a possible hostile action.

In the meantime Mitchell ordered all files pertaining to the Society sent to his office. During a panic situation, the Panic officer of the day automatically assumes awesome power. He virtually runs much of the entire Agency until personally relieved by a deputy director. Only seconds after Mitchell ordered the files, Records called him back.

'Sir, the computer check shows all primary files on Section 9, Department 17, are missing.'

'They're *what*?'

'Missing, sir.'

'Then send me the secondary set, and God damn it, send it under guard!' Mitchell slammed the phone down before the startled clerk could reply. Mitchell grabbed another phone and connected immediately. 'Freeze the base,' he ordered. Within seconds all exits from the compound were sealed. Anyone attempting to leave or enter the area would have been shot. Red lights flashed throughout the buildings. Special security teams began clearing the corridors, ordering all those not engaged in Panic or Red priority business to return to their base offices. Reluctance or even hesitance to comply with the order meant a gun barrel in the stomach and handcuffs on the wrists.

The door to the Panic Room opened just after Mitchell froze the base. A large man strode firmly past the security guard without bothering to return the cursory salute. Mitchell was still on the phone, so the man settled down in a chair next to the second in command.

'What the hell is going on?' The man would normally have been answered without question, but right now Mitchell was God. The second looked at his chief. Mitchell, though still barking orders into the phone, heard the demand. He nodded to his second, who in turn gave the big man a complete synopsis of what had happened and what had been done. By the time the second had finished, Mitchell was off the phone, using a soiled handkerchief to wipe his brow.

The big man stirred in his chair. 'Mitchell,' he said, 'if it's all right with you, I think I'll stay around and give you a hand. After all, I am head of Department 17.'

'Thank you, sir,' Mitchell replied, 'I'll be glad of any help you can give us.'

The big man grunted and settled down to wait.

If you had been walking down Southeast A just behind the Library of Congress, at 1.09 on that cloudy Thursday afternoon, you would have been startled by a sudden flurry of activity. Half a dozen men sprang out of nowhere and converged on a three-storey white building. Just before they reached the door, two cars, one on each side of the road, double-parked almost in front of the building. A man sat in the back seat of each car, peering intently at the building and cradling something in his arms. The six men on foot went through the gate together, but only one climbed the steps. He fiddled with a large ring of keys and the lock. When the door clicked he nodded to the others. After throwing the door wide open and hesitating for an instant, the six men poured inside, slamming the door behind them. A man got out of each car. They slowly began to pace up and down in front of the building. As the cars pulled away to park, the drivers both nodded at men standing on the corners.

Three minutes later the door opened. A man left the building and walked slowly towards the closest parked car. Once inside, he picked up a phone. Within seconds he was talking to Mitchell.

'They were hit all right, hard!' The man speaking was Allan Newbury. He had seen combat in Vietnam, at the Bay of Pigs, in the mountains of Turkey, dozens of alleys, dark buildings, and basements all over the world, yet Mitchell could feel uneasy sickness in the clipped voice.

'How and how bad?' Mitchell was just beginning to believe.

'Probably a two- to five-man team, no sign of forcible entry. They must have used silenced machine guns of some sort or the whole town would have heard. Six dead in the building, four men, two women. Most of them probably didn't know what hit them. No signs of an extensive search, security camera and film destroyed. Phones are dead, probably cut somewhere. A couple of bodies will have to be worked on before identity can be definitely established. Neat, clean, and quick. They knew what they were doing down to the last detail, and they knew how to do it.'

Mitchell waited until he was sure Newberry had finished. 'O.K. This is beyond me. I'm going to hold definite action until somebody upstairs orders it. Meantime you and your men sit tight. Nothing is to be moved. I want that place frozen and sealed but good. Use whatever means you must.'

Mitchell paused, both to emphasise his meaning and to hope he wasn't making a mistake. He had just authorised Newberry's team to do anything, including premeditated, non-defensive kills, Stateside action without prior clearance. Murder by whim, if they thought the whim might mean something. The consequences of such a rare order could be very grave for all concerned. Mitchell continued. 'I'm sending out more men to cover the neighborhood as additional security. I'll also send out a crime lab team, but they can only do things that won't disturb the scene. They'll bring a communications setup, too. Understand?'

'I understand. Oh, there's something a little peculiar we've found.'

Mitchell said, 'Yes?'

'Our radio briefing said there was only one door. We found two. Make any sense to you?'

'None,' said Mitchell, 'but nothing about this whole thing makes sense. Is there anything else?'

'Just one thing.' The voice grew colder. 'Some son of a

bitch butchered a little girl on the third floor. He didn't hit her, he butchered her.' Newberry signed off.

'What now?' asked the big man.

'We wait,' said Mitchell, leaning back in his wheelchair. 'We sit and wait for Condor to call.'

At 1.40 Malcolm found a phone booth in the Capitol. With change acquired from a bubbly teen-age girl he dialed the panic number. It didn't even finish one complete ring.

'493-7282.' The voice on the phone was tense.

'This is Condor, Section 9, Department 17. I'm in a public phone booth, I don't think I was followed, and I'm pretty sure I can't be heard.'

'You've been confirmed. We've got to get you to Langley, but we're afraid to let you come in solo. Do you know the Circus 3 theaters in the Georgetown district?'

'Yes.'

'Could you be there in an hour?'

'Yes.'

'O.K. Now, who do you know at least by sight who's stationed at Langley?'

Malcolm thought for a moment. 'I had an instructor codenamed Sparrow IV.'

'Hold on.' Through priority use of the computer and communications facilities, Mitchell verified Sparrow IV's existence and determined that he was in the building. Two minutes later he said, 'O.K., this is what is going to happen. Half an hour from now Sparrow IV and one other man will park in a small alley behind the theaters. They'll wait exactly one hour. That gives you thirty minutes leeway either direction. There are three entrances to the alley you can take on foot. All three allow you to see anybody in front of you before they see you. When you're sure you're clean, go down the alley. If you see anything or anybody suspicious, if Sparrow IV and his partner aren't there or somebody is with them, if a God damn pigeon is at their feet, get your ass out of there, find someplace safe, and call in. Do the same if you can't make it. O.K.?'

'OKahahaachoo!'

Mitchell almost shot out of his wheelchair. 'What the hell was that? Are you O.K.?'

Malcolm wiped the phone off. 'Yes, sir, I'm fine. Sorry, I have a cold. I know what to do.'

'For the love of Christ.' Mitchell hung up. He leaned back in his chair. Before he could say anything, the big man spoke.

'Look here, Mitchell. If you have no objection, I'll accompany Sparrow IV. The Department is my responsibility, and there's no young tough around here who can carry off what might be a tricky situation any better, tired old man as I may be.'

Mitchell looked at the big, confident man across from him, then smiled. 'O.K. Pick up Sparrow IV at the gate. Use your car. Have you ever met Condor?'

The big man shook his head. 'No, but I think I've seen him. Can you supply a photo?'

Mitchell nodded and said, 'Sparrow IV has one. Ordnance will give you anything you want, though I suggest a hand gun. Any preference?'

The big man walked towards the door. 'Yes,' he said, looking back, 'a .38 Special with silencer just in case we have to move quietly.'

'It'll be waiting in the car, complete with ammo. Oh,' said Mitchell, stopping the big man as he was halfway out the door, 'thanks again, Colonel Weatherby.'

The big man turned and smiled. 'Think nothing of it, Mitchell. After all, it's my job.' He closed the door behind him and walked towards his car. After a few steps he began to wheeze very softly.

'Faulty execution of a winning combination has lost many a game on the very brink of victory. In such cases a player sees the winning idea, plays the winning sacrifice and then inverts the order of his follow-up moves or misses the really clinching point of his combination.'

— Fred Reinfeld, The Complete Chess Course

Thursday Afternoon

Malcolm had little trouble finding a taxi, considering the weather. Twenty minutes later he paid the driver two blocks from the Circus theaters. Again he knew it was all-important that he stay out of sight. A few minutes later he sat at a table in the darkest corner of a bar crowded with men. The bar Malcolm chose is the most active male homosexual hangout in Washington. Starting with the early lunch hour at eleven and running until well after midnight, men of all ages, usually middle to upper middle class, fill the bar to find a small degree of relaxation among their own kind. It's a happy as well as a 'gay' bar. Rock music blares, laughter drifts into the street. The levity is strained, heavy with irony, but it's there.

Malcolm hoped he looked inconspicuous, one man in a bar crowded with men. He nursed his tequila Collins, drinking it as slowly as he dared, watching faces in the crowd for signs of recognition. Some of the faces in the crowd watched him too.

No one in the bar noticed that only Malcolm's left hand rested on the small table. Under the table his right hand held a gun, a gun he pointed at anyone coming near him.

At 2.40 Malcolm jumped from his table to join a large group leaving the bar. Once outside, he quickly walked away from the group. For several minutes he crossed and recrossed Georgetown's narrow streets, carefully watching the people around him. At three o'clock, satisfied he was clean, he headed towards the Circus theaters.

Sparrow IV turned out to be a shaky, spectacled instructor of governmental procedure. He had been given no choice concerning his role in the adventure. He made it quite clear that this was not what he was hired for, he most definitely objected, and he was very concerned about his wife and four children. Mostly to shut him up, Ordnance dressed him in a bulletproof vest. He wore the hot and heavy armor under his shirt. The canvas frustrated his scratching attempts. He had no recollection of anyone called Condor or Malcolm; he lectured Junior Officer Training classes by the dozen. The people at Ordnance didn't care, but they listened anyway.

Weatherby briefed the drivers of the crash cars as they walked towards the parking lot. He checked the short gun with the sausage-shaped device and nodded his approval to the somber man from Ordnance. Ordinarily Weatherby would have had to sign for the gun, but Mitchell's authority rendered such procedures unnecessary. The Ordnance man helped Weatherby adjust a special shoulder holster, handed him twenty-five extra rounds, and wished him luck. Weatherby grunted as he climbed into his light blue sedan.

The three cars rolled out of Langley in close formation with Weatherby's blue sedan in the middle position. Just as they exited from the Beltway turnpike to enter Washington, the rear car 'blew' a tire. The driver 'lost control' of his vehicle, and the car ended up across two lanes of traffic. No one was hurt, but the accident blocked traffic for ten minutes. Weatherby closely followed the other crash car as it turned and twisted its way through the maze of Washington traffic. On a quiet residential street in the city's southwest quadrant the crash car made a complete U-turn and started back in the opposite direction. As it passed the blue sedan, the driver flashed Weatherby the O.K. sign, then sped out of sight. Weatherby headed towards Georgetown, checking for tails all the way.

Weatherby figured out his mistake. When he dispatched the assassination team, he ordered them to kill everyone in the building. He had said everyone, but he hadn't specified how many that was. His men had followed orders, but the orders hadn't been complete enough to let them know one man was missing. Why the man wasn't there Weatherby didn't know and he didn't care. If he had known about the missing man, this Condor, he could have arranged a satisfactory solution. He had made the mistake, so now he had to rectify it.

There was a chance Condor was harmless, that he wouldn't remember his conversation with the Heidegger man, but Weatherby couldn't take that chance. Heidegger questioned all the staff except Dr. Lappe. Those questions could not be allowed to exist. Now one man knew about those questions, so, like the others, that man must die even if he didn't realise what he knew.

Weatherby's plan was simple, but extremely dangerous. As soon as Condor appeared he would shoot him. Self-defense. Weatherby glanced at the trembling Sparrow IV. An unavoidable side product. The big man had no qualms concerning the instructor's pending death. The plan was fraught with risks: Condor might be better with his weapon than anticipated, the scene might be witnessed and later reported, the Agency might not believe his story and use a guaranteed form of interrogation, Condor might turn himself in some other way. A hundred things could go wrong. But no matter how high the risks, Weatherby knew they were not the certainty that faced him should he fail. He might be able to escape the Agency and the rest of the American intelligence network. There are several ways, ways that have been successfully used before. Such things were Weatherby's forte. But he knew he would never escape the striking-looking man with strange eyes. That man never failed when he acted directly. Never. He would act directly against Weatherby the dangerous bungler, Weatherby the threat. This Weatherby knew, and it made him wheeze painfully. It was this knowledge that made any thought of escape or betrayal absurd. Weatherby had to account for his error. Condor had to die.

Weatherby drove through the alley slowly, then turned around and came back, parking the car next to some garbage cans behind the theaters. The alley was empty just as Mitchell said it would be. Weatherby doubted if anyone would enter it while they were there: Washingtonians tend to avoid alleys. He knew Mitchell would arrange for the area to be free of police so that uniforms wouldn't frighten

Condor. That was fine with Weatherby. He motioned for Sparrow IV to get out. They leaned against the car, prominent and visibly alone. Then, like any good hunter staging an ambush, Weatherby blanked his mind to let his senses concentrate.

Malcolm saw them standing there before they knew he was in the alley. He watched them very carefully from a distance of about sixty paces. He had a hard time controlling sneezes, but he managed to stay silent. After he was certain they were alone, he stepped from behind the telephone pole and began to walk towards them. His relief built with every step.

Weatherby spotted Malcolm immediately. He stepped away from the car, ready. He wanted to be very, very sure, and sixty paces is only a fair shot for a silenced pistol. He also wanted to be out of Sparrow IV's reach. Take them one at a time, he thought.

Recognition sprang on Malcolm twenty-five paces from the two men, five paces sooner than Weatherby anticipated any action. A picture of a man in a blue sedan parked just up from the Society in the morning rain flashed through Malcolm's mind. The man in that car and one of the men now standing in front of him were the same. Something was wrong, something was very wrong. Malcolm stopped, then slowly backed up. Almost unconsciously he tugged at the gun in his belt.

Weatherby knew something was wrong, too. His quarry had quite unexpectedly stopped short of the trap, was now fleeing, and was probably preparing an aggressive defense. Malcolm's unexpected actions forced Weatherby to abandon his original plan and react to a new situation.

While he quickly drew his own weapon, Weatherby briefly noted Sparrow IV, frozen with fright and bewilderment. The timid instructor still posed no threat.

Weatherby was a veteran of many situations requiring rapid action. Malcolm's pistol barrel had just cleared his belt when Weatherby fired.

A pistol, while effective, can be a difficult weapon to use under field conditions, even for an experienced veteran. A pistol equipped with a silencer increases this difficulty, for while the silencer allows the handler to operate quietly, it cuts down on his efficiency. The bulk at the end of the barrel is an unaccustomed weight requiring aim compensation by the user. Ballistically, a silencer cuts down on the bullet's velocity. The silencer may affect the bullet's trajectory. A silencer-equipped pistol is cumbersome, difficult to draw and fire quickly.

All these factors worked against Weatherby. Had he not been using a silenced pistol – even though his quarry's retreat forced him to take time to revise his plans – there would have been no contest. As it was, the pistol's bulk slowed his draw. He lost accuracy attempting to regain speed. The veteran killer tried for the difficult but definite head shot, but he overcompensated. Milliseconds after the soft *plop!*, a heavy chunk of lead cut through the hair hanging over Malcolm's left ear and whined off to sink in the Potomac.

Malcolm had only fired one pistol in his life, a friend's .22 target model. All five shots missed the running gopher. He fired Mrs. Russell's gun from the waist, and a deafening roar echoed down the alley before he knew he had pulled the trigger.

When a man is shot with a .357 magnum he doesn't grab a neat little red hole in his body and slide slowly to the ground. He goes down hard. At twenty-five paces the effect is akin to being hit by a truck. Malcolm's bullet smashed through Weatherby's left thigh. The force of the blast splattered a large portion of Weatherby's leg over the alley; it flipped him into the air and slammed him face down in the road.

Sparrow IV looked incredulously at Malcolm. Slowly Malcolm turned towards the little instructor, bringing the gun into line with the man's quivering stomach.

'He was one of them!' Malcolm was panting though he hadn't exerted himself. 'He was one of them!' Malcolm slowly backed away from the speechless instructor. When he reached the edge of the alley, Malcolm turned and ran.

Weatherby groaned, fighting off the shock of the wound. The pain hadn't set in. He was a very tough man, but it took everything he had to raise his arm. He had somehow held on to the gun. Miraculously, his mind stayed clear. Very carefully he aimed and fired. Another *plop!*, and a bullet shattered on the theater wall, but not before it tore through the throat of Sparrow IV, instructor of governmental procedure, husband, father of four. As the body crumpled against the car, Weatherby felt a strange sense of elation. He wasn't dead yet, Condor had vanished again, and there would be no bullets for Ballistics to use in determining who shot whom. There was still hope. He passed out.

A police car found the two men. It took them a long time to respond to the frightened shopkeeper's call, because all the Georgetown units had been sent to check out a sniper report. The report turned out to be from a crank.

Malcolm ran four blocks before he realised how conspicuous he was. He slowed down, turned several corners, then hailed a passing taxi to downtown Washington.

Sweet Jesus, Malcolm thought, he was one of them. He was one of them. The Agency must not have known. He had to get to a phone. He had to call ... Fear set in. Suppose, just suppose the man in the alley wasn't the only double. Suppose he had been sent there by a man who knew what he was. Suppose the man at the other end of the Panic Line was also a double.

Malcolm quit his suppositions to deal with the immediate problem of survival. Until he thought it out he wouldn't dare call in. And they would be looking for him. They would have looked for him even before the shooting, the only survivor of the section, they ... But he wasn't! The thought raced through his mind. He wasn't the only survivor of the section. Heidegger! Heidegger was sick, home in bed, sick! Malcolm searched his brain. Address, what did Heidegger say his address was? Malcolm had heard Heidegger tell Dr. Lappe his address was ... Mount Royal Arms!

Malcolm explained his problem to the cabby. He was on his way to pick up a blind date, but he had forgotten the address. All he knew was she lived in the Mount Royal Arms. The cabby, always eager to help young love, called his dispatcher, who gave him the address in the northwest quadrant. When the cabby let him out in front of the aging building, Malcolm gave him a dollar tip.

Heidegger's name tape was stuck next to 413. Malcolm buzzed. No return buzz, no query over the call box. While he buzzed again, an uneasy but logical assumption grew in his mind. Finally, he pushed three other buzzers. No answer came, so he punched a whole row. When the jammed call box squealed, he yelled, 'Special delivery!' The door buzzer rang and he ran inside.

No one answered his knock at Apartment 413, but by then he didn't really expect an answer. He got on his knees and looked at the lock. If he was right, only a simple spring night lock was on. In dozens of books he'd read and in countless movies, the hero uses a small piece of stiff plastic and in a few seconds a locked door springs open. Plastic – where could he find a piece of stiff plastic? After several moments of frantic pocket slapping, he opened his wallet and removed his laminated C.I.A. identification card. The card certified he was an employee of Tentrex Industries, Inc., giving relevant information regarding his appearance and identity. Malcolm had always liked the two photos of himself, one profile, one full face.

For twenty minutes Malcolm sneezed, grunted, pushed, pulled, jiggled, pleaded, threatened, shook, and finally hacked at the door with his card. The plastic lamination finally split, shooting his I.D. card through the crack and into the locked room.

Frustration turned to anger. Malcolm relieved his cramped knees by standing. If nobody has bothered me up till now, he thought, a little more noise won't make much difference. Backed with the fury, fear, and frustration of the day, Malcolm smashed his foot against the door. Locks and doors in the Mount Royal Arms are not of the finest quality. The management leans towards cheap rent, and the building construction is similarly inclined. The door of 413 flew inward, bounced off its doorstop, and was caught on the return swing by Malcolm. He shut the door a good deal more quietly than he had opened it. He picked his I.D. card out of the splinters, then crossed the room to the bed and what lay on it.

Since time forestalled any pretense, they hadn't bothered to be gentle with Heidegger. If Malcolm had lifted the pajama top, he would have seen the mark a low-line punch leaves if the victim's natural tendency to bruise is arrested by death. The corpse's face was blackish blue, a state induced by, among other things, strangulation. The room stank from the corpe's involuntary discharge.

Malcolm looked at the beginning-to-bloat body. He knew very little about organic medicine, but he knew that this state of decomposition is not reached in a couple of hours. Therefore Heidegger had been killed before the others. 'They' hadn't come here after they discovered him missing from work but before they hit the building. Malcolm didn't understand.

Heidegger's right pajama sleeve lay on the floor. Malcolm didn't think that type of tear would be made in a fight. He flipped the covers back to look at Heidegger's arm. On the underside of the forearm he found a small bruise, the kind a tiny bug would make. Or, thought Malcolm, remembering his trips to the student health service, a clumsily inserted hypodermic. They shot him full of something, probably to make him talk. About what? Malcolm had no idea. He began to search the room when he remembered about fingerprints. Taking his handkerchief from his pocket, he wiped everything he remembered touching, including the outside of the door. He found a pair of dusty handball gloves on the cluttered dresser. Too small, but they covered his fingers.

After the bureau drawers he searched the closet. On the top shelf he found an envelope full of money, fifty- and one-hundred-dollar bills. He didn't take the time to count it, but he estimated that there must be at least ten thousand dollars.

He sat on the clothes-covered chair. It didn't make sense. An ex-alcoholic, an accountant who lectured on the merits of mutual funds, a man frightened of muggers, keeping all that cash stashed in his closet. It didn't make sense. He looked at the corpse. At any rate, he thought, Heidegger won't need it now. Malcolm put the envelope inside his shorts. After a last quick look around, he cautiously opened the door, walked down the stairs, and caught a downtown bus at the corner.

Malcolm knew his first problem would be evading his pursuers. By now there would be at least two 'they's after him: the Agency and whatever group hit the Society. They all knew what he looked like, so his first move would have to be to change his appearance.

The sign in the barbershop said 'No Waiting', and for once advertising accurately reflected its product. Malcolm took off his jacket facing the wall. He slipped the gun inside the bundle before he sat down. His eyes never left the jacket during the whole haircut.

'What do you want, young fellow?' The graying barber snipped his scissors gleefully.

Malcolm felt no regrets. He knew how much the

haircut might mean. 'A short butch, just a little longer than a crew cut, long enough so it will lay down.'

'Say, that'll be quite a change.' The barber plugged in an electric clipper.

'Yeah.'

'Say, young man, are you interested in baseball? I sure am. I read an article in the *Post* today about the Orioles and spring training, and the way this fellow figures it…'

After the haircut Malcolm looked in the mirror. He hadn't seen that person for five years.

His next stop was Sunny Surplus. Malcolm knew a good disguise starts with the right attitude, but he also knew good props were invaluable. He searched through the entire stock until he found a used field jacket with the patches intact that fitted reasonably well. The name patch above the left pocket read 'Evans'. On the left shoulder was a tricolored eagle patch with the word 'Airborne' in gold letters on a black background. Malcolm knew he had just become a veteran of the 101st Airborne Division. He bought and changed into a pair of blue stretch jeans and an outrageously priced set of used jump boots ('$15, guaranteed to have seen action in Vietnam'). He also bought underwear, a cheap pullover, black driving gloves, socks, a safety razor, and a toothbrush. When he left the store with the bundle under his arm, he pretended he had a spike rammed up his ass. His steps were firm and well measured. He looked cockily at every girl he passed. After five blocks he needed a rest, so he entered one of Washington's countless Hot Shoppe restaurants.

'Can Ah have a cup of caufee?' The waitress didn't bat an eye at Malcolm's newly acquired southern accent. She brought him his coffee. Malcolm tried to relax and think.

Two girls were in the booth behind Malcolm. A lifetime habit made him listen to their conversation.

'So you're not going anywhere for your vacation?'

'No, I'm just going to stay home. For two weeks I'll shut the world out.'

'You'll go crazy.'

'Maybe, but don't try calling me for a progress report, because I probably won't even answer the phone.'

The other girl laughed. 'What if it's a hunk of man who's just pining for companionship?'

The other girl snorted. 'Then he'll just have to wait for two weeks. I'm going to relax.'

'Well, it's your life. Sure you won't have dinner tonight?'

'No, really, thanks, Anne. I'm just going to finish my coffee and then drive home, and starting right now I won't have to hurry for another two weeks.'

'Well, Wendy, have fun.' Thighs squeaked across plastic. The girl called Anne walked towards the door, right past Malcolm. He caught a glimpse of a tremendous pair of legs, blond hair, and a firm profile vanishing in the crowd. He sat very still, sniffling occasionally, nervous as hell, for he had found the answer to his shelter problem.

It took the girl called Wendy five minutes to finish her coffee. When she left she didn't even look at the man sitting behind her. She couldn't have seen much anyway, as his face was hidden behind a menu. Malcolm followed her as soon as she paid and started out the door. He threw his money on the counter as he left.

All he could tell from behind was that she was tall, thin but not painfully skinny like Tamatha, had short hair, and only medium legs. Christ, he thought, why couldn't she have been the blond? Malcolm's luck held, for the girl's car was in the back section of a crowded parking lot. He casually followed her past the fat attendant leering from behind a battered felt hat. Just as the girl unlocked the door of a battered Corvair, Malcolm yelled, 'Wendy! My God, what are you doing here?'

Startled, but not alarmed, the girl looked up at the smiling figure in the army jacket walking towards her.

'Are you talking to me?' She had narrow-set brown eyes, a wide mouth, a little nose, and high cheekbones. A perfectly ordinary face. She wore little or no makeup.

'I shore am. Don't you remember me, Wendy?' He was only three steps from her now.

'I ... I don't think so.' She noticed that his one hand held a package and his other was inside his jacket.

Malcolm stood beside her now. He set the package on the roof of her car and casually placed his left hand behind her head. He tightly grabbed her neck, bending her head down until she saw the gun in his other hand.

'Don't scream or make any quick moves or I'll splatter you all over the street. Understand?' Malcolm felt the girl shiver, but she nodded quickly. 'Now get in the car and unlock the other door. This thing shoots through windows and I won't even hesitate.' The girl quickly climbed into the driver's seat, leaned over, and unlocked the other door. Malcolm slammed her door shut, picked up his package, slowly walked around the car, and got in.

'Please don't hurt me.' Her voice was much softer than in the restaurant.

'Look at me.' Malcolm had to clear his throat. 'I'm not

going to hurt you, not if you do exactly as I say. I don't want your money, I don't want to rape you. But you must do exactly as I say. Where do you live?'

'In Alexandria.'

'We're going to your apartment. You'll drive. If you have any ideas about signaling for help, forget them. If you try, I'll shoot. I might get hurt, but you'll be dead. It's not worth it. O.K.?' The girl nodded. 'Let's go.'

The drive to Virginia was tense. Malcolm never took his eyes off the girl. She never took her eyes off the road. Just after the Alexandria exit she pulled into a small courtyard surrounded by apartment units.

'Which one is yours?'

'The first one. I have the top two floors. A man lives in the basement.'

'You're doing just fine. Now, when we go up the walk, just pretend you're taking a friend to your place. Remember, I'm right behind you.'

They got out and walked the few steps to the building. The girl shook and had trouble unlocking the door, but she finally made it. Malcolm followed her in, gently closing the door behind him.

'I have treated this game in great detail because I think it is important for the student to see what he's up against, and how he ought to go about solving the problems of practical play. You may not be able to play the defense and counterattack this well, but the game sets a worthwhile goal for you to achieve: how to fight back in a position where your opponent has greater mobility and better prospects.'

– Fred Reinfeld, The Complete Chess Course

Thursday Evening
– Friday Morning

'I don't believe you.' The girl sat on the couch, her eyes glued to Malcolm. She was not as frightened as she had been, but her heart felt as if it was breaking ribs.

Malcolm sighed. He had been sitting across from the girl for an hour. From what he found in her purse, he knew she was Wendy Ross, twenty-seven years old, had lived and driven in Carbondale, Illinois, distributed 135 pounds on her five-foot-ten frame (he was sure that was an overestimated lie), regularly gave Type O Positive blood to the Red Cross, was a card-carrying user of the Alexandria Public Library and a member of the University of Southern Illinois Alumni Association, and was certified to receive and deliver summonses for her employers, Bechtel, Barber, Sievers, Holloron, and Muckleston. From what he read on her face, he knew she was frightened and telling the truth when she said she didn't believe him. Malcolm didn't blame her, as he really didn't believe his story either, and he knew it was true.

'Look,' he said, 'if what I said wasn't true, why would I try to convince you it was?'

'I don't know.'

'Oh, Jesus!' Malcolm paced the room. He could tie her up and still use her place, but that was risky. Besides, she could be invaluable. He had an inspiration in the middle of a sneeze.

'Look,' he said, wiping his upper lip, 'suppose I could at least prove to you I was with the C.I.A. Then would you believe me?'

'I might.' A new look crossed the girl's face.

'O.K., look at this.' Malcolm sat down beside her. He felt her body tense, but she took the mutilated pieces of paper.

'What's this?'

'It's my C.I.A. identification card. See, that's me with long hair.'

Her voice was cold. 'It says Tentrex Industries, not C.I.A. I can read, you know.' He could see she regretted her inflection after she said it, but she didn't apologise.

'I know what it says!' Malcolm grew more impatient and nervous. His plan might not work. 'Do you have a D.C. phone book?'

The girl nodded toward an end table. Malcolm crossed the room, picked up the huge book, and flung it at the girl. Her reactions were so keyed she caught it without any trouble. Malcolm shouted at her, 'Look in there for Tentrex Industries. Anywhere! White pages, yellow pages, anywhere. The card gives a phone number and an address on Wisconsin Avenue, so it should be in the book. Look!'

The girl looked, then she looked again. She closed the book and stared at Malcolm. 'So you've got an I.D. card for a place that doesn't exist. What does that prove?'

'Right!' Malcolm crossed the room excitedly, bringing the phone with him. The cord barely reached. 'Now,' he said, very secretively, 'look up the Washington number for the Central Intelligence Agency. The numbers are the same.'

The girl opened the book again and turned the pages. For a long time she sat puzzled, then with a new look and a questioning voice she said, 'Maybe you checked this out before you made the card, just for times like this.'

Shit, thought Malcolm. He let all the air out of his lungs, took a deep breath, and started again. 'O.K., maybe I did, but there's one way to find out. Call that number.'

'It's after five,' said the girl. 'If no one answers am I supposed to believe you until morning?'

Patiently, calmly, Malcolm explained to her. 'You're right. If Tentrex is a real company, it's closed for the day. But C.I.A. doesn't close. Call that number and ask for Tentrex.' He handed her the phone. 'One thing. I'll be listening, so don't do anything wrong. Hang up when I tell you.'

The girl nodded and made the call. Three rings.

'W.E. 4-3926.'

'May I have Tentrex Industries, please?' The girl's voice was very dry.

'I'm sorry,' said a soft voice. A faint click came over the line. 'Everyone at Tentrex has gone for the day. They'll be back in the morning. May I ask who is calling and what the nature of your business …'

Malcolm broke the connection before the trace had a chance to even get a general fix. The girl slowly replaced the receiver. For the first time she looked directly at Malcolm. 'I don't know if I believe everything you say,' she said, 'but I think I believe some of it.'

'One final piece of proof.' Malcolm took the gun out of his pants and laid it carefully in her lap. He walked across the room and sat in the beanbag chair. His palms were damp, but it was better to take the risk now than later. 'You've got the gun. You could shoot me at least once before I got to you. There's the phone. I believe in you enough to think you believe me. Call anybody you want. Police, C.I.A., F.B.I., I don't care. Tell them you've got me. But I want you to know what might happen if you do. The wrong people might get the call. They might get here first. If they do, we're both dead.'

For a long time the girl sat still, looking at the heavy gun in her lap. Then, in a soft voice Malcolm had to strain to hear, she said, 'I believe you.'

She suddenly burst into activity. She stood up, laid the gun on the table and paced the room. 'I … I don't know what I can do to help you, but I'll try. You can stay here in the extra bedroom. Umm.' She looked towards the small kitchen and meekly said, 'I could make something to eat.'

Malcolm grinned, a genuine smile he thought he had lost. 'That would be wonderful. Could you do one thing for me?'

'Anything, anything, I'll do anything.' Wendy's nerves unwound as she realised she might live.

'Could I use your shower? The hair down my back is killing me.'

She grinned at him and they both laughed. She showed him the bathroom upstairs and provided him with soap, shampoo, and towels. She didn't say a word when he took the gun with him. As soon as she left him he tiptoed to the top of the stairs. No sound of a door opening, no telephone dialing. When he heard drawers opening and closing, silverware rattling, he went back to the bathroom, undressed, and climbed into the shower.

Malcolm stayed in the shower for thirty minutes, letting the soft pellets of water drive freshness through his body. The steam cleared his sinuses, and by the time he shut off the water he felt almost human. He changed into his new pullover and fresh underwear. He automatically looked in the mirror to straighten his hair. It was so short he did it with two strokes of his hand.

The stereo was playing as he came down the stairs. He recognised the album as Vince Guaraldi's score for *Black Orpheus*. The song was 'Cast Your Fate to the Wind'. He had the album too, and told her so as they sat down to eat.

During green salad she told Malcolm about smalltown life in Illinois. Between bites of frozen German beans he heard about life at Southern Illinois University. Mashed potatoes were mixed with a story concerning an almost fiancé. Between chunks of the jiffy-cooked Swiss steak he learned how drab it is to be a legal secretary for a stodgy corporate law firm in Washington. There was a lull for Sara Lee cherry covered cheesecake. As she poured coffee she summed it all up with, 'It's really been pretty dull. Up till now, of course.'

During dishes he told her why he hated his first name.

She promised never to use it. She threw a handful of suds at him, but quickly wiped them off.

After dishes he said good night and trudged up the stairs to the bathroom. He put his contact lenses in his portable carrying case (what I wouldn't give for my glasses and soaking case, he thought). He brushed his teeth, crossed the hall to a freshly made bed, stuck a precautionary handkerchief under his pillow, laid the gun on the night stand, and went to sleep.

She came to him shortly after midnight. At first he thought he was dreaming, but her heavy breathing and the heat of her body were too real. His first fully awake thought noted that she had just showered. He could faintly smell bath powder mingling with the sweet odor of sex. He rolled on his side, pulling her eager body against him. They found each other's mouth. Her tongue pushed through his lips, searching. She was tremendously excited. He had a hard time untangling himself from her arms so he could strip off his underwear. By now their faces were wet from each other. Naked at last, he rolled her over on her back, pulling his hand slowly up the inside of her thigh, delicately trailing his fingers across rhythmically flowing hips, up across her flat, heaving stomach to her large, erect nipples. His fingers closed on one small breast, easily gathering the mound of flesh into his hand. From out of nowhere he thought of the girl who walked past the Society's building: she had such fine, large breasts. He softly squeezed his hand. Wendy groaned loudly and pulled his head to her chest, his lips to her straining nipples. As his mouth slowly caressed her breasts, he ran his hand down, down to the wet fire between her legs. When he touched her she sucked in air, softly but firmly arching her back. She found him, and a second later softly moaned, 'Now, please now!' He mounted her, clumsily as first-time lovers do. They pressed together. She tried to cover every inch of her body with him. His hard thrusts spread fire through her body. She ran her hands down his back, and just before they exploded he felt her fingernails digging into his buttocks, pulling him ever deeper.

They lay quietly together for half an hour, then they began again, slowly and more carefully, but with a greater intensity. Afterwards, as she lay cradled on his chest, she spoke. 'You don't have to love me. I don't love you, I don't think so anyway. But I want you, and I need you.'

Malcolm said nothing, but he drew her closer. They slept.

Other people didn't get to bed that night. When Langley heard the reports of the Weatherby shooting, already frazzled nerves frazzled more. Crash cars full of very determined men beat the ambulance to the alley. Washington police complained to their superiors about 'unidentified men claiming to be federal officers' questioning witnesses. A clash between two branches of government was averted by the entrance of a third. Three more official-looking cars pulled into the neighborhood. Two very serious men in pressed white shirts and dark suits pushed their way through the milling crowd to inform commanders of the other departments that the F.B.I. was now officially in charge. The 'unidentified federal officers' and the Washington police checked with their headquarters and both were told not to push the issue.

The F.B.I. entered the case when the powers-that-were

adopted a working assumption of espionage. The National Security Act of 1947 states, 'The agency [C.I.A.] shall have no police, subpoena, law-enforcement powers, or internal security functions.' The events of the day most definitely fell under the heading of internal subversive activities, activities that are the domain of the F.B.I. Mitchell held off informing the sister agency of details for as long as he dared, but eventually a deputy director yielded to pressure.

But the C.I.A. would not be denied the right to investigate assaults on its agents, no matter where the assaults occurred. The Agency has a loophole through which many questionable activities funnel. The loophole, Section 5 of the Act, allows the Agency to perform 'such other functions and duties related to intelligence affecting the national security as the National Security Council may from time to time direct.' The Act also grants the Agency the power to question people inside the country. The directors of the Agency concluded that the extreme nature of the situation warranted direct action by the Agency. This action could and would continue until halted by a direct order from the National Security Council. In a very polite but pointed note they so informed the F.B.I., thanking them, of course, for their co-operation and expressing gratitude for any future help.

The Washington police were left with one corpse and a gunshot victim who had disappeared to an undisclosed hospital in Virginia, condition serious, prognosis uncertain. They were not pleased or placated by assurances from various federal officers, but they were unable to pursue 'their' case.

The jurisdictional mishmash tended to work itself out in

the field, where departmental rivalry meant very little compared to dead men. The agents in charge of operations for each department agreed to co-ordinate their efforts. By evening one of the most extensive man hunts in Washington's history began to unfold, with Malcolm as the object of activity. By morning the hunters had turned up a good deal, but they had no clues to Malcolm's whereabouts.

This did little to brighten a bleak morning after for the men who sat around a table in a central Washington office. Most of them had been up until very late the night before, and most of them were far from happy. The liaison group included all of the C.I.A. deputy directors and representatives from every intelligence group in the country. The man at the head of the table was the deputy director in charge of Intelligence Division. Since the crisis occurred in his division, he had been placed in charge of the investigation. He summed up the facts for the grim men he faced.

'Eight Agency people dead, one wounded, and one, a probable double, missing. Again, we have only a tentative – and I must say doubtful – explanation of why.'

'What makes you think the note the killers left is a fake?' The man who spoke wore the uniform of the United States Navy.

The Deputy Director sighed. The Captain always had to have things repeated. 'We're not saying it's a fake, we only think so. We think it's a ruse, an attempt to blame the Czechs for the killings. Sure, we hit one of their bases in Prague, but for tangible, valuable intelligence. We only killed one man. Now, they go in for many things, but melodramatic revenge isn't one of them. Nor is leaving notes on the scene neatly explaining everything. Especially when it gains them nothing. Nothing.'

'Ah, may I ask a question or two, Deputy?'

The Deputy leaned forward, immediately intent. 'Of course, sir.'

'Thank you.' The man who spoke was small and delicately old. To strangers he inevitably appeared to be a kindly old uncle with a twinkle in his eye. 'Just to refresh my memory – stop me if I'm wrong – the one in the apartment, Heidegger, had sodium pentothal in his blood?'

'That's correct, sir.' The Deputy strained, trying to remember if he had forgotten any detail in the briefing.

'Yet none of the others were 'questioned', as far as we can tell. Very strange. They came for him in the night, before the others. Killed shortly before dawn. Yet your investigation puts our boy Malcolm at his apartment that afternoon after Weatherby was shot. You say there is nothing to indicate Heidegger was a double agent? No expenditures beyond his income, no signs of outside wealth, no reported tainted contacts, no blackmail vulnerability?'

'Nothing, sir.'

'Any signs of mental instability?' C.I.A. personnel are among the highest groups in the nation for incidence of mental illness.

'None, sir. Excepting his former alcoholism, he appeared to be normal, though somewhat reclusive.'

'Yes, so I read. Investigation of the others reveal anything out of the ordinary?'

'Nothing, sir.'

'Would you do me a favor and read what Weatherby said to the doctors? By the way, how is he?'

'He's doing better, sir. The doctors say he'll live, but they are taking his leg off this morning.' The Deputy shuffled papers until he found the one he sought. 'Here it is. Now, you must remember he has been unconscious most of the time, but once he woke up, looked at the doctors, and said, "Malcolm shot me. He shot both of us. Get him, hit him".'

There was a stir at the end of the table and the Navy captain leaned forward in his chair. In his heavy, slurred voice he said, 'I say we find that son of a bitch and blast him out of whatever rat hole he ran into!'

The old man chuckled. 'Yes. Well, I quite agree we must find our wayward Condor. But I do think it would be a pity if we "blasted" him before he told us why he shot poor Weatherby. Indeed, why anybody was shot. Do you have anything else for us, Deputy?'

'No, sir,' said the Deputy, stuffing papers into his briefcase. 'I think we've covered everything. You have all the information we do. Thank you all for coming.'

As the men stood to leave, the old man turned to a colleague and said quietly, 'I wonder why.' Then with a smile and a shake of his head he left the room.

Malcolm woke up only when Wendy's caresses became impossible for even a sick man to ignore. Her hands and mouth moved all over his body, and almost before he knew what was happening she mounted him and again he felt her fluttering warmth turn to fire. Afterwards, she looked at him for a long time, lightly touching his body as if exploring an unseen land. She touched his forehead and frowned.

'Malcolm, do you feel O.K.?'

Malcolm had no intention of being brave. He shook his head and forced a raspy 'No' from his throat. The one word seemed to fuel the hot vise closing around his throat. Talking was out for the day.

'You're sick!' Wendy grabbed his lower jaw. 'Let me see!' she ordered, and forced his mouth open. 'My God, it's red down there!' She let go of Malcolm and started to climb out of bed. 'I'm going to call a doctor.'

Malcolm caught her arm. She turned to him with a fearful look, then smiled. 'It's O.K. I have a friend whose husband is a doctor. He drives by here every day on his way to a clinic in D.C. I don't think he's left yet. If he hasn't, I'll ask him to stop by to see my sick friend.' She giggled. 'You don't have to worry. He won't tell a soul because he'll think he's keeping another kind of secret. O.K.?'

Malcolm looked at her for a second, then let go of her arm and nodded. He didn't care if the doctor brought Sparrow IV's friend with him. All he wanted was relief.

The doctor turned out to be a paunchy middle-aged man who spoke little. He poked and prodded Malcolm, took his temperature, and looked down his throat so long Malcolm thought he would throw up. The doctor finally looked up and said, 'You've got a mild case of strep throat, my boy.' He looked at an anxious Wendy hovering nearby. 'Nothing to worry about, really. We'll fix him up.' Malcolm watched the doctor fiddle with something in his bag. When he turned towards Malcolm there was a hypodermic needle in his hand. 'Roll over and puff your shorts down.'

A picture of a limp, cold arm with a tiny puncture

flashed through Malcolm's mind. He froze.

'For Christ's sake, it won't hurt that much. It's only penicillin.'

After giving Malcolm his shot, the doctor turned to Wendy. 'Here,' he said, handing her a slip of paper. 'Get this filled and see that he takes them. He'll need at least a day's rest.' The doctor smiled as he leaned close to Wendy. He whispered, 'And Wendy, I do mean total rest.' He laughed all the way to the door. On the porch, he turned to her and slyly said, 'Whom do I bill?'

Wendy smiled shyly and handed him twenty dollars. The doctor started to speak, but Wendy cut his protest short. 'He can afford it. He – we – really appreciate you coming over.'

'Hmph,' snorted the doctor sarcastically, 'he should. I'm late for my coffee break.' He paused to look at her. 'You know he's the kind of prescription I've thought you needed for a long time.' With a wave of his hand he was gone.

By the time Wendy got upstairs, Malcolm was asleep. She quietly left the apartment. She spent the morning shopping with the list Malcolm and she had composed while waiting for the doctor. Besides filling the prescription, she bought Malcolm several pairs of underwear, socks, some shirts and pants, a jacket, and four different paperbacks, since she didn't know what he liked to read. She carted her bundles home in time to make lunch. She spent a quiet afternoon and evening, occasionally checking on her charge. She smiled all day long.

Supervision of America's large and sometimes cumbersome intelligence community has classically posed the problem of *sed quis custodiet ipsos Custodes:* who guards the guardians? In addition to the internal checks existing independently in each agency, the National Security Act of 1947 created the National Security Council, a group whose composition varies with each change of presidential administration. The Council always includes the President and Vice-President and usually includes major cabinet members. The Council's basic duty is to oversee the activities of the intelligence agencies and to make policy decisions guiding those activities.

But the members of the National Security Council are very busy men with demanding duties besides overseeing a huge intelligence network. Council members by and large do not have the time to devote to intelligence matters, so most decisions about the intelligence community are made by a smaller Council 'sub-committee' known as the Special Group. Insiders often refer to the Special Group as the '54/12 Group', so called because it was created by Secret Order 54/12 early in the Eisenhower years. The 54/12 Group is virtually unknown outside the intelligence, community, and there only a handful of men are aware of its existence.

Composition of the 54/12 Group also varies with each administration. Its membership generally includes the director of the C.I.A., the Under Secretary of State for Political Affairs or his deputy, and the Secretary and Deputy Secretary of Defense. In the Kennedy and early Johnson administrations the presidential representative and key man on the 54/12 Group was McGregor Bundy. The other members were McCone, McNamara, Roswell Gilpatric (Deputy Secretary of Defense), and U. Alexis

Johnson (Deputy Under Secretary of State for Political Affairs).

Overseeing the American intelligence community poses problems for even a small, full-time group of professionals. One is that the overseers must depend on those they oversee for much of the information necessary for regulation. Such a situation is naturally a delicate perplexity.

There is also the problem of fragmented authority. For example, if an American scientist spies on the country while employed by N.A.S.A., then defects to Russia and continues his spying but does it from France, which American agency is responsible for his neutralisation? The F.B.I., since he began his activities under their jurisdiction, or the C.I.A., since he shifted to activities under their purview? With the possibility of bureaucratic jealousies escalating into open rivalry, such questions take on major import.

Shortly after it was formed, the 54/12 Group tried to solve the problems of internal information and fragmented authority. The 54/12 Group established a small special security section, a section with no identity save that of staff for the 54/12 Group. The special section's duties included liaison work. The head of the special section serves on a board composed of leading staff members from all intelligence agencies. He has the power to arbitrate jurisdictional disputes. The special section also has the responsibility of independently evaluating all the information given to the 54/12 Group by the intelligence community. But most important, the special section is given the power to perform 'such necessary security functions as extraordinary circumstances might dictate, subject to Group [the 54/12 Group] regulation'.

To help the special section perform its duties, the 54/12 Group assigned a small staff to the section chief and allowed him to draw on other major security and intelligence groups for needed staff and authority.

The 54/12 Group knows it has created a potential problem. The special section could follow the natural tendency of most government organisations and grow in size and awkwardness, thereby becoming a part of the problem it was created to solve. The special section, small though it is, has tremendous power as well as tremendous potential. A small mistake by the section could be a lever of great magnitude. The 54/12 Group supervises its creation cautiously. They keep a firm check on any bureaucratic growth potentials in the section, they carefully review its activities, keeping the operational work of the section at a bare minimum, and they place only extraordinary men in charge of the section.

While Malcolm and Wendy waited for the doctor, a large, competent-looking man sat in an outer office on Pennsylvania Avenue, waiting to answer a very special summons. His name was Kevin Powell. He waited patiently but eagerly: he did not receive such a summons every day. Finally a secretary beckoned, and he entered the inner office of a man who looked like a kindly, delicate old uncle. The old man motioned Powell to a chair.

'Ah, Kevin, how wonderful to see you.'

'Good to see you, sir. You're looking fit.'

'As do you, my boy, as do you. Here.' The old man tossed Powell a file folder. 'Read this.' As Powell read, the old man examined him closely. The plastic surgeons had done a marvelous job on his ear, and it took an experienced eye to detect the slight bulge close to his left armpit. When Powell raised his eyes, the old man said, 'What do you think, my boy?'

Powell chose his words carefully. 'Very strange, sir. I'm not sure what it means, though it must mean a great deal.'

'Exactly my thoughts, my boy, exactly mine. Both the Agency and the Bureau [F.B.I.] have squads of men scouring the city, watching the airports, buses, trains, the usual routine, only expanded to quite a staggering level. As you know, it's these routine operations that make or break most endeavors, and I must say they are doing fairly well. Or they were up until now.'

He paused for breath and an encouraging look of interest from Powell. 'They've found a barber who remembers giving our boy a haircut – rather predictable yet commendable action on his part – some time after Weatherby was shot. By the way, he is coming along splendidly. They hope to question him late this evening. Where was I … Oh, yes. They canvassed the area and found where he bought some clothes, but then they lost him. They have no idea where to look next. I have one or two ideas about that myself, but I'll save them for later. There are some points I want you to check me on. See if you can answer them for me, or maybe find some questions I can't find.

'Why? Why the whole thing? If it was Czechoslovakia, why that particular branch, a do-nothing bunch of analysts? If it wasn't, we're back to our original question.

'Look at the method. Why so blatant? Why was the man Heidegger hit the night before? What did he know that the others didn't? If he was special, why kill the others too?

If Malcolm works for them, they didn't need to question Heidegger about much. Malcolm could have told them.

'Then we have our boy Malcolm, Malcolm with the many "why's". If he is a double, why did he use the Panic procedure? If he is a double, why did he set up a meeting – to kill Sparrow IV, whom he could have picked off at his leisure had he worked at establishing the poor fellow's identity? If he isn't a double, why did he shoot the two men he called to take him to safety? Why did he go to Heidegger's apartment after the shooting? And, of course, where, why, and how is he now?

'There are a lot of other questions that grow from these, but I think these are the main ones. Do you agree?'

Powell nodded and said, 'I do. Where do I fit in?'

The old man smiled. 'You, my dear boy, have the good fortune to be on loan to my section. As you know, we were created to sort out the mishmashes of bureaucracy. I imagine some of those paper pushers who shuffled my poor old soul here assumed I would be stuck processing paper until I died or retired. Neither of those alternatives appeal to me, so I have redefined liaison work to mean a minimum of paper and a maximum of action, pirated a very good set of operatives, and set up my own little shop, just like in the old days. With the official maze of the intelligence community, I have a good deal of confusion to play with. A dramatist I once knew said the best way to create chaos is to flood the scene with actors. I've managed to capitalise on the chaos of others.

'I think some of my efforts,' he added in a modest tone, 'small though they may be, have been of some value to the country.

'Now we come to this little affair. It isn't really much of my business, but the damn thing intrigues me. Besides, I think there is something wrong with the way the Agency and the Bureau are handling the whole thing. First of all, this is a very extraordinary situation, and they are using fairly ordinary means. Second, they're tripping over each other, both hot to make the pinch, as they say. Then there's the one thing I can't really express. Something about this whole affair bothers me. It should never have happened. Both the idea behind the event and the way in which the event manifested itself are so … wrong, so out of place. I think it's beyond the parameters of the Agency. Not that they're incompetent – though I think they have missed one or two small points – but they're just not viewing it from the right place. Do you understand, my boy?'

Powell nodded. 'And you are in the right place, right?'

The old man smiled. 'Well, let's just say one foot is in the door. Now here's what I want you to do. Did you notice our boy's medical record? Don't bother looking, I'll tell you. He has many times the number of colds and respiratory problems he should. He often needs medical attention. Now, if you remember the transcript of the second panic call, he sneezed and said he had a cold. I'm playing a long shot that his cold is much worse, and that wherever he is, he'll come out to get help. What do you think?'

Powell shrugged. 'Might be worth a try.'

The old man was gleeful. 'I think so, too. Neither the Agency nor the Bureau has tumbled to this yet, so we have a clear field. Now, I've arranged for you to head a special team of D.C. detectives – never mind how I managed it, I did. Start with the general practitioners in the metropolitan area. Find out if any of them have treated anyone like our boy – use his new description. If they haven't, tell them to report to us if they do. Make up some plausible story so they'll open up to you. One other thing. Don't let the others find out we're looking too. The last time they had a chance, two men got shot.'

Powell stood to go. 'I'll do what I can, sir.'

'Fine, fine, my boy. I knew I could count on you. I'm still thinking on this. If I come up with anything else, I'll let you know. Good luck.'

Powell left the room. When the door was shut, the old man smiled.

While Kevin Powell began his painstakingly dull check of the Washington medical community, a very striking man with strange eyes climbed out of a taxi in front of Sunny's Surplus. The man had spent the morning reading a Xeroxed file identical with the one Powell had just examined. He had received the file from a very distinguished-looking gentleman. The man with the strange eyes had a plan for finding Malcolm. He spent an hour driving around the neighborhood, and now he began to walk it. At bars, newspaper stands, public offices, private buildings, anywhere a man could stop for a few minutes, he would stop and show an artist's projected sketch of Malcolm with short hair. When people seemed reluctant to talk to him, the man flashed one of five sets of credentials the distinguished man had obtained. By 3.30 that afternoon he was tired, but it didn't show. He was more resolute than ever. He stopped at a Hot Shoppe for coffee. On the way out he flashed the picture and a badge at the cashier in a by now automatic manner. Almost anyone else would have registered the shock he felt when the clerk said she recognised the man.

'Yeah, I saw the son of a bitch. He threw his money at me he was in such a hurry to leave. Ripped a nylon crawling after a rolling nickel.'

'Was he alone?'

'Yeah, who would want to be with a creep like that?'

'Did you see which way he went?'

'Sure I saw. If I'd have had a gun I'd have shot him. He went that way.'

The man carefully paid his bill, leaving a dollar tip for the cashier. He walked in the direction she had pointed. Nothing, no reason to make a man looking for safety hurry that particular way. Then again … He turned into the parking lot and became a D.C. detective for the fat man in the felt hat.

'Sure, I seen him. He got into the car with the chick.'

The striking man's eyes narrowed. 'What chick?'

'The one that works in them lawyers. The firm rents space for all the people that work there. She ain't so great to look at, but she's got class, if you know what I mean."

'I think so,' said the fake detective, 'I think so. Who is she?'

'Just a minute.' The man in the hat waddled into a small shack. He returned carrying a ledger. 'Let's see, lot 63 … lot 63. Yeah, here it is. Ross, Wendy Ross. This here is her Alexandria address.'

The narrow eyes glanced briefly at the offered book and recorded what they saw. They turned back to the man in the felt hat. 'Thanks.' The striking man began to walk away.

'Don't mention it. Say, what's this guy done?'

The man stopped and turned back. 'Nothing, really. We're just looking for him. He ... he's been exposed to something – it couldn't hurt you – and we just want to make sure he's all right.'

Ten minutes later the striking man was in a phone booth. Across the city a distinguished-looking gentlemen picked up a private phone that seldom rang. 'Yes,' he said, then recognised the voice.

'I have a firm lead.'

'I knew you would. Have someone check it out, but don't let him act on it unless absolutely unavoidable circumstances arise. I want you to handle it personally so there will be no more mistakes. Right now I have a more pressing matter for your expert attention.'

'Our sick mutual friend?'

'Yes. I'm afraid he has to take a turn for the worse. Meet me at place four as soon as you can.' The line went dead.

The man stayed in the phone booth long enough to make another short call. Then he hailed a taxi and rode away into the fading light.

A small car parked across and up the street from Wendy's apartment just as she brought a tray of stew to Malcolm. The driver could see Wendy's door very clearly, even though he had to bend his tall, thin body into a very strange position. He watched the apartment, waiting.

'*Overconfidence breeds error when we take for granted that the game will continue on its normal course; when we fail to provide for an unusually powerful resource — a check, a sacrifice, a stalemate. Afterwards the victim may wail, "But who could have dreamt of such an idiotic–looking move?"*'

— Fred Reinfeld, *The Complete Chess Course*

Saturday

'Are you feeling any better?'

Malcolm looked up at Wendy and had to admit that he was. The pain in his throat had subsided to a dull ache and almost twenty-four hours of sleep had restored a good deal of his strength. His nose still ran most of the time and talking brought pain, but even these discomforts were slowly fading.

As the discomforts of his body decreased, the discomforts of his mind increased. He knew it was Saturday, two days after his co-workers had been killed and he had shot a man. By now several very resourceful, very determined groups of people would be turning Washington upside down. At least one group wanted him dead. The others probably had little affection for him. In a dresser across the room lay $9,382 stolen from a dead man, or at least removed from his apartment. Here he was, lying sick in bed without the foggiest notion about what had happened or what he was to do. On top of all that, here on his bed sat a funny-looking girl wearing a T shirt and a smile.

'You know, I really don't understand it,' he rasped. He didn't. In all the hours he had devoted to the problem he could find only four tentative assumptions that held water: that the Agency had been penetrated by somebody; that somebody had hit his section; that somebody had tried to frame Heidegger as a double by leaving the 'hidden' money; and that somebody wanted him dead.

'Do you know what you're going to do yet?' Wendy used her forefinger to trace the outline of Malcolm's thigh under the sheet.

'No.' He said exasperatedly, 'I might try the panic number later tonight, if you'll take me to a phone booth.'

She leaned forward and lightly kissed his forehead. 'I'll take you anywhere.' She smiled and lightly kissed him, his eyes, his cheek, down to his mouth, down to his neck. Flipping back the sheet, she kissed his chest, down to his stomach, down.

Afterwards they showered and he put in his contacts. He went back to bed. When Wendy came back into his room, she was fully dressed. She tossed him four paperbacks. 'I didn't know what you liked, but these should keep you busy while I'm gone.'

'Where are –' Malcolm had to pause and swallow. It still hurt. 'Where are you going?'

She smiled. 'Silly boy, I've got to shop. We're low on food and there are still some things you need. If you're very good – and you're not bad – I might bring you a surprise.' She walked away but turned back at the door. 'If the phone rings, don't answer unless it rings twice, stops, then rings again. That'll be me. Aren't I learning how to be a good spy? I'm not expecting anybody. If you're quiet, no one will know you're here.' Her voice took on a more serious tone. 'Now, don't worry, O.K.? You're perfectly safe here.' She turned and left.

Malcolm had just picked up one book when her head popped round the doorjamb. 'Hey,' she said, 'I just thought of something. If I get strep throat, will it classify as venereal disease?' Malcolm missed when he threw the book at her.

When Wendy opened her door and walked to her car, she didn't notice the man in the van parked across the street stirring out of lethargy. He was a plain-looking man. He wore a bulky raincoat even though spring sunshine ruled the morning. It was almost as if he knew the good weather couldn't last. The man watched Wendy pull out of the parking lot and drive away. He looked at his watch. He would wait three minutes.

Saturday is a day off for most government employees, but not for all. This particular Saturday saw a large number of civil servants from various government levels busily and glumly drawing overtime. One of these was Kevin Powell. He and his men had talked to 216 doctors, receiving nurses, interns, and other assorted members of the medical profession. Over half the general practitioners and throat specialists in the Washington area had been questioned. It was now eleven o'clock on a fine Saturday morning. All Powell had to report to the old man behind the mahogany desk could be summed up in one word: nothing.

The old man's spirits weren't dimmed by the news. 'Well, my boy, just keep on trying, that's all I can say, just keep on trying. If it's any consolation, let me say we're in the same position as the others, only they have run out of things to do except watch. But one thing has happened: Weatherby is dead.'

Powell was puzzled. 'I thought you said his condition was improving.'

The old man spread his hands. 'It was. They planned to question him late last night or early this morning. When the interrogation team arrived shortly after one a.m., they found him dead.'

'How?' Powell's voice held more than a little suspicion.

'How indeed? The guard on the door swears only medical personnel went in and out. Since he was in the Langley hospital, I'm sure security must have been tight. His doctors say that, given the shock and the loss of blood, it is entirely possible he died from the wound. They were sure he was doing marvelously. Right now they're doing a complete autopsy.'

'It's very strange.'

'Yes it is, isn't it? But because it's strange, it should have been almost predictable. The whole case is strange. Ah, well, we've been over this ground before. I have something new for you.'

Powell leaned closer to the desk. He was tired. The old man continued, 'I told you I wasn't satisfied with the way the Agency and the Bureau were handling the case. They've run into a blind wall. I'm sure part of the reason is that their method led them there. They've been looking for Malcolm the way a hunter looks for any game. While they're skilled hunters, they're missing a thing or two. I want you to start looking for him as though you were the prey. You've read all the information we have on him, you've been to his apartment. You must have some sense of the man. Put yourself in his shoes and see where you end up.

'I have a few helpful tidbits for you. We know he needed transportation to get wherever he is. If nothing else, a man on foot is visible, and our boy wants to avoid that. The Bureau is fairly certain he didn't take a cab. I see no reason to fault their investigation along those lines. I don't think he would ride a bus, not with the package the man at the store sold him. Besides, one never knows who one might meet on a bus.

'So there's your problem. Take a man or two, men who can put themselves in the right frame of mind. Start from where he was last seen. Then, my boy, get yourself hidden the way he has.'

Just before Powell opened the door, he looked at the smiling old man and said, 'There's one other thing that's strange about this whole business, sir. Malcolm was never trained as a field agent. He's a researcher, yet look how well he's made out.'

'Yes, that is rather strange,' answered the old man. He smiled and said, 'You know, I'm getting rather keen to meet our boy Malcolm. Find him for me, Kevin, find him for me quickly.'

Malcolm needed a cup of coffee. The hot liquid would make his throat feel better and the caffeine would pep him up. He grinned slowly, being careful not to stretch tender neck muscles. With Wendy, a man needed a lot of pep. He went downstairs to the kitchen. He had just put a pot on to boil when the doorbell rang.

Malcolm froze. The gun was upstairs, right next to his bed where he could reach it in a hurry, provided, of course, that he was in bed. Quietly, Malcolm tiptoed to the door. The bell rang again. He sighed with relief when he saw through the one-way glass peephole that it was only a bored-looking mailman, his bag slung over one shoulder, a package in one hand. Then he became annoyed. If he didn't answer the door, the mailman might keep coming back until he delivered his package. Malcolm looked down at his body. He only had on jockey shorts and a T shirt. Oh well, he thought, the mailman's probably seen it all before. He opened the door.

'Good morning, sir, how are you today?'

The mailman's cheer seemed to infect Malcolm. He smiled back, and said hoarsely, 'Got a little cold. What can I do for you?'

'Got a package here for a Miss …' The mailman paused and slyly smiled at Malcolm. 'A Miss Wendy Ross. Special delivery, return receipt requested.'

'She's not here right now. Could you come back later?'

The mailman scratched his head. 'Well, could, but it would sure be easier if you signed for it. Hell, government don't care who signs, long as it's signed.'

'O.K.,' said Malcolm. 'Do you have a pen?'

The mailman slapped his pockets unsuccessfully.

'Come on in,' Malcolm said. 'I'll get one.'

The mailman smiled as he entered the room. He closed the door behind him. 'You're making my day a lot easier by going to all this trouble,' he said.

Malcolm shrugged. 'Think nothing of it.' He turned and went into the kitchen to find a pen. As he walked through the door, his mind abstractedly noted that the mailman had put the package down and was unslinging his pouch.

The mailman was very happy. His orders had been to determine whether Malcolm was in the apartment, to reconnoiter the building, and to make a hit only if it could be done with absolute safety and certainty. He knew a bonus would follow his successful display of initiative in hitting Malcolm. The girl would come later. He pulled the silenced sten gun out of his pouch.

Just before Malcolm came around the corner from the kitchen he heard the click when the mailman armed the sten gun. Malcolm hadn't found a pen. In one hand he carried the coffeepot and in the other an empty cup. He thought the nice mailman might like some refreshment. That Malcolm didn't die then may be credited to the fact that when he turned the corner and saw the gun swinging toward him he didn't stop to think. He threw the pot of boiling coffee and the empty cup straight at the mailman.

The mailman hadn't heard Malcolm coming. His first thought centered on the objects flying towards his face. He threw up his arms, covering his head with the gun. The coffeepot bounced off the gun, but the lid flew off and hot coffee splashed down on bare arms and an upturned face.

Screaming, the mailman threw the gun away from him. It skidded across the floor, stopping under the table holding Wendy's stereo. Malcolm made a desperate dive for it, only to be tripped by a black loafer. He fell to his hands and staggered up. He quickly looked over his shoulder and ducked. The mailman flew over Malcolm's head. Had the flying side kick connected, the back of Malcolm's head would have shattered and in all probability his neck would have snapped.

Even though he hadn't practiced in a dojo for six months, the mailman executed the difficult landing perfectly. However, he landed on the scatter rug Wendy's grandmother had given her as a birthday present. The rug slid along the waxed floor and the mailman fell to his hands. He bounced up twice as fast as Malcolm.

The two men stared at each other. Malcolm had at least ten feet to travel before he could reach the gun on his right. He could probably beat the mailman to the table, but before he could pull the gun out the man would be all over his back. Malcolm was closest to the door, but it was closed. He knew he wouldn't have the precious seconds it would take to open it.

The mailman looked at Malcolm and smiled. With the toe of his shoe he tested the hardwood floor. Stick. With deft, practiced movements he slipped his feet out of the loafers. He wore slipperlike socks. These too came off when he rubbed his feet on the floor. The mailman came prepared to walk quietly, barefoot, and his preparations served him in an unexpected manner. His bare feet hugged the floor.

Malcolm looked at his smiling opponent and began to accept death. He had no way of knowing the man's brown belt proficiency, but he knew he didn't stand a chance. Malcolm's knowledge of martial arts was almost negligible. He had read fight scenes in numerous books and seen them in movies. He had had two fights as a child, won one, lost one. His physical education instructor in college had spent three hours teaching the class some cute tricks he had learned in the Marines. Reason made Malcolm try to copy the man's stance, legs bent, fists clenched, left arm in front and bent perpendicular to the floor, right arm held close to the waist.

Very slowly the mailman began to shuffle across the fifteen feet that separated him from his prey. Malcolm began to circle towards his right, vaguely wondering why he bothered. When the mailman was six feet from Malcolm he made his move. He yelled and with his left arm feinted a backhand snap at Malcolm's face. As the mailman anticipated, Malcolm ducked quickly to his right side. When the mailman brought his left hand back, he dropped his left shoulder and whirled to his right on the ball of his left foot. At the end of the three-quarters circle his right leg shot to meet Malcolm's ducking head.

But six months is too long to be out of practice and expect perfect results, even when fighting an untrained amateur. The kick missed Malcolm's face, but thudded into his left shoulder. The blow knocked Malcolm into the wall. When he bounced off he barely dodged the swinging hand chop follow-through blow.

The mailman was very angry with himself. He had missed twice. True, his opponent was injured, but he should have been dead. The mailman knew he must get back into practice before he met an opponent who knew what to do.

A good karate instructor will emphasise that karate is three-quarters mental. The mailman knew this, so he devoted his entire mind to the death of his opponent. He concentrated so deeply he failed to hear Wendy as she opened and shut the door, quietly so as not to disturb

Malcolm's sleeping. She had forgotten her checkbook.

Wendy was dreaming. It wasn't real, these two men standing in her living room. One her Malcolm, his left arm twitching to life at his side. The other a short, stocky stranger standing so strangely, his back towards her. Then she heard the stranger very softly say, 'You've caused enough trouble!' and she knew it was all frighteningly real. As the stranger began to shuffle towards Malcolm, she carefully reached around the kitchen corner, and took a long carving knife from a sparkling set held on the wall by a magnet. She walked towards the stranger.

The mailman heard the click of heels on the hardwood floor. He quickly feinted towards Malcolm and whirled to face the new challenge. When he saw the frightened girl standing with a knife clutched awkwardly in her right hand, the worry that had been building in his brain ceased. He quickly shuffled towards her, dodging and dipping as she backed away trembling. He let her back up until she was about to run into the couch, then he made his move. His left foot snapped forward in a roundhouse kick and the knife flew from her numbed hand. His left knuckles split the skin just beneath her left cheekbone in a vicious backhand strike. Wendy sank, stunned, to the couch.

But the mailman had forgotten an important maxim of multiple-attackers situations. A man being attacked by two or more opponents must keep moving, delivering quick, alternate attacks to each of his opponents. If he stops to concentrate on one before all of his opponents have been neutralised, he leaves himself exposed. The mailman should have whirled to attack Malcolm immediately after the kick. Instead he went for the *coupe de grâce* on Wendy.

By the time the mailman had delivered his backhand blow to Wendy, Malcolm had the sten gun in his hand. He could use his left arm only to prop the barrel up, but he lined the gun up just as the mailman raised his left hand for the final downward chop.

'Don't!'

The mailman whirled towards his other opponent just as Malcolm pulled the trigger. The coughing sounds hadn't stopped before the mailman's chest blossomed with a red, spurting row. The body flew over the couch and thudded on the floor.

Malcolm picked Wendy up. Her left eye began to puff shut and a trickle of blood ran down her cheek. She sobbed quietly, 'My God, my God, my God.'

It took Malcolm five minutes to calm her down. He peered cautiously through the blinds. No one was in sight. The yellow van across the street looked empty. He left Wendy downstairs with the machine gun huddled in her arms pointed at the door. He told her to shoot anything that came through. He quickly dressed, and packed his money, his clothes, and the items Wendy had bought him in one of her spare suitcases. When he came downstairs., she was more rational. He sent her upstairs to pack. While she was gone, he searched the corpse and found nothing. When she came down ten minutes later, her face had been washed and she carried a suitcase.

Malcolm took a deep breath and opened the door. He had a coat draped over his revolver. He couldn't bring himself to take the sten gun. He knew what it had done. No one shot him. He walked to the car. Still no bullets. No one was even visible. He nodded to Wendy. She ran to the car dragging their bags. They got in and he quietly drove away.

Powell was tired. He and two other Washington detectives were covering covered ground, walking along all the streets in the area where Malcolm had last been sighted. They questioned people at every building. All they found were people who had been questioned before. Powell was leaning against a light pole, trying to find a new idea, when he saw one of his men hurrying towards him.

The man was Detective Andrew Walsh, Homicide. He grabbed Powell's arm to steady himself. 'I think I've found something, sir.' Walsh paused to catch his breath. 'You know how we've found a lot of people who were questioned before? Well, I found one, a parking-lot attendant, who told the cop who questioned him something that isn't in the official reports.'

'For Christ's sake, *what*?' Powell was no longer tired.

'He made Malcolm, off a picture this cop showed him. More than that, he told him he saw Malcolm get into a car with this girl. Here's the girl's name and address.'

'When did all this happen?' Powell began to feel cold and uneasy.

'Yesterday afternoon.'

'Come on!' Powell ran down the street to the car, a panting policeman in his wake.

They had driven three blocks when the phone on the dash buzzed. Powell answered. 'Yes?'

'Sir, the medical survey team reports a Dr. Robert Knudsen identified Condor's picture as the man he treated for strep throat yesterday. He treated the suspect at the apartment of a Wendy Ross, R-o...'

Powell cut the dispatcher short. 'We're on our way to her apartment now. I want all units to converge on the area, but do not approach the house until I get there. Tell them to get there as quickly but as quietly as they can. Now give me the chief.'

A full minute passed before Powell heard the light voice come over the phone. 'Yes, Kevin, what do you have?'

'We're on our way to Malcolm's hideout. Both groups hit on it at about the same time. I'll give you details later. There's one other thing: somebody with official credentials has been looking for Malcolm and not reporting what he finds.'

There was a long pause, then the old man said, 'This could explain many things, my boy. Many things. Be very careful. I hope you're in time.' The line went dead. Powell hung up, and resigned himself to the conclusion that he was probably much too late.

Ten minutes later Powell and three detectives rang Wendy's doorbell. They waited a minute, then the biggest man kicked the door in. Five minutes later Powell summed up what he found to the old man.

'The stranger is unidentifiable from here. His postman's uniform is a fake. The silenced sten gun was probably used during the hit on the Society. The way I see it, he and someone else, probably our boy Malcolm, were fighting. Malcolm beat him to the gun. I'm sure it's the mailman's because his pouch is rigged to carry it. Our boy's luck seems to be holding very well. We've found a picture of the girl, and we've got her car license number. How do you want to handle it?'

'Have the police put out an A.P.B. on her for … murder. That'll throw our friend who's monitoring us and using our credentials. Right now, I want to know who the dead man is, and I want to know fast. Send his photo and prints to every agency with a priority rush order. Do not include any other information. Start your teams looking for Malcolm and the girl. Then I guess we have to wait.'

A dark sedan drove by the apartment as Powell and the others walked towards their cars. The driver was tall and painfully thin. His passenger, a man with striking eyes hidden behind sunglasses, waved him on. No one noticed them drive past.

Malcolm drove around Alexandria until he found a small, dumpy used-car lot. He parked two blocks away and sent Wendy to make the purchase. Ten minutes later, after having sworn she was Mrs. A. Edgerton for the purpose of registration and paid an extra hundred dollars cash, she drove off in a slightly used Dodge. Malcolm followed her to a park. They transferred the luggage and removed the license plates from the Corvair. Then they loaded the Dodge and slowly drove away.

Malcolm drove for five hours. Wendy never spoke during the whole trip. When they stopped at the Parisburg, Virginia, motel, Malcolm registered as Mr. and Mrs. Evans. He parked the car behind the motel 'so it won't get dirty from the traffic passing by'. The old lady running the motel merely shrugged and went back to her T.V. She had seen it before.

Wendy lay very still on the bed. Malcolm slowly undressed. He took his medicine and removed his contacts before he sat down next to her.

'Why don't you undress and get some sleep, honey?'

She turned and looked at him slowly. 'It's real, isn't it.' Her voice was softly matter-of-fact. 'The whole thing is real. And you killed that man. In my apartment, you killed a man.'

'It was either him or us. You know that. You tried, too.'

She turned away. 'I know.' She got up and slowly undressed. She turned off the light and climbed into bed. Unlike before, she didn't snuggle close. When Malcolm went to sleep an hour later, he was sure she was still awake.

'Where there is much light there is also much shadow.'

– Goethe

Sunday

'Ah, Kevin, we seem to be making progress.'

The old man's crisp, bright words did little to ease the numbness gripping Powell's mind. His body ached, but the discomfort was minimal. He had been conditioned for much more severe strains than one missed rest period. But during three months of rest and recuperation, Powell had become accustomed to sleeping late on Sunday mornings. Additionally, the frustration of his present assignment irritated him. So far his involvement had been *post facto*. His two years of training and ten years' experience were being used to run errands and gather information. Any cop could do that, and many cops were. Powell didn't share the old man's optimism.

'How, sir?' Frustrated as he was, Powell spoke respectfully. 'Some trace of Condor and the girl?'

'No, not yet.' Despite a very long night, the old man sparkled. 'There's still a chance she bought that car, but it hasn't been seen. No, our progress is from another angle. We've identified the dead man.'

Powell's mind cleared. The old man continued.

'Our friend was once Calvin Lloyd, sergeant, United States Marine Corps. In 1959 he left that group rather suddenly while stationed in Korea as an adviser to a South Korean Marine unit. There is a good chance he was mixed up in the murder of a Seoul madam and one of her girls. The Navy could never find any direct evidence, but they think the madam and he were running a base commuter service and had a falling out over rebates. Shortly after the bodies were found, Lloyd went A.W.O.L. The Marines didn't look for him very hard. In 1961 Navy Intelligence received a report indicating he had died rather suddenly in Tokyo. Then in 1963 he was identified as one of several arms dealers in Laos. Evidently his job was technical advice. At the time, he was linked to a man called Vincent Dale Maronick. More on Maronick later. Lloyd dropped out of sight in 1965, and until yesterday he was again believed dead.'

The old man paused. Powell cleared his throat, signaling that he wanted to speak. After receiving a courteous nod, Powell said, 'Well, at least we know that much. Besides telling us a small who, how does it help?'

The old man held up his left forefinger. 'Be patient, my boy, be patient. Let's take our steps slowly and see what paths cross where.

'The autopsy on Weatherby yielded only a probability, but based on what has happened, I'm inclined to rate it very high. There is a chance his death may be due to an air bubble in the blood, but the pathologists won't swear to it. His doctors insist the cause must be external – and therefore not their fault. I'm inclined to agree with them. It's a pity for us Weatherby isn't around for questioning, but for someone it's a very lucky break. Far too lucky, if you ask me.

'I'm convinced Weatherby was a double agent, though for whom I have no idea. The files that keep turning up missing, our friend with credentials covering the town just ahead of us, the setup of the hit on the Society. They all smell of inside information. With Weatherby eliminated, it follows he could have been the leak that became too dangerous for someone. Then there's that whole shooting scene behind the theaters. We've been over that before, but something new occurred to me.

'I had both Sparrow IV's and Weatherby's bodies examined by our Ballistics men. Whoever shot Weatherby almost amputated his leg with the bullet. According to our man it was at least a .357 magnum with soft lead slugs. But Sparrow IV had only a neat round hole in his throat. Our Ballistics man doesn't think they were shot with the same gun. That, plus the fact Weatherby wasn't killed, makes the whole thing look fishy. I think our boy Malcolm, for some reason or other, shot Weatherby and then ran. Weatherby was hurt, but not hurt so bad he couldn't eliminate witness Sparrow IV. But that's not the interesting piece of news.

'From 1958 until late 1969, Weatherby was stationed in Asia, primarily out of Hong Kong, but with stints in Korea, Japan, Taiwan, Laos, Thailand, Cambodia, and Vietnam. He worked his way up the structure from special field agent to station head. You'll note he was there during the same period as our dead mailman. Now for a slight but very interesting digression. What do you know about the man called Maronick?'

Powell furrowed his brow. 'I think he was some sort of special agent. A freelancer, as I recall.'

The old man smiled, pleased. 'Very good, though I'm

not sure if I understand what you mean by "special". If you mean extremely competent, thorough, careful, and highly successful, then you're correct. If you mean dedicated and loyal to one side, then you are very wrong. Vincent Maronick was – or is, if I'm not mistaken – the best freelance agent in years, maybe the best of this century for his specialty. For a short-term operation requiring cunning, ruthlessness, and a good deal of caution, he was the best money could buy. The man was tremendously skilled. We're not sure where he received his training, though it's clear he was American. His individual abilities were not so outstanding that they couldn't be matched. There were and are better planners, better shots, better pilots, better saboteurs, better everything in particular. But the man had a persevering drive, a toughness that pushed his capabilities far beyond those of his competitors. He's a very dangerous man, one of the men I could fear.

'In the early sixties he surfaced working for the French, mainly in Algeria, but, please note, also taking care of some of their remaining interests in Southeast Asia. Starting in 1963, he came to the attention of those in our business. At various times he worked for Britain, Communist China, Italy, South Africa, the Congo, Canada, and he even did two stints for the Agency. He also did a type of consulting service for the I.R.A. and the O.A.S. (against his former French employers). He always gave satisfaction, and there are no reports of any failures. He was very expensive. Rumor has it he was looking for a big score. Exactly why he was in the business isn't clear, but my guess is it was the one field that allowed him to use his talents to the fullest and reap rewards quasi-legally. Now here's the interesting part.

'In 1964 Maronick was employed by the Generalissimo on Taiwan. Ostensibly he was used for actions against mainland China, but at the time the General was having trouble with the native Taiwanese and some dissidents among his own immigrant group. Marionick was employed to help preserve order. Washington wasn't pleased with some of the Nationalist government's internal policies. They were afraid the General's methods might be a little too heavy-handed for our good. The General refused to agree, and began to go his own merry way. At the same time, we began to worry about Maronick. He was just too good and too available. He had never been employed against us, but it was just a matter of time. The Agency decided to terminate Maronick, as both a preventive measure and as a subtle hint to the General. Now, who do you suppose was station agent out of Taiwan when the Maronick termination order came through?'

Powell was 90 per cent sure, so he ventured, 'Weatherby?'

'Right you are. Weatherby was in charge of the termination operation. He reported it successful, but with a hitch. The method was a bomb in Maronick's billet. Both the Chinese agent who planted the bomb and Maronick were killed. Naturally, the explosion obliterated both bodies. Weatherby verified the hit as an eyewitness.

'Now let's back up a little. Whom do you suppose Maronick employed as an aide on at least five different missions?

It wasn't a guess. Powell said, 'Our dead mailman, Sergeant Calvin Lloyd.'

'Right again. Now here's yet another clincher. We never

had much on Maronick, but we did have a few foggy pictures, sketchy descriptions, whatnot. Guess whose file is missing?' The old man didn't even give Powell a chance to speak before he answered his own question. 'Maronick's. Also, we have no records of Sergeant Lloyd. Neat, yes?'

'Yes indeed.' Powell was still puzzled. 'What makes you think Maronick is involved?'

The old man smiled. 'Just playing an inductive hunch. I racked my brain for a man who could and would pull a hit like the one on the Society. When, out of a dozen men, Maronick's file turned up missing, my curiosity rose. Navy Intelligence sent over the identification of Lloyd, and his file noted he had worked with Maronick. Wheels began to turn. When they both linked up with Weatherby, lights flashed and a band played. I spent a very productive morning making my poor old brain work when I should have been feeding pigeons and smelling cherry blossoms.'

The room was silent while the old man rested and Powell thought. Powell said, 'So you figure Maronick is running some kind of action against us and Weatherby was doubling for him, probably for some time.'

'No,' said the old man softly, 'I don't think so.'

The old man's reply surprised Powell. He could only stare and wait for the soft voice to continue.

'The first and most obvious question is why. Given all that has happened and the way in which it has happened, I don't think the question can practically and logically be approached. If it can't be approached logically, then we are starting from an erroneous assumption, the assumption that the C.I.A. is the central object of an action. Then there's the next question of who. Who would pay – and I imagine pay dearly – for Maronick with Weatherby's duplicity and at least Lloyd's help to have us hit in the way we have been hit? Even given that phony Czech revenge note, I can think of no one. That, of course, brings us back to the why question, and we're spinning our wheels in a circle going nowhere. No, I think the proper and necessary question to ask and answer is not who or why, but what. What is going on? If we can answer that, then the other questions and their answers will flow. Right now, there is only one key to that what, our boy Malcolm.'

Powell sighed wearily. 'So we're back to where we started from, looking for our lost Condor.'

'Not exactly where we started from. I have some of my men digging rather extensively in Asia, looking for whatever it is that ties Weatherby, Maronick, and Lloyd together. They may find nothing, but no one can tell. We also have a better idea of the opposition, and I have some men looking for Maronick.'

'With all the machinery you have at your disposal we should be able to flush one of the two, Malcolm or Maronick – sounds like a vaudeville team, doesn't it?'

'We're not using the machinery, Kevin. We're using us, plus what we can scrounge from the D.C. police.'

Powell choked. 'What the hell! You control maybe fifty men, and the cops can't give you much. The Agency has hundreds of people working on this thing now, not counting the Bureau and the N.S.A. and the others. If you give them what you have given me, they could ...'

Quietly but firmly the old man interrupted. 'Kevin, think a moment. Weatherby was the double in the Agency, possibly with some lower-echelon footmen. He, we assume, acquired the false credentials, passed along the needed information, and even went into the field himself. But if he was the double, then who arranged for his execution, who knew the closely guarded secret of where he was and enough about the security setup to get the executioner (probably the competent Maronick) in and out again?' He paused for the flicker of understanding on Powell's face. 'That's right, another double. If my hunch is correct, a very highly placed double. We can't risk any more leaks. Since we can't trust anyone, we'll have to do it ourselves.'

Powell frowned and hesitated before he spoke. 'May I make a suggestion, sir?'

The old man deliberately registered surprise. 'Why, of course you may, my dear boy! You are supposed to use your fine mind, even if you are afraid of offending your superior.'

Powell smiled slightly. 'We know, or at least we are assuming, there is a leak, a fairly highly placed leak. Why don't we keep after Malcolm but concentrate on stopping the leak from the top? We can figure out what group of people the leak could be in and work on them. Our surveillance should catch them even if so far they haven't left a trail. The pressure of this thing will force them to do something. At the very least, they must keep in touch with Maronick.'

'Kevin,' the old man replied quietly, 'your logic is sound, but the conditions of your assumptions invalidate your plan. You assume we can identify the group of people who could be the source of the leak. One of the troubles with our intelligence community – indeed, one of the reasons for my own section – is that things are so big and so complicated such a group easily numbers over fifty, probably numbers over a hundred, and may run as high as two hundred persons. That's if the leak is conscious on their part. Our leak may be sloppy around his secretary, or his communications man may be a double.

'Even if the leak is not of a secondary nature, through a secretary or a technician, such surveillance would be massive, though not impossible. You've already pointed out my logistical limitations. In order to carry out your suggestion, we would need the permission and assistance of some of the people in the suspect group. That would never do.

'We also have a problem inherent in the group of people with whom we would be dealing. They are professionals in the intelligence business. Don't you think they might tumble to our surveillance? And even if *they* didn't, each one of their departments has its own security system we would have to avoid. For example, officers in Air Force Intelligence are subject to unscheduled spot checks, including surveillance and phone traps. It's done both to see if the officers are honest and to see if someone else is watching them. We would have to avoid security teams *and* a wary, experienced suspect.

'What we have,' the old man said, placing the tips of his fingers together, 'is a classic intelligence problem. We have possibly the world's largest security and intelligence organisation, an entity ironically dedicated to both stopping the flow of information from and increasing the flow to this country. At a moment's notice we can assign a hundred trained men to dissect a fact as minuscule as a misplaced luggage sticker. We can turn the same horde loose on any given small group and within a few days we would know everything the group did. We can bring tremendous pressure to bear on any point we can find. There lies the problem: on this case we can't find the point. We know there's a leak in our machine, but until we can isolate the area it's in, we can't dissect the machine to try to pinpoint the leak. Such activity would be almost certainly futile, and possibly dangerous, to say nothing of awkward. Besides, the moment we start looking, the opposition will know we know there's a leak.

'The key to this whole problem is Malcolm. He might be able to pinpoint the leak for us, or at least steer us in a particular direction. If he does, or if we turn up any links between Maronick's operation and someone in the intelligence community, we will, of course, latch on to the suspect. But until we have a firm link, such an operation would be sloppy, hit-and-miss work. I don't like that kind of job. It's inefficient and usually not productive.'

Powell covered his embarrassment with a formal tone. 'Sorry, sir. I guess I wasn't thinking.'

The old man shook his head. 'On the contrary, my boy,' he exclaimed, 'you were thinking, and that's very good. It's the one thing we've never been able to train our people to do, and it's one thing these massive organisations tend to discourage. It's far better to have you thinking and proposing schemes which, shall we say, are hastily considered and poorly conceived, here in the office, than it is for you to be a robot in the street reacting blindly. That gets every one into trouble, and it's a good way to wind up dead. Keep thinking, Kevin, but be a little more thorough.'

'So the plan is still to find Malcolm and bring him home safe, right?'

The old man smiled. 'Not exactly. I've done a lot of thinking about our boy Malcolm. He is our key. They, whoever they are, want our boy dead, and want him dead badly. If we can keep him alive, *and* if we can make him troublesome enough to them so that they center their activities on his demise, then we have turned Condor into a key. Maronick and company, by concentrating on Malcolm, make themselves into their own lock. If we are careful and just a shade lucky, we can use the key to open the lock. Oh, we still have to find our Condor, and quickly, before anyone else does. I'm making some additional arrangements to aid us along that line too. But when we find him, we prime him.

'After you've had some rest, my assistant will bring you instructions and any further information we receive.'

As Powell got up to go, he said, 'Can you give me anything on Maronick?'

The old man said, 'I'm having a friend in the French secret service send over a copy of their file on the flight from Paris. It won't arrive until tomorrow. I could have had it quicker, but I didn't want to alert the opposition. Outside of what you already know, I can only tell you that physically Maronick is reportedly a very striking man.'

Malcolm began to wake just as Powell left the old man's office. For a few seconds he lay still, remembering all that had happened. Then a soft voice whispered in his ear, 'Are you awake?'

Malcolm rolled over. Wendy rested on one elbow, shyly looking at him. His throat felt better and he sounded almost normal when he said, 'Good morning.'

Wendy blushed. 'I'm … I'm sorry about yesterday, I mean how mean I was. I just … I just have never seen or done anything like that and the shock …'

Malcolm shut her up with a kiss. 'It's O.K. It was pretty horrible.'

'What are we going to do now?' she asked.

'I don't know for sure. I think we should hole up here for at least a day or two.' He looked around the sparsely furnished room. 'It may be a little dull.'

Wendy looked up at him and grinned. 'Well, not too dull.' She kissed him lightly, then again. She pulled his mouth down to her small breast.

Half an hour later they still hadn't decided anything.

'We can't do that *all* the time,' Malcolm said at last.

Wendy made a sour face and said, 'Why not?' But she sighed acceptance. 'I know what we can do!' She leaned half out of the bed and groped on the floor. Malcolm grabbed her arm to keep her from falling.

'What the hell are you doing?' he asked.

'I'm looking for my purse. I brought some books we can read out loud. You said you liked Yeats.' She rummaged under the bed. 'Malcolm, I can't find them, they aren't here. Everything else is in my purse, but the books are missing. I must have … Owww!' Wendy jerked back on the bed and pried herself loose from Malcolm's suddenly tightened grip. 'Malcolm, what are you doing? That hurt …'

'The books. The missing books.' Malcolm turned and looked at her. 'There is something about those missing books that's important! That has to be the reason!'

Wendy was puzzled. 'But they're only poetry books. You

can get them almost anywhere. I probably just forgot to bring them.'

'Not those books, the Society's books, the ones Heidegger found missing!' He told her the story.

Malcolm felt the excitement growing. 'If I can tell them about the missing books, it'll give them something to start on. The reason my section was hit must have been the books. They found out Heidegger was digging up old records. They had to hit everybody in case someone else knew. If I can give the Agency those pieces, maybe they can put the puzzle together. At least I'll have something more to give them than my story about how people get shot wherever I go. They frown on that.'

'But how will you tell the Agency? Remember what happened the last time you called them?'

Malcolm frowned. 'Yes, I see what you mean. But the last time they set up a meeting. Even if the opposition has penetrated the Agency, even if they know what goes over the Panic Line, I still think we're O.K. With all that has gone on, I imagine dozens of people must be involved. At least some of them will be clean. They'll pass on what I phone in. It should ring some right bells somewhere.' He paused for a moment. 'Come on, we have to go back to Washington.'

'Hey, wait a minute!' Wendy's outstretched hand missed its grasp on Malcolm's arm as he bounded out of bed and into the bathroom. 'Why are we going back there?'

The shower turned on. 'Have to. A long-distance phone call can be traced in seconds, a local one takes longer.' The tempo of falling water on metal walls increased.

'But we might get killed!'

'What?'

Wendy yelled, but she tried to be as quiet as possible. 'I said we might be killed.'

'Might get killed here too. You scrub my back and I'll scrub yours.'

'I'm very disappointed, Maronick.' The sharp words cut through the strained air between the two men. The distinguished-looking speaker knew he had made a mistake when he saw the look in his companion's eyes.

'My name is Levine. You will remember that. I suggest you do not make a slip like that again.' The striking man's crisp words undercut the other man's confidence, but the distinguished-looking gentleman tried to hide his discomposure.

'My slip is minor compared to the others that have been happening,' he said.

The man who wished to be called Levine showed no emotion to the average eye. An acute observer who had known him for some time *might* have detected the slight flush of frustrated anger and embarrassment.

'The operation is not yet over. There have been setbacks, but there has been no failure. Had there been failure, neither of us would be here.' As if to emphasise his point, he gestured towards the crowds milling around them. Sunday is a busy day for tourists at the Capitol building.

The distinguished-looking man regained his confidence. In a firm whisper he said, 'Nevertheless there have been setbacks. As you so astutely pointed out, the operation is not yet over. I need not remind you that it was scheduled for completion three days ago. Three days.

A good deal can happen in three days. For all our bumbling we have been very lucky. The longer the operation continues, the greater the risk that certain things will come to the fore. We both know how disastrous that could be.'

'Everything possible is being done. We must wait for another chance.'

'And if we don't get another chance? What then, my fine friend, what then?'

The man called Levine turned and looked at him. Once again the other man felt nervous. Levine said, 'Then we make our chance.'

'Well, I certainly hope there will be no more … setbacks.'

'I anticipate none.'

'Good. I shall keep you informed of all the developments in the Agency. I expect you to do the same with me. I think there is nothing further to say.'

'There is one other thing,' Levine said calmly. 'Operations such as this sometimes suffer certain kinds of internal setbacks. Usually these … setbacks happen to certain personnel. These setbacks are planned by operation directors, such as yourself, and they are meant to be permanent. The common term for such a setback is double cross. If I were my director, I would be most careful to avoid any such setback, don't you agree?' The pallor crossing the other man's face told Levine there was no disagreement. Levine smiled politely, nodded farewell, and walked away. The distinguished man watched him stalk down the marble corridors and out of sight. The gentleman shuddered slightly, then went home to Sunday brunch with his wife, son, and a fidgety new daughter-in-law.

While Malcolm and Wendy dressed and the two men left the Capitol grounds, a telephone truck pulled up to the outer gates at Langley. After the occupants and their mission were cleared, they proceeded to the communications center. The two telephone repairmen were accompanied by a special security officer on loan from another branch. Most of the Agency men were looking for a man called Condor. The security officer had papers identifying him as Major David Burros. His real name was Kevin Powell, and the two telephone repairmen, ostensibly there to check the telephone tracing device, were highly trained Air Force electronics experts flown in from Colorado less than four hours before. After their mission was completed, they would be quarantined for three weeks. In addition to checking the tracing device, they installed some new equipment and made some complicated adjustments in the wiring of the old. Both men tried to keep calm while they worked from wiring diagrams labeled Top Secret. Fifteen minutes after they began work, they electronically signaled a third man in a phone booth four miles away. He called a number, let it ring until he received another signal, then hung up and walked quickly away. One of the experts nodded at Powell. The three men gathered their tools and left as unobtrusively as they had come.

An hour later Powell sat in a small room in downtown Washington. Two plainclothes policemen sat outside the door. Three of his fellow agents lounged in chairs scattered around the room. There were two chairs at the desk where

Powell sat, but one was unoccupied. Powell talked into one of the two telephones on the desk.

'We're hooked up and ready to go, sir. We've tested the device twice. It checked out from our end and our man in the Panic Room said everything was clear there. From now on, all calls made to Condor's panic number will ring here. If it's our boy, we'll have him. If it's not … Well, let's hope we can fake it. Of course, we can also nullify the bypass and just listen in.'

The old man's voice told his delight. 'Excellent, my boy, excellent. How's everything else working out?'

'Marian says the arrangements with the *Post* should be complete within the hour. I hope you realise how much our ass is in the fire on this. Someday we'll have to tell the Agency we tapped their Panic Line, and they won't appreciate that at all.'

The old man chuckled. 'Don't worry about that, Kevin. It's been in the fire before and it will be there again. Besides, theirs is roasting too, and I imagine they won't feel too bad if we pull it out for them. Any reports from the field?'

'Negative. Nobody reports a sign of Malcolm or the girl. When our boy goes to ground, he goes to ground.'

'Yes, I was thinking much the same thing myself. I don't think the opposition has got him. I'm rather proud of his efforts so far. Do you have my itinerary?'

'Yes, sir. We'll call you if anything happens.' The old man hung up, and Powell settled down for what he hoped would be a short wait.

Wendy and Malcolm arrived in Washington just as the sun was setting. Malcolm drove to the center of the city. He parked the car at the Lincoln Memorial, removed their luggage, and locked the vehicle securely. They came into Washington via Bethesda, Maryland. In Bethesda they purchased some toiletries, clothes, a blond wig, and a large padded 'visual disguise and diversionary' bra for Wendy, a roll of electrical tape, some tools, and a box of .357 magnum shells.

Malcolm took a carefully calculated risk. Using Poe's 'Purloined Letter' principle that the most obvious hiding place is often the safest, he and Wendy boarded a bus for Capitol Hill. They rented a tourist room on East Capitol Street less than a quarter of a mile from the Society. The proprietress of the dingy hostel welcomed the Ohio honeymooners. Most of her customers had checked out and headed home after a weekend of sightseeing. She didn't even care if they had no rings and the girl had a black eye. In order to create a believable image of loving young marrieds (or so Malcolm whispered), the young couple retired early.

'In war it is not men, but the man who counts.'

– Napoleon

Monday, Morning to Midafternoon

The shrill scream from the red phone jarred Powell from his fitful nap. He grabbed the receiver before a second ring. The other agents in the room began to trace and record the call. Concentrating on listening, Powell only half saw their scurrying figures in the morning light. He took a deep breath and said, '493-7282.'

The muffled voice on the other end seemed far away. 'This is Condor.'

Powell began the carefully prepared dialogue. 'I read you, Condor. Listen closely. The Agency has been penetrated. We're not sure who, but we're pretty sure it's not you.' Powell cut the beginning of a protest short. 'Don't waste time protesting your innocence. We accept it as a working assumption. Now, why did you shoot Weatherby when they came to pick you up?'

The voice on the other end was incredulous. 'Didn't Sparrow IV tell you? That man – Weatherby? – shot at me! He was parked outside the Society Thursday morning. In the same car.'

'Sparrow IV is dead, shot in the alley.'

'I didn't ...'

'We know. We think Weatherby did. We know about you and the girl.' Powell paused to let this sink in. 'We traced you to her apartment and found the corpse. Did you hit him?'

'Barely. He almost got us.'

'Are you injured?'

'No, just a little stiff and woozy.'

'Are you safe?'

'For the time being, fairly.'

Powell leaned forward tensely and asked the hopeless and all-important question. 'Do you have any idea why your group was hit?'

'Yes.' Powell's sweaty hand tightened on the receiver as Malcolm quickly told of the missing books and financial discrepancies Heidegger had discovered.

When Malcolm paused, Powell asked in a puzzled voice, 'But you have no idea what it all means?'

'None. Now, what are you going to do about getting us to safety?'

Powell took the plunge. 'Well, that's that going to be a little problem. Not just because we don't want you set up and hit, but because you're not talking to the Agency.'

Five miles away, in a phone booth at a Holiday Inn, Malcolm's stomach began to chum. Before he could say anything, Powell spoke again.

'I can't go into the details. You will simply have to trust us. Because of the penetration of the Agency at what is probably a very high level, we've taken over. We plugged into the Panic Line and intercepted your call. Please don't hang up. We've got to blow the double in the Agency and find out what this was all about. You're our only way, and we want you to help us. You have no choice.'

'Bullshit, man! You might be another security agency, and then again you might not. Even if you are O.K., why the hell should I help you? This isn't my kind of work! I read about this stuff, not do it.'

'Consider the alternatives.' Powell's voice was cold. 'Your luck can't hold forever, and some very determined and competent people besides us are looking for you. As you said, this isn't your line of work. Someone will find you. Without us, all you can do is hope that the right someone does find you. If we're the right someone, then everything is already O.K. If we're not, then at least you know what we want you to do. It's better than running blind. Any time you don't like our instructions, don't follow them. There's one final clincher. We control your communication link with the Agency. We even have a man on the listed line.' (This was a lie.) 'The only other way you can go home is to show up at Langley in person. Do you like the idea of going in there cold?'

Powell paused and got no answer. 'I thought not. It won't be too dangerous. All we basically want is for you to stay hidden and keep rattling the opposition's cage. Now, here's what we know so far.' Powell gave Malcolm a concise rundown of all the information he had. Just as he finished, his man in charge of tracing the call came to him and shrugged his shoulders. Puzzled, Powell continued. 'Now, there's another way we can communicate with you. Do you know how to work a book code?'

'Well … You better go over it again.'

'O.K. First of all pick up a paperback copy of *The*

Feminine Mystique. There is only one edition. Got that? O.K. Now, whenever we want to communicate with you, we will run an ad in the *Post*. It will appear in the first section, and the heading will read, "Today's Lucky Sweepstakes Winning Numbers Are:" followed by a series of hyphenated numbers. The first number of each series is the page number, the second is the line number, and the third is the word number. When we can't find a corresponding word in the book, we'll use a simple number–alphabet code. A is number one, B is number two, and so on. When we code such a word, the first number will be thirteen. The *Post* will forward any communication you want to send us if you address it to yourself, care of Lucky Sweepstakes, Box 1, *Washington Post*. Got it?'

'Fine. Can we still use the Panic Line?'

'We'd rather not. It's very chancy.'

Powell could see the trace man across the room whispering furiously into another phone. Powell said, 'Do you need anything?'

'No. Now, what is it you want me to do?'

'Can you call the Agency back on your phone?'

'For a conversation as long as this?'

'Definitely not. It should only take a minute or so.'

'I can, but I'll want to shift to another phone. Not for at least half an hour.'

'O.K. Call back and we will let the call go through. Now, here's what we want you to say.' Powell told him the plan. When both men were satisfied, Powell said, 'One more thing. Pick a neighborhood you won't have to be in.'

Malcolm thought for a moment. 'Chevy Chase.'

'O.K.,' Kevin said. 'You will be reported in the Chevy

Chase area in exactly one hour. Thirty minutes later a Chevy Chase cop will be wounded while chasing a man and a woman answering your descriptions. That should make everyone concentrate their forces in Chevy Chase, giving you room to move. Is that enough time?'

'Make it an hour later, O.K.?'

'O.K.'

'One more thing. Who am I talking to, I mean personally?'

'Call me Rogers, Malcolm,' The connection went dead. No sooner had Powell placed the phone in the cradle than his trace man ran to him.

'Do you know what that little son of a bitch did? Do you know what he did?' Powell could only shake his head. 'I'll tell you what he did, that little son of a bitch. He drove all over town and wired pay phones together, then called and hooked them all up so they transmitted one call through the lines, but each phone routed the call back through the terminal. We traced the first one in a little over a minute. Our surveillance team got there right away. They found an empty phone booth with homemade Out of Order signs and his wiring job. They had to call back for a trace on the other phone. We've gone through three traces already and there are probably more hookups to go, that son of a bitch!'

Powell leaned back and laughed for the first time in days. When he found the part in Malcolm's dossier that mentioned his summer employment with the telephone company, he laughed again.

Malcolm left the phone booth and walked to the parking lot. In a rented U-Haul pickup with Florida plates a chesty blonde wearing sunglasses sat chewing gum. Malcolm stood in the shade for a few moments while he checked the lot. Then he walked over and climbed in the truck. He gave Wendy the thumbs-up sign, then began to chuckle.

'Hey,' she said, 'what is it? What's so funny?'

'You are, you dummy.'

'Well, the wig and the falsies were your idea! I can't help it if …' His protesting hand cut her short.

'That's only part of it,' he said, still laughing. 'If you could only see yourself.'

'Well, I can't help it if I'm good.' She slumped in the seat. 'What did they say?'

As they drove to another phone booth, Malcolm told her.

Mitchell had been manning the Panic phone since the first call. His cot lay a few feet from his desk. He hadn't seen the sun since Thursday. He hadn't showered. When he went to the bathroom the phone followed. The head of the Panic Section was debating whether to give him pep shots. The Deputy Director had decided to keep Mitchell on the phone, as he stood a better chance than a new man of recognising Malcolm should he call again. Mitchell was tired, but he was still a tough man. Right now he was a tough *determined* man. He was raising his ten-o'clock coffee to his lips when the phone rang. He spilled the coffee as he grabbed the receiver.

'493-7282.'

'This is Condor.'

'Where the hell …'

'Shut up. I know you're tracing this call, so there isn't

147

much time. I would stay on your line, but the Agency has been penetrated.'

'What!'

'Somebody out there is a double. The man in the alley' – Malcolm almost slipped and said 'Weatherby' – 'shot at me first. I recognised him from when he was parked in front of the Society Thursday morning. The other man in the alley must have told you that, though, so …' Malcolm slowed, anticipating interruption. He got it.

'Sparrow IV was shot. You …'

'I didn't do it! Why would I want to do it? Then you didn't know?'

'All we know is we have two more dead people than when you first called.'

'I might have killed the man who shot at me, but I didn't kill Maronick.'

'Who?'

'Maronick, the man called Sparrow IV.'

'That wasn't Sparrow IV's name.'

'It wasn't? The man I shot yelled for Maronick after he hit the ground. I figured Maronick was Sparrow IV.' (Easy, thought Malcolm, don't overdo it.) 'Never mind that now, time is running short. Whoever hit us was after something Heidegger knew. He told all of us about something strange he found in the records. He said he was going to tell somebody out at Langley. That's why I figure there is a double. Heidegger told the wrong man.

'Listen, I've stumbled onto something. I think I might be able to figure some more out. I found something at Heidegger's place. I think I can work it out if you give me time. I know you must be looking for me. I'm afraid to come in or let you find me. Can you pull the heat off me until I figure out what I know that makes the opposition want me dead?'

Mitchell paused for a moment. The trace man frantically signaled him to keep Malcolm talking. 'I don't know if we can or not. Maybe if ...'

'There's no more time. I'll call you back when I find out some more.' The line went dead. Mitchell looked at his trace man and got a negative shake of the head.

'How the hell do you figure that?'

Mitchell looked at the speaker, a security guard. The man in the wheelchair shook his head. 'I don't, but it's not my job to figure it. Not this one.' Mitchell looked around the room. His glance stopped when it came to a man he recognised as a veteran agent. 'Jason, does the name Maronick mean anything to you?'

The nondescript man called Jason slowly nodded his head. 'It rings a bell.'

'Me too,' said Mitchell. He picked up a phone. 'Records? I want everything you got on people called Maronick, any spelling you can think of. We'll probably want several copies before the day is out, so hop to it.' He broke the connection, then dialed the number of the Deputy Director.

While Mitchell waited to be connected with the Deputy Director, Powell connected with the old man. 'Our boy did fine, sir.'

'I'm delighted to hear that, Kevin, delighted.'

In a lighter voice Powell said, 'Just enough truth mingled with some teasing tidbits. It'll start the Agency rolling the right way, but hopefully they won't catch up to us. If you're right, our friend Maronick may begin to feel nervous. They'll be more anxious than ever to find our Condor. Anything new on your end?'

'Nothing. Our people are still digging into the past of all concerned. Outside of us, only the police know about the connection between Malcolm and the man killed in the girl's apartment. The police are officially listing it and her disappearance as parts of a normal murder case. When the time is right, that little tidbit will fall into appropriate hands. As far as I can tell, everything is going exactly according to plan. Now I suppose I'll have to go to another dreary meeting with a straight face, gently prodding our friends in the right direction. I think it best if you stay on the line, monitoring, not intercepting, but be ready to move any time.'

'Right, sir.' Powell hung up. He looked at the grinning men in the room and settled back to enjoy a cup of coffee.

'I'll be damned if I can make head or tail of it!' The Navy captain thumped his hand on the table to emphasise his point, then leaned back in his spacious padded chair. The room was stuffy. Sweat stains grew under the Captain's armpits. Of all the times for the air conditioning to break down, he thought.

The Deputy Director said patiently, 'None of us are really too sure what it means, either, Captain.' He cleared his throat to take up where he had been cut off. 'As I was saying, except for the information we received from Condor – however accurate it may be – we are really no further than at our last meeting.'

The Captain leaned to his right and embarrassed the man from the F.B.I. sitting next to him by whispering, 'Then why call the God damn meeting?' The withering glance from the Deputy Director had no effect on the Captain.

The Deputy continued. 'As you know, Maronick's file is missing. We've requested copies of England's files. An Air Force jet should have them here in three hours. I would like any comments you gentlemen might have.'

The man from the F.B.I. spoke immediately. 'I think Condor is partially right. The C.I.A. has been penetrated.' His colleague from the Agency squirmed. 'However, I think we should put it in the past tense and say "had" been penetrated. Obviously Weatherby was the double. He probably used the Society as some sort of courier system and Heidegger stumbled onto it. When Weatherby found out, the Society had to be hit. Condor was a loose end that had to be tied up. Weatherby goofed. There are probably some members of his cell still running around, but I think fate has sealed the leak. As I see it, the important thing for us to do now is bring in Condor. With the information he can give us, we can try to pick up those few remaining men – including this Maronick, if he exists – and find out how much information we've lost.'

The Deputy Director looked around the room. Just as he was about to close the meeting, the old man caught his eye.

'Might I make an observation or two, Deputy?'

'Of course, sir. Your comments are always welcome.'

The men in the room shifted slightly to pay better attention. The Captain shifted too, though obviously out of frustrated politeness.

Before he spoke, the old man looked curiously at the representative from the F.B.I. 'I must say I disagree with our colleague from the Bureau. His explanation is very plausible, but there are one or two discrepancies I find disturbing. If Weatherby was the top agent, then how and why did he die? I know it's a debatable question, at least until the lab men finish those exhaustive tests they've been making. I'm sure they will find he was killed. That kind of order would have to come down from a high source. Besides, I feel there is something wrong with the whole double agent-courier explanation. Nothing for sure, just a hunch. I think we should continue pretty much as we have been, with two slight changes.

'One, pry into the background of all concerned and look for crossing paths. Who knows what we may find? Two, let's give the Condor a chance to fly. He may find something yet. Loosen up the hunt for him, and concentrate on the background search. I have some other ideas I would like to work on for your next meeting, if you don't mind. That's all I have now. Thank you, Deputy.'

'Thank you, sir. Of course, gentlemen, the ultimate decision lies with the director of the Agency. However, I've been assured our recommendations will carry weight. Until we have a definite decision, I plan to continue as we have been.'

The old man looked at the Deputy Director and said, 'You may be sure we shall give you whatever assistance we can.'

Immediately the F.B.I. man snapped, 'That goes for us too!' He glared at the old man and received a curious smile in reply.

'Gentlemen,' said the Deputy Director, 'I would like to thank all of you for the assistance you have given us, now as well as in the past. Thank you all for coming. You'll be notified of the next meeting. Good day.'

As the men were leaving, the F.B.I. man glanced at the old man. He found himself staring into a pair of bright, curious eyes. He quickly left the room. On the way out, the Navy captain turned to mutter to a representative from the Treasury Department, 'Jesus, I wish I had stayed on line duty! These dull meetings wear me out.' He snorted, put on his naval cap, and strode from the room. The Deputy was the last to leave.

'I don't like this at all.'

The two men strolled along the Capitol grounds just on the edges of the shifting crowds. The afternoon tourist rush was waning, and some government workers were leaving work early. Monday is a slow day for Congress. j205

'I think he shouldn't be the only one.' The rare Washington wind carried the striking man's voice to his companion, who shivered in spite of the warm weather.

'What do you mean?'

The reply was tinged with disgust. 'It doesn't make sense. Weatherby was a tough, experienced agent. Even though he was shot, he managed to kill Sparrow IV. Do you really believe a man like that would yell out my name? Even if he made a slip, why would he yell for me? It doesn't make sense.'

'Pray tell, then, what does make sense?'

'I can't say for sure. But there's something we don't know going on. Or at least something I don't know.'

Nervous shock trembled in the distinguished man's voice. 'Surely you're not suggesting I'm withholding information from you?'

The wind filled the long pause. Slowly, Levine-Maronick answered. 'I don't know. I doubt it, but the possibility exists. Don't bother to protest. I'm not moving on the possibility. But I want you to remember our last conversation.'

The men walked in silence for several minutes. They left the Capitol grounds and began to stroll leisurely past the Supreme Court Building on East Capitol Street. Finally the older man broke the silence. 'Do your men have anything new?'

'Nothing. We've been monitoring all the police calls and communications between the Agency and Bureau teams. With only three of us, we can't do much field work. My plan is to intercept the group that picks Condor up before they get him to a safe house. Can you arrange for him to be brought to a certain one, or at least find out what advance plans they've made? It will cut down on the odds quite a bit.' The older man nodded, and Maronick continued.

'Another thing that strikes me wrong is Lloyd. The police haven't linked him with this thing yet, as far as I can tell. Condor's prints must have been all over that place, yet the police either haven't lifted them – which I doubt – or reported them on the A.P.B. I don't like that at all. It doesn't fit. Could you check on that in such a way that you don't stir them into activity?'

The older man nodded again. The two continued their

stroll, apparently headed home from work. By now they were three blocks from the Capitol, well into the residential area. Two blocks down the street a city bus pulled over to the side, belched diesel smoke, and deposited a small group of commuters on the sidewalk. As the bus pulled away, two of the commuters detached themselves from the group and headed towards the Capitol.

Malcolm had debated about turning in the rented pickup. It gave them relatively private transportation, but it was conspicuous. Pickups are not common in Washington, especially pickups emblazoned with 'Alfonso's U-Haul, Miami Beach'. The truck also ran up a bill, and Malcolm wanted to keep as much of his money in reserve as he could. He decided public transportation would suffice for the few movements he planned. Wendy halfheartedly agreed. She liked driving the pickup.

It happened when they were almost abreast of the two men walking towards them on the other side of the street. The gust of wind proved too strong for the bobby pin holding Wendy's loose wig. It jerked the blond mass of hair from her head, throwing it into the street. The wig skidded to a stop and lay in an ignoble heap almost in the center of the road.

Excited and shocked, Wendy cried out, 'Malcolm, my wig! Get it, get it!' Her shrill voice carried above the wind and the slight traffic. Across the street Levine-Maronick pulled his companion to an abrupt halt.

Malcolm knew Wendy had made a mistake by calling out his name. He silenced her with a gesture as he stepped between the parked cars and into the street on a retrieval mission. He noticed the two men across the street watching him, so he tried to appear nonchalant, perhaps embarrassed for his wife.

Levine-Maronick moved slowly but deliberately, his keen eyes straining at the couple across the street, his mind making point-to-point comparisons. He was experienced enough to ignore the shock of fantastic coincidence and concentrate on the moment. His left hand unbuttoned his suit coat. Out of the corner of his eye and in the back of his mind Malcolm saw and registered all this, but his attention centered on the lump of hair at his feet. Wendy reached him just as he straightened up with the wig in his hands.

'Oh, shit, the damned thing is probably ruined.' Wendy grabbed the tangled mass from Malcolm. 'I'm glad we don't have far to go. Next time I'll use two …'

Maronick's companion had been out of the field too long. He stood on the sidewalk, staring at the couple across the street. His intent gaze attracted Malcolm's attention just as the man incredulously mouthed a word. Malcolm wasn't sure of what the man said, but he knew something was wrong. He shifted his attention to the man's companion, who had emerged from behind a parked car and begun to cross the street. Malcolm noticed the unbuttoned coat, the waiting hand flat against the stomach.

'Run!' He pushed Wendy away from him and dove over the parked sports car. As he hit the sidewalk, he hoped he was making a fool of himself.

Maronick knew better than to run across an open area charging a probably armed man hiding behind bulletproof cover. He wanted to flush his quarry for a clear shot. He also knew part of his quarry was escaping. That had to be prevented. When his arm stopped moving, his body had snapped into the classic shooting stance, rigid, balanced. The stubby revolver in his right hand barked once.

Wendy had taken four very quick steps when it occurred to her she didn't know why she was running. This is silly, she thought, but she slowed only slightly. She dodged between two parked cars and slowed to a jog. Four feet from the shelter of a row of tour buses she turned her head, looking over her left shoulder for Malcolm.

The steel-jacketed bullet caught her at the base of the skull. It spun her up and around, slowly, like a marionette ballerina turning on one tiny foot.

Malcolm knew what the shot meant, but he still had to look. He forced his head to the left and saw the strange, crumpled form on the sidewalk twenty feet away. She was dead. He knew she was dead. He had seen too many dead people in the last few days to miss that look. A stream of blood trickled downhill towards him. The wig was still clutched in her hand.

Malcolm had his gun out. He raised his head and Maronick's revolver cracked again. The bullet screeched across the car's hood. Malcolm ducked. Maronick quickly began to angle across the street. He had four rounds left, and he allowed two of them for further harassing fire.

Capitol Hill in Washington has two ironic qualities: it has both one of the highest crime rates and one of the highest concentrations of policemen in the city. Maronick's shots and the screams of frightened tourists brought one of the traffic policemen on the run. He was a short, portly man named Arthur Stebbins. In five more years he planned to retire. He lurched towards the scene of a possible crime with full confidence that a score of fellow officers were only seconds behind him. The first thing he saw was a man edging across the street, a gun in his hand. This was also the last thing he saw, for Maronick's bullet caught him square in the chest.

Maronick knew he was in trouble. He had hoped for another minute before the police arrived. By that time Condor would have been dead, and he could be far away. Now he saw two more blue forms a block away. They were tugging at their belts. Maronick swiftly calculated the odds, then turned, looking for a way out.

At this instant a rather bored congressional aide heading home from the Rayburn House Office Building drove up the side street just behind Maronick. The aide stopped his red Volkswagen beetle to check for traffic on the main artery. Like many motorists, he paid little attention to the areas he passed through. He barely realised what happened when Maronick jerked his door open, pulled him from the car, whipped the pistol across his face, and then sped away in the beetle.

Maronick's companion stood stiff through the whole episode. When he saw Maronick make his getaway, he too took flight. He ran up East Capitol Street. Less than fifty feet from the scene he climbed into his black Mercedes Benz and sped away. Malcolm raised his head in time to see the license plate of the car.

Malcolm looked down the street to the policemen. They huddled around the body of their comrade. One of them spoke into his belt radio, calling in the description of Maronick and the red Volkswagen and asking for reinforcements and an ambulance. It dawned on Malcolm that they hadn't seen him yet, or that if they had, they thought of him as only a passerby-witness to a police killing. He looked around him. The people huddled behind parked cars and along the clipped grass were too frightened to yell until he was out of sight. He quickly walked away in the direction the Volkswagen had come. Just before he turned the corner he looked back at the crumpled form on the sidewalk. A policeman was bending over Wendy's still body. Malcolm swallowed and turned away. Three blocks later he caught a cab and headed downtown. As he sat in the back seat, his body shook slightly, but his mind burned.

'The first step toward becoming a skilful defensive player, then, is to handle the defense in an aggressive spirit. If you do that, you can find subtle defensive resources that other players would not dream of. By seeking active counterplay, you will often upset clever attacking lines. Better yet, you will upset your opponent.'

— Fred Reinfeld, The Complete Chess Course

Late Monday

'All hell has broken loose, sir.' Powell's voice reflected the futility he felt.

'What do you mean?' On the other end of the telephone line the old man strained to catch every word.

'The girl has been shot on Capitol Hill. Two witnesses tentatively identified that old photo of Maronick. They also identified the girl's companion who fled as Malcolm. As far as we can tell, Malcolm wasn't injured. Maronick got a cop, too.'

'Killing two people in one day makes Maronick rather busy.'

'I didn't say she was dead, sir.'

After an almost imperceptible pause the tight voice said, 'Maronick is not known for missing. She is dead, isn't she?'

'No, sir, although Maronick didn't miss by much. Another fraction of an inch and he would have splattered her brain all over the sidewalk. As it is, she has a fairly serious head wound. She's in the Agency hospital now. They had to do a little surgery. This time I made the security arrangements. We don't want another Weatherby. She's unconscious. The doctors say that she'll probably stay that way for a few days, but they think she'll eventually be O.K.'

The old man's voice had an eager edge as he asked, 'Was she able to tell anyone anything, anything at all?'

'No, sir,' Powell replied disappointedly. 'She's been unconscious since she was shot. I've got two of my men in her room. Besides double-checking everyone who comes in, they're waiting in case she wakes up.

'We've got another problem. The police are mad. They want to go after Maronick with everything they've got. A dead cop and a wounded girl on Capitol Hill mean more to them than our spy chase. I've been able to hold them back, but I don't think I can for long. If they start looking using the tie-ins they know, the Agency is bound to find out. What should I do?'

After a pause, the old man said, 'Let them. Give them a slightly sanitised report of everything we know, enough to give them some leads on Maronick. Tell them to go after him with everything they can muster, and tell them they'll have lots of help. The only thing we must insist on is first questioning rights once they get him. Insist on that, and tell them I can get authority to back up our claim. Tell them to find Malcolm too. Does it look like Maronick was waiting for them?'

'Not really. We found the boarding house used by Malcolm and the girl. I think Maronick was in the neighborhood and just happened to spot them. If it hadn't been for the police, he probably would have nailed Condor. There's one other thing. One witness swears

Maronick wasn't alone. He didn't get a good look at the other man, but he says the guy was older than Maronick. The older man disappeared.'

'Any confirmation from other witnesses?'

'None, but I tend to believe him. The other man is probably the main double we are after. The Hill is an excellent rendezvous. That could explain Maronick stumbling onto Malcolm and the girl.'

'Yes. Well, send me everything you can on Maronick's friend. Can the witness make an I.D. sketch or a license-plate number? Anything?'

'No, nothing definite. Maybe we'll get lucky and the girl can help us with that if she wakes up soon.'

'Yes,' the old man said softly, 'that would be lucky.'

'Do you have any instructions?'

The old man was silent for a few moments, then said, 'Put an ad – no, better make it two ads – in the *Post*. Our boy, wherever he is, will expect to hear from us. But he's probably not too organised, so put a simple, uncoded ad to run on the same page as the coded one. Tell him to get in touch with us. In the coded ad tell him the girl is alive, the original plan is off, and we're trying to find some way to bring him in safe. We'll have to take the chance that he either has or can get a copy of the code book. We can't say anything important in the uncoded ad because we don't know who else besides our boy might be reading the *Post*.'

'Our colleagues will guess something is up when they see the uncoded ad.'

'That's an unpleasant fact, but we knew we would have to face them eventually. However, I think I can manage them.'

'What do you think Malcolm will do?'

There was another short pause before the old man replied. 'I'm not sure,' he said. 'A lot depends on what he knows. I'm sure he thinks the girl is dead. He would have responded differently to the situation if he thought she was alive. We may be able to use her somehow, as bait for either Malcolm or the opposition. But we'll have to wait and see on that.'

'Anything else you want me to do?'

'A good deal, but nothing I can give you instructions for. Keep looking for Malcolm, Maronick, and company, anything which might explain this mess. And keep in touch with me, Kevin. After the meeting with our colleagues, I'll be at my son's house for dinner.'

'I think it's disgusting!' The man from the F.B.I. leaned across the table to glare at the old man. 'You knew all along that the murder in Alexandria was connected with this case, yet you didn't tell us. What's worse, you kept the police from reporting it and handling it according to form. Disgusting! Why, by now we could have traced Malcolm and the girl down. They would both be safe. We would be hot after the others, provided, of course, that we didn't already have them. I've heard of petty pride, but this is national security! I can assure you, we at the Bureau would not behave in such a manner!'

The old man smiled. He had told them only about the link between Maronick and the murder in Alexandria. Imagine their anger if they realised how much more he knew! He glanced at the puzzled faces. Time to mend fences, or at least to rationalise. 'Gentlemen, gentlemen, I can understand your anger. But of course you realise I had a reason for my actions.

'As you all know, I believe there is a leak in the Agency. A substantial leak, I might add. It was and is my opinion that this leak would thwart our efforts on this matter. After all, the end goal – whether we admit it or not – is to plug that very leak. Now, how was I to know that the leak was not in this very group? We are not immune from such dangers.' He paused. The men around the table were too experienced to glance at each other, but the old man could feel the tension rising. He congratulated himself.

'Now then,' he continued, 'perhaps I was wrong to conceal so much from the group, but I think not. Not that I'm accusing anyone – or, by the way, that I have abandoned the possibility of the leak's being here. I still think my move prudent. I also believe it wouldn't have made much difference, despite what our friend from the F.B.I. says. I think we would still be where we are today. But that is not the question, at least not now. The question is, Where do we go from here and how?'

The Deputy Director looked around the room. No one seemed eager to respond to the old man's question. Of course, such a situation meant he should pick up the ball. The Deputy dreaded such moments. One always had to be so careful about stepping on toes and offending people. The Deputy felt far more at ease on his field missions when he only had to worry about the enemy. He cleared his throat and used a ploy he hoped the old man expected. 'What are your suggestions, sir?'

The old man smiled. Good old Darnsworth. He played the game fairly well, but not very well. In a way he hated to do this to him. He looked away from his old friend and stared into space. 'Quite frankly, Deputy, I'm at a loss for suggestions. I really couldn't say. Of course, I think we should keep, on trying to do something.'

Inwardly the Deputy winced. He had the ball again. He looked around the table at a group of men now suddenly not so competent and eager-looking. They looked everywhere but at him, yet he knew they were watching his every move. The Deputy cleared his throat again. He resolved to end the agony as quickly as possible. 'As I see it, then, no one has any new ideas. Consequently, I have decided that we will continue to operate in the manner we have been.' (Whatever that means, he thought.) 'If there is nothing further …' He paused only momentarily. '… I suggest we adjourn.' The Deputy shuffled his papers, stuffed them into his briefcase, and quickly left the room.

As the others rose to leave, the Army Intelligence representative leaned over to the Navy captain and said, 'I feel like the nearsighted virgin on his honeymoon who couldn't get hard: I can't see what to do and I can't do it either.'

The Navy captain looked at his counterpart and said, 'I never have that problem.'

Malcolm changed taxis three times before he finally headed for northeast Washington. He left the cab on the fringes of the downtown area and walked around the neighborhood. During his ride around town he formed a plan, rough and vague, but a plan. His first step was to find all-important shelter from the hunters.

It took only twenty minutes. He saw her spot him and discreetly move in a path parallel to his. She crossed the street at the corner. As she stepped up to the sidewalk she 'tripped' and fell against him, her body pressed close to his.

Her arms ran quickly up and down his sides. He felt her body tense when her hands passed over the gun in his belt. She jerked away and a pair of extraordinarily bright brown eyes darted over his face.

'Cop?' From her voice she couldn't have been more than eighteen. Malcolm looked down at her stringy dyed blond hair and pale skin. She smelled from the perfume sampler at the corner drugstore.

'No.' Malcolm looked at the frightened face. 'Let's say I'm involved in a high-risk business.' He could see the fear on her face, and he knew she would take a chance.

She leaned against him again, pushing her hips and her chest forward. 'What are you doing around here?'

Malcolm smiled. 'I want a lay. I'm willing to pay for it. Now, if I'm a cop, the bust is no good, cause I entrapped you. O.K.?'

She smiled. 'Sure, tiger. I understand. What kind of party are we going to have?'

Malcolm looked down at her. Italian, he thought, or maybe Central European. 'What do you charge?'

The girl looked at him, judging possibilities. It had been a slow day. 'Twenty dollars for a straight lay?' She made it clear she was asking, not demanding.

Malcolm knew he had to get off the streets soon. He looked at the girl. 'I'm in no hurry,' he said. 'I'll give you … seventy-five for the whole night. I'll throw in breakfast if we can use your place.'

The girl tensed. It might take her a whole day and half the night to make that kind of money. She decided to gamble. Slowly she moved her hand into Malcolm's crotch, covering her action by leaning into him, pushing her breast against his arm. 'Hey, honey, that sounds great, but …' She almost lost her nerve. 'Could you make it a hundred? Please? I'll be extraspecial good to you.'

Malcolm looked down and nodded. 'A hundred dollars. For the full night at your place.' He reached in his pocket and handed her a fifty-dollar bill. 'Half now, half afterwards. And don't think about any kind of setup.'

The girl snatched the money from his hand. 'No setup. Just me. And I'll be real good – real good. My place isn't far.' She linked her arms in his to guide him down the street.

When they reached the next corner, she whispered, 'Just a second, honey, I have to talk to that man.' She released his arm before he could think and hurried to the blind pencil hawker on the corner. Malcolm backed against the wall. His hand shot inside his coat. The gun butt was sweaty.

Malcolm saw the girl slip the man the fifty dollars. He mumbled a few words. She walked quickly to a nearby phone booth, almost oblivious of a boy who jostled her and grinned as her breasts bounced. The sign said Out of Order, but she opened the door anyway. She looked through the book, or so Malcolm thought. He couldn't see too well, as her back was towards him. She shut the door and quickly returned.

'Sorry to keep you waiting, honey. Just a little business deal. You don't mind, do you?'

When they came abreast of the blind man, Malcolm stopped and pushed the girl away. He snatched the thick sunglasses off the man's face. Carefully watching the astonished girl, he looked at the pencil seller. The two empty sockets made him push the glasses back quicker than he had taken them off. He staffed a ten-dollar bill into the man's cup. 'Forget it, old man.'

The hoarse voice laughed. 'It's done forgotten, mister.'

As they walked away, the girl looked at him. 'What did you do that for?'

Malcolm looked down at the puzzled, dull face. 'Just checking.'

Her place turned out to be one room with a kitchen–bath area. As soon as they were safely inside, she bolted and locked the door. Malcolm fastened the chain. 'Be right with you, honey. Take off your clothes. I'll fix you up real good right away.' She darted into the curtained-off bathroom area.

Malcolm looked out the window. Three stories up. No one could climb in. Fine. The door was solid and double-locked. He didn't think anyone had followed them, or even really noticed them. He slowly took off his clothes. He put the gun on the small table next to the bed and covered it with an old *Reader's Digest*. The bed squeaked when he lay down. Both his mind and his body ached, but he knew he had to act as normal as possible.

The curtains parted and she came to him, her eyes shining. She wore a long-sleeved black nightgown. The front hung open. Her breasts dangled – long, skinny pencils. The rest of her body matched her breasts, skinny, almost emaciated. Her voice was distant. 'Sorry I took so long, sugar. Let's get down to business.'

She climbed on the bed and pulled his head to her breasts. 'There, baby, there you go.' For a few minutes she ran her hands over him, then she said, 'Now I'll take real good care of you.' She moved to the base of the bed and buried her head in his crotch. Minutes later she coaxed his body into a response. She got up and went to the bathroom. She returned holding a jar of Vaseline. 'Oh, baby, you were real good, real good, sugar.' She lay down on the bed to apply the lubricant to herself. 'There, sugar, all ready for you. All ready for you whenever you want.'

For a long time they lay there. Malcolm finally looked at her. Her body moved slowly, carefully, almost laboriously. She was asleep. He went to the bathroom. On the back of the stained toilet he found the spoon, rubber hose, matches, and homemade syringe. The small plastic bag was still three-quarters full of the white powder. Now he knew why the nightgown had long sleeves.

Malcolm searched the apartment. He found four changes of underwear, three blouses, two skirts, two dresses, a pair of jeans,, and a red sweater to match the purple one laying on the floor. A torn raincoat hung in the closet. In a shot box in the kitchen be found six of the possession return receipts issued upon release from a Washington jail. He also found a two-year-old high-school identification card. Mary Ruth Rosen. Her synagogue address was neatly typed on the back. There was nothing to eat except five Hersheys, some coconut, and a little grapefruit juice. He ate everything. Under the bed he found an empty Mogen David 20/20 wine bottle. He propped it against the door. If his theory worked, it would crash loudly should the door open. He picked up her inert form. She barely stirred. He put her on the torn armchair and threw a blanket over the limp bundle. It wouldn't make any difference if her body wasn't comfortable in the night. Malcolm took out his lenses and lay down on the bed. He was asleep in five minutes.

'In almost every game of chess there comes a crisis that must be recognized. In one way or another a player risks something – if he knows what he's doing, we call it a "calculated risk".

'If you understand the nature of this crisis; if you perceive how you've committed yourself to a certain line of play; if you can foresee the nature of your coming task and its accompanying difficulties, all's well. But if this awareness is absent, then the game will be lost for you, and fighting back will do no good.'

– Fred Reinfeld, The Complete Chess Course

Tuesday, Morning through Early Evening

Malcolm woke shortly after seven. He lay quietly until just before eight, his mind going over all the possibilities. In the end he still decided to carry it through. He glanced at the chair. The girl had slid onto the floor during the night. The blanket was wrapped over her head and she was breathing hard.

Malcolm got up. With a good deal of clumsy effort he put her on the bed. She didn't stir through the whole process.

The bathroom had a leaky hose and nozzle hooked up to the tub, so Malcolm took a tepid shower. He successfully shaved with the slightly-used safety razor. He desperately wanted to brush his teeth, but he couldn't bring himself to use the girl's toothbrush.

Malcolm looked at the sleeping form before he left the

apartment. Their agreement had been for a hundred dollars, and he had only paid her fifty. He knew where that money went. Reluctantly, he laid the other fifty dollars on the dresser. It wasn't his money anyway.

Three blocks away he found a Hot Shoppe where he breakfasted in the boisterous company of neighbors on their way to work. After he left the restaurant he went to a drugstore. In the privacy of a Gulf station rest room he brushed his teeth. It was 9.38.

He found a phone booth. With change from the Gulf station he made his calls. The first one was to Information and the second one connected him with a small office in Baltimore.

'Bureau of Motor Vehicle Registration. May I help you?'

'Yes,' Malcolm replied. 'My name is Winthrop Estes, of Alexandria. I was wondering if you could help me pay back a favor.'

'I'm not sure what you mean.'

'You see, yesterday as I was driving home from work, my battery tipped over right in the middle of the street. I got it hooked up again, but there wasn't enough charge to fire the engine. Just as I was about to give up and try to push the thing out of the way, this man in a Mercedes Benz pulled up behind me. At great risk to his own car, he gave me the push necessary to get mine started. Before I had a chance to even thank him, he drove away. All I got was his license number. Now, I would at least like to send him a thank-you note or buy him a drink or something. Neighborly things like that don't happen very often in D.C.'

The man on the other end of the line was touched.

'They certainly don't. With his Mercedes! Phew, that's some nice guy! Let me guess. He had Maryland plates and you want me to check and see who he is, right?'

'Right. Can you do it?'

'Well ... Technically no, but for something like this, what's a little technicality? Do you have the number?'

'Maryland 6E-49387.'

'6E-49387. Right. Hold on just one second and I'll have it.' Malcolm heard the receiver clunk on a hard surface. In the background, footsteps faded into a low office murmur of typewriters and obscure voices, then grew stronger. 'Mr. Estes? We've got it. Black Mercedes sedan, registered to a Robert T. Atwood, 42 Elwood – that's E-l-w-o-o-d – Lane, Chevy Chase. Those people must really be loaded. That's *the* country-squire suburb. He could probably afford a scratch or two on his car. Funny, those people usually don't give a damn, if you know what I mean.'

'I know what you mean. Listen, thanks a lot.'

'Hey, don't thank me. For something like this, glad to do it. Only don't let it get around, know what I mean? Might tell Atwood the same thing, O.K.?'

'O.K!'

'You sure you got it? Robert Atwood, 42 Elwood Lane, Chevy Chase?'

'I've got it. Thanks again.' Malcolm hung up and stuffed the piece of paper with the address on it into his pocket. He wouldn't need it to remember Mr. Atwood. For no real reason, he strolled back to the Hot Shoppe for coffee. As far as his watchful eyes could tell, no one noticed him.

The morning *Post* lay on the counter. On impulse he began to thumb through it. It was on page twelve. They hadn't taken any chances. The three-inch ad. was set in bold type and read, 'Condor call home.'

Malcolm smiled, hardly glancing at the coded sweepstakes ad. If he called in, they would tell him to come home or at least lie low. That wasn't what he intended. There was nothing they could say in the coded message that could make any difference to him. Not now. Their instructions had lost all value yesterday on Capitol Hill.

Malcolm frowned. If his plan went wrong, the whole thing might end unsatisfactorily. Undoubtedly that end would also mean Malcolm's death, but that didn't bother him too much. What bothered him was the horrible waste factor that failure would mean. He had to tell someone, somehow, just in case. But he couldn't let anyone know, not until he had tried. That meant delay. He had to find a way of delayed communication.

The sign flashing across the street gave him the inspiration. With the materials he had at hand he began to write. Twenty minutes later he stuffed curt synopses of the last five days and a prognosis for the future into three small envelopes begged from the waitress. The napkins were to the F.B.I. The pieces of junk paper from his wallet filled the envelope addressed to the C.I.A. The map of D.C. he had picked up at the Gulf station went to the *Post*. These three envelopes went into a large manila envelope he bought at the drugstore. Malcolm stuck the big envelope in a mailbox. Pickup was scheduled for 2.00 p.m. The big envelope was addressed to Malcolm's bank, which for some reason closed at 2.00 p.m. on Tuesdays. Malcolm reckoned it would take the bank until at least tomorrow to find and mail the letters. He had a minimum of twenty-four hours to operate in, and he had passed on what he knew. He considered himself free of obligations.

While Malcolm spent the rest of the day standing in the perpetually long line at the Washington Monument, security and law-enforcement agencies all over the city were quietly going bananas. Detectives and agents tripped over each other and false reports of Malcolm. Three separate carloads of officials from three separate agencies arrived simultaneously at the same boarding house to check out three separate leads, all of which were false. The proprietress of the boarding house still had no idea what happened after the officials angrily drove away. A congressional intern who vaguely resembled Malcolm's description was picked up and detained by an F.B.I. patrol. Thirty minutes after the intern was identified and released from federal custody, he was arrested by Washington police and again detained. Reporters harassed already nervous officials about the exciting Capitol Hill shootout. Congressmen, senators, and political hacks of every shade kept calling the agencies and each other, inquiring about the rumored security leak. Of course, everyone refused to discuss it over the phone, but the senator-congressman-department chief wanted to be personally briefed. Kevin Powell was trying once again to play Condor and retrace Malcolm. As he walked along East Capitol Street, puzzling, perturbing questions kept disturbing the lovely spring day. He received no answers from the trees and buildings, and at 11.00 he gave up the chase to meet the director of the hunt.

Powell was late, but when he walked quickly into the room he did not receive a reproachful glance from the old man. Indeed, the old man's congeniality seemed at a new height. At first Powell thought the warmth was contrived for the benefit of the stranger who sat with them at the small table, but he gradually decided it was genuine.

The stranger was one of the biggest men Powell had ever seen. It was hard to judge his height while he sat, but Powell guessed he was at least six feet seven. The man had a massive frame, with at least three hundred pounds of flesh supplying extra padding beneath the expensively tailored suit. The, thick black hair was neatly greased down. Powell noticed the man's little piggy eyes quietly, carefully taking stock of him.

'Ah, Kevin,' said the old man, 'how good of you to join us. I don't believe you know Dr. Lofts.'

Powell didn't know Dr. Lofts personally, but he knew the man's work. Dr. Crawford Lofts was probably the foremost psychological diagnostician in the world, yet his reputation was known only in very tightly controlled circles. Dr. Lofts headed the Psychiatric Evaluation Team for the Agency. P.E.T. came into its own when its evaluation of the Soviet Premier convinced President Kennedy that he should go ahead with the Cuban blockade. Ever since then, P.E.T. had been given unlimited resources to compile its evaluation of major world leaders and selected individuals.

After ordering coffee for Powell, the old man turned and said, 'Dr. Lofts has been working on our Condor. For the last few days he has talked to people, reviewed our boy's work and dossiers, even lived in his apartment. Trying to build an action profile, I believe they call it. You can explain it better, Doctor.'

The softness of Loft's voice surprised Powell. 'I think

you've about said it, old friend. Basically, I'm trying to find out what Malcolm would do, given the background he has. About all I can say is that he will improvise fantastically and ignore whatever you tell him unless it fits into what he wants.' Dr. Lofts did not babble about his work at every opportunity. This too surprised Powell, and he was unprepared when Lofts stopped talking.

'Uh, what are you doing about it?' Powell stammered, feeling very foolish when he heard his improvised thoughts expressed out loud.

The Doctor rose to go. At least six-seven. 'I've got field workers scattered at points throughout the city where Malcolm might turn up. If you'll excuse me, I want to get back to supervising them.' With a curt, polite nod to the old man and Powell, Dr. Lofts lumbered from the room.

Powell looked at the old man. 'Do you think he has much of a chance?'

'No, no more than anyone else. That's what he thinks, too. Too many variables for him to do much more than guess. The realisation of that limitation is what makes him good.'

'Then why bring him in? We can get all the manpower we want without having to pull in P.E.T.'

The old man's eyes twinkled, but there was coldness in his voice. 'Because, my dear boy, it never hurts to have a lot of hunters if the hunters are hunting in different ways. I want Malcolm very badly, and I don't want to miss a trick. Now, how are you coming from your end.'

Powell told him, and the answer was the same as it had been from the beginning: no progress.

★

At 4.30 Malcolm decided it was time to steal a car. He had considered many other ways of obtaining transportation, but crossed them off his list as too risky. Providence combined with the American Legion and a Kentucky distillery to solve Malcolm's problem.

If it hadn't been for the American Legion and their National Conference on Youth and Drugs, Alvin Phillips would never have been in Washington, let alone at the Washington Monument. He was chosen by the Indiana state commander to attend the expense-paid national conference to learn all he could about the evils of drug abuse among the young. While at the conference, he had been given a pass which would enable him to avoid the lines at the Monument and go straight to the top. He lost his pass the night before, but he felt obligated to at least see the Monument for the folks back home.

If it hadn't been for a certain Kentucky distillery, Alvin would not have been in his present state of intoxication. The distillery kindly provided all conference participants with a complimentary fifth of their best whiskey. Alvin had become so upset by the previous day's film describing how drugs often led to illicit sex among nubile teen-age girls that the night before he drank the entire bottle by himself in his Holiday Inn room. He liked the whiskey so much that he bought another fifth to help him through the conference and 'kill the dog that bit him'. He finished most of that fifth by the time the meetings broke up and he managed to navigate to the Monument.

Malcolm didn't find Alvin, Alvin found the line. Once there, he made it plain to all who could hear that he was standing in this hot God damn sun out of patriotic duty.

He didn't have to be here, he could have gone right to the God damn top, except for that God damn hustling floozy who lifted his wallet and the God damn pass. He sure fooled her God damn ass with those traveler's checks – best God damn things you could buy. She sure had God damn big jugs, though. God damn it, all he wanted to do was take her for a ride in his new car.

When Malcolm heard the word 'car', he immediately developed a dislike for cheap God damn floozies and a strong affection for the American Legion, Indiana, Kentucky whiskey, and Alvin's band-new Chrysler. After a few short introductory comments, he let Alvin know he was talking to a fellow veteran of American wars, one whose hobby just happened to be automobiles. Have another drink, Alvin, old buddy.

'S'at right? You really dig cars?' The mention of important matters pulled Alvin part way out of the bottle. It didn't take a lot of effort for bosom companionship to slide him back down. 'You wanna see a real good 'un? Got me bran'-new one. Jus' drove 't here from Indiana. Ever been to Indiana? Gotta come, come see me. An' the old lady. She ain't much to look at – we're forry-four, you know. I don't look forry-four, do I? Where was I? Oh yeah, ol' lady. Good woman. A li'l fat, but what the hell, I always say …'

By this time Malcolm had manoeuvered Alvin away from the crowd and into a parking lot. He had also shared half a dozen swigs from the bottle Alvin carefully kept hidden under his soggy suit coat. Malcolm would raise the bottle to his closed lips and move his Adam's apple, in appreciation. He didn't want alcohol slowing him down for the night. When Alvin took his turn, he more than made up for Malcolm's abstention. By the time they reached the parking lot, only two inches remained in the bottle.

Malcolm and Alvin talked about those God damn kids and their God damn drugs. Especially the girls, the teen-age girls, just like the cheerleaders in Indiana, hooked on that marijuana and ready to do anything, 'anything', for that God damn drug. Anything. Malcolm casually mentioned that he knew where two such girls were hanging around, just waiting to do anything for that God damn marijuana. Alvin stopped him and plaintively said, 'Really?' Alvin thought very, hard when Malcolm ('John') assured him that such was the case. Malcolm let the discussion lag, then he helped Alvin suggest meeting these two girls so Alvin could tell the folks back in Indiana what it was really like. Really like. Since the girls were in kind of a public place, it probably would be best if 'John' went and picked them up and brought them back here. Then they could all go to Alvin's room and talk. Better to talk to them there than here. Find out why they'd do anything, *anything*, for that God damn marijuana. Alvin gave Malcolm the keys just as they reached the shiny new car.

'Got lotsa gas, lotsa gas. Sure ya don't need any money?' Alvin fumbled with his clothes and extracted a weather-beaten wallet. 'Take watcha need, bitch last night only got traveler's checks.' Malcolm took the wallet. While Alvin shakily tipped the bottle to his lips, his new friend removed all identification papers from the wallet, including a card with his car license number. He gave the wallet back to Alvin.

'Here,' he said. 'I don't think they'll want any money. Not now.' He smiled briefly, secretively. When Alvin saw the smile his heart beat a shade faster. He was too far gone to show much facial expression.

Malcolm unlocked the car. A crumpled blue cap lay on the front seat. On the floor was a six-pack of beer Alvin had brought to help ease the heat. Malcolm put the cap on his friend's head and exchanged the now empty whiskey bottle for the six-pack of beer. He looked at the flushed face and blurred eyes. Two hours in the sun and Alvin should pass out. Malcolm smiled and pointed to a grassy mall.

'When I come back with the girls, we'll meet you over there, then go to your room. You'll recognise us because they both have big jugs. I'll be back with them just after you finish the six-pack. Don't worry about a thing.' With a kindly push he sent Alvin staggering off to the park and the tender mercies of the city. When he pulled out of the parking lot, he glanced at the rearview mirror in time to see Alvin lurch to a sitting position on a portion of grass well away from anyone else. Malcolm turned the corner as Alvin opened a beer can and took a long, slow swig.

The car had almost a full tank of gas. Malcolm drove to the expressway circling the city. He stopped briefly at a drive-in restaurant in Chevy Chase for a cheeseburger and use of the rest room. In addition to relieving himself, he checked his gun.

Number 42 Elwood Lane was indeed a country estate. The house was barely visible from the road. Direct access to it was through a private lane closed off by a stout iron gate. The closest neighboring house was at least a mile away. Dense woods surrounded the house on three sides.

The land between the house and the road was partially cleared. From Malcolm's brief glance he could tell that the house was large, but he didn't stop for a closer look. That would be foolish.

From a small gas station just up the road he obtained a map of the area. The woods behind the house were uninhabited hills. When he told the gas-station attendant he was a vacationing ornithologist and that he might have seen a very rare thrush, the attendant helped him by describing some unmapped country roads which might lead to the bird's nesting area. One such road ran behind 42 Elwood Lane.

Because of the attendant's anxious help, Malcolm found the proper road. Bumpy, unpaved, and with only traces of gravel, the road wound around hills, through gullies, and over ancient cowpaths. The woods were so dense that at times Malcolm could see only twenty feet from the road. His luck held, though, and when he topped a hill he saw the house above the trees to his left, at least a mile away. Malcolm pulled the car off the road, bouncing and lurching into a small clearing.

The woods were quiet, the sky was just turning pink. Malcolm quickly pushed his way through the trees. He knew he had to get close to the house before all light faded or he would never find it.

It took him half an hour of hard work. As the day shifted from sunset to twilight, he reached the top of a small hill. The house was just below him, three hundred yards away. Malcolm dropped to the ground, trying to catch his breath in the crisp, fresh air. He wanted to memorise all he could see in the fading light. Through the windows of the house he caught fleeting glimpses of moving figures. The yard was big, surrounded by a rock wall. There was a small shed behind the house.

He would wait until dark.

Inside the house Robert Atwood sat back in his favorite easy chair. While his body relaxed, his mind worked. He did not want to meet with Maronick and his men tonight, especially not here. He knew the pressure was on them, and he knew they would press him for some sort of alternate solution. At present Atwood didn't have one. The latest series of events had changed the picture considerably. So much depended on the girl. If she regained consciousness and was able to identify him ... well, that would be unfortunate. It was too risky to send Maronick after her, the security precautions were too tight. Atwood smiled. On the other hand, the girl's survival might pose some interesting and favorable developments, especially in dealing with Maronick. Atwood's smile broadened. The infallible Maronick had missed. True, not by much, but he had missed. Perhaps the girl, a living witness, might be useful against Maronick. Just *how* Atwood wasn't sure, but he decided it might be best if Maronick continued thinking the girl was dead. She could be played later in the game. For the time being Maronick must concentrate on finding Malcolm.

Atwood knew Maronick had insisted on meeting him at his home in order to commit him even further. Maronick would make it a point to be seen by someone in the neighborhood whom the police might later question should things go wrong. In this way Maronick sought to further ensure Atwood's loyalty. Atwood smiled. There were ways around that one. Perhaps the girl might prove a useful lever there. If ...

'I'm going now, dear.' Atwood turned towards the speaker, a stocky gray-haired woman in an expensively-cut suit. He rose and walked with his wife to the door. When he was close to his wife, his eyes invariably traveled to the tiny scars on her neck and the edge of her hairline where the plastic surgeon had stretched and lifted years from her skin. He smiled, wondering if the surgery and all her hours at an exclusive figure salon made her lover's task any more agreeable.

Elaine Atwood was fifty, five years younger than her husband and twenty-four years older than her lover. She knew the man who had driven her wild and brought back her youth as Adrian Queens, a British graduate student at American University. Her husband knew all about her lover, but he knew that Adrian Queens was really Alexy Ivan Podgovich, an aspiring K.G.B. agent who hoped to milk the wife of a prominent American intelligence officer for information necessary to advance his career. The 'affair' between Podgovich and his wife amused him and served his purposes very well. It kept Elaine busy and distracted and provided him with an opportunity to make an intelligence coup of his own. Such things never hurt a man's career, if he knows how to take advantage of opportunity.

'I may just stay over at Jane's after the concert, darling. Do you want me to call?'

'No, dear, I'll assume you are with her if you aren't home by midnight. Don't worry about me. Give Jane my love.'

The couple emerged from the house. Atwood delivered a perfunctory kiss to his wife's powdered cheek. Before she reached the car in the driveway (a sporty American car, not the Mercedes) her mind was on her lover and the long night ahead. Before Atwood closed the front door his mind was back on Maronick.

Malcolm saw the scene in the doorway, although he couldn't discern features at that distance. The wife's departure made his confidence surge. He would wait thirty minutes.

Fifteen of that thirty minutes had elapsed when Malcolm realised there were two men walking up the driveway towards the house. Their figures barely stood out from the shadows. If it hadn't been for their motion, Malcolm would never have seen them. The only thing he could distinguish from his distant perch was the tall leanness of one of the men. Something about the tall man triggered Malcolm's subconscious, but he couldn't pull it to the surface. The men, after ringing the bell, vanished inside the house.

With binoculars, Malcolm might have seen the men's car. They had parked it just off the road inside the gate and walked the rest of the way. Although he wanted to leave traces of his visit to Atwood's house, Maronick saw no point in letting Atwood get a look at their car.

Malcolm counted to fifty, then began to pick his way towards the house. Three hundred yards. In the darkness it was hard to see tree limbs and creepers reaching to trip him and bring him noisily down. He moved slowly, ignoring the scratches from thornbushes. Halfway to the house, Malcolm stumbled over a stump, tearing his pants and wrenching his knee, but somehow he kept from crying out. One hundred yards. A quick, limping dash through brush stubble and long grass before he crouched behind the stone wall. Malcolm eased the heavy magnum into his hand while he fought to regain his breath. His knee throbbed, but he tried not to think about it. Over the stone wall lay the house yard. In the yard to the right was the crumbling tool shed. A few scattered evergreens stood between him and the house. To his left was blackness.

Malcolm looked at the sky. The moon hadn't risen yet. There were few clouds and the stars shone brightly. He waited, catching his breath and assuring himself his ears heard nothing unusual in the darkness. He vaulted the low wall and ran to the nearest evergreen. Fifty yards.

A shadow quietly detached itself from the tool shed to swiftly merge with an evergreen. Malcolm should have noticed. He didn't.

Another short dash brought Malcolm to within twenty-five yards of the house. Glow from inside the building lit up all but a thin strip of grass separating him and the next evergreen. The windows were low. Malcolm didn't want to chance a fleeting glance to the outside catching him running across the lawn. He sprawled to his belly and squirmed across the thin shadowed strip. Ten yards. Through open windows he could hear voices. He convinced himself different noises were his imagination playing on Mother Nature.

Malcolm took a deep breath and made a dash for the bush beneath the open window. As he was taking his second step, he heard a huffing, rushing noise. The back of his neck exploded into reverberating fire.

'The truth, the whole truth, and nothing but the truth.

— Traditional oath

Late Tuesday Night, Early Wednesday Morning

Consciousness returned abruptly to Malcolm. He felt a dim awareness around his eyes, then suddenly his body telegraphed a desperate message to his brain: he had to vomit. He lurched forward, up and had his head thrust into a thoughtfully provided bucket. When he stopped retching, he opened his aching eyes to take in his plight.

Malcolm blinked to clear his contacts. He was sitting on the floor of a very plush living room. In the opposite wall was a small fireplace. Two men sat in easy chairs between him and that wall. The man who shot Wendy and his companion. Malcolm blinked again. He saw the outline of a man on his right. The man was very tall and thin. As he turned to take a closer look, the man behind him jerked Malcolm's head so he again faced the two seated men. Malcolm tried to move his hands, but they were tied behind his back with a silk tie that would leave no marks.

The older of the two men smiled, obviously very pleased with himself. 'Well, Condor,' he said, 'welcome to my nest.'

The other man was almost impassive, but Malcolm thought he saw curious amusement in the cold eyes.

The older man continued. 'It has taken us a long time to find you, dear Malcolm, but now that you are here, I'm really rather glad our friend Maronick didn't shoot you too. I have some questions to ask you. Some questions I already know the answers to, some I don't. This is the perfect time to get those answers. Don't you agree?'

Malcolm's mouth was dry. The thin man held a glass of water to his lips. When Malcolm finished, he looked at the two men and rasped, 'I have some questions too. I'll trade you answers.'

The older man smiled as he spoke. 'My dear boy. You don't understand. I'm not interested in your questions. We won't even waste our time with them. Why should I tell you anything? It would be so futile. No, you shall talk to us. Is he ready yet, Cutler, or did you swing that rifle a little too hard?'

The man holding Malcolm had a deep voice. 'His head should be clear by now.' With a quick flick of his powerful wrists the man pulled Malcolm down to the floor. The thin man pinned Malcolm's feet, and Maronick pulled down Malcolm's pants. He inserted a hypodermic needle into Malcolm's tensed thigh, sending the clear liquid into the main artery. It would work quicker that way, and the odds that a coroner would notice a small injection on the inside of a thigh are slim.

Malcolm knew what was happening. He tried to resist the inevitable. He forced his mind to picture a brick wall, to feel a brick wall, smell a brick wall, become a brick wall. He lost all sense of time, but the bricks stood out. He heard the voices questioning him, but he turned their sounds to bricks for his wall.

Then slowly, piece by piece, the truth serum chiseled away at the wall. His interrogators carefully swung their hammers. Who are you? How old are you? What is your mother's name? Small, fundamental pieces of mortar chipped away. Then bigger hunks. Where do you work? What do you do? One by one bricks pried loose. What happened last Thursday? How much do you know? What have you done about it? Why have you done it?

Little by little, piece by piece, Malcolm felt his wall crumble. While he felt regret, he couldn't will the wreckage to stop. Finally his tired brain began to wander. The questions stopped and he drifted into a void. He felt a slight prick on his thigh and the void filled with numbness.

Maronick made a slight miscalculation. The mistake was understandable, as he was dealing with milligrams of drugs to obtain results from an unknown variable, but he should have erred on the side of caution. When he secretly squirted out half the dosage in the syringe Atwood gave him, Maronick thought he had still used enough to produce unconsciousness. He was a little short. The drug combined with the sodium pentothal as predicted, but it was only strong enough to cause stupor, not unconsciousness.

Malcolm was in a dream. His eyelids hung low over his contacts, but they wouldn't shut. Sounds came to him through a stereo echo box. His mind couldn't connect, but it could record.

– Shall we kill him now? (The deep voice.)

– No, on the scene.

– Who?

– I'll let Charles do it, he likes blood. Give him your knife.

– Here, you give it to him. I'll check this again.

Receding footsteps. A door opens, closes. Hands running over his body. Something brushes his face.

– Damn.

A pink slip of paper on the floor by his shoulder. The tears fogging his contacts, but on the paper, '# 27, T.W.A., National, 6 a.m.'

The door opens, closes. Footsteps approaching.

– Where are Atwood and Charles?

– Checking the grounds in case he dropped anything.

– Oh. By the way, here's that reservation I made for you. James Cooper.

Paper rustles.

– Fine, let's go.

Malcolm felt his body lift off the floor. Through rooms. Outside to the cooling night air. Sweet smells, lilacs blooming. A car, into the back seat. His mind began to record more details, close gaps. His body was still lost, lying on the floor with a pair of heavy shoes pressed in his back. A long, bumpy ride. Stop. Engine dies and car doors open.

– Charles, can you carry him into the woods, up that way, maybe fifty yards. I'll bring the shovel in a few minutes. Wait until I get there. I want it done a certain way.

A low laugh. – No trouble.

Up into the air, jammed onto a tall, bony shoulder, bouncing over a rough trail, pain jarring life back into the body.

By the time the tall man dropped Malcolm on the ground, consciousness had returned. His body was still numb, but his mind was working and his eyes were bright. He could see the tall man smile in the dimly lit night. His eyes found the source of the series of clicks and snaps cutting through the humid air. The man was opening and closing the switchblade in eager anticipation.

Twigs snapped and dead leaves crunched under a light foot. The striking man appeared at the edge of the small clearing. His left hand held a flashlight. The beam fell on Malcolm as he tried to rise. The man's right hand hung close to his side. His clear voice froze Malcolm's actions. 'Is our Condor all right?'

The tall man broke in impatiently. 'He's fine, Maronick, as if it mattered. He sure came out of that drug quickly.' The thin man paused to lick his lips. 'Are you ready now?'

The flashlight beam moved to the tall man's eager face. Maronick's voice came softly through the night air. 'Yes, I am.' He raised his right arm and with a soft plop! from the silencer shot the tall man through the solar plexus.

The bullet buried itself in Charles's spine. The concussion knocked him back on his heels, but he slumped forward to his knees, then to his face. Maronick walked over to the long, limp form. To be very sure, he fired one bullet through the head.

Malcolm's mind reeled. He knew what he saw, but he didn't believe it. The man called Maronick walked slowly towards him. He bent over and checked the bonds that held Malcolm's feet and hands. Satisfied, he sat on a handily-placed log, turned off the flashlight, and said, 'Shall we talk?

'You stumbled into something and you blundered your way through it. I must say I've developed a sort of professional admiration for you during the last five days. However, that has nothing to do with my decision to give you a chance to come out of this alive – indeed, a hero.

'In 1968, as part of their aid to a beleaguered, anti-communist government, the C.I.A. assisted certain Meo tribes in Laos with the main commercial activity of that area, narcotics production. Mixed among all the fighting going on in that area there was a war between competing commercial factions. Our people assisted one faction by using transport planes to move the unprocessed opiate product along its commercial route. The whole thing was very orthodox from a C.I.A. point of view, though I imagine there are many who frown on the U.S. government pushing dope.

'As you know, such enterprises are immensely profitable. A group of us, most of whom you have met, decided that the opportunity for individual economic advancement was not to be overlooked. We diverted a sizable quantity of unprocessed, high-quality morphine bricks from the official market and channeled them into another source. We were well rewarded for our labor.

'I disagreed with Atwood's handling of the matter from the start. Instead of unloading the stuff in Thailand to local processing labs and taking a reasonable profit, he insisted on exporting the morphine bricks directly to the States and selling them to a U.S. group who wanted to avoid as many middlemen as possible. To do that, we needed to use the Agency more than was wise.

'We used your section for two purposes. We

compromised a bursar – not your old accountant – to juggle and later rejuggle the books and get us seed money. We then shipped the morphine Stateside in classified book cases. They fitted quite nicely into those boxes, and since they were shipped as classified materials, we didn't have to worry about customs inspection. Our agent in Seattle intercepted the shipment and delivered it to the buyers. But this background has little to do with your being here.

'Your friend Heidegger started it all. He had to get curious. In order to eliminate the possibility that someone might find something fishy, we had to eliminate Heidegger. To cover his death and just in case he told someone else, we had to hit the whole section. But you botched our operation through blind luck.'

Malcolm cleared his throat. 'Why are you letting me live?'

Maronick smiled. 'Because I know Atwood. He won't feel safe until my associates and I are dead. We're the only ones who can link him to the whole mess. Except you. Consequently, we have to die. He is probably thinking of a way to get rid of us. We are supposed to pick up those envelopes at the bank tomorrow. I'm quite sure we would be shot in a holdup attempt, killed in a car wreck, or just "disappear". Atwood plays dumb, but he's not.'

Malcolm looked at the dark shape on the ground. 'I still don't understand. Why did you kill that man Charles?'

'I like to cover my tracks too. He was dangerous dead weight. It will make no difference to me who reads the letters. The powers-that-be already know I'm involved. I shall quietly disappear to the Middle East, where a man of my talents can always find suitable employment.

'But I don't want to turn a corner someday and find American agents waiting for me, so I'm giving the country a little present in hopes it will regard me as a sheep gone astray but not worth chasing. My farewell present – Robert Atwood. I'm letting you live for somewhat the same reason. You also have the chance to deliver Mr. Atwood. He has caused you a lot of grief. After all, it was he who necessitated all those deaths. I am merely a technician like yourself. Sorry about the girl, but I had no option. *C'est la guerre.*'

Malcolm sat for a long time. Finally he said, 'What's the immediate plan?'

Maronick stood. He threw the switchblade at Malcolm's feet. Then he gave him still another injection. His voice was impassive. 'This is an extremely strong stimulant. It would put a dead man on his feet for half a day. It should give you enough oomph to handle Atwood. He's old, but he's still very dangerous. When you cut yourself free, get back to the clearing where we parked the car. In case you didn't notice, it's the same one you used. There are one or two things that might help you in the back seat. I would park just outside his gate, then work my way to the rear of the house. Climb the tree and go in through the window on the second floor. It somehow got unlocked. Do what you like with him. If he kills you, there are still the letters and several corpses for him to explain.'

Maronick looked down at the figure by his feet. 'Goodbye, Condor. One last word of advice. Stick to research. You've used up all your luck. When it comes right down to it, you're not very good.' He vanished in the woods.

After a few minutes of silence, Malcolm heard a car start and drive away. He wormed his way towards the knife.

It took him half an hour. Twice he cut his wrists, but each time it was only minor and the bleeding stopped as soon as he quit using his hands.

He found the car. There was a note taped to the window. The body of the man called Cutler sprawled by the door. He had been shot in the back. The note had been written while the tall man carried Malcolm into the woods. It was short, to the point: 'Your gun jammed with mud. Rifle in back has 10 rds. Hope you can use automatic.'

The rifle in back was an ordinary .22 varmint rifle. Cutler had used it for target practice. Maronick left it for Malcolm, as he figured any amateur could handle so light a weapon. He left the automatic pistol with silencer just in case. Malcolm ripped the note off and drove away.

By the time he coasted the car to a stop outside Atwood's gate, Malcolm felt the drug taking effect. The pounding in the back of his neck and head, the little pains in his body, all had vanished. In their place was a surging, confident energy. He knew he would have to fight the overestimation and over-confidence the drug brought.

The oak tree proved simple to climb and the window was unlocked. Malcolm unslung the rifle. He worked the bolt to arm the weapon. Slowly, quietly, he tiptoed to the dark hall, down the carpeted hallway to the head of the stairs. He heard Tchaikovsky's '1812' Overture booming from the room where he had been questioned. Every now and then a triumphant hum would come from a familiar voice. Slowly Malcolm went down the stairs.

Atwood had his back to the door when Malcolm entered the room. He was choosing another record from the rack in the wall. His hand paused on Beethoven's Fifth.

Malcolm very calmly raised the rifle, clicked off the safety, took aim, and fired. Hours of practice on gophers, rabbits, and tin cans guided the bullet home. It shattered Atwood's right knee, bringing him screaming to the floor.

Terror and pain filled the old man's eyes. He rolled over in time to see Malcolm work the action again. He screamed as Malcolm's second bullet shattered his other knee. His mouth framed the question, 'Why?'

'Your question is futile. Let's just say I didn't want you going anywhere for a while.'

Malcolm worked in a frenzy of activity. He tied towels around the moaning man's knees to slow the bleeding; then he tied his hands to an end table. He ran upstairs and aimlessly rifled rooms, burning up the energy coursing through his blood. He fought hard and was able to control his mind. Maronick chose his drugs well, he thought. Atwood the planner, the director, the thinker was downstairs, Malcolm thought, in pain and harmless. The secondary members of the cell were all dead. Maronick was the only one left, Maronick the enforcer, Maronick the killer. Malcolm thought briefly of the voices on the other end of the Panic Line, the professionals, professionals like Maronick. No, he thought, so far it has been me. Them against me. Maronick had made it even more personal when he killed Wendy. To the professionals it was just a job. They didn't care. Hazy details of a plan formed around his ideas and wants. He ran to Atwood's bedroom, where he exchanged his tattered clothes for one of several suits. Then he visited the kitchen and devoured some cold chicken and pie. He went back to the room where Atwood lay, took a quick look around, then dashed to his car for the long drive.

Atwood lay very still for some time after Malcolm had left. Slowly, weakly, he tried to pull himself and the table across the floor. He was too weak. All he succeeded in doing was knocking a picture off the table. It fell face up. The glass didn't break into shreds he could use to cut his bonds. He resigned himself to *his* fate. He slumped prone, resting for whatever might lie ahead. He looked briefly at the Picture and sighed. It was of him. In his uniform of a captain in the United States Navy.

Wednesday Morning

Mitchell had reached what Agency psychiatrists call the Crisis Acclimatisation Level, or Zombie Stage 4. For six days he had been stretched as tight as any spring could be stretched. He adjusted to this state and now accepted the hypertension and hyperactivity as normal. In this state he would be extremely competent and extremely effective as long as any challenge fell within the context of the conditions causing the state. Any foreign stimulus would shatter his tensed composure and tear him apart at the seams. One of the symptoms of this state is the ignorance of the subject. Mitchell merely felt a little nervous. His rational process told him he must have overcome the exhaustion and tension with a sort of second wind. That was why he was still awake at 4.20 in the morning. Disheveled and smelly from six days without bathing, he sat behind his desk going over reports for the hundredth time. He hummed softly. He had no idea that the two additional security men standing by the coffee urn were for him. One was his backup and the other was a psychiatrist protégé of Dr. Lofts. The psychiatrist was there to watch Mitchell as well as monitor any of Malcolm's calls.

Brrring!

The call jerked all the men in the room out of relaxation. Mitchell calmly held up one hand to reassure them While he used the other hand to pick up the receiver. His easy movements had the quiet quickness of a natural athlete or a well-oiled machine.

'493-7282.'

'This is Condor. It's almost over.'

'I see. Then why don't you …'

'I said almost. Now listen, and get it right. Maronick, Weatherby, and their gang were working under a man called Atwood. They were trying to cover their tracks from a smuggling operation they pulled off in 1968. They used Agency facilities and Heidegger found out. The rest just sort of came naturally.

'I've got one chore left. If I don't succeed, you'll know about it. At any rate, I've mailed some stuff to my bank. You better pick it up. It will be there this morning.

'You better send a pretty good team to Atwood's right away. He lives at 42 Elwood Lane, Chevy Chase.' (Mitchell's second picked up a red phone and began to speak softly. In another part of the building men raced toward waiting cars. A second group raced towards a Cobra combat helicopter kept perpetually ready on the building roof.) 'Send a doctor with them. Two of Maronick's men are in the woods behind the house, but they're dead. Wish me luck.'

The phone clicked before Mitchell could speak. He looked at his trace man and got a negative shake of the head.

The room burst into activity. Phones were lifted and all through Washington people woke to the shrill ring of a special bell. Typewriters clicked, messengers ran from the room. These who could find nothing definite to do paced. The excitement around him did not touch Mitchell. He sat at his desk, calmly running through the developed procedure. His forehead and palms were dry, but deep in his eyes a curious light burned.

Malcolm depressed the phone hook and inserted another dime. The buzzer only sounded twice.

The girl had been selected for her soft, cheery voice. 'Good morning. T.W.A. May I help you?'

'Yes, my name is Henry Cooper. My brother is flying out today for an overdue vacation. Getting away from it all, you understand. He didn't tell anyone where he was going for sure because he hadn't made up his mind. What we want to do is give him a last-minute going-away present. He's already left his apartment, but we think he's on Flight 27, leaving at six. Could you tell me if he has a reservation?'

There was a slight pause, then, 'Yes, Mr. Cooper, your brother has booked a reservation on that flight for ... Chicago. He hasn't picked up his ticket yet.'

'Fine, I really appreciate this. Could you do me another favor and not tell him we called? The surprise is named Wendy, and there's a chance she'll be either flying with him or taking the next plane.'

'Of course, Mr. Cooper. Shall I make a reservation for the lady?'

'No, thank you. I think we better wait and see how it works out at the airport. The plane leaves at six, right?'

'Right.'

'Fine, we'll be there. Thank you.'

'Thank you, sir, for thinking of T.W.A.'

Malcolm stepped out of the phone booth. He brushed some lint off his sleeve. Atwood's uniform fitted him fairly well, though it was somewhat bulky. The shoes were a loose fit and his feet tended to slip in them. The highly polished leather creaked as he walked from the parking lot into the main lobby of National Airport. He carried the raincoat draped over his arm and pulled the hat low over his forehead.

Malcolm dropped an unstamped envelope addressed to the C.I.A. in a mailbox. The letter contained all he knew, including Maronick's alias and flight number. The Condor hoped he wouldn't have to rely on the U.S. postal system.

The terminal was beginning to fill with the bustling people who would pass through it during the day. A wheezing janitor swept cigarette butts off the red rug. A mother tried to coax a bored infant into submission. A nervous coed sat wondering if her roommate's half-fare card would work. Three young Marines headed home to Michigan wondering if she would work. A retired wealthy executive and a penniless wino slept in adjoining chairs, both waiting for daughters to fly in from Detroit. A Fuller Brush executive sat perfectly still, bracing himself for the effects of a jet flight on a gin hangover. The programmer for the piped-in music had decided to jazz up the early-morning hours, and a nameless orchestra played watered-down Beatle music.

Malcolm strode to a set of chairs within hearing range of the T.W.A. desk. He sat next to the three Marines, who respectfully ignored his existence. He held a magazine so it obscured most of his face. His eyes never left the T.W.A.

desk. His right hand slipped inside the Navy jacket to bring the silenced automatic out. He slipped his gun-heavy hand under the raincoat and settled back to wait.

At precisely 5.30 Maronick walked confidently through the main doors. The striking gentleman had developed a slight limp, the kind observers invariably try to avoid looking at and the kind they always watch. The limp dominates their impression and their mind blurs the other details their eyes record. A uniform often accomplishes the same thing.

Maronick had grown a mustache with the help of a theatrical supply house, and when he stopped at the T.W.A. desk Malcolm did not recognise him. But Maronick's soft voice drew his attention, and he strained to hear the conversation.

'My name is James Cooper. I believe you have a reservation for me.'

The desk clerk flipped her head slightly to place the wandering auburn lock where it belonged. 'Yes, Mr. Cooper, Flight 27 to Chicago. You have about fifteen minutes until boarding time.'

'Fine.' Maronick paid for his ticket, checked his one bag, and walked aimlessly away from the counter. Almost empty, he thought. Good. A few servicemen, everything normal; mother and baby, normal; old drunks, normal; college girl, normal. No large preponderance of men standing around busily doing nothing. No one scurrying to phones, including the girl behind the desk. Everything normal. He relaxed even more and began to stroll, checking the terminal and giving his legs the exercise they would miss on the long flight. He didn't notice the Navy captain who slowly joined him at a distance of twenty paces.

Malcolm almost changed his mind when he saw Maronick looking so confident and capable. But it was too late for that. Help might not arrive in time and Maronick might get away. Besides, this was something Malcolm had to do himself. He fought down the drug-edged nervousness. He would get only one chance.

National Airport, while not breath-takingly beautiful, is attractive. Maronick allowed himself to admire the symmetry of the corridors he passed through. Fine colors, smooth lines.

Suddenly he stopped. Malcolm barely had time to dodge behind a rack of comic books. The proprietress gave him a withering glance but said nothing. Maronick checked his watch and held a quick debate with himself. He would just have time. He began to move again, substituting a brisk walk for his leisurely stroll. Malcolm followed his example, carefully avoiding loud footsteps on the marble stretches. Maronick took a sudden right and passed through a door, which swung shut behind him.

Malcolm trotted to the door. His hand holding the gun under the raincoat was sweating from the heat, the drug, and his nerves. He stopped outside the brown door. Gentlemen. He looked around him. No one. Now or never. Being careful to keep the gun between his body and the door, he pulled the weapon out from under the coat. He tossed the heavy raincoat to a nearby chair. Finally, his heart beating against his chest, he leaned on the door.

It opened easily and quietly. One inch. Malcolm could

see the glistening white brightness of the room. Mirrors sparkled on the wall to his far left. He opened the door a foot. The wall with the door had a line of three shiny sinks. He could see four urinals on the opposite wall, and he could make out the corner of one stall. No one stood at the sinks or the urinals. Lemony disinfectant tingled his nose. He pushed the door open and stepped in. It closed behind him with a soft *woosh* and he leaned heavily against it.

The room was brighter than the spring day outside the building. The piped-in music found no material capable of absorbing its volume, so the sound echoed off the tile walls – cold, crisp, blaring notes. There were three stalls opposite Malcolm. In the one on the far left he could see shoes, toes pointed towards him. Their polish added to the brightness of the room. The flute in the little box on the ceiling posed a gay musical question and the piano answered. Malcolm slowly raised the gun. The sound of toilet paper turning a spindle cued the band. The flute piped a more melancholy note, as it inquired once more. A tiny click from the gun's safety preceded the sound of tearing paper and the piano's soft reply.

The gun jumped in Malcolm's hand. A hole tore through the thin metal stall door. Inside the stall the legs jerked, then pushed upward. Maronick, slightly wounded in the neck, desperately reached for the gun in his back pocket, but his pants were around his ankles. Maronick normally carried his gun holstered either at his belt or under his arm, but he had planned to ditch the weapon before passing through the security screening at the airport. There would probably be no need of a gun at this stage of the plan, especially at a large, crowded airport, but the cautious Maronick put his gun in his back pocket, unobtrusive but sometimes awkward to reach, just in case.

Malcolm fired again. Another bullet tore through screeching metal to bury itself in Maronick's chest and fling his body against the wall. Malcolm fired again, and again and again and again. The gun spat the spent cartridge cases in to the tile floor. Bitter cordite mixed with the lemony smell. Malcolm's third bullet ripped a hole through Maronick's stomach. Maronick sobbed softly, and fell down along the right side of the metal cage. His weakening arm depressed the plunger. The *woosh* of water and waste momentarily drowned out his sobs and the coughs from the gun. As Malcolm fired the fourth time, a passing stewardess hearing the muffled cough remembered it was cold season. She vowed to buy some vitamins. That bullet missed Maronick's sinking form. The lead shattered on the tile wall, sending little pieces of shrapnel into the metal walls and tile roof. A few hit Maronick's back, but they made no difference. Malcolm's fifth bullet buried itself in Maronick's left hip, positioning the dying man on the stool.

Malcolm could see the arms and feet of a man slumped on a toilet. A few red flecks stained the tile pattern. Slowly, almost deliberately, Maronick's body began to slide off the toilet. Malcolm had to be sure before he confronted the man's face, so he squeezed the trigger for the last two rounds. An awkward knee on a naked and surprisingly hairless leg jammed against a stall post. The body shifted slightly as it settled to the floor. Malcolm could see enough of the pale face. Death replaced Maronick's striking appearance with a rather common, glassy dullness. Malcolm dropped the gun to the floor. It skidded to a stop near the body.

It took Malcolm a few minutes to find a phone booth. Finally a pretty oriental stewardess helped the rather dazed naval officer. He even had to borrow a dime from her.

'493-7282.' Mitchell's voice wavered slightly.

Malcolm took his time. In a very tired voice he said, 'This is Malcolm. It's over. Maronick is dead. Why don't you send somebody to pick me up? I'm at National Airport. So is Maronick. I'm the guy in the Navy uniform by the Northwest terminal.'

Three carloads of agents arrived two minutes ahead of the squad car summoned by the janitor who had found more than dirty toilets in his rest room.

'The whole is equal to the sum of its parts.'

— Traditional mathematical concept

Wednesday Afternoon

'It was like shooting birds in a cage.' The three men sipped their coffee. Powell looked at the smiling old man and Dr. Lofts. 'Maronick didn't stand a chance.'

The old man looked at the doctor. 'Do you have any explanation for Malcolm's actions?'

The large man considered his answer, then said, 'Without having talked to him at great length, no. Given his experiences of the last few days, especially the deaths of his friends and his belief that the girl was dead, his upbringing, training, and the general situation he found himself in, to say nothing of the drug's possible effect, I think his reaction was logical.'

Powell nodded. He turned to his superior and said, 'How's Atwood?'

'Oh, he will live, for a while at least. I always wondered about his oafishness. He did too well to be the idiot he played. He can be replaced. How are we handling Maronick's death?'

Powell grinned. 'Very carefully. The police don't like it, but we've pressured them into accepting the idea that the Capitol Hill Killer committed suicide in the men's room of National Airport. Of course, we had to bribe the janitor to forget what he saw. No real problems, however!

A phone by the old man's elbow rang. He listened for a few moments, then hung up. He pushed the button next to the phone and the door opened.

Malcolm was coming down from the drug. He had spent three hours bordering on hysteria, and during that time he had talked continually. Powell, Dr. Lofts, and the old man heard six days compressed into three hours. They told him Wendy was alive after he finished, and when they took him to see her he was dazed by exhaustion. He stared at the peacefully sleeping form in the bright, antiseptic room and seemed not to be aware of the nurse standing beside him. 'Everything will be fine.' She said it twice but got no reaction. All Malcolm could see of Wendy was a small head swathed in bandages and a sheet-covered form connected by wires and plastic tubing to a complicated machine. 'My God,' he whispered with mixed relief and regret, 'my God.' They let him stand there in silence for several minutes before they sent him out to be cleaned up. Now he had on clothes from his apartment, but he looked strange even in them.

'Ah, Malcolm, dear boy, sit down. We won't keep you long.' The old man was at his charming best, but he failed to affect Malcolm.

'Now, we don't want you to worry about a thing. Everything is taken care of. After you've had a nice long rest, we want you to come back and talk to us. You will do that, won't you, my boy?'

Malcolm slowly looked at the three men. To them his voice seemed very old, very tired. To him it seemed new. 'I don't have much choice, do I?'

The old man smiled, patted him on the back, and,

mumbling platitudes, led him to the door. When he returned to his seat, Powell looked at him and said, 'Well, sir, that's the end of our Condor.'

The old man's eyes twinkled. 'Don't be so sure, Kevin, my boy, don't be so sure.'

LAST DAYS

OF THE

CONDOR

JAMES GRADY

NO EXIT PRESS

for

Desmond Jack Grady . . .
. . . running toward tomorrow

1

SOMETHING'S HAPPENING HERE
- Buffalo Springfield, 'For What It's Worth'

A cover team locked on him that rainy Washington, D.C., Monday evening as he left his surface job, flipped up his hood and stepped outside the brass back door for the Library of Congress's John Adams Building.

A white car.

Indicator One on the white car as a cover team: Tinted windows and windshield.

Indicator Two: A car engine suddenly purred to life as raindrops tapped the blue mountaineering coat's hood over his silver-haired skull. He spotted the white car parked illegally at the Third Street corner of A Street, SE, a town house–lined road that ran from Congress's turf through Capitol Hill's residential neighborhood.

Indicator Three: The chill in the rain let him see wisps of gray exhaust from behind the purring white car. As it didn't pull out into traffic. As it sat there, wipers off, heaven's tears dotting the tinted-glass windshield.

Indicator Four: No one hurried to the white car from a nearby home. No commuter leaving work splashed through the rain toward it to be greeted with a spouse's kiss.

Indicator Five: He felt the cover team. Chinese martial artists talk about the weight of a stalker's eyes, feeling the pressure of an enemy's *chi*. Kevin Powell - who got his throat cut in an Amsterdam brothel the year the CIA-backed Shah fell in Iran and the Soviet Union invaded Afghanistan - Kevin insisted you must pay attention to your guts, your feelings. Or you'll get butchered on some midnight street. Or wake up screaming in a windowless steel room. That Monday D.C. evening, the silver-haired man standing on hard cement in the chilly spring rain knew what his tingles meant.

One, two, three, four, five. Like fingers of a hand, a hand that meant *cover team.*

He looked to his left along the sidewalk running past the Adams Building with its six stories of white stone plus basements of knowledge and secrets. The brass door behind him could withstand a car ramming into it or a giant gorilla banging on its locked metal.

Walking down Third Street as if to pass the Adams Building came a man: Caucasian, dark hair, late thirties, white-collar-warrior suit and tie under a tan coat, brown shoes not built for running, holding a black umbrella in one brown-gloved hand, the other holding a cell phone pressed to his face as he said: 'Where are you located?'

Could have been a cover team communications ploy.

Feed data via a phony phone conversation.

But the silver-haired man didn't think so: *Too unnecessary.*

Suit & Tie Cell Phone Umbrella Man walked closer, now nearly perpendicular to him, brown shoe step by brown shoe step rippling puddles on the dark, wet sidewalk.

A stream of strangers joined Mister Cell Phoning Suit & Tie, all looking like innocent Americans headed somewhere after work on a Monday evening.

If your cover team is there for wet work, sometimes a better option than running from them is to imbue your assassination with Elevated Exposure Costs.

The silver-haired man in the blue hooded coat put his hands in its storm pockets as he stepped away from the Adams Building. Run, he did not run. He joined that stream of eight pedestrians, five of whom walked under umbrellas. Like a blue penguin, he wove a crooked course to the center of the umbrella group - innocent bystander casualties being a classic EEC.

The smart move.

Unless the cluster of strangers he'd slid into belonged to the cover team.

The Israelis used a twenty-nine-member cover team for the Dubai hotel room assassination of one Hamas executive back in 2010.

Of course, a cover team didn't necessarily mean a hit or mere surveillance: these strangers walking with him under their umbrellas on a Washington, D.C., Capitol Hill sidewalk could be a snatch crew which he'd now let surround him.

But none of his fellow pedestrians vibed *hunter* as they marched toward the restaurant row on Pennsylvania Avenue just up from the House of Representatives' three castle-like office buildings. He flashed on sixth grade, walking to school with other kids. He remembered the smell of bicycles.

We're all kids on bicycles, he thought. *A flock of birds.*

Wondered if *whoosh* his flock of umbrella strangers would sense a shift in the universe and bank another direction and *no*, he hadn't run to join them, though he remembered the joys of long-distance jogging before his knees, back, and the bullet remnants in his left shoulder all conspired against him.

Back then, he'd been passing through Washington as the powers that governed this hydrogen bomb–blessed country argued about blow jobs in the White House. When he jogged during that work trip, his aches & pains decoded as *no more running for fun & fitness*. He accepted that evolution.

But like he remembered blow jobs, he remembered how if you run fast and there's a littler kid near you, you've got a better chance because Beirut snipers prioritize wounding the littlest kids to tempt rescuers. *Run*, you can make it to that doorway if only that doorway were there instead of the intersection of Third Street, SE, and Independence Avenue where it's tonight, you don't have a bicycle, and there is no sheltering doorway or black-smoke stench of burning rubber tires at street barricades.

Focus: This is here. This is now. Washington, D.C. A chilly rainy evening.

Hold on to that.

You can hold on to that.

Sure.

There's a cover team on you.

If nothing else, have some pride. Make them work for it. Whatever *it* is.

Third Street, SE, is a one-way route from busy Pennsylvania Avenue, passes Independence Avenue that heads out of D.C. like an illusion of escape. Third Street means rows of parked cars on both its Adams side and across the road in front of town houses often harboring political action committees for Congressmen whose public offices are two blocks away, only a four-minute walk from their official duties to private property where they can make legal phone calls whoring money for elections. Any car -

Say a cover team's white car.

- any car parked facing the Adams Building on A Street, a block up from Independence Avenue, was stuck with a right-hand turn: the only legal choice. Parking where they had meant they couldn't pull out of their surveillance spot, turn, and drive down Third Street the wrong way against traffic, the route he always walked home, so -

So the cover team knew his predictable route. So they were that kind of *they*: informed, *briefed*. Knew he wouldn't - *couldn't* - walk past them, put his shoes on the sidewalk of A Street, SE, that close to *where*. Once they knew he was out & on the move, on foot, going toward Independence Avenue, the white car would turn right with the one-way traffic flow as if they weren't covering him.

Then circle the block. Given rush-hour traffic, rainy weather, odds are they'd be at the intersection of Pennsylvania Avenue and Third Street, SE, in time to spot whether he diverted down to Pennsylvania's main street of bars & restaurants or continued on his normal route up Independence. Odds are, he'd be walking with the outbound traffic, so the white car could slowly drive behind him, leapfrog parking to keep him ahead of their windshield. Eyes on him the whole way home.

Just in case they'd put shoes on him too, he didn't look back.

Instead, he scanned the bright lights of the restaurants and chain-store coffee shops and bars that served both Congressional staffers on beer-bottle budgets and lobbyists who made champagne flow. He cranked his head as far as he could toward the giant yellow-bulbed traffic sign that had been set up after 9/11, with its insistent arrow ordering all trucks to turn off Pennsylvania Avenue's route between the House of Representatives' office buildings and the Congress's iconic Capitol building.

He saw the Congressional cop standing in the rain beside a cruiser parked next to the flashing detour sign. Wouldn't matter if the truck that disobeyed the detour warnings was a cargo of dead tree products driven by a lost fool or a suicide bomber's rental truck packed with fertilizer in a concoction powerful enough to devastate two city blocks, the cop knew he'd need to risk holding position in the kill zone and try to shoot out the truck's tires before it blasted America's core of government.

The silver-haired man peered past the cop outside his cruiser and the yellow detour arrow. Told himself that through the bare trees and over two blocks away, he could see the edge of the Capitol building; visualize its dome, white and slick in the rain.

Before and for a while after Watergate, the FBI maintained a covert station on Pennsylvania Avenue in the first block of private commercial buildings he saw as he turned back from staring at Congress's domain. That former FBI lair had been a flat-faced concrete building with an underground garage, always shut. He'd learned about the building back when *this life* began. That the three-story gray building belonged to the FBI was gossiped about by all sorts of people who worked on Capitol Hill, including many of Congress's members and staffs. If any of them had the guts and power to ask the Bureau about the building at the corner of Congress & the world, the official FBI response labeled the substation 'a translation center.'

Sure, he thought: *And how does that translate?*

He stood on the corner of the block where he now worked, obeying the traffic light, faced down Independence Avenue with his head turned in its blue hood just enough so his peripheral vision might pick up the appearance in traffic of, *say*, a white car.

The DON'T WALK traffic signal he faced glowed orange with a line slashed across the orange stick figure image of a walker and counting-down flashes:

. . . 30 . . . 29 . . . 28 . . .

On the way to his rampage in 1998, a lone gunman from Montana who killed two Congressional cops while trying to shoot his way into the U.S. Capitol visited the for-decades town house headquarters of a fringe political group across the street from where the silver-haired man now stood. What the diagnosed paranoid schizophrenic gunman wanted from that political group is unknown, but he was drawn to them. The since-moved political group's revered but deceased founder kept a life-sized black metal statue of Adolf Hitler at the foot of his bed and the group openly but illegally sold the same phony cancer-curing drug that failed to save movie star Steve McQueen.

. . . 3 . . . 2 . . . 1 . . . WALK flashed in traffic-light white and freed a white stick figure.

Hope you get where you're going, telepathed the silver-haired man to the white stick figure in the signal light as he himself crossed the road for his eight-block journey with the traffic flowing along Independence Avenue.

He didn't flinch when his peripheral glimpse of the intersection showed the rain-slick black street reflecting a red light and an idling white car.

At the next corner, Fourth Street, he let the green light send him to the right, across the road. Didn't look behind him up that street to *where it happened back then*. Didn't look sideways to see the white car he hoped was blocked a few vehicles back, not at this crosswalk revving its engine to roar off the slick street, smash into his blue-hooded figure, hurtle him to his death or under crushing wheels.

Rundowns are tricky.

What's the Mission Risk Allotment for the cover team in the white car?

He made it to the curb. Didn't look back as he turned left, his usual route.

Don't let them know the weight of your eyes.

The rain stopped two blocks later as he slogged past the long low barn of Eastern Market where J. Edgar Hoover had worked as a grocery delivery boy before his left-wing subversive hunting days during the last century's Palmer Raids.

Cars whooshed by his lone man walking. Homeward-bound citizens.

Four blocks later, as he neared his corner of Eleventh Street, he spotted the white hat and dark blue sweater of a Navy officer leaving the neighborhood dry cleaner's that often served personnel stationed at the nearby Commandant of the Marine Corps. Flashed to cradling a Marine corporal shot in Afghanistan as that man, *that boy*, who'd saved his life flopped, gurgled, and died without ever knowing the truth about his fellow American or having it told to his family back in Oklahoma.

The Navy officer at the dry cleaner's that evening drove away in a minivan outfitted with an empty child's car seat.

The silver-haired man noted the red neon sign in the dry cleaner's barred window:

ALTERATIONS

If only.

He focused on an address just past the corner: 309, a two-story blue-brick town house, four black metal steps up to its turquoise door, walked one step after another until *finally*, as he slid his key into the lock, he looked behind him, checked his four to eight.

The white car cruised past him, made a languid U-turn into one of the parking spots across the street, tinted windshield facing where he stood on his front stoop.

The white car's engine turned off.

No one got out of the white car. Those tinted windows stayed closed.

He slid his key into the turquoise door, unlocked it, turned the doorknob. His eyes caught a downward flutter by his thigh, as low as he could reach without showing what he was doing every day when he put a stolen leaf in the crack of that door he pulled closed. Last summer, he'd worried his neighbors might notice their bushes being nibbled in this neighborhood that had yet to be invaded by the deer who bred madly in D.C.'s Rock Creek Park.

But no one mentioned that to him. Not even the wild-haired witch next door who often stood inside the low black iron fence around her front yard with her yippy filthy white dog to scream: '*This place ain't near nothing like North Carolina!*' She was wrong, but like everyone else, he never risked correcting her.

Today's torn leaf fluttered from the doorjamb.

But it could have been replaced.

Someone could still have opened that door. Be inside.

Fuck 'em.

Then he was in the house, his back pressed against the door he slammed shut. Sundown pinked his landlord's lair, the furniture she'd left when she had to rush move to her new GS insurance & pension federal job in Boston on seventeen days' notice in order to hold her place for computation in the next budget. The flat-screen TV his Settlement Specialist insisted on delivering to him hung over the fireplace in which he burned papers along with pine wood bought from pickups from West Virginia that cruised the city during the cold months. The green sofa belonged to the landlord, as did the brass bed upstairs in the front bedroom where he slept. The rest of the household contents - a couple chairs, a little of this and less of that, what was on the walls, a satellite radio with speakers, those things belonged to him.

No one attacked him in pink light streaming through the house's barred windows.

Yet.

This row house with common walls was six paces wide and twenty-one paces deep. That journey from the front door back to the kitchen took a jag around the bathroom under the stairs leading up to where he showered and slept. He walked toward the kitchen, glanced at the brown wooden stair eye level to him, and saw that the clear dental floss strand strung there had not been blown or pushed away by a passing shoe.

Or the strand had been replaced.

If they were that good, that compulsive, waiting upstairs in his bedroom or in the junk-filled back room, hiding in a closet, then *fuck it: call him already deleted.*

He checked the downstairs half bath: toilet seat up. Only his reflection haunted the mirror above the sink. He pushed the blue hood off his silvered head.

No one waited in the kitchen, the inside back door still shut and the outer iron-bars door locked in place. Beyond those black iron bars waited a wooden slab deck in a tiny fenced backyard with nothing but a waist-high Japanese maple tree rising from an engineered square opening in the deck. The hook & eye latch on the weathered gray back gate looked in place, but anyone who walked past that wooden fence in the alley knew such security was a joke.

They let him have knives.

For cooking.

The Settlement Specialist casually mentioned that need as she filled his shopping cart on their Household Establishment visit to the Fort Meade PX between D.C. and Baltimore where the National Security Agency keeps its official headquarters. He had a set of steak knives, plus a kitchen counter wooden slotted 'display holder' with a knife sharpener, a rapier-strong filleting blade, a serrated-edge bread knife, a monstrous isosceles triangle–bladed *très Français* carver, and a butcher blade that reminded him of Jim Bowie and the Alamo.

He refused to clutch one of those knives, sit *waiting* like a doomed fool on the living room couch.

His blue shell mountaineering coat was soaked. He shivered with that chill. Took the coat off, started back toward the living room -

Stopped in the bathroom to urinate. Told himself that wasn't nerves.

Heard the flush shut off as he hung his wet coat up on the living room coat rack.

They were out there. *Of course they were out there!*

But they might not come tonight.

Or ever.

The cover team might be taggers on a Sit & See, or -

The turquoise front door boomed with a knock.

2

THE ONES WE DON'T KNOW WE DON'T KNOW
- U.S. Secretary of Defense Donald Rumsfeld

Faye Dozier eased the front passenger door shut on the car they parked on Washington, D.C's Eleventh Street, SE, unbuttoned her mid-thigh black coat and kept her eyes on the blue brick town house with the turquoise door. She flexed her empty bare hands. That comfortable metal weight rode on her right hip.

Her partner, Peter, slammed his driver's door shut, didn't give a damn who heard it or looked through the evening light to see her walk around the car to him. He wore a tan raincoat with something bigger than a book bulging its inside pocket and carried a silver briefcase.

'Remember,' he told Faye. 'You're lead on this one.'

'Why him?' she said as she stared at the house, calculated approach angles. 'Why now? He's not on today's action list.'

'After that thing we just did over across the D.C. line in P.G. County, the Taliban guy who was fucking worried about his son getting into college, this guy is between there and base, due to hit our screen, so . . .'

'We got a shot,' said Peter. 'Might as well take it now.'

Like two hawks dropping off the same tree branch, this man and woman stepped together across the street toward the blue brick house.

'Not like you've got anything better to do with your night, right?' he said.

Then laughed.

Like he knew, thought Faye, knowing he didn't, no one did, no one could.

Peter said: 'Heads up on this one, rookie.'

'When did I become a rookie?'

'Out here, with me, rookie is who you are. You're lead on this one because I say so. Because it's time for you to pop your cherry.'

'You're such a charmer.'

'So people keep saying.'

They reached the side of the street of the blue brick house with the turquoise door.

'Listen,' he said to this *Okay, so she wasn't a rookie* partner he'd never asked for, never wanted. 'Take your time. Do it smart, do it thorough, do it right.

'And then,' he added as they reached the four black iron steps leading up to that narrow row house on the edge of Capitol Hill, 'do the same for the report.'

'*Wait*: What are you going to be doing while I'm doing that?'

'My report, my identifier, *your* work, my seniority time off-line, because, like you said, you got nothing better to do with the rest of your night.' He smiled.

'I didn't say.' She held the palm of her left hand low where anyone but another professional like him might have missed the *hang back* signal.

Peter retreated from the black iron steps. Stood where optics let him catch *movement* in the windows on both floors of the blue brick town house, where his sight line included her on the black iron stoop:

As she knocked on the turquoise door.

3

RUNAWAY AMERICAN DREAM
- Bruce Springsteen, 'Born to Run'

This is how you live or die.

Answer the knock on your front door.

That turquoise slab swung open to the rush of the world and *they* filled his vision.

Woman standing on front stoop.

Man posting on the miniscule front yard made of dirt and stone inside the black metal fence.

She's the shooter if this is a Buzz & Bang.

But she just stands there on the front porch, green eyes reflecting him.

Call her thirty, maybe older. Black coat unbuttoned. Pretty, but you might not spot her in a crowd. Brown hair long enough for *styled*, not so long it's an easy grab. An oval face from the stirred ethnicity of modern America. A nose that looked like it had been reset above unpainted lips. She carried her shoulders like a soldier. Her hands hung open by her side, her right strobed *gun hand*. No rings. Dark slacks. Sensible black shoes for running or a snap kick.

She waited in this sundown that smelled like rain on city streets.

The hardest thing.

Waiting.

For the right moment. The right move. For the target to appear.

Her backup man cleared his throat. *Familiar, he seems . . .* Older than her, say fifty, a bald white guy. Muscle in the mass under his tan raincoat. Silver metal briefcase in his left hand, right hand open by his side. He posted backup, a line of sight past her to whoever opened the turquoise door or moved in the front windows, yet the way he cleared his throat marked him as a boss, or maybe -

Standing on the black iron front stoop, she said: 'How are you?'

Tell her the truth: 'I don't know.'

'Can we come in?'

Her backup man added: 'You can't say no.'

'I could, but what good would that do?' Walk backwards into the living room.

They follow. The man in the tan coat shut the door to the rest of the world.

Her smile lied: '*Damn*, I hope we got the right guy! Your name is . . . ?'

'I always hated my born-with-it name: *Ronald*. For a while, I think I was *Joe*. Sometimes I think I'm other names like *Raul, Nick, Jacques*, and oddly, *Xin Shou*.'

The bald man said: 'Call him - '

Peter! The bald backup man's name is Peter!

' - Condor.'

There it is.

The silver-haired man said: 'That's a fluke.'

'Why?' she asked.

'Because the Agency rotates code names. An earlier Condor was Frank Sturgis, a Watergate burglar. Then me. With a code name back then, I felt like two people. One was regular *me*, one was like the movie version of your life where you're better-looking and smarter and get the right girl. While I was locked up, the code name rotated.

226

Something happened to that guy, they won't tell me what. But they redesignated me Condor.'

'Right here, right now,' she asked: 'What's your work name?'

'Vin.'

'Why Vin?'

'*The Magnificent Seven*. Steve McQueen played him. As long as I'm a lie, I might as well be a cool one.'

'My name is Faye Dozier. What do you want me to call you? Condor or Vin?'

'Your choice.'

Bald Peter set his silver briefcase on the floor, pulled an iPad out of his tan raincoat. 'Remember the drill?'

'You made the first home evaluation visit after my Reintroduction Settlement.'

Faye said: 'Was he a charmer back then, too?'

'He had more hair.'

'I was as bald then as - *never mind*.'

Faye caught the flicker of Condor/Vin's *gotcha* smile.

Peter told the silver-haired man: 'Kick off your shoes, go stand with your heels and head pressed against that bit of bare wall next to your fancy radio.'

Your black stocking feet press the wooden floor. Don't get caught flexing your knees or bending your hips to sink your weight but make yourself smaller, the option *no shoes* gave you. The wall of bricks grinds against your skull.

Bald Peter raised the iPad to scan the man with his back against the wall.

'Hold it,' said Peter. 'Calculations for metrics and . . .'

The iPad snapped that picture with a FLASH!

'Turn to your right,' said Peter. 'Face your radio setup.'

Faye asked: 'So you like radio? NPR, the news networks?'

FLASH!

'I'm lucky. I can afford a radio that pulls in more than that from satellites.'

'Tell her about *clongs*.' Disdain filled the voice of the bald man with the iPad. 'Messages from outer space. And turn with your other shoulder to the wall.'

'She knows.'

'No I don't.'

'Sure you do. You're somewhere doing something or thinking something. Maybe driving in a car. A song comes on and it's dead on target for whatever's happening, for who you are right then. The universe dialing in the exactly right soundtrack as everything epiphanies the message and feels perfect, feels . . . *yes!*'

FLASH!

'That's a *clong*. I don't like news on the radio. That's the invisibles telling me *what is*. No *clongs*. Songs coming out of the cosmos show me something, lining up *what could be*, something about me, us. Like poetry. A movie or a novel.'

'But one kind of radio broadcast is about your real life,' she argued.

'Yeah.'

Peter muttered: 'Instead of voices in his head, he gets *clongs*.'

Condor said: 'What helps you make sense of it all?'

'Me?' Peter held up his iPad. 'I follow the program.'

She asked Vin: 'Any problems at work?'

'I show up. Do what's there. Come home.'

'Just so you know,' she told him, 'there's no record of complaints.'

'And yet, here you are.' He smiled: 'How do you like your job?'

'Better than some.'

'Better than some people like their jobs, or better than some jobs you've had?'

'Yeah.' She strolled toward the kitchen.

Bald Peter stared at the wall covered by taped-up newspaper articles and photographs, torn-out color bursts of magazine art, poems and paragraphs ripped from books destined for the furnace, scissored chunks of phonograph album covers and insert sleeves of lyrics from that all-but-dead medium. He raised the iPad.

FLASH! Working his way along the wall. FLASH!

Okay! It's okay, routine, just routine. The crazy's collage wall. Random weirdness. Textbook predictable. Nothing to see. Nothing to analyze.

Get your shoes on, go after her!

Faye stared into the kitchen's refrigerator.

'Milk, hope it's fresh. OJ, that's good. Styrofoam boxes of leftovers, butter. Vanilla yogurt: for the granola on the frig? Blueberries. Your bread looks dead. Mind if I throw out those single-serving boxes of white rice? You must eat a lot of Chinese.'

'We all do.'

She stared through the bars over the back door to the wooden deck.

Said: 'You look like you're in good shape.'

See the tile floor come rushing toward your face then you bounce up away from it again. Your arms burn. Set after set after set of pushups on prison time.

Then in the Dayroom where the murder has yet to happen, Victor comes over, says: 'It's about your root, not your muscle. Your center, not your fist.'

Faye, *if that's not just her work name,* Faye angled her head toward the fenced-in back deck beyond the bars, and with genuine curiosity said: 'Is that where you do *t'ai chi*?'

'That's where I practice the form. I "do" *t'ai chi* all I can.'

'Like now?'

Give her the void of no answer.

She said: 'Show me upstairs - *no*: after you.'

They passed Peter on his way into the kitchen to make another FLASH!

'Do you always make your bed?' she asked after she'd glanced into his upstairs clutter room, moved to the room with the brass bed where dreams made him fly.

'Who would do it for me?' He shrugged. 'It's a rule of lockup. A symptom.'

She looked at his clothes hanging in the closet. Peter will photograph them, too.

Then she led him into the bathroom. Blue towel over the shower rod. The toilet seat up. She opened the mirrored door for the medicine cabinet above his sink.

'*Holy shit.*'

On two shelves of the medicine cabinet stood lines of prescription pill bottles like squads of brave soldiers. Pill bottles labeled with words ending in '-*zines*' and '-*mine*.' Drugs whose names contain an abundance of "*x*"s.' The pills famous for clearing cholesterol-clogged arteries. Blue pills. White pills. Football-shaped pills. Gel tabs. Hard yellow circle pills. Green spheres.

She pointed to one prescription bottle: 'The TV commercial shows that drug is for a man and a woman sitting naked in side-by-side bathtubs as the sun sets.'

'The daily dose is also used for us guys with certain . . . *gotta go* issues.'

'Really?' She pushed him with her stare. 'What's her name?'

'There is no *her*.'

'Or he, I don't - '

'Romance is not as easy as just popping a pill.'

'Tell me about it.' She softened her eyes. 'If there's nobody now, who was your last somebody?'

Ruby lips pucker: '*Shhh*.'

'I'm not sure.'

Faye said: 'There are other medications for guys who need to go to the bathroom all the time. Maybe your doctors want the best you can be for you.'

'Sure, that must be it.'

She looked at him. Looked back at the army of pills. Her eyes scanned the chart taped to the inside of the medicine cabinet door. 'Thirteen pills a day.'

'*Everybody must get stoned*.' Looking at her, even as young as she was, she recognized that Bob Dylan quote.

'Is there anything they're not treating you for?'

'Cancer or similar assassins.'

'You think a lot about assassins?'

'*Really?* That question? From you?'

Peter's heavy footsteps clumped up the stairs outside his bathroom.

She asked: 'What's your diagnosis?'

'Post-Traumatic Stress Disorder. Paranoid Psychosis. Delusional. Alienation. Anxiety. Depression. Recurrent Temporal Disfunctionality. Identity Integration Flux.'

'That means . . . ?'

'Sometimes it's like I'm in a movie. I get lost in time. Can't handle remembering. The pills, the program, you: all to help me keep forgetting and move on.'

'How's that working?'

'I get flashes. Dreams. Ghosts. But I'm functional. Mainstreamable.'

They heard Peter enter the cluttered back room to upload its data with flashes.

'Names drift,' Condor told her, Vin told her. 'Like Kevin Powell. I can tell you how he died but who he was . . . *Beats me.* I remember Victor and four other friends locked up with me in the CIA's secret insane asylum but not my first boss in the Agency. I remember reading books for something called Section 9, Department 17, where something happened I can't think about it *don't make me think about it don't* . . .

'The big blur ends when I got out last year. What came before that . . . I remember the first woman who showed me herself naked, but not who I killed. Sometimes when I think about killing, I smell a men's room. I remember alleys in Beirut. Bars in Amsterdam. Airports in jungles. A Brooklyn diner. L.A. freeways. Getting shot. Shooting back. How to snap your neck. The Dewey Decimal System. The triggering event that made Dashiell Hammett a political lefty. Lying and laughing and creepy-crawlies on the back of my neck as I'm walking down some city street I can't remember the name of and that a 1911 Colt .45 automatic is my weapon of choice.'

'Any changes lately?'

Lie. 'All the time is all the same. Okay, as long as I keep taking the drugs.'

'Medicines,' she corrected.

'Aren't medicines supposed to make you better?'

She shrugged. But his question made her join him in a smile.

He said: 'The diagnosis says what's best for me is not knowing what I don't know I don't know.'

'But you know what real is.'

'If you say so. I know I'm really here, or really at work. But sometimes . . .

'Sometimes I'm sitting on a park bench. Blue sky, trees. No sounds - or maybe whooshing. Smells like human sweat. I'm holding an iPad in my lap. In the tablet, I watch what a drone is seeing. Broadcasting. Wispy clouds. Clear air. My view drops from the sky. Buildings get distinct, bigger, then rushing closer in the center of the screen comes a park and benches and I know that if I can just keep sitting where I am, what I'll see any second now in the iPad screen is the drone's view of me.'

She's staring at you, jaw dropped.

Bald Peter clunked his aluminum briefcase down outside the bathroom. Said: 'Could you step out so I can get my data snaps?'

In the hall, Faye pointed to the bedroom, then to the junk room. 'I didn't spot any computer. Do you have one? A laptop? A tablet? A diary or dream journal or - '

'No, I comply with the conditions. And you know my cell phone is barely smart enough to call the Agent In Trouble line, plus you've got all its records.'

From inside the bathroom came FLASH!

'Hey, Condor!' yelled Peter. 'You know what's going to come out in the pee test, so tell us: you still buying pot from that anthropologist at the Smithsonian?'

FLASH!

'*Jah* provides.'

The grin Peter carried out of the bathroom held no sympathy: 'You get busted, you're busted and gone.'

'Guess we all better be careful then.'

Faye said: 'What does the pot do for you?'

'I get stoned. On my own terms. Well, at least on the terms of my own drugs. I also drink a couple glasses of red wine now and then, but that's almost on doctor's orders. Clean out my All-American arteries and veins.'

'Whatever,' said Peter as he clicked open the silver briefcase on the floor. 'Drop your pants so I can be sure your business is your business, fill this plastic cup for me.'

Peter's black marker pen wrote CONDOR on a specimen cup's white label.

'Sorry. I went right before I answered your knock on the door.'

'Motherfucker!' said Peter.

'Are you talking to me?'

Faye freed the wisp of a smile.

Does she know that movie? Or is that just about you? Or is it all swirling data?

Peter shook the thirsty specimen cup at the man he'd come to see: 'There's a glass pot of cold coffee on your kitchen stove, figure it's from this morning. I'm going to microwave a cup of it, you're going to drink it *pronto*, no matter how hot it comes out of the zap, then you're gonna fill this cup so we can go!'

'Milk.'

'What?' said Peter.

'I like milk in my coffee. Won't take much longer to zap.'

'Motherfucker.' Peter clumped down the stairs.

Vin said: '*Motherfucker*. I wonder if I ever got to have kids.' He blinked. Stared at her. 'You could have been my kid.'

'You're nothing like my father.'

'Why not?'

'You're here,' she said. Too quickly looked away. 'We should go with Peter.'

'If I'd have asked, would your credentials have matched his?'

'What do you think?' she said.

'He's Homeland Security, has been for so long *before* doesn't matter. You're . . . You're with the Firm. My old Firm. The CIA.'

'We're both with Home Sec's National Resources Operations Division.'

'By choice?'

'Let's go downstairs,' said Faye.

'And speaking of *going*,' she added as her inertia pulled him away from where he'd been: 'Where's your car parked?'

'You know my release disallows having a car,' he said at the top of the stairs. 'My driver's license is just so I carry passable pocket litter. But I remember driving. The car skidding sideways on black ice.'

'Me, too.'

They clumped down the stairs.

'Lucky for you,' she said as they stood alone in the living room, 'the Metro has a subway stop nearby.'

'It's a Blue Line.'

'Yeah, but it connects to - '

'I don't like to ride the Blue Line.'

BEEP! The microwave in the kitchen.

'So . . .'

'The Blue Line is blue. I like the Red Line.'

She closed her eyes. Rubbed the bridge of her nose with a pinch of her fingers. No nail polish. She smelled of no perfume. Stretched her eyes open wide.

'Eyes tired?'

She shrugged.

'Glare off your white car even with the tinted glass?' asked Condor.

Faye said: 'We didn't come here in a white car.'

4

ZOMBIE JAMBOREE
- The Kingston Trio

Faye swung open the turquoise door, stepped out to the twilight target zone.

The safest scenario put her walking down this side of the street, the line of cars slumbering along the curb putting at least some metal between her and the white car with tinted windows parked down the block and across the road.

She stepped off the black iron stairs. . . Slid between two parked cars.

Thought she heard Peter shouting curses from where he was covering her - crouched behind the cold glass of the blue brick house's front upstairs bedroom window.

Figured he always took the safest scenario as she marched onto Eleventh Street to stride a direct diagonal intercept angle toward the white car, eleven, now nine vehicles away.

She heard a car engine start.

Keep both hands down! she ordered herself.

Power steering whined. Tires cried.

The white car snapped on a dragon's yellow eyes.

She froze like a deer caught by the headlights.

The white car whipped out of its opposite-curb parking, swung through a U-turn, a 180-degree speed-away *gone*, red-eye taillights vanishing into the coming night.

Faye thumbed STOP on the iPhone she'd kept hidden in her low-hanging right hand and pointed toward the white car.

'You got nothing about nothing,' Peter told her five minutes later in the kitchen that smelled like hot coffee as they watched the replay in her cell phone:

The waist-high wobble view of the sidewalk . . .

Parked cars she'd slid between . . .

This neighborhood's long line of cars slumbering across the street . . .

Two seconds of wild-shot bare trees and rooftops/jerk back to the parked cars -

Blinding yellow headlights, a blur of white, red taillights zooming away.

Condor said: 'The white car is something. And turns out, real.'

'*Real?*' said Peter. 'You say a white car followed you home. We didn't see that. Then *gee*, what are the odds? A white car *really* was parked out front, but . . . went away?'

Condor looked at her. 'What do you think?'

'What I think is, I don't know,' she answered.

'That's something.'

'Oh yeah,' said Peter. 'Maybe actionable data will come to her in a *clong* on the way back to base. Me, I think you hit your herbal medication before we knocked on the door. Now take this cup, drop your drawers and give us the sample so we can go.

'And for the record,' he added as Condor took the plastic cup: 'Is there anything we representatives of a grateful nation need to do for you?'

Condor said: 'You've already done me.'

He told Faye: 'I don't care, but you don't need to watch.'

Unbuttoned his pants, let them fall to the kitchen floor.

She left the two men, walked back to the living room through the gauntlet of ripped newspapers, book pages, and torn trinkets taped or thumbtacked to the walls.

Maybe because of what she knew she had to do later, when those two men joined her, she let *Condor* shimmer into *Vin*. Saw him as a silver-haired man, blue eyes she figured the Agency fixed with laser surgery to increase his operational index. Strong cheekbones, clean jaw. *Fit* like she'd said, but showing six decades of wear & tear. Yet electricity crackled through him: *Is he more than just his diagnoses?*

'Vin,' she said, 'I put my Home Sec card on the mantel.'

Peter packed up his silver briefcase: 'He's got more Agent In Trouble and help-line numbers than he can use, plus shrink team monitors. Let's go.'

'If you see that white car again,' said Faye as Bald Peter's impatience pulled at her, 'or anything else . . . *Call*.'

She left Vin with a real smile she lost as soon as she heard the turquoise door slam behind her, locked onto the tan raincoat back of Peter.

Faye stormed her partner: 'What the Hell! Why were you such a dick to him?'

Peter stopped in the middle of the street. Whirled to face her. His briefcase cut a silver streak in the night. 'There are only two kinds of people - '

'Bullshit! There are as many kinds of people as there are people. Don't sell me some "*us and everybody else*" crap to justify you doing our job like a jerk to that guy!'

'What I was gonna say is, there are only two kinds of people who end up doing *our* job: *agents who fucked up* and *agents who don't give a fuck.*

'We're *so* fucking essential to national security. We check on old men who defected from the Soviet Union that has been gone almost as long as you've been alive. We make sure an al Qaeda guy who came over to us in Morocco six years ago is getting his checks while sitting on his ass with nothing to tell us now we don't already know. And now from what I saw back there with Condor, you give a fuck.'

Peter shook his bald head. 'That means they stuck me with a fuckup. Once a fuckup, always a fuckup, so woe the fuck is me.

'What did you do, huh?' he said. 'Give a fuck about the wrong thing?'

'Maybe I shot my supervising agent.'

'Like I care,' he told her. 'Like you could now. Hell, you're too busy wasting energy on a long-gone-to-crazy-town stoner like Condor.'

'You saw that medicine cabinet. It's more like he's being stoned.'

'Lucky him. He's got his legs, arms, his dick. He's together enough to bring in a paycheck plus *agent down* benefits. And teams of us check on him to see if he's all right.'

He stabbed his forefinger at her: 'Who's gonna check on me and you?'

'Maybe he deserves it. Earned it when he got fucked up on some mission.'

'Or,' said Bald Peter, 'maybe we're just babysitting to keep Condor from fucking up. I don't give a fuck, so fuck him, I don't have to make nice to stoner fantasies.'

He gave her his back and walked toward the car, whose keys he had.

'There are three kinds of people,' Faye called out in the night: '*The living, the dead*, and *the turned-off*. Guess which you are. It's this era's *big thing*. Movies, TV, political metaphors, fashion shows in New York. You're a *"don't give a fuck"* zombie.'

'Yeah,' said Bald Peter. 'And there are a lot of us. Get in the car.'

5

A CANDY-COLORED CLOWN THEY CALL THE SANDMAN
- Roy Orbison, 'In Dreams'

Condor stared at his reflection trapped in the big-screen TV above the fireplace. That dark screen flowed with ghosts.

He looked at the business card left by the woman spy: Faye Dozier. *Is any of her data true?*

She and her bald partner had seen his walls. Uploaded flashing photos.

Flashings swirled Condor to a warehouse in some American nowhere.

Where one room held a sweat-stinking wrestling mat.

Where the schedule had him make gunshots *bang!* inside the baffled Shoot Room.

Where in the musty upstairs office amidst empty desks and silent typewriters stood a blurred man who had Saigon scars in his heart and a white Styrofoam cup of steaming coffee in his hand as he told twenty-something Condor: '*Learn to live your secrets in plain sight so when the bad Joes go looking, there's nothing to find*.'

Then he tossed the scalding coffee in Condor's face.

On that rainy 2013 night in Washington, in his rented home, Condor flinched.

Scanned what he'd hidden amidst oddities taped to his wall - newspaper photos, pages cut from books or magazines. So he'd remember, he poked tiny triangles into the 'intelligence indicators.' Other articles taped to his bricks also had holes, but only items patterned with three dots were clues hidden in plain sight on his seemingly mad wall.

If only he knew what the clues meant:

A *New York Times* photo of a black Predator drone flying in a blue sky with a silver full moon and a cutline that read: 'Like our other less-lethal high-tech toys, unmanned crafts feed our addiction to instant gratification.'

Cut from a book, a photo of a black-hooded British SAS commando peeking over the roof wall of the Iranian embassy in London during 1980's terrorist siege.

The 9/11 smoke-billowing World Trade Towers.

A 2013 newspaper photo showing Chinese citizens wearing white medical masks as they practice *t'ai chi* in a Beijing smog so thick people standing ten feet apart were barely visible to each other or the camera.

A movie review's black & white photo showing the black leather trench coat hero in a swirling sci-fi *kung fu* battle.

A *Washington Post* portrait of Bruce Springsteen that claimed 'The Tao of Bruce' transcended the bitter battles of America's two ruling political parties.

A news service snapshot of a running man ablaze with orange flames from gas he poured over himself in the streets called Arab Spring.

Newspaper photos of paintings: Edward Hopper's lonesome American gas station, another artist's portrait of a woman, black hair tumbling around her shoulders, her face a pink blur.

The one *easy* triggering image: a newspaper photo of a soaring condor.

If only.

Call him *Vin* as he microwaved leftover Chinese food, ate a meal that tasted like cardboard and soy mush.

He carried a glass of water and a razor blade upstairs.

Strung a web of clear dental floss across the top of the stairs - a flimsy barricade, but it might startle an assassin, create noise of his arrival.

Vin used the razor blade to shave that night's prescribed pills, his gamble that a low but correct percentage of those drugs in the Home Sec/NROD urine test could pass as a testing, marijuana masked, or other aberration within Tasers & straitjackets-enforced limits. He swallowed his chop-shopped pills, flushed their shavings down his toilet with a pang of conscience for the fish swimming at the end of the sewer pipe in the Potomac River.

Condor raised his gaze from the bathroom sink.

Through his diminishing medication state saw the bathroom mirror reflecting a face that somehow had become his. He saw his eyes: impenetrable whites surrounding scarred blue orbs centered by zooming-ever-wider black pupils.

6

WE DEAL IN LEAD
- Steve McQueen, *The Magnificent Seven*

Faye hid the flash drive in her closed fist as she navigated through a maze of cubicles in search of her target on the limbo level.

Or as it is officially known: the Situation Center for Task Force Umbrella of the Office of the Director of National Intelligence, the SC for TFU of ODNI, a vast spy factory that fills the fourth level of the ODNI Complex Zed building in Washington, D.C., not far from Wisconsin Avenue's 'upper Georgetown' strip of stores and a private high school with an annual tuition that exceeded the cost of two years at the state university where Faye punched her ticket.

Call it the limbo level.

She always had, back when she was at the CIA.

Now I'm in limbo, she thought as she searched for her target in this windowless cavern's overhead lighting. Blue lightning bolts pulsated atop the walls of green cubicles. The blue lightning bolts zapped upward like Jacob's Ladders, only instead of being designed to inspire intellectual curiosity in hormone-frazzled teenagers, these blue lightning bolts block hostile rays beamed at the cubicles' computers. The limbo level hums and crackles like Dr Frankenstein's laboratory. Electrified ozone wafts through the cavern's smog of cubicle-caged office workers.

The limbo level houses units shuffled off the flow charts of America's sixteen officially admitted intelligence agencies, a catch-all centralization of crews whose duties drift across bureaucratic lines. A dozen desks are designated PITS - Personnel In Transition Stations, sometimes given to an agent, analyst, or exec on the way up some secret ladder, more often assigned as the pre-pension parking place for burnouts or screwups or rebels who were right but failed to cover their ass.

At least I dodged the PITS, thought Faye.

So far.

The hidden flash drive burned in her closed fist.

The National Resources Operations Division she'd been exiled to fills one corner of the limbo level's factory floor, looks like a Smithsonian museum diorama with plastic walls encasing a replica of a police detective squad consisting of twelve workstation desks shared by Faye and nineteen other field agents plus a plastic-walled 'inner office' of command stations for the two executives in charge of monitoring defectors, PINSS (Persons In Need of Security Supervision) like Condor, and miscellaneous but unglamorous national security/intelligence tasks shoved by agencies like the CIA, ODNI, FBI, NSA, Secret Service, DIA, and DEA into the post–9/11 beast called Homeland Security.

She glanced at the time display on a workstation's computer: 7:22 P.M. outside in the real world of Washington, D.C. - ninety-eight minutes until 9 P.M.

You can make it. If you find Alex, you can still –

She spotted him inside a cubicle where the blue lightning bolts were turned off.

'You got a sec?' said Faye as she plopped down beside the thin redheaded man wearing a white shirt, striped tie, and khaki slacks.

'Barely,' Alex said as he packed tools he'd used to install a hard drive in the cubicle's computer. 'I got called off the bench!'

'Good for you.'

'Hey, the Dumpster I backed into still works. I drove by and checked.'

'Great, I'm kind of - '

'Anxious to tell me what you did to end up here?'

'No. What I can tell you is I need to cover my partner's ass to get out of here.'

She handed the flash drive to her instructor, Alex, from a CIA Technical Services' training class whom she'd spotted wandering the limbo's floor the week before.

'That's cell-phone video. A white car flipping a U-turn, twilight. The headlights blur the license plate, but as it drives away, maybe between the taillights' red eyes . . .'

Took Alex four minutes, most of which was spent pulling software from the classified national security grid onto this cubicle computer's new hard drive.

'Virginia tag,' he said as they stared at the screen's enhanced image. 'I live in Virginia. You can tell me if you do, too. It's not like your real name or - '

A new window appeared on the computer screen: a completed government form.

'Weird,' said Alex. 'The DMV check says that plate belongs on a green Jeep Cherokee, not a white Nissan like you got here.'

Faye suppressed the urge to grab her cell phone.

The white car knows we - somebody - was there. Drove away. If it comes back, it won't come back until it's sure it's safe, so time, I - we - Condor's got time.

He's a crazy old burnout who no opposition cares about, she told herself.

And if I bust protocol, go around my Supervising Agent Peter before officially filing the report I'm inputting in his name, trigger Alarm Status because of a license plate anomaly . . . *First*, given *my* status, nobody will do anything except cover their ass. *Second*, another strike on me, and I'll be lucky if I end up nailed to a PITS.

Plus she only had eighty-four minutes until *then*.

Took Faye twenty-three minutes to finish the F409 SIDER - Subject In Domicile Evaluation Report. She used the desktop her partner Peter favored, his sign-ins, prose style. Noted Condor's occasional irrationality yet lucidity and mainstream functionality, the log number for his urine sample, even their discussion of marijuana, and in Recommendations, after describing Condor's 'possible paranoia' about the white car and its license plate anomaly, keyboarded: '*My partner Agent Faye Dozier strenuously urges immediate elevated security response and follow-up to potential hostile surveillance of subject as inferred by observation & verification of suspicious vehicle.*' Clicks of the desktop mouse attached iPad shots of Condor and his house, plus the white car video and DMV files.

She read the electronic report one last time.

Saw nothing that would get her into trouble she couldn't handle.

Addressed it to the proper data submission points, cc'd it to her NROD agent email account and her CIA agent account, plus her legendary CIA crew chief who, after her *horror show*, fought to be sure she *only* got detailed from the Agency to Home Sec's NROD and the limbo's floor. She cc'd Bald Peter's agent email account, wondered whether he'd spin on whatever bar stool he'd snuck off to and check his phone when it *pinged!* with this report he'd officially written. Whatever shit he'd give her because of her recommendation would stay between them. Unless he believed in payback. If so, that would come at her as if by chance, without his fingerprints. But they'd both know.

She stared at the text on the glowing computer screen.

Made sure the F409 SIDER designation read CONDOR.

Clicked SEND.

The report shot into the cyber ether like a bullet into the darkness.

She needed five minutes to log off duty, leave the limbo level, ride the elevator down to the ground floor, get through exit security screening and visibly *not hurry* out the revolving door in the plexiglass walls that separate Complex Zed from a stone plaza with its anti-truck bomber cement planters and sentinel lights that hold back the night.

Security cameras recorded her walk from the building to her car in the bottom level of the employee garage. She employed no obvious counter-surveillance measures. Drove her middle-American maroon Ford clear of the parking garage.

Forty-nine minutes. I've got forty-nine minutes.

Faye lived in an apartment building on the edge of the cupcake emporiums, art theater movie chain, and yoga businesses district known as Bethesda-*landia*. That '*landia*' slang suffix came to life early in the twenty-first century when the middle-class but staid Maryland suburb of Bethesda morphed into one of the ritziest inside-the-Beltway 'hoods as Georgetown and upper northwest D.C. became too crowded to house all the lawyers & lobbyists & corporate & media stars who turned America's Martin Luther King assassination riot–scarred capital into the big-money burg it became beginning with *beat-an-assassin* President Ronald Reagan.

She scanned her mirrors as she drove.

Jumped a red light. Careened through a quick left she didn't need to take, another right, another left, zoomed down an alley past green Dumpsters like the one tech guru Alex expensively backed an Agency car into after two too many beers at a Thai dinner with Army officers from that country who he was training and who the case officer masquerading as his assistant was scouting for recruitment.

Faye's mirrors revealed no yellow-eyed cover team beasts behind her.

Security cameras logged her driving into her apartment building's underground parking lot with thirty-eight minutes to go. She backed the Ford into her space on the second level, pushed the *wee-oo* lock button on her key fob as she marched through the gasoline-musty light of the concrete car barn to the elevator, rode it to the LOBBY. Found nothing in her snail mailbox, but it could have looked suspicious if she hadn't checked.

Faye guessed right: no one presided at the front desk. Night clerk Mr Abdullah was probably sneaking onto the manager's computer, searching for news about his family in Somalia who were trapped amidst drought, famine, pirates, a United Arab Emirates funded anti-pirates army with its own Washington, D.C., law firm, fundamentalist Muslim revolutionaries, and twelve thousand blue-helmeted African Union peacekeeper troops trained by outsourced CIA contractors operating from a razor wire–surrounded complex at Mogadishu's airport that Somalis called 'the pink house.'

She spotted no one else in the lobby. Security cameras for the front door, the lobby, and the rear exit logged her as she walked past the elevators to the stairwell. A routine analysis might conclude she was an office worker who felt in need of exercise.

Stairwell security cameras only covered the first flight of concrete steps and the top-floor stairwell with its roof exit. She floated up two flights of stairs, her heart pounding hard but not from the climb - every day before work, she ran a paratrooper's six miles on a park trail and then home here to run up and down the building's nine flights of stairs.

Faye stopped at the cinder-block walls' switchback between the fourth and her fifth floor. Used her cell phone to link with the computer in her home, checked the log of her computer's camera she'd interfaced with motion detectors aimed at her unit's entrance and the sliding-glass-door balcony for her one-bedroom apartment's living room: NO ACTIVITY. The computer camera via her cell phone screen showed the inside of her locked apartment door and the shadowed living room *empty* of any intruder.

She went to her apartment. Slid inside. All was silent. Shadowed.

Faye stared out her balcony's closed sliding glass door to the purple night shotgunned with twinkles of city lights. Imagined that off in that darkness, she could see the glow of the Lincoln Memorial, the White House and Capitol she'd driven past earlier that day, the place where she'd once escaped termination.

A wall switch snapped on a lamp of here & now. The couch, the chairs, the coffee table from some garage sale. A chin-up bar filled the top of her bedroom door.

The clock read 8:31 - twenty-nine minutes *until*.

Risk a shower.

She tossed her black coat over a chair, hurried to the dark bathroom, snapped the light on and shed her suitable-for-running-or-kicking shoes. The holstered .40 Glock on her right hip went on the back of the closed toilet, hilt toward the open shower. The cell phone and her credentials went on the sink. She unbuttoned her blouse.

The bathroom mirror captured her image. She wore a black bra. The thick pink scar slashed from her sternum to her right hip. Her slacks opened easily: a year after the last surgery, she still liked to wear them loose. They drifted to the floor. She laughed as she imagined insisting to some Boss In The Sky that *black bikini underwear is indeed professional attire suitable for the office* and less likely to bind if you throw a kick. Those black panties peeled off as she stood tall in the mirror. Black bra, arms like thick silk curtain sashes, smooth stomach. That scar.

She unhooked her black bra. Let it fall.

This is me.

Head of short hair. Green eyes special only in how they see, not how they look. Mouth special only for what it never will be allowed to say. *No wrinkles on my neck, not like Mom, not yet, and there'll be a 'yet,' there will be and* . . . Breasts some guys think are too small but only afterward. She felt her nipples pucker with the chill in the apartment.

Turned the shower on full blast, as hot as she dared, tried to lose what she had to do and an old man named *Condor* or *Vin* in the steam and the wet. She spun the shower handle. Icy water flooded her to *focused*.

Drying with a white towel, standing in the tub, tossing the towel over the shower rod, stepping out of the tub, pulling on her slacks, slipping into the blouse and buttoning the four buttons up to her neck. *Unfasten the top button.*

She shoved the black bra and panties into the hamper.

Tossed her shoes into the bedroom, heard them clunk against the wall, the floor.

Stared into the bathroom mirror.

Be you.

But a little lip gloss wouldn't be wrong.

The mirror watched her slide the gloss tube's smooth tip over her lips.

A snap off of the bathroom light and that reflection became only a black shape.

She took her credentials and gun with her, put them in the bedside night table drawer. Slid the drawer shut. All the way shut.

Don't think about the black pistol-grip shotgun in your closet. The Glock rigged under the other side of the bed. The snub-nose .38 revolver hidden for a quick grab in the kitchen, or the 9mm Beretta strapped under the couch. Or where the knives are.

You gotta do this with your own hands.

Nine minutes until nine o'clock.

What if he's late? What will that tell you? What will that mean?

What if you can't go through with it?

She was never supposed to need to do this.

Her left hand floated to her bedroom doorjamb like it was the dance studio bar across a mirror as she straightened her spine, rose to her full height in Third Position, let that motion float her right arm up to a graceful half-moon curve above her head, then sank straight down with her knees bending out and her bare heels rising off the bedroom carpet with *Le Grand Plié*. She held that deep crouch, felt her inner thigh muscles stretch and loosen and then *up* she came with a swoop of her hand as the ballet motion became grabbing & pulling the incoming punch of an invisible attacker while smashing her palm strike into his hyperextended elbow.

The digital clock on her night table read 8:53.

Seven minutes.

The lamp in the living room cast more shadows than light. Scant illumination came from the white bulb under the metal hood over her stove.

Faye unlocked her door to the world.

Stood far enough away not to get overwhelmed by a charge-in breach.

Stood in the flow of the indigo night beyond her walls of glass.

Stared at the unlocked wooden door. At the chain dangling from its mount.

You spend your life waiting for whoever walks through your door.

The tick-tock world fell away as she stood there. She made herself breathe from her belly. Made herself not look at any clock. Made herself *wait*.

The knock - *one two three*, soft but strong.

She stretched from her neck cords to her at-her-sides empty hands.

'Come in,' she said.

The door swung open. There he stood, backlit by the yellow light in the hall.

He said: 'How's my timing?'

'You're here now,' said Faye.

BOLO (Be On Look Out *for*) data: male, Caucasian, early thirties, six foot two, 177 pounds. California-surfer prematurely thinning blond hair, face like a handsome eagle, glasses over blue eyes giving him a scholarly look, but muscled, graceful.

She faked a light tone: 'Shut the door behind you. And lock it.'

He even put the chain on.

The government lawyer–like black shoes he wore were a workweek away from their last shine. His dark blue suit complemented his classic blue dress shirt and nicely offset his red cloth tie that dangled like a leash knotted around his neck.

The best move against a man wearing a tie is to charm your way in close, half your arm's length away. *Smile.* Slide the tie into your loose two-handed grip and lift it off the man's chest like you're admiring -

- grip the tie, whirl & duck so it's pulled across your shoulder as you slam your hips back into him and snap forward/down, jerking the tie toward the floor. Odds are, he'll flip over your back like judo's *Moroteseoi-nage* throw, crash at your feet as you go with inertia, drop your knees into his chest. Even if your knees don't explode his heart, his skeletal shock, vertigo, and blasted-away breath let you grip the tie's knot with one hand as your weight presses through that fist to his throat and your other hand pulls the slack end of the tie. His face turns purple, seventeen seconds to unconsciousness if the strangling tie cinches the right blood vessels as you choke off rescuing air.

Other options include *ring the bell*, the quick grab & jerk the tie to slam him bent *over/down*, but it's easy to miss the debilitating knee-to-face contact. The *garrote from behind* technique is more likely to fail and put you in position to get fucked up by his spinning counter than it is to be your clean kill.

Still, grab a man by his tie and you're halfway home.

He filled his eyes with Faye, said: 'How was your Monday?'

'Same-old, same-old.'

'I'll pretend that's good.'

He watched her barefoot pad toward him, nine steps away, eight.

'Getting to see you,' he said, six steps away, five, 'that's not good, that's the best.'

Faye slid her arms under his suit coat, along his *empty* belt until they met at his spine. Her face pressed against him. Her head reached the knot on his tie, his red cloth tie that smelled like wool and *smell*, she could smell him, his heat, his skin.

Arms wrapped around her - strong, eager.

She said: 'Did anybody see you come here?'

'I hope the world.'

When she said nothing, he told her: 'I saw nobody who knew they saw me.'

'Did you tell anybody?' she asked.

'I know your deal,' he said.

Your: Subtle assertion through a possessive adjective.

Faye mimicked a TV game-show host: '*And the answer is* . . . ?'

He moved her just far enough away so they could see each other face-to-face.

Said: 'We're our secret.'

Then he kissed her. She felt his surprise - *joy* - as she opened her lips and flicked her tongue to his, led it into her mouth. Lifetimes later as she pulled her face away from his, her hands still holding his sides, their chests heaving, he brushed her cheek with his right hand, said: 'So you said tonight has got to be special?'

He watched her nod as she said: 'One time.'

'Not just one-time special,' he said. 'We've got - '

She pursed her lips. '*Shhh.*'

Her hands slid from his spine, under his suit coat, along the sides of his blue shirt.

'I have to know something,' she said.

'What?'

Faye's fingers found his tie, his red cloth tie. Held it. Stroked it.

'If I can trust you.'

'I've - '

Her fingers closed on the tie with a slight tug to snap short his sentence.

She said: 'It's not you, it's me. I have to know I can allow myself to trust.'

'What more - '

Her finger covered his lips as if now he were supposed to say *shhh*. She slid her fingers to his shirt collar. Watched his blue eyes dance behind his minimalist-frame glasses that would have been dorky on anyone else but on him . . .

Just right.

He blinked as he felt her undo the knot of his tie.

Pull it off his neck with a *snap!*

She turned and walked away from him, barefoot, red tie dangling from her hand.

As she walked toward the open-door bedroom where he, where they'd been before, yes and yes and even *yes*, but now . . .

She felt him pulled into her wake. Felt the burn of his eyes as she unbuttoned her blouse and let it fall, her back naked as she reached the bedroom. She unfastened her slacks, stepped out of them. Knew he was close behind her, his eyes on her bare ass, *like my whole world's globe* he'd said to her once as he ran his hand over its curve while she lay on her stomach hiding her smile, as his lips pressed against her flesh *there*.

The lamp on her night table glowed.

Naked, on her knees, she worked her way to the black iron headboard, heard his shoes hitting the floor, the zip of his pants as she lashed the thick end of the tie to the black iron. Kept her back to him as she knelt on her bed facing the wall where she'd mounted a framed poster-sized sepia art photograph, a wild horse plunging through a blizzard. She knotted the skinny end of his red tie around her wrists with loops she'd learned at E&E (Escape & Evasion Course). Her teeth tightened the last loop.

Trapped, unable to undo the tie alone, she turned, the short bond making her stretch out on her back, lie naked there in front of him.

He'd undressed. Put his glasses somewhere. Stared at her with wonder.

Said: 'What - '

'Now be who you are,' she said. 'Do whatever you want, not what you think won't piss me off or will make me happy. Forget about me - fuck that, *fuck me*. I'm tied up because I have to know that I can't guide or stop you. I have to know that I've still got the ability to trust. To tie myself up without a chance, without a choice.'

He climbed on the bed beside her, rose on her right side as she lay stretched out naked, her hands lashed up to the bed above her head.

And he kissed her *oh* and she kissed him back -

- nothing in her need said she couldn't take what she could get on the way to what she had to know -

- deep wet kisses, probing gnawing each other's mouths, faces, neck, *he's kissing my neck, down and oh yes, squeeze I'm not big yes yes I am squeeze oh!* he sucked her nipple into his mouth, his tongue rubbing it, lush and full and wet, she was so wet as his kisses marched down between her breasts, past the scar, not dwelling on it, not ignoring it *yes*, kissing down she saw his blond hair as he pushed her thighs wider -

Spun like by a strong wind, Faye felt and watched him pull her to the edge of the bed, stretch her out from her hands lashed above her head, turning her so she was straight, legs dangling over the edge of the bed where he knelt between them and *oh, oh yes, his mouth, his tongue and then his hands on me, liquid fire caressing my breasts heart going to explode his hands won't stop don't* -

She heard herself scream, a guttural animal cry as again and again -

Then he was up on the bed.

Pushing her.

Rolling her over.

Lashed wrists and she was on her stomach, face down on the bed.

Then *oh*, rolling her on her right side: pressed against her, kissing her, *taste us, yes* her left leg up over his before his hand came down, pulled her leg higher guiding himself *in* and he cupped her ass pulled her so tight/deep to him and -

He pressed his left hand over her mouth.

So she couldn't scream.

Tied to the bed, I'm an idiot can't strike, deep in me, he's deep in me, pulling me closer, his hands pressing my hips wet hard to his, can't fight -

He said: 'I love you.'

Her world spun. She felt the push of one hand over her mouth, cupped like the perfect take-out of a sentry, pressing her against her spine so she couldn't look away, his other hand pulling her hips into him *oh* so she can't spin free, use her legs *oh* . . .

Can't turn away from his blue eyes: '*I love you*. You can't say anything back even if you want to or think you need to. Even if you're afraid, don't know what to say. Because you trusted me to take that away from you. You trusted me to do what I'm afraid you'll reject. But you can't reject a thing because no one can hear you scream.

'Whatever you want to say, you're not ready. Too soon. Too much. Too *not now*.

'So after I take my hand off your mouth, you got nothing to say. I'm gonna say it when I want to, when it bursts out of me because I'm all tied up in loving you. But you can't tell me you love me or you don't. Not now. Someday that's gotta come and now you know you can trust somebody - *me* because I love you, I love you!'

One hand pushed her smothered mouth back against her spine, one hand pulled her thrusting hips against his and he must have felt her come & come again as he cried out *I love you* like a mantra, faster and faster until he cried out beyond words as she screamed against his hand that cupped her mouth and muffled the sounds of her soul.

Done, frenzy slipping away, muscles relaxing, her leg heavy over him, his left hand now cupping her right cheek, the brush of his thumb against her swollen lips.

She had to coach him on how to free her hands.

That made them laugh and the laugh was everything, let them hold each other, slide down on the bed, let her lie across his chest, put her right cheek on his flesh where if she listened, she could hear every beat of his heart.

He kissed the top of her head, the coconut shampoo smell of her hair.

They held each other loosely. They held each other for forever.

His name is Chris Harvie.

'Don't worry,' he said. 'Love isn't lethal.'

Faye said: 'Sure it is.'

7

'Now, it's now!' shouted ghosts to Condor as he woke the next morning.

He rolled out of bed.

Eased back the window's white curtains.

Dawn in Washington. Headlights still glowed on vehicles driving past his home. A seagull's shadow flickered across the morning's sunlit wall of town houses across the street. The dog next door barked at a passing jogger. A car horn honked.

Vin imagined he heard a bugle blowing reveille three blocks away at the redbrick-walled, block-sized barracks for the Commandant of the Marine Corps. The Marines host public parades there on summer Friday nights. Bands play rousing patriotic horn & snare drum anthems. Rows of brave & brilliant men and women in snappy white hats, tan shirts, and bright blue trousers march to the beat of political witches banging spoons against a low-bid government black pot boiling on the bonfire of time. What the witches see & sip from that brew helps decide if flag-draped coffins get shipped home to Beaver Crossing, Nebraska, and Truth or Consequences, New Mexico, and Shelby, Montana.

No white car lurked beyond the cool glass of the second-floor bedroom window.

Not seeing them means the oppo has great street smarts.

Or they're not there, thought Condor. *Or something else happened.*

Today, it'll happen today.

Condor let the white curtain drop back over his window.

Didn't look in the mirror on the cabinet of stoned sanity as he used the bathroom.

No matter what's coming, when you gotta go, you gotta go.

He didn't look at the mirror as he washed his hands.

Left the bathroom with the gurgle of the flushing toilet.

Like a Marine on patrol, he descended the staircase. Turquoise door, still shut. No ninja crouched in the living room. Nothing seems disturbed on the wall of secrets. No vampire waited in the downstairs bathroom. *Do not look in the mirror!* Seen through the back door bars, the weathered gray wooden fence surrounding his blond pressure-treated wooden back deck contained no ambushers, only the lonely Japanese maple tree.

He flipped the wall switch. *A miracle*: light arrived. He filled the teakettle on the gas stove where he lit a blue flame with a *whump*. Vin ground his coffee. Threw out the leftover old brew, rigged the coffeepot to receive the new. Padded back upstairs in his bare feet to change. As the water boiled.

Wearing a torn black sweatshirt over a thermal top, gray sweatpants, white socks and black, hard-soled Chinese *gung fu* shoes, the silver-haired man had to be careful not to slip on the wooden stairs as he came back downstairs to rescue the whistling kettle.

Get your coffee cup later:

If your hands can't be strategically full, be sure they're operationally empty.

He flipped the locks and jerked open the turquoise door.

No one shot him.

No visible watchers hunched in the cars parked on both sides of the street, in the neighborhood windows, on the roofs. A Metro bus rumbled past: *Commuters. Citizens.*

On his front step waited thinly filled plastic sheaths of *The Washington Post* and *The New York Times*. He fetched them inside and locked the turquoise door. Put the newspapers on the breakfast bar in his kitchen. The refrigerator didn't explode when he opened the door to get his carton of milk from cows adulterated with antibiotics. He splashed milk into his cup, added coffee, set the cup on the breakfast bar. Shook *The Post* and *The Times* out of their condom sheaths. Turned on his satellite receiver and the radio blasted dead Warren Zevon singing 'Lawyers, Guns and Money' and -

A civvies-clad Marine Recon Major clutches a stack of newspapers in some D.C. room. There's a not-so-secret war in Nicaragua. A murdered secret agent in L.A. The Marine doesn't know you exist, you're his shadow backup, and why, why are we reading the newspapers' horoscopes?

Hello! thought Vin to those new ghosts: *Who are you?*

But *like that*, like the steam coming from his coffee cup . . . Gone.

Must be the drugs not working.

Yes!

He read the news, *oh boy*. Didn't find his name in the reports of what's supposed to be real and who's supposed to be dead. Finished two cups of coffee. Knew he'd miss newspaper comics when they went extinct. Used the bathroom two more times (usual). And never looked in that downstairs mirror, not even a glance.

Outside on the back deck, he flowed through *t'ai chi*. Cool air surrounding him smelled like a city alley but so far D.C.'s stench is not the smog that strangles Beijing like in the three-dotted photo taped to Condor's brick wall. *T'ai chi* moving from his center snapped Condor's arms and hands up & out *to Ji* - press posture.

Victor in the asylum saying: 'Power generates from your hips'.

Hips thrusting Wendy's naked body astride him, he's on his back, Wendy says: 'They lied to you. I was shot dead in the head.' Her eyes close, she whispers: 'You got it! You - '

Gone. Here, now, whenever: she was really gone.

But good to see her again. *Whoever she was.*

The *remember* caught Condor in his shower: W. The Marine Major was named *Wes*. *Wendy* and *Wes*. Wendy was long dead when Wes . . . when Wes . . .

Clouds of knowing vanished in the shower's pounding steam where it felt good to shave with hand soap and his own safety razor, not have to shave with a blue-handled disposable razor at one of the mirrored sinks in a communal bathroom watched over by two orderlies who weren't as tough as they thought. Condor considered modifying the shave-off of his morning antipsychotics and anxiety meds - if that's what they were.

Naw. Too late to turn back now.

He razor-bladed his morning *stay-sane* doses down a full two-thirds.

Chose a blue shirt over a clean thermal undershirt. All his pants were black, kept him from getting lost in indecision or fashion indecency. Gray socks. Black shoes suitable for running or kicking.

Walk downstairs. Listen to the radio. Stare at the wall of secrets.

Nothing. Not a whisper. Not a *clong*.

'Well, that sucks,' he told his empty home.

Yesterday the weather report said sunny and it rained. Today the report said rain and the sun shined. He thought about wearing the black leather sports jacket that his Settlement Specialist claimed was out of covert guidelines, too flashy, made him look like someone, made him look . . . intense.

'Yeah,' he'd told her.

She'd decided not to push.

And that morning, he decided to wear the gray wool sports jacket instead: *You don't want to ring the wrong bells.*

Condor locked and left his house to walk to work. It was Tuesday, 7:42 A.M.

The crazy woman's dog barked at him as he walked to the corner of Eleventh Street and Independence Avenue, turned left and retraced his steps from the night before on sidewalks he'd tramped hundreds of -

Paris, Hartwell stalking you twenty meters back at your eight o'clock across the cobblestone road. Popped up smack where he wasn't supposed to be. Good that he's a bad brick man, you spot him, is he alone, what's he packing, and at the U.S. embassy where you can't go, can never go, they won't give you shelter, embassy walls draped red, white and bicentennial blue and you're out here quickening through a swirl of French impressionism while behind you, with his every hungry step, with fanatic's fire blazing his eyes, Hartwell yells: 'I know who you are, mother-fucker!'

Now *here*, standing in the giant doorway of the Adams Building, a castle-like structure, the white-shirted Library of Congress cop wears a brass name tag: SCOTT BRADLEY.

The cop wears a holstered 9mm pistol you could grab.

But don't.

'Hi, Vin,' says Officer Scott Bradley.

Condor gave him a smile like this was just another day. Emptied his pockets. Passed through the metal & bomb detector archway without setting off a *beep*. Collected his personals and walked to the elevator bank, pushed the lone brass button for DOWN. Only then did he glance back at the open doorway's *noir* shaft of tall light where Officer Bradley stood as the first overt line of defense. Saw no ghosts.

As if Badge Bradley could stop them.

Call him *Condor*, call him *Vin*: he rode an elevator down alone.

His underground office waited behind a brown steel fireproof slab he opened by tapping a code into the digital lock that transmitted to the Library of Congress's central security computer linked to Homeland Security's NROD and its data flow to Bald Peter and Faye, the woman who wasn't his daughter.

His watch read 7:58 A.M. - more or less two hours *until*.

If I'm lucky.

Condor stood in his basement office's open doorway. Reached to an inside shelf for the rubber wedge he'd conned out of the carpenter's shop. Propped the door wide open to secure a view of the hall. Flipped on the lights for his domain.

Regular Library of Congress workers called it *the Grave Cave*.

Janitors had helped him move his scarred gray steel desk so he sat behind a restricted-internet computer on his left and two carts to his right, everything rigged so he could stare out to see anyone who passed by. Or tried to charge in. As he sat there.

Who cared if propping open his door created a firing lane to his heart.

Some ways we get shot are too sweet to forbid.

Eight in the morning. Underground at the Grave Cave. Two hours *until*.

Plain pine boxes made chest-high walls around his desk. On any given day, there'd be fifty boxes. Condor relished the smell of pine. Appreciated that the aroma of forests covered odors of must & dust & rot from the contents of the crates.

Books.

Blond white pine crates packed full of books.

Books from de-acquisitioning Air Force bases. Books from veterans' hospitals. Books from Army bases in

Germany near where their Soviet Union counterparts no longer existed. Books from deactivated ICBM Minuteman silos dotting the northern prairies. Books from black site prisons that considered vetted knowledge about the outside world as acceptable torture more than rebellious escape. Books from classified CIA staging centers and duty stations. Obama-era books already cycling back from the under-construction, $3 billion-plus secret NSA spy data center in the same mountains of Utah that also shelter nine thousand members of the country's leading Mormon polygamous sect. Books snagged & bagged on commando raids of terrorist lairs. Books CIA *closers* retrieved from the rubble of dead spies.

But not just any books.

Novels. Short story collections. Scripts. Barely read books of poetry.

Volumes of what wasn't real - but was maybe, *just maybe*, true.

Histories, technical manuals, biographies, *how-tos*, TV-famous authors' declarations about *what I say really happened & what it means*, self-motivation manuals by parroting strangers, tomes of faith or brilliant insight and other nonfictions were vetted and disappeared further back up the chain of Review & Resolution.

What came to Condor in the one-room underground Grave Cave at the Library of Congress were stories swirled out of our ether by souls who couldn't stop screaming.

Mistakes were made, *sure*.

More than once Condor crowbarred open a crate and found stacks of what the previous century called *record albums*, cardboard-jacketed, flat black petroleum-based discs containing aural transmissions accessible only with technology most American homes no longer possessed. Sometimes he cried for what he found that he knew he knew but knew not from where. *Clongs* seized him. He'd scissor out an album jacket photo of a singer-songwriter or a scene that riveted his eyes. He hid such photos down the back of his pants and carefully walked home through the security detector arches to tape the stolen photos on his wall alongside newspaper salvages and prose or poetry lines also scissor-stolen from R&R crates.

Magazines sometimes survived R&R's usual toss straight to the trash. Condor tore out the *Spy vs. Spy* cartoon page of a satirical *Mad* magazine from 1968 when revolution fired the streets of Paris, of Prague, of Mexico City and Memphis, Tennessee. Two months out of the secret Ravens' asylum and into this job, Condor uncrated a stack of *Playboy* magazines - the publication starring a centerfold of women photographed nude with makeup & touched-up flesh. Many such photo fictions had already been torn from those magazines, but one surviving image nailed his eyes: a quarter-page color snap of a 1970s beauty 'revisited' a decade later, a photo of her leaning on a brass bed, the mirror behind her reflecting a tumble of mature honey hair, a black garter belt above her moon of curved hips, black stockings on dancer-long legs in ridiculously decorative black stiletto heels, breasts heavy & low & full maroon *there*, her smile wide as her eyes look to see who's looking at her.

Condor taped that garter-belted photo to his brick wall a respectable distance from his newspaper art portrait of a lone woman with black hair tumbling to her simple blue sleeveless blouse and a pink surreal featureless swirl for her face.

One image reveals so much, one image reveals so little. The space between is enough to drive you mad.

Still, he stole and poked them both with the secret three holes: *Pay attention!*

But that wasn't his job.

What *they*'d told Condor to do was glance at each book, each discard of vision, and in as few possible heartbeats, decide which cart claimed the work.

Cart A went to Permanent Storage.

Cart B carried its captives to the pulp machine.

Condor once convinced a transport team to take him along to Cart B's disposal site, a thirty-seven-minute drive in the cramped truck's front seat with two men who argued about professional football and how fucked up the Navy had been and wasn't that the best time and when could they smoke with this *what the hell* stranger sitting between them? Seagulls circled the packed earth landfill, a wasteland where putting a pulping plant probably made environmental sense. Condor watched books he'd tossed onto Cart B get dumped into a green steel maw, heard them sprayed with chemicals and the whining gear clanging crunch as they became a gooey mass poured into vats on other trucks and taken away to be turned into . . . *What?*

Rules prohibited Condor from saving more than one Cart A of books a week.

He agonized over filling Cart B with doomed books. As ordered, flipped their pages. Looked for indications this volume had been the key to a book code. Scanned for spy notes cribbed in the pages or classified documents slid in there and forgotten. He pondered *security risk quotient* amidst coming-of-age novels, con artist swaggers, flesh peddles, *noir* sagas, soul-revealing classics, cop stories, alternative times fantasies or science fictions, heaving bosomed romances about the President's lost love. A book could earn Cart A salvation with its reputation for *getting it right*, for tradecraft revealed or created, secrets shared.

Every workday made Condor unpack crates.

'You're a reader,' said the Settlement Specialist. 'This is like your first spy job.'

'You mean it's not something the CIA made up so they know where I am?'

She smiled.

Helped him keyboard cover lies to his Library of Congress employee file.

Now it's now!

No shit, he told the new ghosts that Tuesday morning as he sat at his desk framed by the open doorway of the Grave Cave. At 9:51 he tossed a novel about a gunfighter come home to a small town on Cart B, then stared out his open door.

Waiting.

Clicking heels came up the hallway on the other side of his wall, to his left, his heart side. Footsteps coming louder, drawing closer to his view through the open door.

Here she comes.

You've been here before.

Here and now spy-you spend hours tracking her data. The more you know, the more you need to know. She's fifty-three. Born in the year of the dragon. Never married, no dependents. *That makes no sense.* Employed by the Library of Congress for eighteen years, plus a three-year loan-out to the Smithsonian. First employment line on her résumé: U.S. Senate staff for five years when she was young & smart & schooled and snapped her way over the sidewalks while taxi passengers gawked at her. She rents an apartment in a building not yet transitioned from run-down to hip. Two promotions during her years here at the Library.

She heel-clicks into view beyond your open door.

Curly blond hair with gray roots falls off a widow's peak to brush a sigh of breasts under her form-fitting business black dress. Navy blue trench coat slung through her shoulder purse strap. She's thicker round the waist than she can change, black-stockinged legs yoga-muscled past trim, metronome-swinging arms and black shoes. Her face is softly lean, rectangular, tan skin that pulls sunlight. Smile lines scar her wide, thick-lipped unpainted mouth. Her eyes stare straight ahead and not at you.

She marches past the open doorway. Out of sight.

Heels click on the hallway floor. The elevator whirs.

There you sit.

Again.

Still.

Find out or fail forever.

Vin whirled from behind his desk. Charged out of the Grave Cave in time to see the elevator close. His fingers woodpeckered the brass call button. Magnets pulled his eyes above the elevator to its floor indicator bar: 'G' lit up.

The parallel elevator whirred open.

Vin jumped into that cage, pushed the button labeled 'G.' Got -

There she is! Clearing security. Slipping into her navy blue trench coat.

Once Vin walked behind her and her coworkers as she said: '*I hate the cold.*'

She's going out the tall shaft back door.

Condor made it outside to the cool spring air in time to watch her turn right at the end of the Adams Building's U-shaped driveway.

No white car parked across the street.

You don't see the oppo because they're street smart.

She's walking toward Pennsylvania Avenue with its wall of cafes and bars.

Vin tried not to run, knew he was born to *this* no matter what he could remember.

Get closer behind her. She's got the light, the WALK sign with its white stick man flaunting his freedom and for you turning orange *fuck him* scurry across the street. Call it twenty, call it fifteen steps from the drift of curly blond hair on her navy blue coat as she crosses Pennsylvania Avenue, opens the dinging-bell door of a Starbucks.

Coffee, thought Vin. *She's going for coffee*.

The world flowed around him. A silver-haired man standing still on the sidewalk as tourists and troopers used their time to walk past him. He made a perfect target.

Opened the tinkling-bell door of the Starbucks.

Ten o'clock, coffee hour, but it's only her standing in the line at the counter.

Sapphire blue eyes lightning-bolted him.

She said: 'Sometimes you go crazy if you don't get outside the walls.'

'Screaming doesn't help,' said Vin.

'You've been hawking me for five months and that's the best you've got?'

The espresso steamer hissed.

He said: 'You give what you can.'

'And get what you get.' Her smile seemed sad. 'Not bad.'

'What do you see in those old movies you catalog for the Library?'

Words whispered through her thick, soft lips: 'It's what you don't see.'

Walking toward them on the other side of the counter with a green apron over her white blouse came the young barista whose parents had fled El Salvador's right-wing death squads. Their daughter dreaded the refugee-spawned, international MS 13 gang that now ruled her family's suburban turf five miles away from this Capitol Hill Starbucks. The gang used its websites and Facebook tattoos to stalk for victims and volunteers and you never knew *until*. The barista told the *gringa* who spent drugstore dollars to stay blond: 'Here's your cappuccino, ma'am.'

The '*ma'am*' brought a different smile to the blond woman. She took the steaming white paper cup from the barista, walked to the Starbucks door.

Turned back, looked at the man watching her go, said: 'So who are you?'

'How 'bout Vin?'

'How about Vin.'

He shrugged. 'I wasn't . . . all the way right with what I said before.'

'Confessions don't impress me anymore,' she told him.

'It's not about impressing you. It's about being true.'

He met her sapphire stare.

Said: 'Sometimes screaming lets you know you're there.'

Sapphire eyes blinked.

She said: 'Vin. *Huh.*'

Turned and left the cafe with the tinkle of the bell above her exit.

'Can I help you, sir?' The barista stayed a patient professional.

'I'll take whatever she had.' Vin did not chase the blonde who watched movies.

Some foggy instinct told him too bold *now* might generate *never*.

Plus if his cover team were active, he'd paint her with cross hairs.

Standing outside the Starbucks window, shrouded in black, Giselle presses her hands and face against the glass and screams.

Waves of *I don't know what or why but I'm sorry!* washed Vin back to work.

The barista returned to the counter with a steaming white cup in her hand and before she realized she didn't see him there said: 'Here's your coffee, sir.'

All she ever knew about that and what came after was the strange man's *gone.*

All his empty sidewalks led him from the Starbucks back to the Grave Cave. He ate lunch in the library's cafeteria hoping to spot her at her usual table but knowing he wouldn't and being right. He sat in his office and stared at the open doorway. Come five o'clock, he stepped out onto the Adams Building stoop.

No white car.

No new ghosts.

His gray wool sports jacket kept the cool of the evening away from his bones. Concrete pushed his black shoes toward the home he'd been allowed. Cars rushed past him on Independence Avenue, their headlights turning on to probe the coming dark. The air smelled like spring. No cover team, no brick boys on his tail, no snipers on the rooftops, *no white car*, there was no white car now but there was one yesterday.

Of course there was. Sure there was.

A green leaf fell from its protective wedge when he opened his turquoise door.

As it should.

As it would - if everything is safe.

Condor stepped into his living room. Shut the door behind him. Thought he was merely hallucinating again as he saw the limits of safe.

Bald secret agent Peter sat slumped on the floor in front of the fireplace.

His arms spread wide across that place where Condor would burn wood.

His hands nailed to the fireplace, blood flowing from his palms pierced and nailed to the mantel by knives from Condor's kitchen carving set.

Blood soaked the dead agent's white shirt inside his sports jacket and tan raincoat.

Probably *before* the killer nailed Bald Peter to the fireplace, he cut the man's throat along that crimson gash above the knot of a dampened dark necktie.

Probably the assassin gouged out Peter's eyes *after* the crucifixion.

Call him *Vin*, call him *Condor*, a man who came home from work on an ordinary Tuesday to find a blood-soaked American agent nailed to a fireplace with knives.

Vin saw a crucified man, the corpse's gaping mouth, his cheeks slickened red, eyes gouged to gory black holes.

Condor saw the *trickling* of freshly freed crimson tears.

8

What a glorious Tuesday spring morning it was for Faye as she walked across the plaza toward Complex Zed. She didn't know Condor was right then offering his heart in a Starbucks, but she knew she was going to rock the limbo's floor and -

Walking across the plaza toward her: a stocky, tan-skinned, black-haired man.

'What are you doing here?' said Faye.

They both knew that only Zed's security cameras kept her from hugging him.

'Good to see you, Faye,' said Sami. He gave her a fatherly smile. 'I don't want to hold you up, make you late.'

'Don't worry,' she said. 'I'll say my run took longer than usual.'

'Did it?'

'No.' A forgivable lie of omission. She hadn't run that morning.

'You can tell them we ran into each other. It's natural, and you're cleared.'

'Am I getting off the limbo level? Coming back online?'

'There's cleared and there's *cleared*,' he said.

'So you're not here about me?'

'Wish I was.' He looked around the mid-morning-lit plaza. Looked for who was there. Who wasn't. 'Remember RTDs?'

'Real-Time Drills.'

'Necessary risk even before Boston. A random day. Flash alert. Race to some game scenario site designed to see how you can do better. By noon, every crisis-clear East Coast headhunter worth his bullets will be in your building. But one real bomb go BOOM! under the right conference room table, and it's a great day for the bad guys.'

Sami sighed. 'Oh well, at least I got to run into my most charming colleague. She's kind of okay on the bricks, too.'

'If it weren't for the cameras,' smiled Faye, 'I'd drop you.'

'*A B C*,' grinned Sami. '*Always Be Covered*.'

Risk it, she thought as they walked toward work. Told the man beside her: 'You've been around a long time.'

'You wouldn't have gotten odds on that back when I was a kid in Beirut.'

'Rumors, legends, whispers: you're who knows.'

Sami stopped an arm's length away from a security door in the wall of black glass that reflected the images of him and a younger woman with short hair, slacks, Op shoes.

He said: 'Only three types of people are susceptible to flattery: *men, women -* '

'And *children*,' finished Faye. 'I don't want to talk to a child.'

She said: 'There are rumors about an agent who got caught in the shit in denied territory and called in a drone strike on himself.'

'We're spies, Faye. Starting rumors is one of the *what*s we do.'

'Come on, Sami. It's me asking.'

'No matter what you heard,' said her friend and former boss, 'something like that happens, guy like that . . . Forget about him getting one of the no-name stars on the wall out at Langley. He'd be Congressional Medal of Honor material.

'Or completely nuts,' added Sami. Smiled as he said: 'And dead.'

The breath of spring morning that Sami took seemed completely natural. He let his hand touch her arm. A mentor-to-protégé touch. A soft, sensitive touch. Innocent.

He looked straight into her green eyes. 'Have you got some reason for asking?'

'I don't know what I got,' said Faye. 'If it is something, I'll play it straight.'

'Never a doubt in my mind,' said Sami as he held the door open for her.

Like he held the door for her that day eight months before *when* they didn't pillory her in the soundproofed, plexiglass 'fishbowl' conference room of the Senate Intelligence Committee. That *when* morning, Sami looked away from the two Senators sitting across the table from him and Deputy Directors from both the CIA and the ODNI, looked at Faye in her chair, told her: 'Would you step outside, please?'

Then he got up and held that door for her.

As if her wound might require special care and attention.

Sami loved subtle.

She left that fishbowl deep in the windowless office complex for the Senate Select Committee on Intelligence. Perhaps a dozen cubicles and other executive offices waited between where she stood outside the fishbowl and the Committee entrance. CIA task forces on paper clips have more personnel than this Congressional oversight force charged with keeping track of America's war status intelligence community.

Faye glanced back into the fishbowl. *Sami with four strangers wearing business suits, deciding what they're going to do to me, with me.*

She looked left, saw *him* standing by the coffee bar holding a white Styrofoam cup.

She'd seen him before - one of five Senate staffers in that morning's meeting with Sami, the two spy agency execs, and a Senator from each political party. And her. For the CONFIDENTIAL-level briefing about Paris. Then he'd been sent out with the other Senate staffers, with Faye and Sami still in there as the quorum of two Senators got briefed on America's spies' TOP-SECRET version of blood on *le rue de cobblestones*.

Et moi, thought Faye.

She looked at that Senate staffer. Just a guy, tall, blond, gray suit. Her age.

Fuck him, fuck the doctors, I need coffee.

He didn't retreat when she put a dollar bill in the Styrofoam cup by the coffeepot, filled her own Styrofoam cup. Indeed, he came closer, and *fuck trusting the Committee's metal detectors*, she eyeballed him for a hidden weapon, saw his cup contained only water.

Over the burn of long-heated coffee she had to admit he smelled good. She was drenched in nervous sweat, hoped the perfume she seldom wore covered that with a scent of lilacs. He sent a bespectacled nod to the Senators and spy execs in the fishbowl.

'So,' he said, 'after I left, what did you guys talk about in there?'

'*Seriously?*'

'I know you're CIA so I had to say something that would shock a real response,' he told her. 'Because if talking about what's really going on is out, we have to resort to some kind of disembodied chatter where I start out asking you safe things, like which camp were your parents, Rolling Stones or Beatles?'

'That's your chatter?'

'I was hoping for *our* chatter, but *yeah*. What else can I say to you?'

'Are you hitting on me?'

'If I tried to hit you, you'd break my arm in like six places.'

'Probably only two.'

'Thanks for your restraint.' He shrugged both hands into the air and smiled with his blue eyes. 'And while I'm not hitting on you, per se, the intent is clearly growing.'

'Per se?'

'Sorry, I talk like that sometimes when I'm nervous.'

'I make you nervous?'

'Since the moment I saw you.'

'This oughta be good.'

'It's the way you stood - *stand*. You're here. Stepping right up and taking it. And true to that. Whatever it is.' He waved his fawn-suited hand. 'Blew me away.'

'So you decided to recruit me.'

'There's an idea. Do you play Ultimate?'

'What?'

'Ultimate Frisbee. Like soccer. Only with plastic discs. A stoner sport.'

Faye said: 'So you're a stoner? And think I am?'

'I'm a randomly drug-tested federal employee. Yesterday is gone if not forgotten.

'It's a simple game,' he said. 'You toss, you catch, you run. No contact.'

'Rules,' she said.

'Honor code,' he replied.

'Sounds like a pastime for sophomores.'

He nodded to the fishbowl where Senators frowned to show they were serious. 'I spend all day up on this hill chasing back and forth after whatever gets thrown into the air by them, so getting to catch and toss something real while running in what passes for clean air ... *Yeah*, that feels pretty good. And I'm a long way from being a sophomore.'

'Which way?' *Don't stare at the fishbowl!*

And he laughed. Just ... *did it*. Laughed. Out loud and in the open.

Said: 'Some days that's open to debate.'

'You should come,' he said.

'*What?*'

'More or less seven o'clock tomorrow night unless we get a freak September storm. Down on the Mall, the grass alongside the east wing of the National Gallery.'

'You want me to play?'

'I want you to give you the chance.'

'You're all heart.' She gulped the bitter coffee. Tossed the white cup in the trash, couldn't pretend anymore to ignore what was going on in the fishbowl.

'I'm Chris,' he said. 'Chris Harvie.'

She walked away.

As he said: 'Can I ask your name?'

Faye refused to turn around. Watched the fishbowl that trapped her tomorrows.

Traps my today, she thought that Tuesday seven months later as *après* Starbucks Condor walked back to work over empty sidewalks and she walked across the cubicle-crowded, blue-lightning-bolts limbo level and into NROD's clear-walls corral.

'Where's Peter?' she said to her half-dozen men and women colleagues.

'Did you lose your partner?' said Harris with a snide look that lied and said he knew more than he did.

He's not worth the bullet. Faye claimed an empty desktop computer, checked the online agent duty roster. Frowned. Saw one of the two bosses in NROD's inner office.

Stuck her head in, said: 'Why is my partner detailed to Admin this morning?'

The section co-commander who insisted you call her *Pam* checked the computer at her desk, shrugged. 'Probably some data-processing glitch.'

'Is it about me?' asked Faye.

'Why, did you do something wrong?'

Faye returned Pam's shrug, said: '*Naw*. You know me, boss.'

As she walked away, Faye heard Boss Pam say: 'No, I don't.'

No, Faye hadn't planned on going to that Ultimate Frisbee game the night after Sami worked a miracle, covered everyone's ass with the Senate oversight committee and cut some deals that eventually sent her to Home Sec's NROD in Complex Zed, but that next day she couldn't, she just *couldn't* stay in her new Bethesda apartment staring out at the autumn leaves of the political metropolis she'd need to get used to again.

She went for a late run like she often did, but that evening she and her backpack cleared any brick surveillance, only ran as far as the Bethesda Metro before she caught a train, transferred to the Blue Line, spotted Frisbee players on the grassy Mall, walked to them and watched him watch her (and miss a catch) as she took something from under her sweatshirt, put it in her knapsack that she secured to a tree with a bicycle lock.

He called out: 'She's with us!'

But he cut her no slack when players switched around so they were on opposite sides. Between the post-surgery push-ups, pull-ups, and running, she was in better shape, but he never hesitated to play as hard against her as he could.

Standing beside him as he caught his breath, she said: 'So this is what people do?'

'What people?' he gasped.

'People our age. Normal people.'

'Nobody's normal,' he said. 'You know that.'

Somebody yelled *Go!* They ran to and fro on the green grass under Washington's evening sky. The ivory Capitol dome rose a few blocks beyond one side of their playing field, while a quarter mile from the other sideline rose the Washington Monument topped by blinking red lights.

Faye had her cover story ready, a driver's license from Ohio, but no one hit her with Washington's ubiquitous defining question of '*What do you do?*'

She thought: *They've carved out this time from their imposed reality.*

Still, she deduced that many players were Congressional aides, that one handsome guy with curly hair worked for a telecommunications giant, a woman was a waitress waiting to hear about law school, two other women already were beginning associates in some D.C. legal factory where they'd go back to their desks and work toward midnight.

After the last game, Faye caught a ride with strangers to the chosen burgers & beers bar, watched him smoothly cut her out of the crowd to end up sitting with her and their third-round beers at the far end of the jukebox bar where no one could hear them.

'Nicely maneuvered,' she told him. Told Chris. Chris Harvie.

'I am working my hardest here,' he said.

'Not gonna get you anywhere.'

'You mean besides where we already are.' He shrugged. 'So I might as well give you the worst of it.'

Which was his father walked into a San Francisco fog one kindergarten night and never came back until another family sent high school junior Chris, his sister, and their mother his obituary for *their* husband-father. Which was exceeding law school rules on how much outside employment he could take driving pre-dawn bakery delivery trucks while going to Stanford. Which was a car wreck he shouldn't have walked away from, a few 'bonehead' accidents on the summer-job California state highway crew that helped fill his undergraduate scholarship gap at Brown University, some unspecified 'loutish' behavior with women. Which was breaking into an apartment a heartbeat ahead of a police raid to flush his buddy's LSD stash after the buddy's vindictive ex-girlfriend lied and ratted him out to the police as a dealer on her cell phone right in front of Chris.

'Oh, and I was a virgin until I was twenty-one,' he told Faye.

Shrugged: 'I wanted to get it right.'

'What happened to her?'

'Better things.' He drained what he'd said would be his last beer. 'And the rest, well, you probably already ran a background check.'

'That's the kind of thing you'd have a colleague who owes you do off the books.'

'You sure don't need a lawyer.'

'No, I don't.' She got off the stool, slung her backpack weighted with her holstered gun she hadn't slipped back on under her sweatshirt.

Said: 'My name is Faye Dozier.'

'For real?'

Left him with her smile as she entered that night alone.

Faye worked alone all that Tuesday morning after the night she met Condor - 'morning' being relative, given that NROD agents work staggered shifts and hers started at 10 A.M. She wrote an impassioned report on why Immigration should admit the neighbors of a young man who'd spent three years as an interpreter for U.S. soldiers in Afghanistan, not one betrayal, several acts of heroism, and all he wanted was to marry the girl next door and be free in Kansas.

At 1:23 P.M., she checked the online duty roster.

Peter was still 'Detailed Admin.'

Plus now he was NU/UC - No Unauthorized/Unnecessary Contact.

As per regs, he'd texted his Status Confirm every two hours.

One of the nicer and newer NROD agents, a sharp ex–Brooklyn cop named David, said: 'I hope his Admin deal isn't Internal Affairs calling him out for drinking.'

'We don't call it Internal Affairs,' said Faye as they stared at the computer monitor screen. 'We call it the Office of Professional Responsibility.'

'Oh. Is that what "*we*" call it?'

'I'm a spy,' she told David. 'Not a rat.'

The first Monday night after that Frisbee game, Chris Harvie came home from work to his U Street rented apartment - a neighborhood that went Obama-era *très chic* after being Jimmy Carter–era *très noir* - and found *My name is Faye Dozier* standing in his living room.

'I picked your locks,' she said before he could speak. 'I could have searched your place, but I didn't, I won't. I'll tell you nothing rather than lie. I expect the same from you.'

September chilled that week. She wore ugly jeans. A ratty old sweater and a green nylon flight jacket with zero patches that she'd got in Kandahar. She unfastened the waistband holster heavy with her newly issued Glock, put it on top of a stack of novels on his sofa's cheap end table.

'That comes with me,' she said.

She struggled out of her wool sweater.

Faye'd worn her ugliest, most unflattering white exercise bra.

That night her scar still puckered pink and angry.

'This is me, too. I might never tell you about it, but it's big, you can see, it's big, and no matter that I'm a hundred per cent medically, I fucked up and it fucked me up.'

She watched his blue eyes that hadn't looked away.

His mouth that hadn't said a thing.

Faye said: 'I can walk out that door. No regrets. No blowback. No tears. Just gone. Or I can stay and we can see what we can see.'

He crossed his room to her. Cupped her face in his hands. Said: 'Stay. You already beat my locks.'

Never gonna forget that, Faye was thinking at 5:28 on the evening after the night Chris cupped her mouth & then . . . She blinked back into focus, into her computer monitor at a desk, scrolled down all field agents' mandated daily review of America's on-average 270+ Actions/Alerts.

'A/A is like a cop shop's daily lineup of who got popped the night before,' ex–Brooklyn detective David had described it.

'Only it's all digital, all online, all the time,' Faye'd replied.

At 5:29 P.M. that Tuesday, Faye read the classified A/A report from Los Angeles on how starving sea lion pups which were washing up on Southern California beaches at more than five times the usual frequency had cleared terrorist-linked toxicology analysis and therefore this Event Syndrome's TSR - Threat Spectrum Rating - had dropped from six to one out of one hundred possible data-rated TSR levels.

'Dozier!' yelled the deputy commander named Ralph from the doorway of his box within a box of NROD's dioramic squad room. 'Get in here! David - '

He yelled to the ex–Brooklyn cop.

' - Harris,' yelled the commander to the snide asshole. 'You, too.'

Faye beat the other agents to the huddle with their boss Ralph.

'Nineteen minutes ago,' said the boss, 'our boy Peter missed his two-hour window for routine Status Confirm. His detail contact to Admin gave him fifteen minutes' grace and had the decency to call me before they upload into the system. We all know that Peter sometimes . . . His bald head can be lax about things.'

Harris started a snide drinking remark - ex-cop David elbowed him silent.

'Fuck Peter's *"I'm a star"* with a new NU/UC status,' said his boss. 'I called him. Straight to voicemail. The GPS ping on his phone . . .'

The boss focused on Faye: '. . . puts him on Capitol Hill at the address of a PINSS you two interviewed yesterday.'

'*Condor,*' whispered Faye. *Off work half an hour ago. Probably walked home.*

The boss said: 'Fuck if I know why Peter's doing follow-up, but that's what I just found logged into the system. He's out there, dinging the grid, and we've got . . .'

The boss looked at the nearest row of digital clocks on the wall outside his office.

'We've got to cover his ass and beat some rat squad react team there. Since I ordered a car brought out front *now*, technically we're already primary on this before the routine look-see goes out. Our team picks up its own shit - *hey!*'

Faye was out the boss's door before he ordered David and Harris to go with her.

They caught up with her at the elevator that let them all out at the ground-floor main lobby where they quick-marched past a group of out-of-complex colleagues standing in a friendly cluster to jive about where to go for dinner.

Sami stood on the fringe of that group of headhunters.

Saw Faye emerge from the elevator, and he started to smile . . .

Saw the look on her face.

Saw her see him.

Saw her clench her right fist by her belt buckle: *Running hot.*

Sami watched her gunners' trio stalk outside to a waiting sedan that screamed *badges*, said to his colleagues: 'Let's go to the closest place.'

'And guys,' he added to this mixed-gender group who hung on his every word, 'I'm thinking no beers yet.'

'I thought the alert game was over!' said one of the headhunters, who felt the heat from his colleagues for his error of opposing the guru even as those words left his mouth.

Sami said: 'You never know.'

At 5:33, the Home Sec/NROD sedan peeled away from the curb - Faye drove, ex-cop David rode shotgun, Harris strapped himself into the backseat.

'It's rush hour!' yelled Harris. 'Can't take Rock Creek Parkway!'

David snapped his cell phone into the cradle, on speaker to DISPATCH plus GPS.

At 5:41, they pushed the red light at Connecticut Avenue and Nebraska and sped by the last best independent bookstore in America.

Their boss's voice over the phone: 'Team, be advised, a classified protocol activated automatically when the system posted a possible trouble alert under your destination coordinates and the Condor identifier. Nearest hard-duty unit was protocol triggered. A unit launched that should be on scene before you.'

'Order them as backup!' yelled Faye. 'No action until I - we get there!'

'Understood, but . . . I'm not sure I've got that authority.'

Faye hit the switch for the red emergency lights in the grille and the siren. David pulled out the magnetic light-spinning cherry, slapped it on the roof of the car.

'What the fuck is going on?' yelled Harris from the backseat as they raced through siren-blasted gaps in the steel river of traffic stretching through affluent D.C. toward Capitol Hill.

'I don't know!' yelled Faye. 'Heads up for a white car, tinted windows!'

Washington rush-hour traffic devours high-speed responses. Any other time of day, red lights & siren, they'd have made it from that last phone call to the Eleventh Street, SE, destination in eleven minutes. Took them seventeen minutes, even with Faye taking every possible risk and Harris screaming: *Look out! Look out!*

Their squad car slammed to a stop outside the turquoise door at 6:01 P.M. Faye'd killed the siren four blocks away, but their flashing red lights beat rhythms on the evening sunlit row of town houses.

'Harris - alley out back, gray wood fence. Post up where you can cover it, don't pass anybody I mean *anybody* but me or David. *GO!* Run, we'll give you thirty!'

Yippy dog barking - fenced in next door front yard.

Dirty white yippy dog.

Gun out and so is David, must have *been there before*, too, *fuckup like me not a don't give a fuck*, two-handed combat grip the Glock out front - no citizens, lucky break. Eyes on the turquoise door, white curtains drawn over the two stories of front windows.

'*Yip! Yip yip!*'

Nod to the sidewalk: David moves to that post, eyes on the windows, knowing -

'Freeze!' yells the ex–Brooklyn cop.

Faye whirls -

Male, white, late twenties, *gun, he's got a gun*, black automatic *zeroed on me!*

'I'm Home Sec!' yells the strange man in blue jeans, a blue nylon Windbreaker. 'Yellow initials on my jacket back! You're Faye! Agent Dozier! I'm protocol!'

Seeing him over her gun barrel. Seeing his gun bore zero her face.

'*Yip! Yip!*'

Protocol is tall and lean. Wears a scruffy brass goatee, chopped-short hair, a poorly groomed surfer look.

He whirls. Aims his gun at the turquoise door.

Keep your gun on him.

Why? thinks Faye. But obeys her instincts.

Protocol says: 'That's the place, right?'

Says: 'My partner's posting our red-lights unit in the alley, block and secure.'

Pauses, listens: wireless earpiece.

Protocol says: 'Our two guys have hooked up.'

Harris's voice in David's belt-packed, speaker-on phone confirms.

Faye swung her Glock toward Condor's home.

Protocol said: 'You or me?'

Faye followed the flow of her gun sights to the turquoise door.

9

WHAT ROUGH BEAST
- William Butler Yeats, 'The Second Coming'

A throat-cut American spy slumps crucified by *your* knives over *your* fireplace.

Dark tears trickle from his empty eye sockets: *Fresh. Recent. Run!*

Across town in Complex Zed, Faye Dozier scanned Action/ Alerts. Learned the Threat Spectrum Rating for starving sea lions washing up on Southern California beaches.

In the twilight outside a D.C. house with a turquoise door, the neighbor's dirty white dog yipped once more in triumph, strutted under 'her' front porch, the human who'd dared come near her turf successfully *skedaddled* into its next-door cave.

shh!

Silence. No one alive in here but you. No one in the kitchen. No one upstairs.

What kind of cover team is outside watching?

Condor shook his head.

Impeccable timing. T.O.D. (Time Of Death) matches my known schedule.

Peter, the corpse was Peter. Bald, and that pissed him off. Lots pissed him off.

No blood spray high on the walls, so not a slashing samurai.

Picture it:

Peter knocked out. Killer drags him to the fireplace. Probably finishes him first, *then* crucifies him. Situational genius even if the killer was following some Op script.

If you're going to frame a crazy, build a crazy frame.

A freshly butchered body smells like steamy ham. Feels like a warm beach ball that's lost a breath of inflation. Condor slid his hands around the dead man's waist.

Holster - *empty.*

So officially, you've taken his gun.

Are now obviously armed and dangerous. A trained and crazed murderer.

There'll be a fast behavioral science profile of the fugitive - *you*: 'Crucifying the victim indicates a severe psychotic break. Gouging out the eyes means our subject doesn't want to be seen. And will attack anyone who seems to be stalking him.'

Shoot on sight won't be the Operational Order.

But it will be the street-smart move.

What did the wet-work artist do with the murdered man's eyes?

Mumbo jumbo mind mappers will say: 'Call them trophies or what he didn't know to discard, like a kid saving his graded exam paper.'

If they find the eyes on you or linked to you . . .

So the artist assassin is still active. With a pocketful of eyeballs to plant on you after somebody - *anybody* - takes you off or shoots you down, which means . . .

He's inside the machine.

That's how he got Bald Peter here.

How much time do you have before they nail you?

Across town on the limbo floor of the Office of National Intelligence's Complex Zed, an NROD deputy commander stood in his glass-walled office door and yelled: 'Dozier! Get in here. David, Harris: you, too.'

Condor made himself check the rest of the crucified corpse.

No ankle-holster backup gun to take and be the actual threat you officially are. Forget about the dead man's phone, his IDs maybe imbedded with GPS chips, his credit card, his cash: That'll look like you panicked, didn't scavenge resources.

A bald, gouged-out-eyes, throat-cut agent of America slumps crucified with your knives over your fireplace.

You are so fucked.

On your way to Killed While Resisting.

Or BAM! Extraordinary rendition. No trial, locked forever in some asylum box.

Across town in the lobby of Complex Zed, a headhunter guru named Sami sees one of his protégés scrambling with a team toward a car waiting in the street beyond the glass walls. She spots Sami, clenches her right fist by her belt buckle: *Running hot.*

Condor ran to the kitchen, grabbed a canvas shopping bag from between the refrigerator and the counter, ran back toward the living room -

Stopped. Stared at his collage wall. At his triangle-marked images.

Tell me what I'm trying to say!

Nothing. He heard nothing.

No creaking boards.

No yipping from the dog next door.

No ghosts. No *clongs*. Only the *whoosh* of time outside in the evening street.

Vin grabbed his blue hooded raincoat off the wall hook in the living room, noticed dark splatters of *not rain* on it as he bounded upstairs, ignored whether the dental floss strand had been snapped. *The killers are gone and on their way.*

Three cardboard boxes stacked in his bedroom closet held Vin's junk. Most of it came from who knew where, who knew why, but the middle box . . .

Weighed about forty pounds. Inside were books he could conceivably care about. And a black leather zip-up bomber jacket wrapped around something heavy the size of a loaf of bread. He unwrapped the jacket to reveal a black plaster statue of the Maltese Falcon. But who cared about that bird: he freed his scruffy black leather jacket, the secret he'd been hiding by making it look like mere padding around a fragile treasure.

Or so he hoped any squirrels who black-bagged & tossed his home had thought.

No iPad photos of this jacket, of Vin in it. No data for a BOLO alert.

Condor stuffed the black leather bomber jacket in his shopping bag. Restacked the boxes. Grabbed thermal underwear top and bottoms from a drawer. Clean socks.

Look at your reflection in the bathroom mirror.

Running scared.

Again.

'Yeah,' Condor told his image, told the ghosts. 'But I was young then.'

Grab the pill bottle of pee medicine, pain tablets, beta blockers and baby aspirin for your hyper heart, multivitamins. Drop them and the low-dose Valium into your shopping bag: you'll need to sleep if you live long enough. Take your toothbrush.

Rows of antipsychotic sedations stared at Condor.

Make them kill the real you.

Vin slammed the medicine cabinet door shut.

Grabbed yellow rubber gloves from under the bathroom sink.

Remembered to pocket his Maglite, a black metal flashlight the size of a fat tube of lipstick, perfectly acceptable and prudent for any PINSS-resettled home.

Condor pushed a stepstool against the blank white wall at the top of the stairs where he'd often been tempted to violate *Operational Readiness* and hang a picture or a movie poster of, *say*, Magnum-toting Lee Marvin and *noir* blonde Angie

Dickinson in *Point Blank*, or maybe an art print like the ones tourists buy in the Smithsonian gift shop, Sargent's *Girl in the Street of Venice*, a black-shawled, white-dressed brunette walking past two men, one of them raises his head to -

Focus!

Vin snatched the cloth belt off the black & red checked bathrobe hanging in the bathroom, the seemingly innocent robe he bought for this cloth belt, and *it will work*.

He threaded his leather belt through the canvas handles of the shopping bag so it now both carried the shopping bag and held up his pants.

Vin took off, then tied his laces together to dangle his shoes around his neck.

Tied one end of the bathrobe belt through a slat on the stool, left as much slack as possible when he tied the other end of the robe belt around his left ankle.

Almost forgot!

Condor tossed his cell phone clattering down the hall to the floor of his bedroom.

Pulled on the yellow rubber gloves.

'Yip! Yip yip yip!'

Outside - the neighbor's yippy white dog: *Barking at who?*

Condor climbed on the stool next to the bare *oh so clean* white wall, reached up -

Yellow-rubber-gloved hands left no smudge marks on the white ceiling panel they pushed open to the crawl space between Condor's hallway and his roof.

'Yip! Yip yip!'

Vin grabbed the lip of that portal, stood on his left foot, bathrobe-belt-lashed and with the bag behind him, put his stockinged right foot on the bare white wall, took a deep breath -

Propelled himself up into the crawl space, his elbows held his weight on the frame of the passageway, his left leg stretched below him lashed to the stool launchpad.

In the trapdoor's maw, Condor dangled above the house floor tied to a stool.

'*Yip yip!*'

Outside the turquoise front door, something or someone was driving the yippy white dog mad. Condor shoved open the trapdoor to the roof.

Cool air tumbled over his sweaty face.

He scrambled out to the city sky. Pulled the stool lashed to his ankle up behind him. Slid the square white ceiling panel back in place, unsmudged.

Wood-splintering crash - someone kicked in his downstairs front door.

Condor quietly closed the trapdoor.

'*Yipyipyipyip yip!*'

Peel off the yellow gloves. Shove them in the shopping bag unlashed from your pants. Untie the bathrobe belt from your left ankle. Put on your shoes.

Cop car red lights spun in the alley below and off to his right: *Go left.*

Washington is a horizontal city defined more by what's inside its Beltway's circling eight lanes of whizzing cars, trucks, and bus traffic than by the borders of various legal jurisdictions like the District of Columbia, Maryland, and Virginia. Any of the city's twenty-first-century vertical growth higher than the white marble Washington Monument *by law* begins in outlying neighborhoods that are no longer distinct suburbs.

Condor ran across the top of the city.

Off to the right of that stumbling runner rose a horizon of the Capitol dome. Like most of the central city, wall-to-wall town houses filled his neighborhood. He stumbled over firewalls, past chimneys, toward the edge at end-of-the-block.

The last house on the block. The owner had chopped this three-story-plus-basement property into apartments, rigged a steel fire escape down the back of the top two units. The fire escape zigzagged down toward a minuscule backyard patio inside a tall wooden fence. Other buildings sticking farther into the alley blocked Condor's view back toward his home and where the alley pulsated with cops' red lights.

You can't see them, they can't see you.

The fire escape trembled, but he made it down the top two flights.

A silver-haired man wearing a gray sports jacket with a shopping bag looped on his shoulder dangled by his hands from the fire escape's bottom steel rung.

Let go.

Fall through cool spring air.

Crash to a heap on a postage stamp of lawn.

Everything hurt. Shoulders from climbing and dangling. Sore arms. Legs - *right knee, oh man!* The jarring drop rattled his bones, his teeth. His heart pounded *no no no* against his ribs. He wanted to lie there. Vin stumbled to his feet.

A distant siren wailed.

Steel bars protected the door into the apartment from this backyard. The other exit was the gate through the man-high wood fence. He could run out to the alley . . .

Into whose gun sights from back where the red lights spun?

Condor shoved a lawn chair to the street side of the fence.

One more climb. One more fall.

Sirens screamed closer as he thumped onto the sidewalk screened from the view of his front stoop and back alley by the block of town houses he'd run over. Crossed the street, didn't look to his right down the alley.

Don't pull them with your eyes.

Nobody shot him. Nobody yelled stop. No sounds of running footsteps.

Get out of the cordon zone.

Don't go there.

Condor ducked into the garden-level alcove of a town house, unpacked his black leather jacket, revealed its satiny tan inner lining repaired with an L of gray duct tape. Ripped the tape free, stuck his hand between the inner lining and the outer black leather.

Found the money: four flat packs of bills sorted by denomination from $1s to $20s. Almost a year's worth of hoarding. Never so much his bank accounts plus expenses might alarm his minders' probable audit projections. Dollars short-changed out of waiters' tips. Five-dollar portraits of Abe Lincoln skimmed out of un-receipted sacks of homegrown tomatoes and fresh peaches and white corn and rainbow trout from the fish counter at the Eastern Market four blocks from Vin's house. Twenty-dollar bills palmed from what cover teams could have seen him stuffing in the pots of Christmas bell-ringing Salvation Army warriors. Vin had drawn the line at stealing for his cache: *You are the line you stand on.* Wouldn't dip his hand into an unknown Library of Congress staffer's open purse to snatch a loose twenty he saw in there as she rode beside him in the elevator. Standing in the alcove that night, he knew that if squirrels searching his place hadn't stolen any of his secret funds, he was stuffing $327 into his black jeans.

Enough operational cash to last, what: twenty-four hours in a major American city?

Condor shook his head. *How long did I last that first time?*

Inside the lining, he found the SmarTrip credit card to ride D.C.'s public buses and subways. The SmarTrip was a tradecraft coup: he'd bought it at a drugstore when the clerk was overwhelmed by a distraught mom holding a crying baby. They were the only people in that bright-lights store, no cover team to see what thirty dollars cash got him.

Drugstore, thought Condor as he put the SmarTrip in a cash-stuffed pants pocket.

Marra Drugs Superstore sprawls over the north-side block on Ninth and Pennsylvania, SE, welcomed Condor that Tuesday evening with a SPRING MADNESS SALE! banner over its double glass doors. He kept his face down for security cameras as he slid into a smog of deodorizers. Soulless instrumental music poured from the ceiling.

Don't notice me. His grip on the red plastic shopping cart let him control trembling while he rolled down the aisles. His shopping bag gaped open for any security inspection as he dropped items into his cart. *Don't stop me as a shoplifter*.

From the Close Out & Seasonal Goods aisle:

- A WASHINGTON REDSKINS logoed maroon & gold baseball cap.
- An XXL unlined maroon nylon REDSKINS jacket.
- A knapsack-like Kangaroo Love baby carrier designed to let the wee one ride strapped below Mommy or Daddy's beating heart.

From the Medical Devices aisle:

- Three pairs of Athlete's Foot & Odor Eater cushioned shoe inserts.
- The last pair of giant black plastic, square-framed, no-UV-protection sunglasses that at best evoked *the late, great* rock warbler Roy Orbison.
- A turquoise plastic travel-pack box of 'lemon-fresh hypo-allergenic' baby wipes.

From the Groceries & Sundries aisle:

- The lightest, cheapest, plastic bottle of water.
- Four 'protein' bars.
- The thinnest roll of 'stretch & cling tight' plastic wrap.

- The smallest spool of 'magic' invisible tape.

From the Beauty Products aisle:

- A twelve-pack of silver-dollar-sized coated cotton makeup swabs.
- A dainty cuticle scissors, the only blades he'd seen in the store.
- Three - *no*, two $3.98 palm-sized bottles of HipGirlz liquid cover-up makeup in *Our Darkest Tone Yet!*

Condor rolled his shopping cart toward the cashier line. A white-haired woman shuffled toward the same register. She used a black cane with one hand and clutched a box of microwave popcorn in the other. Wore hearing aids.

The hitch & hide.

'Here,' he said to the woman with a cane as he pushed his cart ahead of her in the checkout line and plucked the popcorn from her hand, 'let me get that for you.'

'What?' said that white-haired woman.

But Condor had already dropped her popcorn on the checkout conveyer belt, stacked his own purchases behind it, whispered to the cashier: 'My wife loves popcorn.'

'Un-huh,' said the cashier, her eyes on her work.

And not seeing us, thought Condor. Because we're over fifty and thus invisible.

Now 'solo fugitive you' were never here, are the silver-haired husband of a white-haired woman with a black cane and bad hearing who joneses for popcorn.

Condor gave the clerk cash, got change. Grabbed the store's giant white plastic bag stuffed with purchases, pushed his cart toward the front door.

Called out to the white-haired cane lady behind him: 'Come on, dear.'

Please, please, please . . .

He heard the *tap tap tap* of her cane following behind him through sliding glass doors to sundown. Heard her not bust him.

'Whoever you are,' said the white-haired woman standing on the sidewalk with him. 'Even back in the day, took more'n popcorn to get me to go.'

Condor gave her the popcorn.

'I could use a Scotch,' she said. 'How about you?'

She was maybe ten years older than him. Came of age before rock 'n' roll. Left fear in some footprints far behind her. Lived alone calmly waiting for *when*.

'I've got to run,' he told her. 'But you're spectacular.'

He hurried up Pennsylvania Avenue toward the Capitol dome. Turned right on Eighth Street before Capitol Hill's commercial blocks where bank ATMs used constantly recording security cameras. With a shopping bag in each hand, walked past a mother with a baby in the car seat of the SUV she was parking. *Don't snatch them for her ride.*

The sky reddened. He spotted a passageway between two brick town houses, slid into that gap. *Peed*, a *call-the-cops* offense for any witness, but he stood with his back to the brick passageway's opening, a stream of his life gurgling into a circular storm drain.

When you gotta go.

Don't go there.

He ripped store tags off the REDSKINS cap, pulled it on. Wore the huge maroon nylon Windbreaker over his gray sports jacket. Calculated that the oversized Roy Orbison sunglasses would attract too much attention in this evening hour.

Everything ached. His head throbbed. His feet hurt. He felt his pulse slow to only 50 per cent too fast. Popped a pain pill with a swallow from the drugstore water bottle. The passageway he stood in stank of his own urine, of wet cement, bricks.

Can't stay here.

Don't. Go. There.

Vin closed his ears to the ghosts, and with a shopping bag weighing down each hand, left the passage, a sports fan shuffling north on Eighth Street. Crossed Independence Avenue and the route he'd taken home from work less than two hours earlier.

These are the streets of your life. Not your hometown but the town you made into someplace you could call home. When they let you. When you weren't on the run.

Washington, D.C., under a bloodred sky.

He marched toward the Adams Building five blocks away at Third and A, SE.

The white car had been parked at that corner *way back when*.

Vin hadn't been able to step on A Street back then when he'd been officially *safe*.

Now he walked *there*.

A white stucco three-story town house filled the corner of A and Fourth Street, SE. The building had long since blended into this neighborhood of town houses, unmemorable except for its size and the brass plaque mounted on the white wall beside the black iron stairs leading to the black wooden main door on the second floor. Blinds covered all the windows. Clearly not a personal home, the building looked like no one ever went in or came out. A low black iron fence surrounded this building the color of Moby Dick.

Vin stood on the corner across the street from the white town house.

Felt time fall away. Heard wind inside his head. Smelled . . .

Gunpowder. Sweat. Blood. Perfume from a pretty woman named . . .

What was her name? What were all their names, the names of the dead?

That was when you became Condor.

So long ago. Yesterday. This morning.

He stared at the brass plaque mounted on the town house white wall. What it said there now didn't matter, wasn't real, *was a lie*.

What it read once and forever was AMERICAN LITERARY HISTORICAL SOCIETY.

And that, too, was a lie.

Gone behind him in time like his shadow he could never shake.

Bags in hand, he marched up Fourth Street, crossed East Capitol. Glanced left at the looming Capitol building, bathed in crimson - then in the wink of his street crossing, darkness fell, freed electric illumination so the Capitol glowed like an ivory skull.

Walk through this chilling Tuesday night.

Walk far away from Union Station with its trains out of town, its subways underground, its buses to New York City, its restaurants and food court and chairs to rest in and its swiveling-high-on-the-marble-walls security cameras to capture your picture.

Darkness covered streets where he slouched past town houses with lit windows that showed him young lovers struggling to figure out what they felt behind their smiles. First-time parents coaxing spoons of food into a pint-sized person who mortgaged them to the future. Office warriors pacing in their living rooms pressed to the cell phones chaining them to careers of political conscience, power, status, and payouts. Group houses with five onetime strangers assuring each other that these days when they could only get paid to serve high-priced coffee weren't their tomorrows.

Real life, thought Condor. *Should have tried it.*

But he was years past blaming anyone for the sum of his choices.

There's something wrong with the car headlights at the end of this block.

Condor stopped by two reeking gray rubber Dumpsters. Headlights filled the town house city canyon ahead of him as a car *crept* not *sped* closer, closer.

One whirl stacked his bags next to the two gray rubber Dumpsters, let him dive and curl up behind them.

Yellow eyes eased down the street toward where two rubber Dumpsters sat in front of an ordinary town house. The purr of a car engine grew to a grumble.

They're nobody, Condor told himself. *Looking for a parking place or a lost dog.*

The view from the creeping-past car showed no one shuffling in the street. No one running away or looking back. Not even a rat on top of the stuffed gray Dumpsters.

Dark sedan. Two shadowed shapes hulking in the front seat.

Don't move. Don't breathe. Don't let your eyes weigh on them so they'll pass by.

Red taillights going . . . going . . . turning the corner . . . Gone.

You'll never know if that was the right move.

Walking on, he heard no sirens for a dozen blocks. Saw no spinning red lights. No roadblocks on New York Avenue he crossed before the neon glows of a McDonald's, a Burger King and kitty-corner gas stations franchised from the surviving multinational oil companies. And as he neared North Capitol Street, the pulsing north-south four-lane artery connecting the skull Capitol dome with the rest of the world, Vin needed fuel.

Risk it: Dark night, two miles from the Op epicenter, wearing sports camouflage, you can shuffle up North Capitol's bright-lights commercial zone and not get tagged.

Vin walked past a rehabbed check cashing store, glanced through the front picture window, saw the new space sparsely filled with surplus government metal desks, tables that could have come from a church bankruptcy sale, two desktop computers where no one sat and a college-vintage laptop that lit the face of a woman in her mid-twenties with light brown hair. Working late. The white letters over the swirling blue wall poster behind her had a logo for The Public Trust Project and the words:

Today we're losing the fish, tomorrow . . . ?

Condor walked on from the sight of a young woman trying to save the world.

Left, left, left right left . . .

Ah, fuck.

We're back!

Vin focused on the yellow glow from a carryout restaurant on the next corner. The red neon sign above the picture windows read:

FULL DRAGON YUM

You step into that Chinese food carryout, into its yellow spotlight box. The L-shaped walls of picture windows make you visible to any cruising-past cars. There's a sense of steam, warmth beyond the humid cool outside, smells of sweat and grease and soy sauce and maybe something from the trash can against one wall. That trash can shows its black plastic bag. Above the trash can hang fourteen faded color pictures of food with labels like Foo Yung and Lo Mein. You face the bulletproof plexiglass separating customers from stoves covered by pots and pans and coolers stacked with soft drink bottles no shoplifter can reach. The white-clad cook wears some kind of hair net, keeps his back to the plexiglass and you, leaves the lookout for the taut tan face of the counterwoman wearing a flower-print blouse who eats you with her ebony eyes.

Watches you watch the black fly buzzing on your side of the bulletproof partition.

The black fly walked across the wall's color photo of Beef With Broccoli.

Vin stepped to the slatted speaker slot. Ordered the beef with broccoli, felt his stomach rumble and added a beef fried rice. Felt the cash dwindling in his black jeans pocket but still asked for a plastic bottle that advertised it contained REAL ORANGE JUICE! and thus, *perhaps*, a dash of Vitamin C and other actual nutrients.

The Chinese woman barked his order back to him, got his nod, yelled something in what Vin thought might be Mandarin to the white-clad cook.

If you can't shoot them through the plexiglass, they can't shoot you either.

There are no stools or chairs or tables for customers to sit down and stay awhile.

Outside cars whiz through the city.

'*Hai!*' The ebony-eyed woman stands on the other side of the plexiglass. The brown paper sacks on the Lazy Susan pass-through in the partition need only a spin from her steady hand to come clear of the smudged plexiglass.

Vin put the exact change for the price she barked at him in the pay slot.

Wait.

He held up an extra dollar bill, pointed to the trash can against the wall: 'I want to buy . . . say five of those black plastic trash can liners, the big thirty-gallon ones.'

Her brow wrinkled. She stood on her tiptoes. Pushed herself up farther with her hands pressing down on the counter, a demonstration of strength Condor feared he barely still had in him. She saw two bags on the floor beside where the man waited, wearing a jacket over a jacket and a smile she didn't believe for a heartbeat.

She told him: 'You *san jia quan*.'

301

Turned and disappeared behind the cooler.

Came back into view clutching a wad of black plastic in one hand, put those bundled-up garbage bags beside the brown paper sack on the Lazy Susan and spun the lot through the bulletproof partition to Vin's waiting hands.

'You keep dollar,' she said. 'Sometime everybody is *trouble-lost dog*.'

He knew better than to force the dollar or a tip on her. But gave her a smile that this time she believed. Her face stayed fixed. Her ebony eyes rode him out the door.

He tramped north like his favorite fictional character - mouse Stuart Little. Shuffled over residential sidewalks. Two foreclosed houses he passed were nailed shut too securely to repurpose. A birthday party pinwheel stuck in a postage-stamp front lawn spun slowly with this cool spring night and fried-rice-smelling air.

Down a street sloping to his right rose a brick high school with a cop car parked out front, its engine idling on watch, just like there'd be armed cops waiting inside the metal detectors of the front door come tomorrow morning.

Streetlights silhouetted trees clustered at the crest of the hill, turf surrounded by a black iron fence. Metal letters arcing over the chained entry gate bars read:

EVERWOOD CEMETERY

A sign on the gate read: WE PROSECUTE ALL TRESPASSERS.

This garden of the dead covered a dozen square blocks of the city looming above North Capitol Street. Commuters to Congress drove past it every day. So did the bus to a Veterans Center where briefly Condor'd been sent to get his drugs - his medicines.

If only I was still as strong as that Chinese woman.

Condor shoved his two bags through the bars of the gate - tossing them over would have dumped everything on the entrance road asphalt.

Got no choice now. Dinner's on the other side of the bars. With your gear.

He jumped, grabbed as high as he could on the bars, flopped to the other side.

Again he dangled above the earth. Again he let go. This fall only jarred him.

Vin adjusted his cap. Took his two bags in one hand, filled his other with the Maglite that sent a pale white cone of light to illuminate the darkness.

Fog. Pale wisps snake through the flashlight beam.

Feel: Wet on your face.

Smell: Wet grass. Stones and pavement. A whiff of cooling fried rice.

Hear: Faraway, city traffic. Rustles of trees. Silence from stone angels on pedestals blowing horns, spreading their wings, beckoning.

Walk behind your flashlight beam over paved paths wide enough for a black hearse. Walk a random path past family plots, marble slabs. MOTHER. LOVING HUSBAND. PRECIOUS DAUGHTER. VETERAN. Amidst stone crosses and angels atop gravestones Vin spotted dozens of ten-foot-tall stone obelisks, miniatures of the Washington Monument rising hundreds of feet into the sky on the not-too-distant Mall.

No moon beamed down on him. No stars dotted the sky. Fog enveloped him. Now and then he glimpsed muted streetlights far off beyond the invisible black iron fence. He mostly saw only as far as his Maglite shone. Didn't worry that some sniper waited off in the darkness, drawing a bead on the wink of the light in his hand.

His shoes crunched pebbles on the looping black pavement path.

Toolsheds he came upon all had locked doors. He discovered an artificial hill with crypts built into its face, but those stone shelters had steel doors and bars and chains with solid padlocks to foil their prisoners' escapes.

Out of the fog and darkness loomed an Asian pavilion. Open walls around a handball-court-sized circle topped two pancaked layers of roof, the smaller one above the larger with a gap in between that come morning would let in the sun. Pavement for a floor and on the down slope, a pebbled Zen garden with a plaque that read:

FREEDOM'S GARDEN OF SCATTERED MEMORIES

This is where they give the wind the ashes of the cremated. *Like a burnt spy.*

On the pavilion floor, Vin sat atop his bundled-up blue raincoat. His Maglite created a cone of visibility as he used a plastic fork to eat cold beef with broccoli and fried rice. He drank all the orange juice. *Ration the water.* The flashlight led him to the edge of the pavilion so he could relieve himself on the shadowed sea of grass.

He made his bed beneath the pavilion roof. Stretched two plastic trash bags lengthwise on the pavement, atop them put the blue blood-splattered raincoat from Peter's iPad pictures and the gray sports jacket he'd worn to work that day.

Cold. Spring, sure, but out here tonight: cold.

Vin stripped in the glow of the Maglite until he wore only his socks.

Ghosts mocked a burlesque striptease: 'Wha-wha wa, wha-wha-wha wha . . .'

Condor pulled on thermal underwear, redressed in his shirt and black jeans, shoes. Used one swallow of the bottled water to take his need-to-pee pill, his heart-soother pill, a keep-calm Valium and a pain pill for aches and soreness that made him want to moan. Zipped into his black leather flight jacket and snapped the maroon nylon football jacket on over that, laid on his wilderness bed with his cloth shopping bag and the Kangaroo Love baby carrier for a pillow. Stuck his feet and legs into one black plastic shopping bag, patted another trash bag over his torso, pulled on the yellow rubber gloves.

Condor thumbed out the Maglite.

Snugged on the maroon cap, lay on his back with its bill sticking straight up.

Bet my target silhouette looks like a duck lying on its back in the darkness.

Vin heard it first.

Pattering on the metal roofs above him.

Pattering becoming drumming like thousands of bullets strafed from the stars.

Then wind that spun down a monster tornado in far-away Oklahoma came through the open walls on all sides of him. Wind cool, cold, *then wet* blown across *and on him* as the dark opened with torrents of rain.

'You've gotta be fucking kidding me!' yelled Condor, yelled Vin to whatever heaven was out there this stormy night. 'Couldn't you pick another time to cry?'

10

Faye leaned against the white wall opposite the brick fireplace where Peter, Bald Peter, her partner - a jerk, sure, *but her partner* - hung crucified by kitchen knives, his throat cut so he could not speak, his eyes stolen from their stare.

My fault. How much of this is my fault?

From outside came the incessant barks of the dog next door: '*Yip yip! Yip!*'

Lean against this wall. Not gonna fall. Just lean against the wall. Breathe.

She dropped her gaze to her watch: 6:42. Still light outside.

Emergency lights on top of unmarked cars beat blasts of red against the house.

'*Yip!*'

White flashes. Another of the gun-toters crowded in here, taking cell phone pictures of the murdered man nailed over a fireplace by *fucking* kitchen knives.

One of us.

Faye's instincts told her not to stare at the horror that had redefined her life, to focus instead on the whispering cluster of three men and one woman who wore suits that could have come from the same tailor. Through the shifting crowd, Faye kept her eyes on that quartet of bosses who thought they had the power to decide her fate.

'*Yip yip!*'

Sami.

Walking through the turquoise door with three men and two women, all wearing street clothes not unlike his shopping-mall slacks and tan Windbreaker. He gave a concerned glance to where Faye leaned against the wall even as he stepped past her, marched to close quarters with the command cluster.

'*Yip yip!*'

Sami demanded: '*Yes* or *no*?'

The black executive who played college ball glared at Sami: 'Excuse me?'

'The question you gotta decide right now,' said Sami. '*Yes or no? Yes*, I and my people are the umbrella covering this scene, in charge of everything, or not - *No.*'

The chewed-lipstick frown on the cluster's lone woman curved like a scimitar as she told Sami: 'Do you know who you're talking to?'

'Yeah. You're a Deputy Director of my CIA who jumped on this rollout because you know this bites our Agency - speaking of which . . . *Harlan!*'

Faye'd worked with the lanky man in Sami's cadre who replied: 'Yo?'

'You got your silencer?' Sami kept his eyes on the command quartet.

'Sure,' said Harlan.

'Shoot that fucking yippy dog.'

Harlan stepped toward the door, one hand suddenly full of steel, the other reaching into his jacket pocket.

'*What!*' chorused the quartet of commanders.

'Cancel, Harlan,' said Sami. 'They're right, not my show. If they weren't smart enough to neutralize a dog attracting a whole lot of public attention, that's on them.

'So,' said Sami to the glaring bosses, 'I know who you all are. You're the dead man's CO from NROD in Home Sec, *sorry*, I know what it's like to lose a man. Standing next to you, we got Supervising Special Agent Bechtel of the FBI, nice to see you again, Rich. I've never met you, Deputy Director Martinez, but the whispers are you seem to know how to navigate the ODNI mess you got.

'But our question is: *Are you putting me in charge of this or not?*

'Our luck means I got nineteen of the best headhunters ever carried a sanction posting up right here in the Action Area, coincidental training gig for a shit storm like this. What I see here and now, you're already behind on the ABCs.'

Deputy Director Martinez from the Office of the Director of National Intelligence who only knew the legends about Sami said to him: 'What alphabet?'

'*A*,' said Sami. '*Action*. This isn't one of our Ops, so any Action we do is part of somebody else's chain of cause and effect. Look at their Action: our guy nailed to the wall in the home listed to a High-Alert disabled vet of ours who's gone nobody knows where. Whatever our Action is, it needs to break free of the other guys' chains to do any good, so it's gotta be big and fast and hard all the way up to extreme prejudice.

'*B*,' said Sami. '*Bounce*. How's this thing gonna bounce around, how are we going to control everybody's everything so nothing more gets broken than it has to?

'But what you're most worried about is *C*,' said Sami. '*Cover*. How are we going to put a cover over all this so it doesn't hurt U.S. national security *or* hurt the *U* and *S* that spells *us*?

'You want to start?' said Sami. 'Get half these people outta here. There's a school parking lot to reconvene at somewhere near here . . .'

A blond woman agent in his cadre shouted out the school name and address.

'Get most everybody gone before the crowd of citizens outside gets any bigger,' said Sami. 'And call an ambulance.'

ODNI DD Martinez said: 'He's - '

'Dead,' said Sami. 'Let's get him down from there, show some respect.'

'Crime Scene Investigators haven't gotten here.'

'If they're en route, wave them off. We're not cops. Unless Rich here is claiming this for the FBI, does anybody really think any of this is going to go to lawyers and rules of evidence some public fucking *trial*?'

ODNI DD Martinez blinked.

Ordered an ambulance called. Ordered 'all non-essentials' out.

'Hold up.' Sami looked at Faye. 'Who rolled on this with you?'

'That would be me,' said David, the ex–Brooklyn cop.

Asshole Harris pleaded with both hands raised: 'I just got logged onto their ride.'

Sami told him: 'Now you're logged on for CPR.'

'*What?*' said Harris.

'Ambulance gets here,' said Sami, 'bundles up our boy, you get on top of him, on top of the stretcher, ride it all the way into the ambulance, kneel on each side of our *man down* and make big show of giving him CPR chest compressions.'

Ex-cop David *got it*, volunteered: 'I'll work squeezing the breathing bag.'

No one - not Faye, not Harris or the ex–Brooklyn cop David, not any of the four national security executives - no one contradicted Sami.

Who said: 'Everybody else except for my team and Faye, drift out of here. Hang around outside. You're concerned. Upset. Responded to one of those commercially available panic alarms for help from a disabled vet, a - ex-FBI, explains the badges, guns, the too fucking many red lights. What was our guy's work name?'

'*UNN!*' grunted one of the suits as he pulled the knife out of dead Peter's left hand. The bald man's body slumped toward the floor.

His pale former Home Sec NROD boss said: 'The knifed agent is - was - '

'Not him,' said Sami. 'What was Condor's work name?'

Faye called out: 'Vin.'

Frowned. Asked Sami: 'Do you know him?'

'*Vin,*' Sami told the agents inside the murder house. 'Every TV watcher knows every badge rolls on any '*officer down*' call. That's why so many of you came here, kicked in the door. Found our guy *Vin*, our colleague, your buddy, *lying on the floor*. No knives. Heart attack. Still alive. Now it's *Vin* going out of here on the stretcher to the ER. Old guys, heart attacks: ordinary news. Be like the cell phone cameras out there, watch them take a' old guy getting CPR away in an ambulance, listen for any dangerous leaks or rumbles gossiping in the bystanders, follow it up soft but certain. Let it be heard out there how the cops' association is asking for volunteer badges - who are gonna be us - to sit on *Vin*'s stuff because of the busted door. *Go!*'

Without waiting for confirmation from the official executives, the herd of America's security and intelligence agents did as Sami said.

That ex-Marine who'd thrived as a teenager in the sniper streets of Beirut turned to the quartet of his fellow Americans who all outranked him, said: 'So?'

Four intelligence commanders looked at the legend in front of them.

Knew there was no more time for phone calls.

Knew they were on the line.

Knew how to hand off to a fall guy.

Martinez of the umbrella agency ODNI got the nods. Told Sami: 'Green light.'

'Full sanction.' Not a question from Sami, but his stare demanded confirmation.

'Yes,' said Martinez.

Within two minutes Sami'd made sure everyone on-scene had the phone number of a command center he'd set up but not activated at Complex Zed before he'd raced from there to here with carloads of his cadre.

'I've got two-man teams already working a wheel-out from here,' said Sami. 'They're driving in circles, progressively working their way out from the house. They got the iPad photos from yesterday's home visit report, the data on Condor.'

He sent teams to Union Station to cover the tracks, its subway entrance, food courts and upper parking lots where buses left for Baltimore, New York, Boston. Made sure TSA at area airports had photos of Condor on their cell phones and alert screens. Made sure Condor's photos got Priority Match status with Facial Recognition Software programs on the grid of federal, state, and local Big Brother cameras.

'Circle a perimeter five blocks out so it won't hit the *looky-loos* who are here,' said Sami. 'Get the D.C. cops to help FBI guys, flash badges, describe Condor, see if him being around tonight hits with any witnesses *without* polluting their timeline credibility of having seen him around before. If we get a hit, confirm with pictures.

'Get our people to the homeless shelters,' he told one of his cadre who was coordinating his commands. 'One inside, backup outside. Stay the night. Gonna be cold out there. Gonna rain. He's not going to hide under bridges because he knows cops drive past with the spotlights on, and make sure they do. Hospitals, museums, any place that's been open since Condor got off work. Come back every four hours.

Agents who officially approach gatekeepers should use a . . . a Department of Social Services rap, a lost Alzheimer tourist - *maybe*: say we don't want to create a false press report in case it's just an old guy sneaking off from visiting his grandkids to get laid.'

The cadre's Harlan asked: 'What Intensity Level?'

The room held its breath.

Sami said: 'One of our guys got cut down. We lose no more people. We let no bad guys get away. Locate, cover, call in a collection team and back up. We got *zero* solid that Condor is a killer, though no doubt he cruises Crazytown. He's a person of extreme interest. We want him. Want to talk to him. But don't let him get away.'

Sami pointed to a woman in his cadre. 'I skimmed the visitation report from yesterday by our dead guy on the way here. A white car, stolen license plate. Go with uniformed cops from that jurisdiction, Virginia suburbs. A low-key investigation, but brace everybody associated with that license plate about a white car, smell out who they really are. If you don't get anything, smile, say thank you, just routine, drive away. But no matter what, full-spectrum geographic and behavior profiles, full cover teams on them.'

He designated three agents to sit on this house, a fourth who was ex–murder police from Baltimore to 'run the janitors, suck up the scene,' bag any physical evidence beyond the bloody knives pulled from Peter's crucified palms.

Walked to where Faye leaned against the wall, said: 'How are you doing?'

'Wasn't him,' said Faye. 'He's crazy, but he's more clever than this.'

'Easy to buy either way, given his record.'

'What record?' she said.

'What you know now is what's important. We'll go over that back at your HQ building. You're in quarantine. There's an ambush team already in your apartment.'

And a squirrel team, she thought. Knew there was nothing there they'd find she couldn't live with. *Nothing in there about Chris.*

Faye said: 'I want the streets.'

'After we debrief,' he said.

She said: 'Do you know Condor?'

'What you don't know won't get in your way,' he told her. 'I want you running free and hard and full-on after you tell me what you can tell me.'

Faye said: 'Besides my two guys you put on the ambulance CPR scam, there were two Homeland Security hard guys who breached this place with me. The guy with the scraggy blond goatee, the other guy - '

'Can they tell me anything about Condor?'

'I don't see why.'

'Then let's keep them on the streets. We want every gun looking.'

'You mean every badge.'

'We'll talk when I get back to the Task Force command center.'

Sami walked away, past the ambulance crew muscling a butchered body onto a waist-high wheeled stretcher.

Harlan came to her and she knew to pass him the car keys before he held out his hand. Faye waited with Harlan inside the bloody living room while the ambulance crew and Brooklyn cop David and asshole Harris kneeling on the stretcher played out the CPR farce on a corpse, roared off in the siren-screaming ambulance.

She left Sami staring at Condor's mad collage wall.

Heard him whisper: 'What are you trying to say?'

11

SECRET HEART OF LONELY (WHAT CONDOR ALWAYS WRONGLY THOUGHT THE SONG SAYS)
- Yardbirds, 'Heart Full of Soul'

Screaming someone's screaming! Wet blood on -

Condor realized: *It's me screaming.*

Bolted upright wrapped in wet plastic bags & jackets. Wearing a cap. Butt on the concrete of a cemetery in the gray of false dawn. Fists in yellow rubber gloves.

Every joint, every muscle, everything ached. *Won't survive another night outside.*

Morning light bathed gravestones in the cemetery. He smelled wet grass.

You're where you're going to end up. Stay.

Your canvas shopping bag holds drugstore scissors.

These are your wrists.

Right here, right now, cut yourself free from the handcuffs of whoever *they* are.

Condor stood with his ghosts amidst a garden of gravestones in a city of marble dreams where so many somebodies wanted him dead or silent or a servant to what they said was sensible. Wind stirred the trees and the sky was blue and he could not fly away.

The only way you're not a lie is to fight to be true.

You're not going to choose to fucking lose.

Ghosts watched Vin eat leftover Chinese food, take *be healthy not cured* pills.

The scissors trimmed the three pairs of footpad inserts but only two sets fit under his feet in his black sneaker-like shoes. He felt taller, no worse balance.

Stones from the Zen garden let him break the dark lenses out of the Roy Orbison sunglasses. Condor taped plastic cling wrap into taut transparencies over the lens holes. Search metrics account for sunglasses or empty frames as disguises. The 'lenses' he made registered on camera scans as existing, let him see - though with distorted translucence. The huge black frames dominated his face, changed his profile.

Condor kept his thermal underwear on under his blue shirt and black jeans, put his blue raincoat in a garbage bag. They have photos of that coat from that Faye and the murdered man's Monday visit two days ago. Yesterday's surveillance footage from the Library of Congress office building would show his gray sports jacket. He dropped the sports jacket into the trash bag. By now, squirrel teams would have cataloged his closets. Two missing jackets/coats doubled the data they had to BOLO.

Condor strapped himself into the Kangaroo Love baby carrier. Stuffed his black leather jacket into the baby pouch over his stomach. Hid that under his maroon nylon jacket.

Maybe discerning eyeballs will notice the jacket isn't really covering too many beers and fast-food hamburgers, but Facial Recognition Software in security cameras around town will register my fat guy as 0 not 1, signal NO MATCH to the grid.

He pulled on the baseball cap: amateur, but every bit of bad data helps.

Bottles of makeup clinked in his jacket pockets as he policed the pavilion. His pill bottles bulged in his shirt pockets. Everything not in the Kangaroo Love or his pockets went into a trash bag he ditched behind a tree. *Keep your hands free.*

Condor shuffled over roads paved through this cemetery in the heart of the city. Found the locked office building. Its windows mirrored this empire of the dead. A stranger emerged in those windows' reflection as he rubbed HipGirlz cover-up over his face, his hands. Turned his skin some disgusting color of mud.

You look marvelous!

And then they laughed.

At 8:02 on the other side of the building, steel gates creaked open, let in workers.

Only ghosts saw Condor walk out of the cemetery.

One formula made sense.

Fuck with them.

Find some chance in the chaos.

Figure out what you can't remember or don't know, who and why.

Fix it. Or at least go down fighting.

He spotted an orange-plastic-wrapped *Washington Post* tossed in front of a house like it was still the twentieth century. Nobody'd come outside to claim this delivered reality while water boiled on the stove for morning coffee. *I would kill for a cup of coffee*, so stealing someone's newspaper seemed like an acceptable moral stretch.

When he started this life, it would have taken Condor twenty minutes to skim *The Post*. That morning, he scanned the newspaper in less time than it took to walk a block.

War in Afghanistan that was officially almost over. Car bombings in Iraq that weren't officially war. Slaughters in Syria that started as hopeful Arab Spring. Strong moves by the strong man in Russia. North Korea ranted. Europeans raged in the streets. Soundbites shouted on the Senate floor. Hong Kong had coughing chickens, we all had whacky weather. Wall Street wages were up for the thirty-first straight year. A factory closed in Indiana. Traffic sucked. Divorcing Hollywood stars vowed to remain friends.

Nowhere in the newspaper did Condor spy a story about a crucified federal agent or a manhunt for a missing Library of Congress employee.

A handmade sign hung taped to the screen door of a corner grocery:

COFFEE.

The grizzled black man behind the store counter blinked at the entering freak.

' 'Need coffee,' said Condor.

The counterman filled a cup from the urn. 'Take this one on me and walk on.'

Vin shuffled down an access street parallel to North Capitol, here a used furniture store, there a nail salon he could imagine no one frequenting except 'beauty students' scamming a few cents out of cash-strapped federal job-training programs.

A Hispanic man wearing a tool belt glanced at the weird gringo sipping coffee beside him while they waited for the traffic light, then watched his fellow crew members on scaffolding across the street. The light turned green. The workman hurried toward the scaffolding. Didn't feel Condor steal the cell phone out of his tool belt pouch.

A pickup truck hauling debris from a house gut idled at the red light.

Padding jiggled under his maroon nylon jacket as Condor hurried toward the idling pickup while tapping the secret CIA Agent In Trouble digits into the stolen cell phone.

The traffic light's changing -

Made it, behind the pickup, in front of a car that honked at his jay-walking as he thumbed SEND on the cell phone he tossed into the pickup's cargo box.

The Panic Line Center at Langley won't recognize the caller ID. Won't hear a voice on the call. Will activate a GPS track. Divert headhunters off Condor. Maybe find the cell phone still *on*, maybe find fingerprints on it, maybe chase *maybes* all morning.

First time you called the panic line was from a pay phone.

Condor blinked. Cooling black coffee trembled in the paper cup he clutched.

Remembering, you're remembering.

Up ahead a man stepped outside of a glass-fronted store: CYBER WEB D.C. A poster read CYBER CAFE. Orange calligraphy on the store's glass read:

NEW AND USED COMPUTERS! LAPTOPS & COMPUTERS & CELL PHONES REPAIRED HERE! DISPOSABLE CELL PHONES! *SE HABLA ESPANOL!*

A man stood outside his store, smoked a cigarette, licked the street with his eyes.

Chicago. California Street, a Friday-night table in a dive bar, sitting with ebony-hued Ethelbert. He wears a perfect suit, Cary Grant confidence. Watches you sip the second shot of Scotch that he insisted you drink as he says:

'Do you think I care about any of that bicentennial happy 1976 going on out there in the good old U.S. of A.? I'm working the deal, two years of schooling you amateurs on short cons, then I'm out of a go-to-jail jacket.'

'I'm a couple tough ops past being an amateur.'

That's you. That's Condor.

'Yet you just blew your cover to show me you've got a big dick.' Ethelbert finished his Scotch. 'But you also got some savvy. Didn't freak when I walked you in here, only white face around, and yes, maybe those days are over, but this has never been about white or black, it's about where you belong, whether you're an insider or an outsider. These are hard-line folks. They been put on it, they walk it and expect you to do the same. You spotted those two bad motherfuckers who are considering clobbering your ass just because. They're gonna clobber somebody tonight, might as well make it easy on themselves and clobber the outsider.

'You've got no money,' said Ethelbert. 'No guns. No knives. Not a two-way wrist-radio the comics keep promising we're going to have someday. You don't have a dime in your pocket for a pay phone, can't pay the tab for our top-shelf Scotch that I'm walking out of here leaving you holding.

'You want to learn, you got to do. You can't do, I can't teach you, so then tell our boss you're quitting the knock-knock who's there school. NOC, "Non-Official Cover" - Hell: everything is official out here in the street.

'Now con your way safe downtown by midnight.

'Remember, if you're an outsider, try working The Sideways Slide.'

Wednesday morning in Washington, D.C., when we have 'two-way wrist-radios.'

The man outside this cyber store lets the smoke drift from his cigarette.

Condor walked up to him. 'I been robbed.'

'What do you want me to do about it?'

'You sell used cell phones,' said Condor. 'Good chance one of them is mine.'

'We aren't that kind of store. We sell disposables. Burners.'

'Whatever I buy, you're giving me my money's worth after what been stole.'

The man laughed. Dropped his cigarette. Made a show of grinding it out.

Flicked *gonna fuck-you-up* eyes onto this freak.

Condor strobed back: *So what?*

Said: 'I'm gonna buy a phone from you, twenty bucks fair, but what I'd really like to buy is what else they stole.'

That Sideways Slide sank the hook into cigarette man.

So it was he who said: 'What else you looking for?'

'My gun.'

'What'd you lose?'

Like that matters. 'An Army .45. Brought it AWOL back from 'Nam.'

'Sentimental guy?'

'Practical,' said the man with the weird dark skin in the Redskins cap and fucked-up glasses and some soft gut under his maroon jacket. 'What works, works.'

'If we did sell guns, we'd do it in the law. We don't do it here.'

'But you might know somebody, and if they kick back to you, who cares?'

Cigarette Man shrugged.

'Here's that twenty. I'm gonna tap on your keyboards in there, and the phone you sell me's gonna work.'

Cigarette Man took Condor's twenty-dollar bill, gestured for him to enter.

Condor swept his hand toward the visibly empty cyber store: *After you.*

Cigarette Man added such caution to whoever he thought this freak was, went into the store's back room, out of sight.

Gonna happen how it's gonna happen.

Condor picked the computer workstation that let him watch the back room. Like he guessed, the desktop machine needed no password: such a legitimate feature created a record for income tax, money laundering, or fraud audits.

His first search engine result dropped him onto the 'Ask Us!' page for the city government's Advisory Neighborhood Commission covering Capitol Hill, a window on the computer screen into which he typed: '*What happened with that murder in his house on Thirteenth Street, SE, of a Homeland Security agent last night?*'

The second search zapped him to the website for the Senate Select Committee on Intelligence where he skipped the thirty-second Hollywood-level movie highlighting the Committee as a streetwise defender of every American voter and found the 'Contact the Committee' click: *Why is the CIA overstepping its jurisdiction and investigating the murder of a Homeland Security agent on Capitol Hill last night?*

Nine clicks in the third search revealed a 'conspiracy center' website that ranked high on popular search results *and* had a flowing 'HAPPENING NOW!' message board system where each posted 'citizen's report' had a click for comments that spun into rants and cross-links to other web entries. Condor typed: *Who's running the cover-up of the murder of a Homeland Security agent in D.C. on Capitol Hill last night that the CIA is somehow involved in, too?*

His next two searches led him to phone numbers Condor wrote on scrap paper.

Cigarette Man came out of the back room waving a cell phone. 'Cheapest one is thirty dollars. Say . . . four hours of use. The strip of white tape on the back shows its number.'

'Say exactly four hours.' Condor cleared his search history, exchanged another of his few bills for the cell phone. 'Say I'll be pissed off if it doesn't. And on that other thing, say I'll be back around four this afternoon to see what's what and who's here.'

'You will or you won't.'

Condor left the store. *You will or you won't. What more is there to say?*

Ten minutes later, he stood in a bus stop, its three plexiglass walls filled by public service posters in Spanish. Condor understood the top banner of a poster that exhorted readers to call 911 in case of emergency, but didn't know that the *Jamas tendras que pagar!* line meant: 'You never have to pay!'

He stared down the street to the entrance of a Metro station - D.C.'s subway.

Sure, there'd be security cameras. He'd done what he could about that.

Washington's subway doesn't run twenty-four hours. Last night, cover teams would have ridden the last train, swept the locking-up stations with Metro cops. Spy shop headhunters probably swept the system again when it opened before dawn. But now it's morning rush hour, deep into double shifts for spook agency headhunters, day shift for straight cops who'd be working only off a 'regular' high-alert BOLO.

No uniformed cops stood scanning the commuters swiping their fare cards through the orange turnstiles. No men or women with *soft clothes & hard eyes* lingered by the escalators up to the platform. Could be patrols, cover teams he didn't see, but could be the hunt for him now focused on Facial Recognition and other search programs across Big Brother's grid.

A bus braked at the stop sheltering Condor. Bus doors freed morning commuters to flock toward the Metro subway stop. Condor slid into that pack of professionals carrying backpacks, a muscled man carrying a hard hat, a white-haired guy who wore a blue blazer and the gaze of someone who sits behind a downtown lobby desk with no hope of a pension.

Condor kept his head down, his cap obscuring his face as he swiped his way into the station, as he rode the UP escalator. His arms swung up from his sides whenever it seemed like someone might brush against his belly-bulging maroon jacket.

Back-to-back security cameras hung from the cement awning over the train platform. Condor stood directly under the cameras, hoped it was a blind spot.

A hundred bodies waited on those red tiles with him. The crowd formed two groups, each facing one of the two sets of tracks and beyond them, the open spaces looking out over low buildings, trees, into block-away high-rise office windows.

But no one else waiting on the subway platform was really there.

They read smartphones held in one hand. Tablets colored their faces with rivers of broadcasting TV or movies or YouTube clips of bacon-loving dogs. Earbuds closed and glazed eyes. A dozen people talked on cell phones Condor could see, a dozen more babbled into cell phones he couldn't spot, seemingly solo chatter as though they, too, experienced ghosts. Dozens of people used thumbs and fingers to text messages. All his fellow travelers existed in data flows they thought they controlled.

Condor cupped his empty left palm toward his face to look like everyone else.

He tapped his left palm with his right finger, with each tap thought: *This is me.*

A silver *whoosh* knifed through the sunlight above the tracks.

This is a train of now. A *whoosh*, a hum, a whine like an electric current, not the *clackety-clack* rhythm of Woody Guthrie, not the clatter on steel rails of bluesmen from Mississippi or settlers headed West to prairie won from the Cheyenne or soldiers coming home from guarding the Berlin Wall. The train of now slides in and out of stations with a whoosh, a whir, a rumble through this new world.

Bells chime. Train doors jump open. The brown-skinned man in the baseball cap and ridiculous glasses and maroon nylon jacket snapped over his big belly got on board.

Condor found a seat facing the direction the train was going. Even though commuters stood in the aisles, no one chose to sit beside him.

The robotic woman's voice over the loudspeaker called out: 'DOORS CLOSING.' Electronic bells chimed. Sliding doors sealed everyone inside. Condor felt himself sucked against his orange padded seat as the train accelerated.

Be more than a moving target.

Condor turned on his new cell phone. Called the *Washington Post* phone number he'd gotten at the *transa* store. Key-tapped through a voice menu of instructions.

The train slowed for a platform of waiting riders.

Could be wet boys waiting to get on board - HURRY!

The robotic woman's voice echoing through Condor's car announced 'DOORS OPENING!' just as the robotic woman's voice speaking for *The Washington Post* in Condor's cell phone said: 'Leave a message or news tip at the beep.'

'*Yeah, are you going to cover how the Capitol Hill ANC is getting the run-around from the cops about a murder of some Federal agent on Thirteenth Street last night?*'

'DOORS CLOSING!'

No one shot him and the train whooshed from that station.

Travelers filled the subway car. Nannies with their charges. Parents who'd left their kids with nannies. Men and women of no fame who worked in buildings identified by initials like EPA and NIH, who did their best for places like the Justice Department, who roamed with the excited herd of twenty-somethings who staff Capitol Hill to sweat out laws and loopholes and to lance attacks approved by American voters via the smiling faces they send to this city from available big-dollar-approved selections. A soldier in green fatigues held on to an overhead bar as he rode standing in the aisle, the double bars of a captain on the rank patch on his chest. Here and there rode students, street dudes.

I hope some of them overheard me. Are emailing, maybe tweeting or Facebooking: 'Anbdy know bout murdered cop on Hill 1st nite?'

Condor dialed the second phone number.

Another robot answered: 'You have reached *The New York Times*.'

They know you.

How? Who? Why?

No answers came to him as the train whooshed through its dark tunnel.

Again he worked his way through an automated phone menu: '*Why are your buddies at* The Washington Post *ignoring a story about a Federal agent getting killed last night on Capitol Hill and there's something about a Congressman, too. Fox News has some woman nosing around.'*

The train roared into an underground station stop.

Bells chimed. Robot Woman alerted. Doors popped open, clunked closed. People shuffled on and off the train and still no one shot him.

So it went through the morning, Condor changing from one train to another at random underground stations, moving with crowds. Never riding one train long, always facing forward, trying to get the train window with the best view of arriving stations.

There! Two casual-clothes headhunters lurking on the coming platform!

Condor bent over in his subway car seat to tie his shoe.

'DOORS CLOSING!'

The train surged.

He sat straight up in his seat.

Those two headhunters hadn't gotten on this car. *If that's who they were.*

He rode this train to the end of its line, a park & ride plaza with blockish stone buildings for county bureaucracies beyond the border for the District of Columbia yet still inside the Beltway. Few people rode to this last stop at eleven in the morning.

Another elevated subway platform, red tiles, blue sky under the awning gaining warmth with the midday sun. He left the train, hit the smell of pine-scented ammonia.

A Metro janitor in his green jumpsuit mopped the red tiles near the escalators.

Two steps from the DOWN escalator, Condor spotted two uniformed Metro cops getting onto the adjoining UP escalator.

'DOORS CLOSING!' The empty train he'd left roared away without him.

Jumping off the sides of the subway platform meant the tracks, the killer third rail, and after it, a chain-link fence. Then a thirty-foot fall to concrete.

The Metro cops were halfway up their escalator ride.

Condor turned to the mopping janitor, smiled: 'Hey man, you okay?'

The janitor blinked. 'Ah . . . yeah, I'm fine.'

'Your family still doing good?'

Radios crackled on the belts of two Metro cops stepping off the escalator, walking behind the freaky fat man in the baseball cap and Redskins maroon nylon jacket - *obviously* a friend of the janitor who was telling him: 'Yeah, the family's okay.'

'Good,' said the fat guy as the cops walked past.

The cops were five steps past the janitor when he whispered to the friendly stranger: 'What's wrong with your face? Looks streaky, like you been crying or - '

'The burns,' ad-libbed Condor.

'Shit, man - I'm sorry.'

The last those cops saw of the fat man was as he shook hands with the janitor.

Outside the subway station, Condor crossed the street to a franchise restaurant named after a Rolling Stones song. Condor's face horrified the hostess. She gave him a booth in the back. Launched a white shirt/black-tied server - '*Get him in, get him out!*' Condor yearned for the soup and salad bar, couldn't stand that kind of exposure, ordered the biggest cheeseburger he could afford and milk, waddled to the MEN'S room.

Shoot him! Shoot him! This is where you shoot him!

Condor blinked into the bathroom mirror. The ghosts vanished. Left him staring at a browned face streaked by teardrops or terror from his sweat. He recolored his image with the last of the makeup.

Sometimes being less of a freak is all you can do.

He wanted to linger over his cheeseburger until the lunch crowd left him behind with only the serious drinkers at the bar who would sit there for hours pretending they were only playing hooky from success. But he couldn't risk staff coming around with *we need that booth*. He paid, slid outside to the midday sun, went next door to a Starbucks.

She's not going to be in here waiting for you. That's so yesterday!

Condor bought a small coffee to justify taking a chair not far from the picture window where he could see across the street to the Metro station.

Steam still floated out of the coffee cup when he spotted them.

An American sedan slid to the drop-off sidewalk near the subway station entrance. The car's rear doors sent a man and a woman into the Metro. They wore open jackets, kept their right hands on their sides as they walked, as their heads swiveled.

The sedan stayed parked out front of the station in a NO PARKING zone. Didn't bother to put on its flashers. Two watchers filled the front seat.

So they got badges to show.

Thirty-seven minutes later, after the third train had come and gone, a zebra team - a white guy and a black guy - stalked out of the station to the sedan.

Cover teams traveling both ways between Metro stops. And now leaving their scheduled train patrols for the next Op maneuver.

But the white headhunter marched from the parked sedan toward the Starbucks.

Take your cup, DON'T RUN toward the back of the -

'Excuse me!' The barista pointed to the end of the counter.

Condor scooped up one of two keys there. Hurried down the hall to the back of the store. Slipped into the WOMEN'S room as he heard the store entrance bell tinkle.

327

Hid in a bathroom's shiny stall.

That's where you shot Maronick! Blasted bullets through the metal walls of his stall without even looking him in the eyes.

Water flushed in the other bathroom: *Go when you can* is a cover team creed.

Condor waited five minutes. Left the bathroom, eased down the hall ...

Saw only the barista.

Who said: 'I thought you were gone.'

'Me, too.' Condor looked out the front window.

No cover team's sedan parked outside the Metro station across the street.

No uniformed cops patrolling inside the station.

He rode the next train out of there.

Maronick turns around in the seat in front of you. Smiles despite the bullet hole in his right cheek. 'We know right where you are.'

Riding tracks and tunnels through the city. Blue pinstripe suits mean K Street. Tourist shoes in tight groups mean Smithsonian, Capitol Hill and White House stations that lead Americans out of the underground passageways to see How Things Really Work. The Dupont Circle stop near where CIA-funded D.C. cops burgled anti–Vietnam War think tanks and tear-gassed protesters now feeds the train bright-eyed young women with yoga mats and tattoos of Asian calligraphy. Condor rode one train sharing a seat with a double-shift nurse in blue scrubs.

On one run out of Union Station through the reddening evening light, Condor's train slid past a long tube-like concrete building deserted and scarred with graffiti: the Washington Coliseum where The Beatles exploded America with their first U.S. concert.

Wearing black suits, white shirts and jiving by the train car's middle doors:

Bullet-holed Maronick. Bald Peter and Kevin Powell, throats cut above their black ties. The young Marine who'd saved Condor's life.

Singing:

> 'Kill, kill you do,
> You know they'll kill you.
> Their aim is true,
> So ple–ee–ee–ease . . . Kill you do.'

The train *whooshed* on.

Toward a Snatch & Stash.

The only play Condor had left.

You've done it before.

Find your mark. Figure a woman. A frail man. Alone. No wedding ring. In the darkening night. Few passengers on the train, on the platform. The end of the line, suburbs of strangers who mind their own business. Exit the station as a shadow. First chance, punch the base of the mark's spine - shocks them forward, knocks the breath out so they can't scream. Grab them, sell: 'I've got a gun.' *Should have risked going back to the transa store.* Let the snatched citizen stash you in his or her home.

Kill the chump.

No! That's not who -

The train he rode roared out of a dark tunnel into the gray light of a concrete cavern.

And through the windows . . . On the stop's red-tiled platform . . . Waiting for him . . .

Condor saw how he would die.

12

TROUBLE-LOST DOG
- Chinese Triad slang, *san jia quan*

Faye told Sami: 'You didn't need to drug me.'

They sat across a card table from each other on gray metal folding chairs in a soundproof glass booth on the vast warehouse floor of Complex Zed.

Sami sat there with his black curly hair, rolled-up sleeves on a rumpled white shirt and shopping-mall khaki slacks.

He shrugged and Faye pictured him as the middle-aged Beirut businessman he could have grown up to be, if not for the pickup trucks full of militiamen who'd driven into his sunny Lebanese neighborhood when he was nine and passed out free AK-47s to all the eagerly waving hands of the young boys who crowded around their coming.

'After we debriefed last night,' Sami told her, 'you spent six hours running the streets. Way past midnight, you got frantic, didn't trust the cover teams at his apartment, at his work. That's when I knew you were on adrenaline burn. I need you clear of your own smoke - mentally and physically.'

'So you stood beside my cot and made me take a sleeping pill.'

'Then I went to my cot and took one, too.'

Faye said: 'Is that all my pill was, Sami? A knockout?'

'I'm not the kind for date rape.'

'But you are such the pro. Divert me with that horror so I don't ask the obvious.'

'What's the obvious?'

'Interrogation drug.'

Sami cocked his head. 'You got me, Faye. I'm that devious. Evidently, so are you. Which is why I need you. But come on: *Really?* Truth serum?

'If the pill was anything extra,' said Sami, 'call it a test of trust. I give you a pill. Tell you it's mission critical that you take it. You got needed rest because you trusted me and I get confirmed trust that you'll do what it takes to nail the mission.'

'I didn't dream. All I had to deal with, I should have.'

'Dreamland isn't our turf, Faye. We live in the *gotta do* world.'

'What do I *gotta do* now, *Boss?*'

'I know everything about what's happening and nothing about what's going on.'

Sami looked at his wristwatch, a black metal chronometer with irradiated dials that glowed green in any darkness.

'It's coming up on six o'clock Wednesday evening,' he told her. 'And now we got a new problem. Seventh-Floor Langley called. There's buzz.'

'Buzz?'

'Gossip, phone calls, web traffic, weird alerts, whispers in halls, maybe some reporter from what's left of the mainstream media, I don't know: *buzz.*

'We're sticking with the cover of an ex–FBI agent named Vin had a heart attack last night, critical at undisclosed hospital, sorry for any confusion. So now we're welded to that story. One contradiction gets believed, becomes a meme on the web, we're lying motherfuckers in a cover-up and facts become irrelevant to fury.'

'I don't understand.'

'Sure you do, but neither of us understands why your partner went back to Condor's place to get killed. There's a text message from his cell phone logged into NROD's system about follow-up on the report you say you wrote under his name.'

'That's not Peter. He was a *don't give a fuck* guy.'

'But there he was. And logged to Admin, not your unit.'

Sami shook his head. 'Oh, Condor.'

Faye said: 'You know him.'

Faye let black-haired Sami who held her life in his hands fill her eyes.

Let the luminous second hand sweep a circle around his watch.

Let him fill the silence in their glass booth with what he thought he dared to say.

'We will never have talked about this.'

'I've got to know if I'm going to help us, help you.'

'Trust, right?' Sami smiled. 'Was a time, no one I trusted more than Condor.'

'He was your partner. Or your case officer.'

'More than that. He was . . . the legend inside the legend.'

Sami spoke a man's name.

Faye said: 'Wait, I - '

'Under that name,' said Sami, 'he was a CIA whistleblower back in the days of truth, justice and the American way after Watergate.'

'He was the one who - '

'Went to *The New York Times*. I don't know the real details. Neither did the newspaper. Something about heroin. Something about Middle East operations. Or the CIA lying about a reason to invade someplace with oil. Something about a bunch of people getting murdered in some undercover facility somewhere.

'The paper printed a bare-bones story. Used that citizen name of Condor's.

'*But nobody cared!* It slid into the deluge of stories about the Agency using the Mafia for assassinations, black-bagging citizens, secret LSD tests, overthrowing governments. Condor became a bit player, didn't get called to testify at the Church Committee Senate Hearings or mentioned in their final report. You'd think that whatever the reality was about Condor, it would have been a big deal, but if enough of the right people don't say *boo*, reality disappears into what's official. Or at least it did before the web made alternate realities easier.'

Faye shook her head. 'The Agency would never forget. Maybe they decided not to prosecute Condor for violating any secrecy laws or oaths, but he would have been . . .'

She saw it.

Whispered: '*Holy shit.*'

'Just like Phil Agee who published a book and blew the covers of a hundred of our people, everybody in our bad-guy streets knew Condor by that civilian name, knew he was on the CIA enemies list. The enemy of my enemy . . .'

'*It was all cover Op to plant him out there!*'

'No,' said Sami. 'Whatever bloody Op gone wrong triggered him, that was real. He started out some first-job-out-of-college guy in the right place at the right time.

'After-Action Evaluation was he'd tried to be on the side of the angels. The Agency rerecruited him. He had the perfect cover: a verifiable enemy of the CIA.

'Nobody knows all he's done. At least two stateside counter-spy Ops, one I think involved China. Mixed with American expat draft dodgers in Europe targeting Soviet agents and terrorists who tried to co-opt the anti-war GIs and draft resisters. Life isn't Hollywood, terrorist or rule-the-world megalomaniac organizations with chrome skyscraper headquarters and pension plans, but I think he ran with Marxist-tinged groups in the seventies. Red Brigade types. Japanese Red Army. And Neo-Nazis like the National Front, he told me about one night on the docks of London. Maybe even some IRA *boyos*, something about Paris. Locked onto the drug cartels early, they're more important politically than most countries. He was the perfect flytrap. They'd come to him. His truth became his cover.'

'But he's been *Vin* for . . .'

'Since he got out of the CIA's secret insane asylum in Maine.'

Faye's frown asked her question.

'No, he really was crazy. Or went crazy. Evidently, still is crazy.

'Your drone rumor,' Sami told her. 'That Op was one of the big ones he thought up after 9/11. That's what he was best at - the wild idea.

'Bottom line, *yeah*, he got cornered in the shit, used one of the first iPads to call in a drone strike on himself. Some al Qaeda wannabes decided he was who he really was, a CIA plant. The bad guys were racing to torture and/or kill him, we couldn't exfilt and evac his ass, he couldn't go under, so he waited until they were right on top of him . . .

'The drone killed bad guys and proved they were wrong: the CIA'd sent a drone to kill Condor, so he must have been their enemy, and the Op he'd created stayed safe.'

'Why didn't he die?'

'Suicide is a hard shot when you've been taught to take out the other guy.'

Sami leaned across the table and his gravity pulled Faye closer to him.

We're whispering in a soundproofed glass box, she thought. *Somehow, that doesn't seem crazy.*

'That part of the world,' said Sami, 'when it does rain, it pours. Lot of runoff goes down the gutters into city parks, so cities like that, they got big storm drainage slits.

'The argument around the Seventh Floor is: Did he plan for the slit being there when he called in the drone, or did he call in the drone *then* suddenly see the slit and change his mind about being a kamikaze?'

'What do you think?' said Faye.

'Doesn't matter,' answered Sami. 'Whatever he decided, he got it done.

'Figure this: Hard as it might have been calling in the drone strike, after he exploded his world, when he was down there in that storm sewer, dust everywhere, a slit of sunlight, the sound of rescuers racing to find survivors . . .

'To be trapped there and *not* shout for rescue because that will reveal your truth . . . That buys him a hell of *get out of jail forever* card from me.

'Night comes, he can't claw his way out, crashes down and tumbles through the storm drains, into the city sewers. We figure fourteen hours he was down there. Saw the sunshine of another storm drain, crawled out with the rats. Had to mess some woman up to steal her cell phone, call the panic line, hide while he was soaked and stinking of shit.'

Sami stared out the glass walls.

Drilled his eyes into Faye.

'When we got him back, he seemed damaged but doable. Had to stay officially dead, of course. Even had some surgery on his face - repair the drone attack damage away from *had been* to *what could be*. Getting older had changed his looks anyway.

'That was when I knew him best. That was back when private contractors were all the rage - Blackwater, a dozen others you know, a dozen more you've never heard of. Contractors still account for about one in four U.S. spooks, but their clout is dropping. Condor set me up in an outsourced Op. If you don't trust who's in charge or how their show might go, stick in a player you rely on. I did what I did, it cost what it cost, never mind now. By the time I got clear of all that - got my head on straight, got back inside Uncle Sam - Condor'd officially gone crazy.'

Sami said, 'They didn't even let me know he'd gotten better.'

'Maybe he hasn't,' said Faye. 'What's going on?'

'That's what I want to know.'

'You're the boss.'

'Really?' Sami smiled. 'What about the buzz? What about "the record" we keep rewriting with our ABCs? What about Seventh-Floor Langley or the West Wing of the White House? What about every hustler looking for anything that gets TV? What about our people out there hunting a fugitive who they think is as good a killer as they are?'

'They're going to shoot first.'

'In their shoes,' said Sami, 'so would you.'

Sami looked at her. 'You're the last known contact with Condor I can trust.'

'You want me to find him.'

'Oh, he'll be found. Forget about the overt global BOLOs, we got great shadow headhunters out there after him. He's not that good, not for long.

'But before that happens, before he gets grabbed up or gunned down, either way out of my control, I want *you* to get found by *him*.'

Faye blinked. 'What makes you think he's looking for me?'

'Crazy as he's supposed to be, he might not be - *not looking for you*, I mean. But if he spots you . . . You're the last known official contact for him, too. If he's looking to escape the sewers, you're someone who might know a way out. Which is me.'

'I have no idea what to do.'

'Hit the bricks. Follow whatever it is that makes you duck before your mind tells you there's a bullet coming your way.'

'There's a million miles of nowhere out there.'

'Yeah.' Sami didn't blink. 'We can't give you a cover team. He spots that, he'll know and go, blood bath or back into hiding. Then the percentages suck for me, for us.'

Sami leaned back in his chair. 'You've got my phone number, I've got yours. I don't want to be the one who calls to say Condor's been got.'

'He was your friend. You like him. Trusted him. You want him alive, right?'

'I want to know what I want to know, and I want this all to go down right.'

Faye stood. 'What about Peter? You would have turned his life inside out.'

'The saddest thing about his dying is he left nothing behind him worth knowing. You ask me, Peter was the wrong guy in the wrong place at somebody's wrong time.'

'What about Condor?'

'Yeah.'

She put her hand on the handle of the glass door.

Looked back at him: 'What, no parting ABCs?'

'*Always Be Careful*.' He shrugged. 'If not: *Accept Being Crucified*.'

She walked through Complex Zed's warehouse, full of portable workstations and data screening posts and folded-up tables in front of giant steel trunks full of hardware and that glowing soundproof glass booth.

Thought: *Act Beyond Crazy*.

She wore post-shower clothes from her GO! bag she kept by her desk. Dark slacks, gray blouse, a business-acceptable blazer to cover the Glock .40 on her belt and carry the folders of official IDs and badge. Faye marched to the locker room and her locker searched by squirrels who were professionally respectful enough to leave it untidy so they wouldn't insult her by pretending not to have been there. She knew everything they found. Unless something had been planted there, in which case, *not knowing* had a better chance of being believed on a polygraph test or with whatever confession drugs the priests used in their interrogations.

Like maybe whatever drug they gave me last night.

Not a problem, she knew. She had nothing mission critical to hide.

So far.

But if they got me to offer up Chris . . .

Some things we don't like to think about.

She snapped the pouch with two ammo magazines on the left side of her belt under the jacket. Her dull metal spring-bladed jackknife had a belt clip on one of its flat handle's sides, rode on her belt over her spine - *tolerable* if she sat in a chair.

Smart tradecraft would have been to unpack the hip, suede leather backpack-like purse *thoughtfully*, put its contents on the locker shelves *in* and *with* some kind of order, a tidy display that implied she believed she was coming back, a trustable clue for profilers and squirrels who'd open her locker after she was gone.

She dumped her backpack purse into her locker, put back in only the pouch of mission toiletries, grabbed her short black raincoat she'd worn when she interviewed Condor, slammed the locker shut.

A handmade poster above the camp made from portable storage and delivery trunks read: EQUIPMENT DISBURSEMENT DETAIL. Two M4 carbine-slung SWAT guards paced near the bulletproof vest over his white shirt & tie Santa sitting behind EDD's unfolded table that would have fit in at a church social.

Faye confirmed her ID through Santa's portable retina scanner, established her Access/Action Level logging her identifier and Op code word into the laptop on the table, negotiated what she wanted out of what Santa said he had and could release.

Two credit cards with a phony female name came from him without a blink.

Cash was no problem, $2,500 in twenties and fifties, two tens, two fives.

Faye unbuttoned her blouse.

Santa stared at the list they'd typed into his iPad.

Said: 'You going to war, Agent?'

'I know what I'm doing,' lied Faye.

Before he disappeared in canyons of locked storage trunks, Santa gave her the advice every good government spymaster bestows on their secret agents: 'Get receipts.'

She laid her blouse on the table and stood there in her black bra.

Santa brought her a charger for her cell phone and spare battery, a forgettable light blue nylon jacket a size too big for her and a ballistic (bulletproof) vest.

'Seven pounds,' he said as she strapped it on. Faye told herself the vest fabric that would show above her blouse's open collar could pass for a hip T-shirt. 'No plates, but rated for most combat pistols. Never had any complaints.'

'If they had to, they couldn't.'

His shrug conceded the point. He returned to the canyon of gear trunks for what he could get. Came back and helped her arrange that weight in her backpack purse.

'You were lucky we got these.' Santa shrugged. 'I'm a sentimentalist.'

'I'm a satisfied shopper,' lied Faye as she walked toward the elevators.

She knew it was useless to divert to the WOMEN'S room. Rub her hands over her body. Use the spring-bladed jackknife to check behind the badge in her folder. Smell the soles of her black sneaker-like shoes for the scent of fresh glue. Sami or her bosses at NROD or Home Sec or the CIA didn't need to plant a tracking bug on her. They and probably the whole world were pinging on the GPS in her cell phone.

Doesn't matter that they know where you are if they can't touch you there.

The elevator let her out at the main lobby.

Our world waited beyond those walls of glass.

Faye pushed her way through the revolving door, walked across the plaza to the sidewalk curb and raised her hand for a taxi.

He's presumed to be on foot, so I should be, too.

A taxi slid to a stop, she got in, told the driver where she wanted to go, didn't recognize him as one of Sami's soldiers - but he'd have used a face unknown to her.

After all, she wasn't *supposed* to have a cover team.

The backpack purse rode heavy on the seat beside her.

Cuts your speed and stamina. That weight better be worth it.

'Rush hour,' said the cabby, a black guy with an accent of where: *Nigeria?* 'Always rush hour where you got to get to, to get where you got to go.'

'Yeah.' She turned so he saw her face in the rearview mirror point toward the sidewalks they whizzed past and no more conversation. Let her eyes scan his side mirror.

The route he chose took them all the way down Wisconsin Avenue to the tricky left-hand turn onto Massachusetts Avenue by the fenced grounds of the Naval Observatory and the vice president's official residence.

Mass Avenue below the vice president's house is Embassy Row, the sprawling brick estate with Winston Churchill's V-fingered bronze statue out front for the Brits, the black glass castle-sized box of Brazil that had seemed *ultra modern* before Faye'd been born, gray stone mansions for European powers, the Islamic Center seized and held bloody hostage along with the headquarters for B'nai Brith and a D.C. government building by radical Hanafi Muslims in 1977.

A few blocks later, her taxi flowed with traffic around Sheridan Circle where in America's bicentennial, the year before the Hanafi siege, a wet squad including a former CIA agent from Waterloo, Iowa, remote-control bombed a car during the rush-hour commute in order to murder a former Chilean diplomat, also killing one American and wounding her husband as part of Operation Condor, the secret spy collaboration between six right-wing South American nations.

Faye had the taxi drop her at the corner of Third Street & Pennsylvania Avenue, SE. The Capitol waited behind her, Condor's Library of Congress office loomed a block-plus off to her left. Pennsylvania Avenue stretched away from the Congress's turf with blocks of cafes and bars and restaurants, there a Starbucks, there a two-story brick building with a street door listing offices for three different groups, all with public policy–sounding names that guaranteed nothing about what they really did.

This was your turf, Condor.

Faye corrected herself: *Is your turf.*

See me, she wished as she stood there, the last cars of rush hour whizzing past her, the crowd of Congressional staffers who'd headed somewhere after work now thinning.

Besides Starbucks, whose interior she cleared with a quick scan through its picture windows, the 'social business' that appeared most in Condor's credit card bills waited down the block near Fourth Street.

The Tune Inn. A flat-fronted beer & burgers saloon sunk like a shaft into the block's wall of coat & tie–friendly restaurants and bars.

Two steps into The Tune and Faye knew why Condor came here.

Three steps into the saloon and she spotted Pulaski sitting at the bar to her left as she walked toward the back end of booths before the bathrooms and kitchen. Pulaski was pure Special Ops, a scraggy beard that would have let him drop from this stakeout cover team mission to the streets of Kabul without much more than a minor wardrobe adjustment from his dirty blue jeans and soiled cloth Windbreaker Faye was sure covered two pistols in shoulder-holster rigs. He kept his eyes on his bottle of Miller beer.

Three stools away from Pulaski sat Georgia, an ex-cop from Alabama, dressed like a hard-luck drinker who didn't take her eyes off the half-full glass of white wine in front of her and kept her hands resting lightly on the scarred bar beside her cell phone.

Sami wouldn't have called off the dogs of Standard Operating Procedure just because he'd sicced her solo into the streets. Beyond headhunter patrols, there'd be cover teams at Condor's house, at his work, at - *say* - the top five places he'd been known to frequent. Faye wondered who she hadn't spotted in the Starbucks, but maybe that cover team coded in the Op plan as an exterior post surveillance, maybe a van parked where the watchers could cover the Starbucks doors and also scan more of the target's turf.

She walked past her colleagues without a sign of recognition amongst them.

Knew one of them would text Control that she was on-site. As if the bosses didn't already know from pinging her cell phone.

'You want a booth, hon?' asked the strong but slumping sixtyish waitress with rusted hair and a face that as a teenager slowed all the pickup truck traffic in whichever small Maryland town she'd gotten this far from. 'Wherever you want.'

This is what Condor sought, thought Faye as she took an empty, black-cushioned booth. The Tune's brown-paneled walls were hung with stuffed animal heads and a rifle rack of guns that clearly wouldn't work, pictures and plaques and beer signs from truck stops along the highways of Out There, America. She smelled beer, cooking grease from the kitchen beyond a half-door, the scent of evening drifting in from the city street.

This was a bar an American could call home. A place that felt like those post–World War II days when everything still seemed possible. You could wear a torn T-shirt or a tux here, and probably both came in during the course of any business week. A sign said the bar had been here longer than any other alcohol stop on Capitol Hill. Faye believed it. Most of the other stools at the bars where Pulaski and Georgia sat held people who'd not gotten where they were on easy roads.

One booth held two facing-fifty women whose blond dye jobs and white mohair sweaters and strings of pearls cost a lot of alimony, while their college-age sons, trying not to look bored or embarrassed, were clearly being shown where it used to be happening *back when*. Try as they might to maintain their aloof, Faye knew those college boys were tracking three scattered groups of Congressional aides who couldn't be more than a few years older than them, 'men' and 'women' who'd beaten the odds, gotten jobs, maybe'd gone to Harvard on Daddy's rep & billions or worked their way through heartland state universities on student loans they'd be repaying for decades, *but whatever*, they'd made it, they were here, 'on the Hill.'

In a bar that felt like the America they all wanted to believe was in their blood.

Faye didn't need to listen to the music above the bar chatter or check the jukebox to know Condor'd come here hoping for his *clongs* amidst sounds of Hank Williams and Dusty Springfield, Bruce Springsteen and a handful of country & western songbirds flying the same skies as Loretta Lynn and other icons Faye recognized only by name.

'What can I get you, hon?' The rust-haired waitress leaned on the back of Faye's booth and gave the customer a real smile - what the hell, we're stuck here, might as well go for the happy we can get.

Faye ordered a hamburger and a Coke. Protein and caffeine. Fuel and fire.

'Not Diet, right? Good for you, hon.' The rust-haired waitress yelled the food order back to the kitchen, swayed toward the bar to get Faye's drink.

Let me count the ways I'm trapped, thought Faye as the jukebox played.

Don't know where I'm going, don't know how to do what I've got to do, don't know how to get found by a killer - the right killer, anyway. Don't know how I ended up here - well, ended up here like this.

Don't know how I can warn off the man who loves me.

Years ago, there'd have been a pay phone in this bar. If there was now, Faye still couldn't use it. The cover team would catch that, zap the pay phone coordinates to the command center, and NSA's MAINWAY computers would flash *who* or *where* Faye called. Same reason she couldn't use her cell phone to call Chris, leave a message for him at work or get him on his cell. Faye considered stealing a phone from one of the Congressional staffers who were one beer away from being more than a little drunk, but every complication on a mission increases risk and the risk of a stolen cell phone scenario equaled why she wanted to steal a phone: keeping Chris clear of all this, of her.

Or so she told herself.

Had nothing to do with wanting to reach out and touch him, know he was safe, know he was there, know he still cared.

Last thing I need, she told herself sitting in that black upholstered bar booth, sipping a Coke as the jukebox played some Sarah Lee Guthrie & Johnny Irion song, *is to worry about him worrying about me.*

Sunset pinked the front windows at the end of the bar as she forced herself to finish the hamburger she couldn't taste, the Coke that didn't quench her thirst.

Her stomach gurgled. She told herself it wasn't nerves, had to be the bar food, maybe the drug she'd swallowed the night before.

She took the heavy purse/backpack with her through the scruffed & scarred brown wooden door labeled WOMEN.

The hook & eye lock would stop a polite customer's pull but not much more.

If only it would be Condor jerking on that door!

But it won't be. And if it were, her two colleagues at the bar would claim him. Not her. Not just her and Sami and what the two of them needed.

She didn't shut the door on the metal stall when she did what she had to do in there: if someone burst into the bathroom, she wanted a chance for a clear shot.

Washing her hands in the white sink, she raised her eyes to the mirror.

Saw the face called hers staring back.

Saw the chance.

Stupid, sure. *Crazy*, sure. *Corny*, sure. *Risky*. With all that, still her best shot.

She found her mission toiletries in the backpack purse, the gold tube of cheap bright red lipstick, the kind Faye as herself would never wear, the kind of *notice me* lip paint that dominates a witness's perception, cheap tradecraft she'd never used.

She turned the dial so the glossy red tip slid up and out of its gold sheath.

On the glass of the mirror she made appear in bright smear cherry-red letters:

Call Chris 202 555 4097
Tell him better roads r
around this bend. Tnx F

Then surrounded her lipstick plea with the outline of a red heart.

Slashed a long bloodred line under her heart on that mirror and -

Saw her second shot.

Do. Not. Run.

Walk out of the bathroom.

Go back to your booth.

She let her eyes sweep over her *sisters* who were in this bar, who were yet to come there tonight, would use the bathroom before the janitor mopped up with his ammonia cleaner and tired eyes. Surely some woman would come to that mirror who had a romantic soul, the courage of her curiosity. And a cell phone.

She counted out the cost of her dinner plus a great tip.

Showed she wasn't hurrying by standing there, dipping a last French fry into the plop of ketchup on her plate. She put the straw between her lips for a last sip of Coke.

Sure, that's all anyone sitting at the bar would see.

And she walked out without showing or saying a thing worth reporting.

Gray twilight muted by streetlamps swallowed her as she stepped onto the sidewalk. Could have turned to the right, but the formula of her epiphany mandated Condor being a sentimental guy, so she turned left as she cell-phoned Control.

Sami's voice in the cell phone pressed to her ear: 'What have you got?'

'A hunch.' Faye quickened her pace past a lucky mother who was her age and pushing a laughing baby boy in a stroller from *Me-ma*. 'Give me room to play it.'

'How?'

'Have cover teams pull back if they spot me come into surveillance Op zones.'

'I'll do what I can, give you as much slack as is Op safe. Tell me - '

'Whatever you know, you'll try to plan ahead of, and that might mess me up.'

'Then don't miss.' Sami hung up.

Faye muttered '*ABC to you, motherfucker*' as she returned her cell phone to the shirt pocket above her bulletproof vest, but she meant it in the nicest possible way.

The white-icing dome of the Capitol slid past her heart side as she marched to Union Station where she thought she saw a homeless woman rolling her shopping cart of rags and remnants away with more purpose than prayer. Could have been a headhunter pulling back as ordered, could have been just another nobody in the night, Faye couldn't let herself care. Rode Union Station's exterior escalator down to the subway platform and stood in front of the poster-sized stations-and-routes map for Metro's subway, the names of the stops in black letters, the subway lines drawn between them in thick colored connectors of orange and blue and green and yellow. And red.

Red like blood.

Red like lipstick.

'*I like the Red Line*.' She'd chalked that up to Condor sounding crazy.

Now hoped he'd told the truth.

Faye saw a man with a Metro patch on the shoulder of his blue sweater giving directions to two tourist-clad senior citizens - *older even than Condor*, thought Faye, buying that both the tourists and the Metro worker were true to those identities. The Metro worker finished with the grateful tourists and Faye caught his eye.

'Can I help you?' he said.

'I'm visiting my father,' she said, and even though she rode the Metro at least three times a week, asked: 'He said there's one stop on the Red Line that after rush hour gets deserted on the platform and that I should ride to the next one. Is there a Red Line stop where, like he said, not many people are on the platform after now?'

The Metro worker blinked. 'Really?'

She gave him her friendliest *What can you do?* shrug.

'Could be . . . I don't know. This one, or this one . . . Maybe that one.'

And Faye pictured *that one*: an underground platform. One set of escalators, the upper entry level with turnstiles visible from the red-tiled platform between the two sets of train tracks, a gray cement cavern with dark tunnels for the trains at either end.

She thanked him.

Rode the first train there.

'DOORS OPENING.'

One person got off the train at that stop with Faye, a businesswoman who barely looked up from answering the endless stream of emails in her smartphone as she rode the escalator up, out through the turnstiles, gone.

This is the picture.

A woman standing alone on the red-tile platform in the gray concrete tunnel.

Me.

Wearing the black raincoat I had on when we met. Coat unbuttoned, Condor'd expect that, believe that. Could see me as any train he rode slowed into the station.

Faye calculated it made more sense to set the backpack purse on the red tiles in front of her shoes. *Sure*, not as in her control, but also, one more thing for his eyes to process. One more thing for her to worry about, but the weight of it during her waiting and the energy that would cost seemed worth avoiding.

*What if*s raced infinitely down each set of tracks. *What if she was wrong and he hadn't chosen to be a moving target on the line he liked? What if a Metro patrol scooped him up? Why hadn't they? What if he didn't see her waiting on the platform or did and rode on anyway or jumped out of the Metro car blazing away with Peter's stolen gun?*

She let all that go.

Waited to deal with what the steel rails brought her.

A train rumbled roared *whooshed* into the station, rectangular windows of light dotting the long silver snake like scales as it slid past her facing eyes, stopped.

'DOORS OPENING!'

No one got off.

None of the three people she looked at through the train windows looked back.

'DOORS CLOSING!'

The train whooshed away.

She refused to look at her watch.

Or count the number of times trains whooshed into the station, stopped, let one or two or three or mostly no one off to ride the escalators up and out into the night.

A rumble roar whoosh, silver train sliding to a stop.

'DOORS OPENING!'

No one getting off, no one -

Standing in the subway car's open doorway twenty paces from her.

A baseball-capped, fatboy freak in brown skin, hands by his sides, *empty, are they empty?*

The freak stepped off the train.

13

DRAGONS FIGHT IN THE MEADOW
- The I-Ching, K'un/The Receptive

A man and a woman stand alone on a red-tiled subway platform.

He's stepped out of the silver train on the track behind him.

She's keeping her stance soft and still, facing a maroon-jacketed, big-bellied apparition with a baseball cap, absurd eyeglasses, brown skin. He knows *she knows*.

'DOORS CLOSING!'

Rubber-edged doors *ca-thunk* shut behind him.

The silver train streaks from the station.

She said: 'If I wanted you dead, you would be.'

Her hands stay at her sides, fingers splayed open to show *empty*. The thirty feet of red tiles between them represent the optimal kill zone for a handgun.

What's that bag on the tiles near her feet? Remote-detonated flash-bang? Gas?

'How are you, Vin?'

'Call me Condor. That's why we're here.'

'Do you remember who I am?'

'Your work ID is Faye something.'

'Faye Dozier. And it's more than a work name, a cover.'

'Who are you right now?'

'Your rescue. Your chaperone. Your minder to bring you in. Get you safe.'

'I think I remember I've been told that before.'

Take a step toward her.

She didn't move. Reposition. Shift her weight. Draw her gun.

Take another step closer. Close the gap.

She said: 'My partner got whacked at your place. I need to know all about that.'

'And you think I know.'

'The white car,' she said as he was three steps from being able to hit her. 'That makes me think you don't know *enough*. So we're stuck on the same bull's-eye.'

He stopped two paces from her. She was out of his striking zone. But close. If she moved to draw a weapon, *theoretically*, at least now he had a chance.

Condor said: 'What's in the bag?'

'Proof you can trust me.'

An electronic marquee on a hollow brown metal column listed glowing lines of train schedules. Rush hour was over, the next train was due in nineteen minutes, the one on the opposite track due three minutes after that. Empty escalators whirred up from and down to this platform where only the two of them stood.

He imagined she heard the slamming thunder of his heart beneath his maroon nylon jacket. Imagined he heard her muffled thunder, too. Inside her black coat that no doubt covered at least one pistol, under her blouse, he saw the thickness of a bulletproof vest.

Where they stood was the lowest level of the subway station. The closed orange doors of the 'Handicap Accessible' elevator leading up to the street waited near the escalators that connected this passengers' platform to an entrance level twenty feet above the top of their heads, an apron of red tiles inside orange turnstiles that *whumped* open & closed. Beyond those turnstiles were fare card machines, and mere steps beyond them, a forty-one-second-long escalator ride connecting our world to these underground arteries. Condor couldn't see much past the top of the escalator up to the entrance level, couldn't see the orange turnstiles, certainly couldn't see the main escalators up to the night.

Faye said: 'How long are we going to just stare at each other?'

'My chaperone.' *What does she think of me: the dark skin, the baseball cap and big glasses, the fat-man jacket?* 'I liked slow dances in high school.'

'This isn't high school, Condor,' she said.

She's worried I'm losing it.

Next train: eighteen minutes.

Concrete columns five times as thick as Condor's fat-man suit rose from the red tiles to the curved gray ceiling. He remembered two FBI agents and two bank robbers in . . . *Miami*, who'd chased each other around a parked car, all four of them blasting away with semi-automatic pistols, two of them reloading on the run, all the bullets missing flesh. The two columns on this subway platform needed fewer steps to race around than a parked car. And down in this tunnel, the perils of ricochets canceled out any advantage the concrete gave over bullet-porous car metal.

'Hey, chaperone,' said Condor: 'Slow dance.'

He took two steps back.

Faye took two steps forward to preserve the distance he'd chosen between them.

Her shoes stopped beside the backpack purse on the red tiles.

Condor said: 'Pick it up. Both hands.'

Oh so slowly, she did.

No BOOM! No *flash-bang* stunning light. No eruption of tear gas or smoke.

'See?' she said. 'So far, so good.'

Green eyes, he thought. Her eyes are green.

'Don't see only what's in front of you.'

Who taught me that? Let that go. Let that ghost dissolve.

Faye said: 'What now?'

'Unzip it. Make sure the opening is toward your face, not mine.'

The zipper *zuzzed* a slow opening of the backpack purse.

Condor said: 'Show me - *easy*.'

She tilted the backpack so he could peek into the bag. 'Take what you want.'

He flicked his eyes up from the bag to meet hers.

'I was right,' he said. 'One way or another, you're how I'm going to die.'

'Not now,' she said. 'Not with me. Not if I can help it.'

'And this is your help?'

She shrugged. 'And my bona fides.'

He took the last step to be close enough to her.

Slid his right hand into the backpack. She didn't close it. Trap him. Try for some aikido or judo throw, she just . . . let him do it.

Feel cool steel, textured wood, the terrible weight of choice.

Condor filled his right fist in the bag with a snub-nosed .38 revolver.

He pulled out the hand-sized pistol. Let its death hole drift aimlessly and casually from side to side, but showing him the gold glint of brass cartridges in the wheel cylinder that implied the gun held ammunition that worked.

Faye said: 'I thought you'd go for the .45 in there. The updated 1911, but still like you said you - '

Thunk! The cold steel bore of the snub-nosed revolver dug into her forehead.

' - prefer,' she finished.

Her green eyes blinked.

But she didn't back away. Whirl/sweep her arm up to beat a bullet to her brain.

A man and a woman stand alone on a red-tiled subway platform.

His arm extended to press a gun's death bore against her third eye.

'I prefer to be murdered with my partner Peter's weapon,' she said.

'Sorry, I don't have it.'

'Then you'd be stupid to shoot me.'

'Stupid comes easy.'

'Here I thought you were a hard guy. If you don't have my partner's gun, then you didn't kill him and somebody took it to package you as armed and dangerous.'

'Great minds,' he said. 'Theirs. Yours.'

Slowly the steel barrel backed off her skull.

Still she didn't counterattack.

Condor put the revolver in his jacket pocket.

Smiled.

Lifted the holstered .45 semi-automatic out of the backpack. That gun came with a pouch of two spare ammunition magazines. He awkwardly shifted the bulk under his jacket to clip both the ammo pouch and the holstered .45 to his belt.

She shook her head. 'You look ridiculous.'

The marquee read fourteen minutes until the next train arrived.

'Moving,' she told him. 'Getting my phone.'

She used her left thumb and forefinger in an overly formal pincer grip to lift her cell from the blouse pocket over her heart.

Told Condor, 'I'll put it on speaker.'

Empty escalators whirred to and from this red-tiled station platform.

The cell phone buzzed once. Buzzed twice.

Condor heard faint background noise coming from the phone.

Faye told the device in her hand: 'Someone's here to talk with you.'

'Who?' said a man.

That voice! Here! D.C. National Airport. A little girl - Amy. A bomb.

Be sure: 'Tell me something.'

Eagerness came through the man's voice in the phone: '*Always Be Cool!* Condor, it's Sami!'

The question ripped from Condor's bones: '*Where have you been?*'

'Trying to bring you home. Where are you - both of you?'

Condor thrust his hand to block Faye's reply. '*Here*. Where's *there*? Langley?'

'No, our friend Faye, she knows where I am. Doesn't matter. GPS says our exfilt team will be to you in fourteen minutes.'

'We'll be gone. See you.'

Condor lifted the phone from the woman's hand and she let him, but her eyes flashed questions as he thumbed the phone here, there . . .

As Sami's voice in the phone said: 'Faye, come - '

. . . Condor killed the call. Gave her back the phone.

'Turn off the power,' he said.

She did.

'We've got to go now.'

'Sami is - '

'Not here. We are.'

Condor took a backward step away from her, his eyes on her as an image, his hand near his maroon nylon jacket's pocket, sagging with the weight of the gun.

Saw her green eyes decide before she gave him a nod.

'Okay, Condor. You're the star.'

The marquee told them twelve minutes before the next train.

'You got a car?' he said as he gave her his back . . .

. . . and she didn't shoot him as he hurried toward the UP escalator.

'No,' said Faye.

He climbed the escalator steps as they carried him up.

Heard her footsteps right behind him.

They hurried across the entrance level toward the orange turnstiles. Condor and Faye slapped their electronic SmarTrip cards over the data-reading strip in side-by-side turnstiles. The turnstiles jumped open to set them free.

Alone in the station, the man and woman quick-walked to the bottom of the three basketball-court-length, forty-one-second-ride UP escalators stretched through a slanting giant straw of concrete to D.C.'s neon blue night sky.

Condor hesitated. Stepped on the rising metal stair . . . and stayed there.

Sighed: 'I wish I was in better shape.

'Or younger,' he added as Faye climbed to ride up on the step below him. He felt energy coursing through her, her strobing urge to run up the stairs, move on, DO IT!

'We're on our way,' she assured her quarry, her *protectee*, her de facto partner, as Condor looked back down the stairs toward her and the sliding-away tunnel of where they'd been, saw the thought light her face: *Not going to lose another one!*

He turned forward.

Looked up the long stairs carrying them toward the neon-blue night.

Said: 'Too late.'

14

GONNA SHOOT YOU RIGHT DOWN
- John Lee Hooker, 'Boom Boom'

Faye spotted them at the top of the escalator carrying Condor and her ever upward toward the blue night: Four, *no*, six backlit silhouettes.

Two shapes moved with military grace at the top of the tunnel onto the DOWN escalator that ran past Faye's left. A man and a woman. *Like us*, thought Faye.

Faye whispered: 'Be cool!'

Nothing! Condor's not answering! Did he hear me? What does he hear?

His right hand slid into the pocket of his maroon nylon jacket.

No! Had to make him trust me! He's not rogue! Or crazy!

Trapped behind Condor on stairs carrying her up toward four *unknowns*.

As sliding down the escalator next to her, *toward her*, came two more strangers.

They could all be innocents. Six total. Six bullets in a revolver.

The escalator trembled Faye with its upward glide. Cooler outside air flowed over her face. The escalator smelled like oiled steel, the black rubber handrails.

Drawing nearer on the DOWN *escalator: Black man, white woman behind him.*

Twenty feet and a few seconds apart, fifteen, ten -

The black man wore a brown leather hip-length coat over weightlifter muscles.

The white woman, hair colored Midwestern brown and -

Whirled her hands up weapon pointing at Condor WUNK!

Taser! Two wire-leashed probes shot out -

Hit the giant belly of Condor's maroon nylon jacket, the *Gotcha!* frenzy on the Midwestern-haired woman's face turning to puzzlement as she squeezed the Taser's control handle to send fifty thousand volts of electricity coursing into . . .

Into non-conductive padding under Condor's maroon nylon jacket.

Condor fired the snub-nose .38 from inside his pocket.

The tunnel boomed with the gunshot roar. The bullet slammed into the Midwestern woman's chest, knocked her off balance on the sliding-down escalator stairs.

No blood spray! Ballistic vest, she's wearing armor!

The Midwestern woman crashed toward her black partner as he cross-drew -

Gun! Silenced pistol! His partner tumbles into him and he falls as he aims -

Faye heard *cough*, a bullet whine past her face.

Found the Glock in her hand, fired twice at the falling man, blood spraying from hits on unarmored flesh, then he was tumbling out of sight on the descending escalator.

BANG! Condor firing up the mouth of the tunnel.

Faye whirled - saw four human shapes dive out of sight of her escalator-up view.

Condor fired again. His bullet smacked into metal at the top of the escalators, whined off into the night *God don't let its ricochet hit some kid!*

'Stop!' she yelled. 'Cease - '

Gun! Poked into the escalator shaft, wink of flame/bullet whines past Faye. She popped two shots into the metal at the top of these stairs. Gun pulled back.

'Condor!' she yelled. 'Roll across to the other escalator, the DOWN stairs!'

Faye spotted motion near the street-level mouth of the escalator. Crashed a bullet into the metal escalator shaft up by where the steel stairs folded into the machine.

Condor lunged across the metal border separating the UP and the DOWN escalators, missed grabbing the moving rubber handrail, flopped into the shaft of the DOWN escalator. His baseball cap flew off, his fake glasses spun away, the Taser probes ripped free from him. A steel stair edge chopped his right arm. He yelled in pain as he somersaulted down the sliding stairs.

The snub-nose .38 flew from Condor's hand, bounced down the moving steel stairs, over the prone & gasping woman whose bulletproof vest had just proven its worth.

Condor tumbled into that Midwestern woman, rolled over her, past her, his feet pointing down on those sliding-into-the-earth steel stairs. He skidded, stopped.

Looked up the steel shaft passage to the receding half-moon of blue night.

Whine over Condor's head clangs into metal.

From escalator beside him Faye's gun roared.

As she ran *backwards* down the steps of the moving UP escalator.

The Midwestern woman jackknifed up in front of Condor. Sat on the stairs, blocked his view up the tunnel as she gripped a black pistol, its bore zeroed on Condor.

Crimson spray flowered in the shiny steel–lit darkness behind her head.

She snapped forward, her ballistic vest springing her back so she sat upright on the descending escalator stairs between Condor and the shooters. A spritz of red mist glistened in her small-town-escapee hair. She rode those downward stairs sitting with dangling low arms at her sides like a '*come unto me*' Madonna.

Another bullet meant for Condor *thunked* into the dead woman, hit her vest-covered spine, not the back of her skull.

The gun she dropped filled his hand. He fired up at the night.

Condor ran down the DOWN escalator.

Chased by the skull-shot Madonna slumped on the stairs.

On the escalator stairs ahead of Condor lay a black man in a brown leather coat with a dark-stained left shoulder. Ooze covered the black man's left ear. He kicked as Condor staggered past him. Condor stomped his face. The black man slumped. Condor ran off the end of the moving-down stairs to the floor of the subway's entry platform where seconds later, the escalator dumped the unconscious black man.

Condor yelled up to Faye: 'Covering you!'

Fired two rounds from the dead woman's Glock.

Faye vaulted onto the metal border between the escalators. Fist-sized knobs are built into that metal border to discourage the sliding Faye tried, so she improvised a scrambling charge and leapt off the escalator to the red tiles beyond Condor.

They ran deeper into the underground subway station.

She vaulted orange turnstiles, whirled to cover their retreat where descending stairs dumped a slumped Madonna on top of an unconscious black man.

'Move!' she yelled to Condor.

No vaulting over orange turnstiles for him. He used the emergency gate.

'Go!' she yelled, backing toward the escalators down to the subway platform.

He ran ahead of her. *Galumped* down the escalator to the red tiles. Staggered to the center of the platform so he could aim back up toward the turnstiles, yelled: 'Now you!'

Faye ran down the last escalator.

Saw the subway schedule marquee:

Next train in five minutes.

Opposite-direction train arriving three minutes later.

A man and a woman stood alone on a red-tiled subway platform.

Both of them aiming guns up to the entrance level toward orange turnstiles they could barely see. They sidestepped apart to not cluster in one easily targetable group.

'Four left, minimum,' said Faye. 'Maybe they broke off.'

'You wouldn't,' said Condor.

The marquee above them displayed four minutes to the next train, but they didn't take their eyes off where shooters might appear.

Your train comes when it comes.

Up on the entrance level: two shapes vaulting the turnstiles.

Faye fired before Condor, then they flowed forward for new defensive positions.

Soaring through the concrete cavern air:

A black stone tossed from that upper entrance level on a soared curving arc to the red-tiled platform where Faye and Condor crouched.

'*Flash-bang!*' Faye leapt alongside the solid sheltering wall of the escalators.

Condor jumped behind the thick concrete pillar.

Both turned their backs toward the grenades. Scrunched their eyes closed. Covered their ears. Opened mouths to ease explosive pressure, dropped low as -

White nova FLASHING seared their closed eyelids.

Ear-stabbing BANG! rocked their equilibrium.

Faye forced her eyes open.

The subway platform shimmered into view.

A giant invisible vacuum cleaner whined in her ears.

Gunpowder smoke tinged this concrete cavern.

Your back's pressed against the solid metal side of the escalators, and -

Condor: beside the concrete column aiming up toward the next level. His gun spits two flashes. He jumped behind the concrete pillar where POP! white dust flowers:

Someone's returning fire!

Charging feet pound down the escalator.

First attacker down the stairs, *a man*, running, squeezing rhythmic shots at the concrete pillar, keeping Condor pinned on the other side, killer closing to there as –

Second attacker, *young guy*, lunges over the escalator, thrusts his gun to shoot –

Faye grabbed her assailant. He toppled over the side of the escalator, crashed into her and they collapsed on the red tiles.

Don't let his gun point at you! He's grabbed your right wrist doing the same!

Faye drove her knee into the man on top of her.

He gasped, flung himself off her, their hands gripping them together like jitterbug dancers from her grandmother's era as he muscled their inertia, jerked her onto her feet.

She spins the man she grips in an airborne half circle.

They fly off the edge of the subway platform.

Crash onto the train tracks.

Third rail! Third rail! Where the fuck is the third –

Won't let go of each other, scramble to stand.

What's that noise . . .

She stomps her foot out to dragon kick his stomach.

He gets knocked back, trips over a rail –

– just a regular steel rail –

– his back hits the concrete edge of the platform.

Bouncing him off with a body slam that rockets her off her feet, barely catching her balance with her shoes on the grille covering the white lights along the tunnel's far wall as she sees her foe drop into a combat shooter's stance and swing his pistol –

Train slams into her attacker, whining stopping only after the silver snake scarfs his body under its steel snout and blood spray trickles down the engineer's window.

Train pins Faye with her back pressed against the curved gray concrete wall, her arms straight out to her sides. *Like I'm crucified.*

See the glow of train windows smack in front of her.

Smell the hot steel brakes.

Smell wet ham.

'DOORS OPENING!'

Bullet hole punched out the train window above her.

Two more shots, holes punched through the plastic windows. Cosmically, she knew the engineer heard *gunshots*, so *get out of here!*

'DOORS CLOSING!'

Faye pressed against the concrete wall as the train roared past her.

Going to suck me off my feet toss me bounce me crushed dead and -

Whump, she saw the butt of the train, red light vanishing down the tunnel *gone*, her feet settling on the steel grille over the tunnel wall floor lights.

From the track bed where she stood Faye stared across the waist-high red-tiled platform at a warrior edging his way around the concrete pillar to gun down Condor.

Faye shot the warrior in the head. Shot him dead.

Condor left the pillar's shelter as Faye hoisted herself out of the track bed.

'Four down!' she gasped to Condor.

The handicap-access elevator by the escalator DINGED!

Metro elevators ease down shafts from the sidewalk to the subway platform. Their metal walls create a closed box big enough to hold four wheelchair travelers. Blurry steel creates mirrors on the inside; on the outside, the elevator's doors are orange.

Take the harder shot, thought Faye, told Condor: 'I got our backs!'

Faye aimed up to the main entrance.

Orange elevator doors slid open.

Faye felt Condor hustle toward that cube that could be their escape route.

Slow dance. She walked backwards in his wake, never wavering her aim.

Quick glance showed her *he's at the elevator, gun barrel moving toward the open doors* and as she swung back to scan the darkness beyond her gun sights.

Condor eased his left foot onto the crack between the elevator and the subway platform's red tiles so that the cage door's rubber guard closed on/bounced off his shoe as he flowed forward and swung the barrel of his gun up to -

The sky fell on Condor.

Dropped from spread-eagled across the top of the elevator cage, Monkey Man, long, whip lean and strong, missing a perfect ambush onto the old guy in the maroon nylon jacket but still grabbing his gun arm BANG!

Faye whirled -

Got knocked off her feet by Monkey Man shoving Condor into her, holding on to Condor, charging past him with a pivoting aikido throw that flung the Glock out of Condor's hand even as the throw also flipped Condor off his feet and onto the red tiles.

Monkey Man spun out of his pivot with a crescent kick that slammed his shoe into Faye's extended gun arm - the kick clattered her gun away on the tiles.

But the crescent kick required heartbeats and space for Monkey Man to settle, balance, recover - and only *then* be able to attack.

Whoosh of silver streaks into the subway station.

Time slows down if you survive enough fights, boxing or martial arts encounters. Doctors claim that's merely the relaxation/suppression of fear instincts and the startle impulse allowing you to be aware of, process and react to the accelerated flood of data generating from the person in front of you trying to rip your head off. Science favors the experienced who know about leverage and coverage and counters, who possess strength and speed and stamina. From the moment Monkey Man touched her, Faye knew she'd need more than science to survive on that subway platform. As she swooped her guard up, she prayed for the deliverance of poetry, of art.

She launched a snap kick, mostly feint, and Monkey Man didn't buy it, flowed back to suck her charge in further and then launched forward to blast through her guard with one of his long-ass punching arms but she dodged sideways, changed her angle of attack, came at him with a three-punch/one-kick combination -

'DOORS OPENING!'

Felt herself flipped over Monkey Man, aikido or judo *who cared* as he powered her head straight down to the red tiles, but she twisted tucked curled landed on the soles of her shoes. Shocked, still held by him, her counter-leveraging his arm only *kind of* worked as she dropped onto her butt. He staggered backward, got his balance -

BANG!

Monkey Man bounced back toward the subway train behind him.

Backlit by that silver snake with its yellow glow of empty windows, Faye saw Monkey Man staggering on his shoes, hand raising to his chest *no blood* and she saw his short-cropped dirty blond hair and scraggy goatee - *Special Ops guys stay bearded in case* - saw him in her mind's eye over her gun sights as he wears a blue nylon Homeland Security jacket and claims *protocol*.

BANG!

Condor, sprawled on the red tiles firing another round from the 1911 .45 created to stop fanatic Muslim Moro warriors from overwhelming American soldiers with a screaming sword-swinging charge.

Monkey Man staggered spun backwards hit in his ballistic-vested chest -

And hurtles through the open doors of the subway train, falls to the orange carpet.

'DOORS CLOSING!'

BANG! Condor blasted a third .45 slug through the train's closed metal doors toward the bottom of fallen Monkey Man's feet.

Whoosh and that train rocketed out of the station.

A man and a woman sprawled alone on a red-tiled subway platform.

Faye got to her feet first. Drew her second gun, scanned the upper platform - *No visible threats!* - quick-stepped over to help Condor stand.

Said: 'I hope your last shot tore him a new asshole.'

'Elevator,' gasped Condor.

She saw those doors had slid closed, pushed the button.

The orange doors slid open.

Condor said: 'Sometimes all you can choose is where you're trapped.'

Faye helped him into the cage.

Pressed the button labeled **STREET.**

Zeroed her pistol out the cage's entrance until that gray cavernous void disappeared beyond sliding-closed doors, orange on the outside, but in here, in the cage, steel walls of smudged silver mirrors showing Faye's crazed reflection, showing Condor's panting grotesqueness.

Lurch, and the elevator lifted them up.

'At least one more hostile posted by top of the escalators,' said Faye, her gun at her side, her heart slamming against the ballistic vest.

'You think nobody called the cavalry?' said Condor.

'Whose cavalry?' muttered Faye.

Lurch. Bounce. Stopped.

Faye posted to one side of the elevator doors.

Condor to the other.

Second date in the cool blue D.C. night, Heather and Marcus as savvy as all twenty-four-year-olds stand on the street near a Metro stop, by the elevator that's sixty feet from the escalators, a perfect site for D.C.'s ecofriendly Bike Share program, lock-up racks all over the city with stand-up-handles orange bicycles to rent & ride & return, Marcus's idea that Heather hoped he, *like*, hadn't needed to get from some magazine or a Perfect Dates *dot com*, meet at the bike stand between their starter jobs downtown, work clothes but *never mind*, they're young and thus in enough shape to not sweat out the ride to the Potomac waterfront, let him buy her a fish sandwich off one of the boat/restaurants floating tied up to the wooden wharf, shame that soft-shell crabs aren't in season, white bread and tartar sauce and *so good*, sitting on benches watching moored yachts rock back and forth in the wide gray river as the sun sets, seagulls screeing, and *hey*, Marcus listens to everything Heather prattles on about and only says one or two not-smart things, then they pedal back close to where she lives and now they're standing there, *aw-kward*, each trying to figure out the next move because even though it's only the second date, *well, you know*, except they don't have much in common even if they're in each other's cute zone, so instead of locking the bikes into the steel rack, they're dawdling, watching something weird going on over by the top of the escalators where maybe two dozen people stand talking about *like* going down or not going down, *what's that* near the bottom of the escalator stairs and *did you see those flashes, did you hear bangs*, people have their cell phones out filming, *like*, nothing Heather and Marcus can see, check out that especially agitated bearded guy in a trench coat by the escalators and -

DING!

Orange metal doors on the Metro elevator beside Heather and Marcus . . .

. . . slide open.

Out of the elevator darts, *like*, somebody's kind of cool, way-intense older sister.

And *OMG!* right after her stumbles some Friday-night slasher-movie monster all silver-haired and shit-brown-smeared-faced with a weird body and maroon nylon jacket.

The older sister spots the bearded guy over by the subway escalators.

But bearded guy stares down the tunnel toward *whatever*, doesn't see her see him.

Older sister zooms right up to Heather and Marcus and *OMG!* that's *like a fucking real gun* as she says: 'Give us the bikes, hold hands, keep your other ones where we can see them and walk *don't run* down the street that way.'

Sister Gun nods the opposite direction of the subway entrance.

'Don't scream, don't cell phone, don't do anything but hold hands *fucking move!*'

Heather and Marcus remember that second date for, *like*, the rest of their lives.

Faye swung onto the orange bike, turned to see Condor struggling onto his bike.

Darted her eyes back toward the subway escalators, through the gathered crowd -

The bearded guy in a trench coat met her stare.

'Go!' she yelled to Condor, gambling that the posted rear guard gunner wouldn't cut loose on a city street for a *less than sure* shot through this small crowd.

Faye powered the bicycle into the street. *No cars* as she pedaled away from the subway, glanced back and saw the weird image that was Condor trying to keep up.

Lumbering across and down the street from Faye comes a Metro bus.

She glanced over her shoulder to check on Condor . . .

Saw a dark sedan skid around the corner behind them.

The sedan fishtailed, locked its headlights on the two bicyclists like a yellow-eyed dragon on rabbits. The sedan gunned its engine.

Faye whipped around, saw the giant Metro bus looming now *four* car lengths away, *three*, and yelled: 'Condor!'

The woman biker zoomed straight into the path of a rushing-closer bus.

Whoosh and she's across that traffic lane, standing hard on the pedals, cranking the steering handles to the left - *Bike's wobbling skidding gonna spill!*

But she bounced off a parked car, pedaled back the way she came.

Condor wheeled his bike behind the bus as a dragon-eyed sedan shuddered past him, brake lights burning the night red. Condor pumped pedals to follow Faye.

Car horns blared behind them as the sedan almost slammed into oncoming traffic while trying to make a U-turn to chase the bicycles.

Spinning red & blue lights on city cop cars, an ambulance, and a fire truck illuminated the entrance to the subway. Faye biked away from that chaos, powered down an alley, heard gravel crunch and Condor curse as he biked after her.

Yellow dragon eyes and a growling engine filled the alley a block behind them.

Two cyclists shot out of the alley and across the side street then into the opposite alley half a block ahead of a yellow-eyed monster roaring in their wake.

There! Off to the right: yellow glowing open door!

A Hispanic man in a kitchen worker's white uniform spotted two bikers charging toward where he stood in an open doorway. His eyes went wide, his jaw dropped. Black plastic trash bags jumped out of his hands as he leapt out of the way. Two bikers shot past him through the open back door under the blue neon back door sign:

Nine Nirvana Noodles

The *Washington Post* review called Nine Nirvana Noodles 'a twenty-first-century culinary revelation' with its menu of peanut sauce *Pad Thai*, Lasagna, *Lo Mein*, Macaroni & Cheese,*Udon*, plus three daily specials, but the restaurant critic had no clue about who really owned this *fabbed-up* former hole-in-the-wall destined for hipness.

Faye ducked her head/braked her bike as she blew into the shiny metal kitchen.

Veer around that chopping table - knife worker leaping out of the way!

The wobbling woman biker pushed her foot off the grill.

Black rubber smoke from the scorched sole of her shoe polluted food aromas.

A redheaded waitress dropped her tray of steaming yellow noodles.

BAM! Faye's front tire banged open twin doors to the dining room, a long box of white-clothed tables below wall-mounted computer monitors that streamed Facebook and YouTube mixed with muted clips from old TV shows, the moon landing, presidential addresses, movies like *Blade Runner* and *Casablanca, Dr. Strangelove.*

A waiter jumped out of Faye's way/fell onto a table of divorced daters.

Exploding dropped plates. Screams from splashed hot tea. Behind her, Faye heard Condor's bike crash into this dining room.

A waiter and a customer crouched to grab the crazy biker woman.

'Police emergency!' Faye threw her GPS-hacked cell phone at the two citizens.

'Open the fucking doors to the hospital!' Faye yelled to the hostess in the white blouse and black leather skirt, hoping 'hospital' would inspire the clearing of an exit.

Whatever worked, *worked*: the front door opened.

Faye shot through it, skidded to a stop outside the restaurant, looked back for -

Crashing tables busting glass screams - *'Don't touch him he's sick!'*

Condor pushed his bike out the restaurant's front door, swung onto it, yelled: 'One's chasing us on foot!'

They sped away from Nirvana, pedaled two more blocks, a zig, a zag, an alley.

Faye heard Condor's bike skid, stop.

Turned in time to see him wave his hand at her, slouch, wheezing, *spent*.

Two bikers staggered in the garbage can alley behind slouching houses where American citizens lived. Near Faye, a gate on a peeling wooden fence as high as her shoulder hung broken in its frame. She swung off her bike, eased inside the gate . . .

Somebody's backyard. What started its existence as a modest middle-class 1950s house was now sixty-some years later probably worth more money than it and all its companions on this block sold for when new. A watch light glowed over the back door, and through rear windows, she saw that a lamp shone deeper into the first floor. No lights on the second floor. Nothing that made her believe anyone was home.

She dropped her bike on the lawn, went back to the alley, muscled Condor and his bike into the backyard, dumped them on the night's spring grass.

Still wearing my backpack!

Faye dropped that gear bag on the lawn.

Stared at the nylon-jacketed mess sprawled in front of her.

A garden hose snake lay in the grass near Condor. She unscrewed its sprinkler, walked to the faucet and turned it on. The hose in her hand gushed cool water.

Faye drank hose water, drank again. Splashed cool wet on her face.

Water tumbled from the hose as she shuffled toward the man sprawled on his back on the grass. Faye sprayed his face: 'Get up! You don't get to die yet.'

Choking, gasping, flopping . . . *Sitting*, Condor sitting on the grass.

She turned the hose away from him.

He said: 'I'm too old for this shit.'

'Shit doesn't care how old you are.'

Pale light from nearby houses and streetlights let them see each other.

He said: 'How much makeup is still on my face?'

'You're a disgusting smear.'

'Squirt it all off.'

And she did as he sat there, raising his hands to clean them, too.

'Enough,' she said.

He rolled onto his hands and knees, pushed and staggered to his feet.

Like Faye, drank and drank again.

She turned off the hose.

Came back to him as he took off the maroon nylon jacket, the baby carrier. From the infant pouch came a black leather jacket, drier than his black jeans or blue shirt.

The .45 rode holstered on his right side, the ammo pouch on his left.

Condor checked his vials of pills, muttered that it felt like they were all there.

Looked at her.

Faye whispered: 'Who did we just kill?'

'Who's trying to kill us?' answered Condor.

'Now?' she said. 'Everybody.'

15

THE WAY I ALWAYS DO
- Warren Zevon, 'Lawyers, Guns and Money'

Taxi, you're in the backseat of a yellow taxi.

Smells like burnt coffee and pine-scented ammonia and passengers' sweat.

Your sweat.

A cool breeze through the driver's open window bathes your sticky face.

Look out your rolled-up window.

The street-lit night streams surreal images. Sidewalks. Stores. Bar lovers hurrying into their neon cathedrals. The window catches your blurred reflection sitting beside someone you barely know. The glass vibrates from your pounding heart.

Condor and Faye stumbled through blocks of alleys toward a 7-Eleven, caught a break when Faye waved down a long-way-from-home taxi.

Condor lied to the cabby about where they were going.

The cabby lied about the shortest way to get there.

Drove through Georgetown.

The yellow taxi glided through that zone of boutiques, bars and restaurants, clothing franchises just like in most malls *back home*, sidewalks where charm mattered less than cash. Houses off these commercial roads sold for millions and still held graying survivors who'd pioneered Georgetown for Camelot's glory of JFK, but the streets now belonged to franchisers with factories in Hong Kong and Hanoi.

The cabby turned up his radio - loud, brassy music not born in the U.S.A.

Condor stared out the taxi window.

Saw him holding a red flower amidst unseeing strangers on the sidewalk.

'Rose men,' whispered Condor.

'What?' Faye's eyes darted from sidewalk to sidewalk to side mirror to side mirror to the rearview mirror to the taxi's windshield and back again.

'Jimmy Carter was President. Middle Eastern guys popping into Georgetown restaurants, table to table, selling single roses for a dollar. They were spies. Savak, Iranian secret police brick boys working for the Shah, tracking dissidents, exiles, allies.'

'Way before my time,' said Faye. 'I'm a Reagan baby.'

'So who are the rose men now?'

'You tell me.'

The taxi rumbled through dark residential streets. Blocks of apartment buildings lined main avenues. Town houses and cramped GI Bill homes filled the side roads.

They drove two blocks past their true destination.

Condor and Faye scanned cars parked along the curbs. Looked for vans. Looked for hulks in the bushes, lingering inside alleys or stairwells to basements. Looked for security cameras. Tracked rooflines for silhouettes under the dark sky.

The cabby stopped at the intersection Condor'd requested.

Said: 'You sure this where you want to go?'

'Sure,' said the old man in the black leather jacket as the woman who could be his daughter paid the fare they all knew was bogus. 'This is where she grew up.'

'Feels familiar.' *True* & *False* intertwined from this woman who slipped into her backpack as the cabby hesitated so the change from the corrupt fee became his tip.

Condor and Faye watched the cab drive away into the night.

Stepped back out of the cone of light from the corner streetlamp.

Faye scanned the surrounding darkness. 'You sure this is where we should go?'

'Everything about you will be lit up in crosshairs,' he said. 'You told me nothing about this is in my target packet for Sami's headhunters.'

'Do you think this is the right thing to do?'

'It's the only *do* I got left,' he told her. 'Don't ask me any more than that. Or come up with a better idea and come up with it fast. I'm dead on my feet.'

'Not yet,' she said. 'Not on my watch.'

Then she let him lead her where he'd never been before, where he'd dreamed, where he already felt falling into déjà vu.

'Nothing's ever like it used to be,' he muttered as they walked through the dark.

He heard concern in her voice as she said: 'Concentrate on here and now.'

This residential neighborhood smelled of bushes and grass and sidewalks damp from the previous night's rain. Freshly budded trees lined the boulevards, spread their thickening branches like nets poised over where Faye and Condor walked.

TV clatter floated from an open window as someone surfed their remote - sitcom laughter, crime drama sirens, dialog from fictional characters viewers could trust.

Coming toward them across the street: a woman in a yellow rain slicker muttering encouragement to the rescue mutt scampering on the end of her leash: '*Come on now, you can do it, yes you can.*'

Out of the apartment building next to their destination came a cleanshaven man zipping up a leather jacket that was brown instead of Condor's black. He didn't notice they slowed their pace until he drove away in a car with taillights like red eyes.

'You sure this is the right address?' asked Faye when they stood outside the glass lobby door to a seven-story apartment building built during the Korean War. Through the glass entrance, they saw no one in the lobby, no one waiting for the elevator.

Condor pointed to the label beside the buzzer for Apartment 513:

M. Mardigian

Because you never know, Faye pulled on this main glass door: locked.

She tapped the 'M. Mardigian' label. 'If we buzz and get a *no*, we're fucked.'

They looked behind them to the night street.

'We can't stand out here exposed, waiting for a chance to try a hitch-in,' she said.

Condor pushed his thumbs down two columns of buzzer buttons for the seventh floor.

The door lock buzzed as a man's voice in the intercom said: '*Yeah?*'

Faye jerked open the heavy glass door, told the intercom: 'Like, thanks, but never mind, I found my key!'

Condor and Faye hurried into the lobby.

'You'd think people would have learned the spy tricks by now,' said Faye.

'If they did, we'd be stuck out in the cold.'

Steel silver elevator doors slid open.

He hesitated. Felt her do the same.

Then she said: 'Come on. We've got nowhere to go but up.'

They got in, pushed the button for five.

Steel doors slid closed. This silver cage rose toward heaven.

Make it work, you can make this work. And nobody will get hurt, it'll be okay.

Faye watched him with skeptical eyes.

Inertia surged their skulls as the elevator stopped. Silver doors slid open.

A lime green hallway. Black doors, brass apartment numbers over peepholes. Dark green indoor-outdoor industrial carpet that smelled long overdue for replacement.

Apartment 513. No name label, no door decorations, nothing to set it apart from other slabs of entry into strangers' lives in this long green hall. The round plastic peephole stared at them, a translucent Cyclops eye beneath brass numbers.

This is where I want to be never wanted this shouldn't do this déjà vu.

Poetry. *Clong.*

Condor whispered to Faye: 'Try to look like just a woman.'

Faced the slab of black.

Raised his fist . . .

Knocked.

16

Let us in.

Faye watched the black door swing open & away from her in this musty green hall. Smiled as she secretly coiled to charge or draw & shoot or . . . *Or.*

Let us in!

But the woman who opened the door just stood there - blocking entry.

M. Mardigian.

She looks younger than fifty-three. *Condor mining her data isn't creepy, you've done that.* M. Mardigian's hair is gray highlighted blond, and unlike most women in Washington, she wears it curling past her shoulder blades. She looks like the part-time yoga instructor Condor says she is, a slow flow, subtle but stocky, strong. Her face is a pleasant rectangle, big nose, unpainted slash of lush lips. Her eyes are set too wide. She lets the two visitors standing in her hall tumble into their slitted blue gaze.

'*Wow,*' she deadpanned. 'You never know who's gonna knock on your door.'

Faye felt the disturbing force of her and Condor in this empty hallway.

Felt peepholes on the other apartment doors staring at them.

LET US IN!

The yoga woman scanned Faye, then her blue gaze settled on Condor, a wrinkle crossing her brow as she said: 'You show up here with your daughter?'

'We're not that lucky,' said Condor.

'Who's "*we*"?'

Faye flashed one of her three sets of credentials. 'Homeland Security. Let's step inside, Ms. Mardigian. You're not in any kind of trouble.'

'If you're here, we all know that's some kind of not true.'

Condor asked the graying blonde blocking the door: 'Can I call you *Merle*?'

She stared at him.

Said: 'Word around work is that you're some kind of spook.'

Bust in, push in, bowl her over in ten, nine, eight -

Call her Merle stepped back out of the doorway and pulled Condor in her wake.

Faye edged between Merle and the black door, wrapped her fist around the lock-button knob, closed that black slab to block out the world. Faye glanced away from their hostess only long enough to shoot the deadbolt home, fasten the door's chain.

Merle's husky voice said: 'Somehow that doesn't make me feel safe.'

'Sorry,' said Condor. 'You're not.'

'Thanks to you?'

'Guilty. At least, in the personal sense.'

'This is personal?' She sent her eyes to Faye. 'So what do you want with me?'

Already got it, got in here, thought Faye. *Just need to stay in control.*

'Would you do me a favor, please, Ms. Mardigian? Sit over there on the couch.'

Yoga woman wore a gold pullover and dark blue jeans. Was barefoot. She settled on her couch. Faye saw the woman force herself to relax, to sit back from poised on the edge of the black leather sofa, to act as if nothing was too wrong.

Faye followed Condor's lead. 'Thanks. Mind if I call you Merle?'

'You've got the credentials to do a whole lot no matter what I mind.'

Condor claimed one of two swivel chairs across the glass coffee table from Merle.

Good, thought Faye. The chair closest to the door. He could probably grab Merle if she made a break for it, definitely catch her before she could defeat the locks and chain.

'Con - *Vin* will keep you company while I follow procedure. Take a quick look through your apartment. To be sure we're alone. To be sure we're safe.'

'Does *safe* come with a warrant?'

'You don't need to worry about that,' said Faye.

Her eyes swept the kitchen: no visible knives, a landline phone on the wall.

The fifth-floor windows showed the night - Jesus, it's only ten o'clock! *Call her Merle* had a balcony big enough to stand on. Or jump from. A wet team could rappel down from the roof, swing *crash* bust through the glass with blazing machine guns.

Faye walked to the bedroom as Merle asked Condor: '*What do you know about me?*'

Faye kept the white bedroom door open so she heard him answer: '*Not enough.*'

In the bedroom. Windows with another suicide-sized balcony. A queen-sized bed. Dressers. Clothes hanging in a closet where a dozen pairs of shoes lined the floor, tidy couples waiting to be wanted.

Voices drifted in as Faye quietly slid open bureau drawers.

Merle asked again: '*What do you want from me?*'

Condor replied: '*That's . . . complicated.*'

380

Underwear, leotards, sweaters. Jeans, yoga-type tops and pants. No gun.

'Complicated is never the answer you want.'

'Let's wait until Faye -'

'So she's the boss? Who I should pay attention to?'

Framed photographs on the bedroom bureaus: Mother. Father. A middle-class house somewhere beyond the Beltway. A 1960s little girl jumping rope. A near-thirty Merle, fierce and glowing as she marches down the steps of the Capitol building. A cell-phone shot of this-age her stretching into a yoga pose while the class watches.

'You should pay attention to what's smart.'

'Who gets to decide "smart"? You?'

No wedding picture. No pictures of children. No pictures of men. Or women. No group photos from an office party. No snapshots of friends' kids, nephews or nieces.

Thumbtacks held picture postcards above the bedside table where a cell phone rested in its charger beside a landline extension. A piazza in some Italian city. The theater district of London at night. The gargoyles on Notre Dame in Paris.

Faye's stomach scar burned when she saw the postcard of Paris. America's trained spy lifted the edge of the Paris postcard, then each of the others: no stamps on the backs, no written notes or Merle's address. Had she gone there, gotten them for herself?

'Please, trust us.'

'Gosh, nobody's ever said that before.'

The bedside table that held the phones had two books - fictions, *Beautiful Ruins* by Jess Walter, a woman named Maile Meloy writing *Both Ways Is The Only Way I Want It*. The bedside table's bottom drawer rattled with tubes of this and jars of that, moisturizers, Vitamin E oil. Bottles of headache meds, over-the-counter sleep aids.

'*Doesn't matter if I trust you.*'

'*Matters to me.*'

Faye found a white cardboard box from a dress shop under the bed.

Pulled it out - filled with photos, letters, a menu from a long-gone cafe.

Closed the lid on that coffin of memories, pushed it back under the bed.

Found nothing under the pillows.

'*What happened to your face? It looks . . . smeared.*'

'*That's left over from trying not to be me.*'

'*How'd that work out?*'

'*I ended up here.*'

On the other side of the bed by the closet, a bedstand held a laptop computer. Faye clicked onto the email - messages about yoga classes from the head teacher at some studio where Merle subbed and taught the 'Sunday seniors seminar.' No Facebook or other social media accounts. Faye didn't bother to snoop for financial records, pushed the **POWER** button until the whisper whine of the laptop turned off.

'*Who are you now?*'

'*Better.*'

Faye slid open that bedstand table's bottom drawer. Odds and ends, an art deco glass pipe plus a plastic baggy with, *say*, a quarter cup of green marijuana.

She closed the drawer. Thought: *Good, Merle chooses to live like an outlaw.*

'*And all this is your "better" plan?*'

'*None of this was any plan until an hour ago.*'

The closet felt . . . culled. Gaps between the hangers with skirts and dresses, blouses, slacks, jackets. Empty spaces on the top shelf. Empty floorboards between the pairs of shoes, mostly office wear, but there, in the back, three pairs of out-of-fashion high-heeled shoes, the kind of rhinestone footwear that once carried a little black dress from one big-dollar event to another to a not-so-quiet end of the night.

'*So if I wasn't part of your plan, why have you been hawking me?*'

'*I was trying to work up the guts to do more than dream.*'

Faye knew she couldn't do a squirrel team full toss of the bedroom. Didn't think she needed to. Her eyes roamed over shelves of books. When she'd been recovering in the private hospital room, Faye'd avoided the TV mounted above her post-surgery bed for the controllable magic of books. Novels, not tomes of facts she knew were hollow of the hidden world where she lived and had just almost died. Now she stared at dozens of books on Merle's walls, knew all but a few were fictions, thought: *So she's looking for visions that make you feel something true, not data about other people trapped with you in a version called history. Looking for escape. Looking for . . .*

Whatever. Maybe Merle just liked the thrill of a good story.

'*This is no dream. This is the edge of a nightmare.*'

'*This is all I got.*'

Faye dropped Merle's cell phone into her black coat's pocket. Closed the laptop, carried it and the receiver for the landline phone in her left hand.

Bathroom, through the door beside the closet. A shower tub. Faye's free right hand opened the mirrored medicine cabinet: Nail scissors, lethal but only if you got lucky and knew what you were doing. More tubes and lotions. A half-full bottle of prescription pills she recognized from Condor's inventory as a generic antidepressant.

Voices in the living room came only as murmurs in this blue bathroom.

Faye toed open the cabinet under the sink. Toilet paper, other junk. Shelves held towels. A white bathrobe hung from a hook on the back of the bathroom door.

She walked back to the living room where Condor sat across from this woman they'd trapped who more and more scored like an innocent bystander.

Merle spotted her electronics under Faye's arm. 'Did you get what you need?'

Faye left the electronics on the glass coffee table.

Opened two closed doors in the living room: a big closet, coats for all seasons, boots, a pillow and blankets on the top shelf; second door, a small bathroom.

Faye took off her backpack purse and her black coat, put their weight over their reluctant hostess's phone and laptop. Felt Merle's eyes drawn to the gun on her belt, the magazine pouch. Felt the ambushed woman's eyes follow her.

Faye sat in the other chair, said: 'You have to understand our situation.'

'No I don't,' said Merle. 'I just have to survive it.'

Condor said: 'Go for more than just that.'

Take over. Faye said: 'I'm a Federal agent, CIA detailed to Homeland Security. Con - *Vin* . . . He's one of us, though how is not what you need to know. Someone penetrated the system, fit Vin for a frame. Now probably just wants him dead. Me, too.'

'Call for help, backup. Rescue. This is America, these are our streets.'

'If we call or email, we're in the system. We won't know who will hear and find us first. This might be America, but the streets belong to whoever makes us run.'

'*Run*? What if I get off the couch here and walk right out - '

'Merle, I'm sorry,' said Faye. 'That's not going to happen.'

Faye bored her hunter's gaze through the older woman sitting on the black couch.

'Oh,' whispered Merle. 'Okay. I get it.'

Merle blinked. 'Why do you keep calling him *Con*?'

Give trust to get trust. 'That's his classified code name. Condor.'

'Is anybody ever who they say they are?' said Merle.

'He is,' said Faye. 'Except . . .'

Condor beat her to it: 'I'm kind of crazy. Sometimes I space out. See ghosts. I'm officially not supposed to remember so that's what I'm trying to do.'

'Remember what?' said Merle.

'Yeah,' said Condor.

Get her to focus, thought Faye, *get her to what she needs to get over.*

Faye said: 'We're sorry for the truth, which is you're stuck with us now. We need a place to hide. Every other place is compromised. We need to figure out what to do, rest. We've hijacked your life - not because of anything you've done but because you're just who we came up with. And sorry, but we're going to keep doing that until we can leave. We're asking you to cooperate. Don't try to call anyone, email, whatever.'

'Got it, but really, I can just go to a hotel and - '

Faye said: 'We can't take that risk. You, out there, alone.'

'What risk did you just pin on me?'

'I won't lie to you. There's been . . . combat. Some deaths.'

'*Some deaths?*'

Condor said: 'Nothing we wanted, nothing we could avoid.'

Merle shook her head. '*Deaths. Combat.* Now you've signed me up for a . . . a *civilian casualty*, as *collateral damage.*'

'No,' said Faye. 'Nobody knows we're here. Nobody will know about you until we get back in with the good guys.'

'Your promise went from *nobody* to *somebody* in a blink.' Merle gave the younger woman a brokenhearted smile. 'It's good to know where I stand.'

'You don't know,' said Faye. 'Neither do we. But we know we're here, we know you're covered when you're with us, we know we'll die to keep you that way.'

'That's a hell of a promise for a first date.' Merle blinked. Let her gaze address both of the strangers in her house. 'Is that all you want?'

'Truthfully,' said Faye, 'we want all we can get.'

'Oh.'

Merle looked around where she called home. Shuddered. Seemed to shrink.

Then Faye saw her inhale this new reality.

Merle whispered: 'What do we do now?'

'Not much,' said Faye. 'Hunker down. We're safe, but we're both wiped out.'

'Are you hungry?' Merle shrugged. 'I buy giant frozen lasagnas, bake and cut it up and refreeze cooked portions for . . .'

She shrugged. 'For my old ordinary everyday life.'

'That's not where we are now,' said Faye. 'But we're still hungry.'

'Then let's deal with that,' said Merle. 'Can I . . . ?'

Faye nodded permission for the older woman to get off the couch, walk into her own kitchen, open her refrigerator and pull out an aluminum baking tub three-quarters full of tomato & meat sauce and pasta, put it on the counter -

Merle froze.

Whispered: *'Jesus!'*

Here it comes, thought Faye.

'You people show up and people are dead and you've got guns and I'm just . . .'

Faye said: 'Breathe. Just breathe. You can do this.'

'All my life, that's what I keep hearing.' Merle's eyes drifted to somewhere other than this kitchen, this apartment, this time of strangers and guns. 'You *can* do this. *You* can do this. *"You wanna do this"* doesn't . . . But you can do *this*.'

'You're doing great,' said Faye, braced for Merle to go off, *full hysterics*, throw the aluminum tub of lasagna through the trapped air of this white-walled kitchen, charge the front door, scream for neighbors, for help, for anyone but who was here to hear her.

The husky-voiced woman muttered: 'If I'm doing great, why am I here?'

Condor walked to two steps from Merle in the kitchen. Silver-haired, still wearing his black leather jacket, staring at this woman he'd stalked, told her: 'You're here because of me. The last thing I ever wanted was for you to be here like this. But you're all I've got, all I know, my only chance. You're who matters.'

Merle whispered: 'I shouldn't have gone for coffee yesterday.'

'Who knows where our *shouldn't-haves* start?' said Condor. 'All we've got is what we do.'

Merle stood in her white-walled kitchen, breathing hard.

Condor *not* touching her.

And here I am, thought Faye. *Two strangers to save while not getting whacked.*

Merle said: 'There's leftover salad.'

Five microwave beeps, clattering dishes, stools scraping across chessboard-sized white square kitchen tiles to the island counter, and there they were, Merle perched on a stool between the stoves and the counter, Condor sitting across from her with his plate of lasagna and leafy green salad and glass of water, the same nourishment in front of Faye, who perched on the stool closest to the door with her back to it but her eyes able to see the older couple on stools in the open kitchen of this apartment.

Where we are all trapped.

Faye and her comrade fugitive were almost done with the food that another time might have had some taste when Merle said: 'What happened?'

Condor said: 'The less you know, the better it will be for you.'

'Really? Ignorance equals safety?' Merle shook her head. 'Forget about trying to sell me that, not while I can't walk out my own front door.'

Faye saw Condor's eyes - tired, drooping, yet following the sway of the captive woman's hair as she shook her head *no*.

'What happened?' whispered Merle.

Faye sighed. 'Again, what we can tell you about this - '

'No,' interrupted Merle. 'That's not what I'm talking about now.

'*What happened?*' she said. 'Do you ever think about that? Here you are. With only who you've been. What you've done. What you thought was going to happen and never did. What little you can still do. Chunks of time fallen backwards away from you, and here you are locked in some landlord's mouse hole . . .'

She shook her head. Stared at the counter and the glass of water she had yet to drink.

'You're walking,' said Condor. 'See a store window that reflects cars, other people, but you don't see yourself in that mirror. Then you do, a face you barely recognize.'

Merle said: 'What kind of crazy are you?'

'Older.'

The two of them laughed.

Faye noted how Condor slumped on the stool. Remembered their captive's medicine cabinet. Asked her silver-haired colleague: 'Do you have any of your meds?'

'None that will make me go back to not seeing,' he said.

From his shirt pockets, from his black leather jacket in the living room, Condor fetched pill bottles he lined out on the counter by his red sauce–smeared dinner plate.

Faye watched Merle scan the bottle labels. Watched Merle read the label for Condor's bladder control pills that also increased his ability to . . . Saw that knowledge flash through Merle but couldn't tell what it meant to the older woman.

Faye said: 'You work at the Library of Congress?'

'Wow,' said Merle. 'Gun on your hip, door locked against *whoever*, you still ask the inescapable Washington question: "*What will you do?*"'

'Funny,' said Merle. 'No one picked me as a library type twenty years ago. Now I could retire. Sit locked in here with what little is left of my little life.'

She shook her head. 'Sorry, I don't usually let myself get that way, but . . .

'Yes, I work at the Library of Congress. The Motion Picture Archives. I watch old black-and-white movies. Catalog them, rank them in the line of movies waiting to be digitalized for whatever survives the apocalypse, artistic worth plus print quality plus . . .

'You don't care.' Merle shrugged. 'I spend my days watching other people's ideas play out on a small white screen in a dark room. I watch what I'm not.'

Condor said: 'Like most of us.'

Merle looked at him.

Turned to Faye. 'So how are you going to negotiate your way out of here and into where you'll get what you want? Or at least not dead.'

'Not a lot of negotiation happening,' said Faye.

'Bullshit,' said Merle, as shocked as her captors by her own force, her candor. 'This town is all one interlocked negotiation. You do what you gotta do to convince whoever's got the power to let you get what you can.'

'More to it than that,' said Condor.

'Don't tell me about more,' said Merle. 'I spent twelve years on the Hill, Congressman's office, Senator's office manager. Come to find out, it's all about power and what you can get from the power that is.'

'We're not there yet,' said Faye.

Merle nodded toward the silver-haired man slumped on a stool in her kitchen. 'You think he's going to get you somewhere?'

'*He*,' said Condor, 'might surprise you.'

'So far,' said Merle, '*yes*.

'But I'm going to call you Vin,' she added. 'Not Condor.'

Faye saw him smile, but with effort, exhaustion.

'Man, do you need to clean up!' Merle told Vin, who reeked of sweat, of gunpowder, who had sticky smears of brown on his face, his wrist.

'We need to sleep more than anything,' said Faye. 'So do you.'

Merle gave her back to the spies as she put their dirty dishes in her sink.

Faye told their captive's back: 'Here are the options.'

Options: such muted honesty.

'Best one,' said Faye, 'toss him in the shower, pop him full of pills he's got - '

'Right here,' said Condor. 'I'm still right here.'

'And we want you to stay,' said Faye. 'But if you don't get real sleep . . .

'The bed is our option,' continued Faye. 'Best is him in it like it is designed. Next best is us making up the mattress for him out here on the floor. I'll take the couch, not big enough for him to stretch comfortably and if he cramps . . .'

Merle turned: 'What about me?'

'You're in your bedroom,' said Faye. 'Don't want to deprive you of that.'

'Plus I'll be another door away from getting out.'

'Safer.'

'Oh. Sure.' Merle shrugged. 'Keep the bed like it is for him. I can sleep on the floor or . . . Or beside him.'

'I'll be out, I'll never know,' said Condor.

'Okay, whatever,' said Faye. 'Condor - *Vin*: leave your gun out here with me.'

'Just in case?' said Merle. 'In case of what? Or who? Me?'

Faye helped Condor unclip the holstered .45 from his belt. Merle watched Faye ask him what pills he should take after his shower, put them in a cup she handed to him, put the glass of water in his other hand.

'Do you have something he can sleep in?' Faye asked.

Merle shrugged. 'Something.'

Condor said: 'Have we said *thank you* yet?'

Before Merle could answer, he shook his head: '*Thank you*'s not enough.'

Condor shuffled into the bedroom.

Faye stopped Merle from following him with a touch on her arm.

She didn't jump, didn't resist, but . . .

Waiting, sensing, not trained, just . . . smart.

Faye said: 'Somehow he's the key to our way out of here. *All* of our way. So we need to keep him going as best as he can be. I'm asking you to keep an eye on him. If he fades more, if he starts to decompensate - '

'*De*compensate? What is he compensating for?'

'You do what you can, make sure I know what's going on with him.'

'And don't touch his gun, right?' Merle smiled. 'Oh, that's right: you took it.'

Faye saw the fierceness caught by the photo of her on the steps of the Capitol flash in those blue eyes, if only for a moment, if only like a memory of what used to be.

Merle walked into the bedroom, pulled the white door closed behind her, *clunk*.

Before Faye went to *call it sleep* on the black couch positioned so she'd bolt awake facing the front door, her Glock and Condor's .45 a grab away on the glass coffee table, she used the living room's half bath, and from its medicine cabinet took dental floss, tied a taut line between the knob of the closed bedroom door and a tall drinking glass on the kitchen counter. Faye pushed one of the living room's black swivel chairs against the front door, knew it would only slow a SWAT breach by a second, maybe two.

But a second, maybe two . . .

In the second, maybe two after she snapped the kitchen into darkness but before she flipped off the light switch in the living room, she stared at the bedroom's white door, that closed white door.

17

BE MY PILLOW
- Jesse Colin Young, 'Darkness, Darkness'

This is how her bedroom smells. Warm cotton sheets whiffed with musk. Vanilla wisps. Or maybe not vanilla. Some other bath & beautify lotion. Plus cirrus clouds of Ben-Gay or another sore-muscles liniment, something practical. But her. Here.

Night spinning tired everything aches skin so yuck clammy!

Behind him, Merle said: 'Are you seeing ghosts?'

She's standing there. You turned around and there she was. Looking at you.

Saying again: 'Ghosts? Are you seeing ghosts?'

Tell her: 'No. Yes.'

She blinked, blushed. 'Let's pretend you're a poet and not a killer, a crazy.'

'I'll be who you need.'

'What about *want*?'

'Can't promise that.'

'Who can?' She frowned.

Took the cup of pills from his hand.

'You're holding on by your fingernails,' she told him. 'Gotta hurt.'

'You can't ever make the hurt stop.'

'Maybe, but you can back it off, get some peace. Like it or not, that's your best choice now. You can pass out where you stand, or if you got enough left in you, you can take a shower - and man, do I recommend that. Then your pills, then bed.

'The bed's just for sleep.' Her blue eyes burned. 'You don't have a gun.'

'I couldn't use it like that. I wouldn't.'

Nodding, agreeing with him to convince herself.

'Take off your shirt,' she said.

And he did.

Gave its blue wrinkle to her.

She tossed it on a chair by the door, the closed white door.

He didn't wait to be told what she wanted.

Kicked off his shoes.

Took off his black jeans.

She held those pants out from her. Felt the weight of whatever was in his pockets, of the ammo mags in their pouch on his belt. Tossed the black jeans onto the chair.

'What are you wearing?' she said, staring at his revealed second skin.

'Thermal underwear,' he said. 'I didn't know how cold it would be out there.'

A slow-motion movie walked her to a brown cardboard box in the far corner of the room. All of her moved when any of her changed. Her blond & gray hair undulated in soft waves on her shoulder, her strong back. Her arms floated with purpose. The roundness of her hips, taut for any age in her blue jeans, rolled from step to step, then he saw them rise out as she bent over, pulled things from that brown cardboard box.

She carried a ragged black sweatshirt and thin gray sweatpants to him.

'Here,' she said.

Could have thrown the sweats, but she chose to hand them to you.

'At the Fifty Plus class I teach, people leave gear and clothes, books, water. I wash the clothes, take the Lost &

Found box to class, but if nobody claims them . . . Every few weeks, there's some charity pickup.'

He held up the black sweatshirt to read its gold logo: **LUX ET VERITAS.** Whatever that meant, what meant a universe more was what else he read emblazoned gold on black.

'*Montana*,' he said. 'How did you know?'

She shook her head. 'It's just a sweatshirt I found.'

'Nothing cosmic. Not a *clong*.'

'A what? Why? Is that where you're from? Montana?'

'That's where I found out I was me.'

'You're a spy,' she said. 'A killer. Not a poet.'

'Yeah.'

'Go shower,' she said. 'There's a blue towel on the shelf. You're not a conditioner kind of guy, but one of the bottles in the tub is shampoo. And on a shelf under the sink, there's an unopened toothbrush: the big-box store makes you buy five.'

'I have my own. I think. Out there,' he said, pointing to the closed white door.

'We're here, don't go drifting back or we'll never get you where you're going.'

She pointed to the bathroom.

In there, slump, your back pressing against the door, your socks gripping tiny white tiles, close your eyes, she's not there, she can't see you, you can let go, let go.

Like inhales shift to exhales, his mind billowed back and forth between clarity and confusion. What kept him conscious in that bright bathroom was the scent of where he was, the pine ammonia of cleanliness, the vanillas of rejuvenation, the damp metal and porcelain hardness of *here* and *now* and *real*.

Fighting off the thermal top was almost more than he could do. He worked it up his chest, both hands inside it as he pulled the shirt over his face - *Stuck!* - staggered around the bathroom, bumped his right shin on the toilet, suffocating, arms pinned crossed over his head inside the clinging -

Off, face clear, dropping the top onto the floor, staring down at his minor victory.

Take what you can get.

He peeled down the long underwear pants, worked them and his socks off. Collapsed more than sat on the toilet, did what he had to do and didn't let his eyes close.

Next thing he knew, he's in the shower, hot water pounding down on him as he reaches back to pull the plastic shower curtain closed -

Psycho, Alfred Hitchcock movie, Janet Leigh showering behind a plastic curtain, not seeing Anthony Perkins come into her bathroom with a butcher knife.

Maronick jerks from bullets you shot into his bathroom stall.

Condor left the shower curtain open.

The water, *oh the water* pounding down on his skull, his face, his closed eyes, steam opening his sinuses, his pores. Ribbons of brown swirled down the drain. He found the shampoo bottle, a bar of soap, used both two or three times, lost count.

His arms burned as he used the blue softness and toweled himself dry, pulled on the gray sweatpants - way too big, barely held up by the frayed drawstring. He struggled into the black sweatshirt. **LUX ET VERITAS** pointed toward the steamed-over mirror. The sleeve he wore wiped the wet fog off that glass.

There you are. Here you are.

'Wow,' whispered Condor.

The toothbrush he found under her sink was red. Her toothpaste was minty fresh.

Merle stood up from sitting on the bed as he opened the bathroom door.

She wore tightly tied green yoga pants. A bulky blue sweatshirt. With no buttons up its front. The woman held the cup of his pills out to him.

Said: 'I put in an extra painkiller. Generic. Over the counter. Works.'

Handed him an aluminum drinking bottle, its top screwed off.

'I make up a bunch of these for class use,' she said. 'With paper cups, or that would defeat the purpose. Store-bought low-cal lemonade with concentrated Vitamin C I dissolve in it. Stopping colds in my class helps me as much as them.'

Lemonade. Cool, tangy.

He swallowed the pills. She took the cup, the now-empty aluminum bottle.

'You should sleep on the side of the bed near the bathroom. Get in, I'll be back.'

She went into the bathroom. Closed that door.

He heard her brushing her teeth. The flush of the toilet. Sink water.

Then she's out, leaving the bathroom door open, snapping off that light.

Condor sank under covers into warmth he hadn't felt in what seemed like forever.

She circled around the foot of the bed.

Watch the ceiling, look up, look at heaven not her.

The bed sagged, the covers fluttered. He felt the heat of her in there with him.

'Forgot,' said Merle.

Condor turned his head to the right.

Saw her blue-sweatshirt-with-no-buttons form bent over her side of the bed.

Sitting up straight, she put an aluminum bottle on her bedstand, turned toward him, a second aluminum bottle in her hand and she's reaching, *leaning* across . . .

Over me.

He lay beneath her as her blue sweatshirt blocked out the lamplit white ceiling. He saw only that blue sweatshirt. Believed in the sway, *the sway* of her breasts.

Clunk went the metal bottle on the bedstand beside him, for him.

She turned out his lamp.

Pulled herself back across him -

Gone, she's gone, pressure heat smell still -

Merle snapped out her lamp, dropped them, this room, this bed, into darkness.

He felt her stretch under the covers. Close enough to reach out and touch.

Falling through soreness and pain . . .

Not yet! Not yet!

Merle whispered: 'Why me?

'You said I wasn't in your plan,' she told the man lying beside her. 'You said "*personal*." You've been . . . eyeing me for months. To "work up your guts." Why me?'

Nothing left but true: 'You're gravity I can't escape.'

His sore heart labored beats in the darkness.

'What am I supposed to do with that?' she said.

'What you can,' he said. 'What you want.'

She whispered his last name.

Said: 'You're the only *Vin* on the Library of Congress's website of staff passes.'

Said: 'The photo's not that good.'

Warm, so warm under here.

Merle let the word come out again: 'Vin.'

Then whispered: 'Condor.'

Swirling warm blackness going g -

18

SAY YOUR LIFE BROKE DOWN
- Richard Hugo, 'Degrees of Gray in Philipsburg'

What have I done?

Faye lay on the black sofa in someone else's dark apartment. She lay absolutely still, as if that would stop time, as if her stillness could make the last two days disappear.

Lay still and do not, DO NOT tremble or shake or vomit or cry.

Or cry.

A drinking glass stood sentry on the kitchen counter. The door's peephole was an eye of distorted light above the chair pushed against that locked portal to buy a second, maybe two for her to not get killed, not get machine-gunned as she tried to rise from this black leather couch of darkness.

Pulitzer Prize–winning reporter David Wood later that year would report that the most common medical trauma immediately suffered by American troops who survived combat in Iraq and Afghanistan translated into plain English as 'deep sorrow.'

What did I do? What did we do?

Hostiles. The Opposition. A wet team targeting her and Condor.

That's who they were in the subway battle.

Not our guys doing their job, my job, doing their duty, their righteous duty.

Playback:

Nobody shouts 'Police!' or 'Federal agents!' or 'Freeze!' *Ambush or oversight?*

The woman on the escalator shot Condor first - but with a Taser, non-lethal.

Not a classic hit. A snatch move? The first-choice neutralization?

Condor shoots her, and I . . .

The black man draws, shoots at me . . . with a silencer-rigged pistol.

You don't use a silencer to take prisoners.

Shot him dropped him he didn't die. *Not from me.*

The team at the top of the escalator stairs threw bullets at us, not selecting who they hit, friendly fire killing their own team member. They didn't care about containing and covering everything as an Eyes Only secret. Taking us out had - *has* - a higher priority than the cost of any casualties or chaos.

The gunner the train hit.

The man I shot on the red-tile platform.

Monkey Man blasted back into a subway car, roared away dead or alive.

Sami said he'd pull our people - *No*: said he'd do what he could. He's the man, the guru, the go-to guy, so if he could, he would, he trusts - *trusted* me that much.

So if not Sami . . . It's them. Whoever they are.

And *if then* it was or *if now* it's become Sami . . . We are so fucked. Dead.

What happened to my life, when did the fall-apart start: Paris?

Or with Chris?

When you let yourself have something to lose, you do.

Faye stared at the bedroom holding Condor and Merle behind a closed door.

Bring him in safe, *yes*, call it an objective, but the mission, *her* mission was to nail who killed her partner, who was trying to kill her, who made her kill.

What's worth all this?

My life. What I pledge it to by what I do.

A deep breath flowed into her, pushed her breasts against the bullet-proof vest and suddenly she felt like an anaconda was squeezing her ribs, the giant snake crushing her and *breathe, just breathe, got to -*

Faye stopped her hyperventilating.

Fall apart when you're finished. If you fall apart now you are finished.

Not me. Not now. Not yet.

Fuck them. Fuck that.

Oh, but *oh* she was so tired. So heavy with the vest, with the weight of two guns waiting on the glass coffee table beside where she lay on this black leather couch, with the weight of a man crucified over a fireplace, a man getting smashed by a train, a man crumpling to the red tiles of a subway platform beyond the smoke from her pistol.

She imagined floating up from the couch, the ballistic vest falling away from her. And the exhaustion and pain and soreness and seared memories . . . floated away, gone.

Faye saw herself naked.

The scar erased from her stomach.

Standing in this apartment. Facing the curtains drawn open from the floor-to-ceiling sliding windows. Standing there naked with no *musts*, no *shoulds*, no *cans*, no *who will die* consequences, no Mission no Op no Duty. With dreams she could believe. Standing in front of a transparent plane as she spreads her arms wide, her chest and heart uncovered as she smiles at the glass that won't shatter from a sniper's bullet.

Or if it does, it won't be her finger on the killing trigger.

Won't be a squeezed betrayal from her *us*.

She stands there, arms spread wide, naked in front of the night.

Waiting for the sound of busting glass.

19

THE TIME TO HESITATE
- The Doors, 'Light My Fire'

From beside you in the dark bed, she says: 'You're awake.'

Condor exhaled the sigh he'd been holding back. She was already awake. His disturbing motion wouldn't matter now.

He told her: 'Yes, but you can go back to sleep.'

'It's almost dawn. You got up in the night - bathroom, I know, it's all right. Sometimes it's nice to hear you're not alone. Are you okay?'

'Are you kidding?'

The bed trembled with their quiet laughter.

'You have to go again.' Not a question from her. Matter of fact.

He slid from the sheets without looking back. Inside the bathroom, door closed, light blasted on, he did what he did, washed his hands.

Looked in the mirror.

You're here. This is real.

Snapped out the light.

Opened the bathroom door to find she'd snapped on a nightlight.

'You look better than before,' she told him.

'Better than before isn't much.' He shrugged. 'Six hours' sleep in a real bed.'

What should you do?

He got back in bed. Under the covers. Lay on his right side. Facing her.

She'd propped herself up on two pillows, lay on her left side, facing him. Her shoulders in the blue sweatshirt were out from under the sheet.

'This could be my last good sleep,' she said. 'Today all your *this* could kill me.'

'Today can always kill you.'

She tossed her head to get strands of long hair off her face. 'Are you scared?'

'Oh yeah.'

'Of dying?'

'Sure, but . . . I'm more scared of you dying. Of not doing what I can right.'

'How's "*doing what you can*" working for you so far?'

'Evidently not so good, I ended up here - I mean: putting you here.'

'So I noticed.' Her smile lacked joy. 'Though I get some of the blame.'

'Why blame?'

'What I *coulda shoulda* to not be here. Where I could have ended up.'

'Where's that?'

'Not stuck in all this alone, waiting for trouble to knock on my door.'

'Why are you alone?'

She stared at him.

'That was one thing I couldn't figure when . . .'

'When you were stalking me.'

'No malice, but . . . okay, I hacked your employment cover sheet. You checked SINGLE. No children. Not married, widowed, divorced. I don't understand why.'

'Why what?'

'No woman as . . . great - '

She laughed.

'. . . like you should be single.'

'I know a dozen women my age and younger who are smarter and more accomplished and way *way* prettier and believe me: far, *far* nicer, but who are walking around with only their shadows. Like me.'

'But why you?'

'You want to know,' she said. Not a question.

'You want to tell me,' he said. Not a question.

'Maybe I don't want to ruin my image in your eyes,' she said. 'Could be risky.'

'I want to see the real you.'

'Your real is crazy.'

Oh so slightly came a smile to his lips.

'I'm a member of the jilted mistresses club,' said Merle.

'Do you want to know *who*?' she said.

Condor shrugged. 'If he's gone, who cares.'

'Who he is makes the story.'

And he guessed. Said: 'You mean *what* he is.'

'Oh, he's an asshole, but made for this town.

'I was twenty-four, nowhere near as smart as I thought. I was born when JFK got elected, thought that was somehow . . . magical. I got here in 1984 when Reagan ruled and things were going to be right, based on principles, an America for everybody.

'He was a freshman Republican Congressman from one state over. Young enough to be cool, old enough to feel like he was more substantive than me. I knew his district, parlayed an internship with my own Senator into working for - for David.'

She told Condor - told *Vin* - the man's last name.

Meant little to Condor, to *Vin*: another cosmetic face on TV.

'His daddy had medium money, the country-club set. David mastered the sincere look, rumpled Ivy League polish. Knew where to stand to catch the light. Great hair. Could make you feel like you were the one in the crowded room he was talking to.

'In college, he knocked up a hometown princess. Her folks had money, too, so they had a white wedding extravagance, a merger, a kid, big fish in a small city, but he . . .

'He didn't have a spy war, an operation, a mission, a *whatever* you're stuck in. He had big ideas. Or so I thought. Nobody knows how to work a soundbite better than David, whether he's talking to TV cameras or across a pillow.'

Vin's cheek burned on the pillow that held him.

'He was crusading, that was why he couldn't leave his wife. A divorce would wreck his re-election. He couldn't jeopardize his chance to serve. How dare I be selfish. Then it was the first Senate race. Then the second Senate race, the one that would set him up to *really* do what had to be done even if by then I wondered what that meant. But I hung in there - *Yeah*, don't tell me: apt image. On camera, he was a no-divorce religion, no abortion, though he didn't blink when it came to paying cash for . . .'

She looked away.

'I'd go to movies alone to be not waiting by the phone or the clock.

'He had great timing,' she said. 'I'd finally admitted he was one of the herd who come here to *be* rather than *do*, that he only followed the big bucks and floodlights and *the right kind of people*. But for "*us*," I was going to give him one more chance, one . . .

'One day. That's all it took to end thirteen years. One conversation in a fucking underground parking garage where nobody could see if I made a scene. "*These things happen.*" And by the way, best *for me* if I left his Senate staff, left Congressional staffing, the only work I knew. "*You like movies, right?*" He'd engineered an archivist post in the Library of Congress. Where I could even earn a pension. As long as he protected my job at the budget table. He made that sound like kindness.

'Two months later, suddenly divorce became okay. Weeks after his, he married a divorcee. They'd been fucking long before either his first wife or I were gone. The bitch's first husband was an internet genius from the defense contractors' sprawl out by Dulles Airport who thought life's reward for his hard work was a willowy model nine years younger than me. She walked with his millions all the way to queen for the now-distinguished white-haired Senator I'd paid my youth to.'

She sighed. 'Still think I'm worth looking at?'

'You're worth a lot of seeing.'

Condor swore she blushed in the soft light as she said: 'What about your exes?'

Flashes.

'Whoever they were, they got me here.'

'In trouble. On the run.'

She closed, then opened her eyes. 'Can I get out of this okay?'

'If we're all lucky.'

'You just got to find the best deal - right?'

'We're meat on some table. I don't know if there's any deal.'

'This is Washington,' she said. 'There's always a deal. If you've got clout.'

'Me, Faye out there: What you see is what we've got.'

'Then maybe you don't know how to look. Or who you have on your side.'

'Besides her?' said Condor.

'Guess that's where we start.'

'*We?*'

'You don't give a girl much choice.'

He said: 'Why did you stay in D.C.? You had experience, education - probably a little clout you could have leveraged from *David*. You could have gone to . . .'

Condor blinked. 'I think I always wanted to live in San Francisco.'

'L.A.,' she said. 'Warm. No fog. You drive away from what goes wrong. And in L.A., people are honest about pretending to be somebody else.'

'Why didn't you go?'

'The falling-apart years,' she said.

'I know about them,' said Condor.

Merle gave him a smile. 'So you said.

'Me,' she continued, 'I might not have been wicked smart, but I was savvy functional when I was with David. Afterwards . . . Depression. Self-pity. Feeling stupid. If you cop to that, you're guilty of it. Inertia and kind bosses kept me in paychecks.

'Just as I was coming out of my cage of mirrors, Mom got everything that steals your last years. All she had was social security and what I could send back to Pennsylvania. I would go up and see her whimpering in a county nursing home that was all we could afford. Red Jell-O and the sound of scampering rats.

'The echo of dirt hitting her coffin was still in the air when I got lucky cancer.'

'There's no such thing as - '

'Yeah there is. It's the kind you survive without too much damage and only a small mountain of medical bills, thanks to health insurance from the job you gotta keep to keep the insurance. Nothing special, only about ten million of us like that.

'So,' she said straight into his stare, 'here I am. With all my reasons *why*. No magic. No second chances. Men look past me for younger women. Women who didn't lose their chance to have babies. But I have a job I don't hate, a life I'm doing. All on my own. And until last night, all I had to fear was the real world.'

'Then I showed up.'

'Knock-knock,' she said.

Sheets rustled. He felt her legs shift somewhere in the bed.

'Let's say you win,' said Merle. 'Then what?'

'Then I'm done being a target getting shot at by whoever, however, why-ever. Then maybe my life gets a new freedom. Depending on what I remember.'

'And what you forget.'

She sat up in the bed. The sheets fell to her lap. Merle turned so he saw the tumble of her gray-and-blond hair on the back of her blue sweatshirt. When she faced him again, she was unscrewing an aluminum water bottle. Held the lid in one hand while she drank, lowered the hard bottle from her lips, her now wet lips, handed a drink to him.

He drank without thought: fortified lemonade.

Passed the hard bottle back to her. Watched her drink again.

'Now we taste the same,' said Merle as she screwed the top back on.

She put the shiny metal bottle back on the bedstand, turned so she sat facing him. Her crossed yoga pants legs were mostly out of the bedcovers.

'If you lose, I'm fucked, right?' she said. 'You made our interests coincide.

'But if you win and get out of this,' she said, 'then what about me?'

'Then I'll do everything I can for you.'

' "Everything" is a whole lot of ransom for a first kidnapping.'

He felt himself smile with her. Felt his heart pounding his ribs. Felt . . .

Merle said: 'Was I *really* the only place you could go?'

'Yes.'

'Truth?'

'Yes, but . . . You were the only place I wanted to go.'

'I've never been somebody's only.'

Breathe. Just breathe.

The dark night outside her bedroom window faded toward morning gray.

Last time I saw that, I was in the garden of the dead.

Like a beautiful Buddha, Merle sat cross-legged and tangled up in the sheets on the bed in front of him. The ends of the drawstring securing her yoga pants dangled to her lap below the edge of her blue sweatshirt that covered trembling roundness he made his eyes leave, look up, see her tousled thick morning gray-and-sunshine hair. Her lemonade lips parted for soft, shallow breaths. He saw her face full on toward his as he sat across the bed from her, only an arm's length away, only that far from his touch. He felt all of him weighed by her cobalt blue eyes.

Her arms crossed and pulled off the blue sweatshirt, let it butterfly away.

She shook her head to settle her long hair. 'You want to see the rest of my real.'

A truth, a question, a dare, a plea, an offer, *everything*.

Her breasts were tears full with time and gravity *oh yes* swollen top-hatted pink.

She whispered: 'Good thing we've got all the right drugs.'

Like a laugh as she unfolded toward him, yoga graceful, sitting again but now right in front of him, between his accommodating open legs, her arm holding her weight through her palm splayed on the bed a breath away from his aching groin as she took his right hand in her heart-side fingers, floated it to her warm breast to fill his grasp.

The lemonade fire of that first real kiss.

20

MAYBE TOGETHER WE CAN GET SOMEWHERE
- Tracy Chapman, 'Fast Car'

Knocking.

On the bedroom door.

Faye turned off the faucets on the sink in the bathroom across from the bedroom. She'd kept that bathroom door open. Refused to be trapped blind in there. Morning light filled this commandeered apartment. Condor's .45 lay on the bathroom sink. Her Glock rode in its holster on her hip. She wore the ballistic vest and pants from yesterday.

Yesterday, that was only yesterday.

She dried her palms on her pant legs.

Tucked Condor's pistol into the belt over her spine.

Stepped out of the bathroom without looking in its mirror so she could better ignore the best chance for Condor and her to escape, survive, and perhaps even triumph.

Knocking.

'Just a minute.'

Faye stepped to the kitchen counter where a water glass stood tethered to the bedroom door. Lifted the glass free of its tether, a strand of dental floss that then fell like a fishing line to the kitchen floor and along the bedroom's white door.

'Okay.' Faye stood back to avoid a charge-out. Her gun hand hung empty.

The bedroom door eased open and out came Merle wearing a clean blue blouse and fresh jeans. Her curly blond-gray hair looked damp, her arms cradled . . .

'Those are Condor's clothes,' said Faye.

'Yes.'

Merle pulled the bedroom door shut before Faye could see much in that room. Her eyes dodged Faye's. The older woman walked with nervous courage to the stainless-steel washer-dryer unit built into her kitchen island. She kept her back to Faye as she loaded the washer-dryer - a tub Faye had already checked for stashed weapons.

'Who told you to knock?' said Faye.

'We thought it would be smart. A good idea.'

We, noted Faye.

'And now you're washing his clothes.'

'They needed it. I can do yours next. I'm making coffee. Want some?'

'What's he doing in there?' Faye nodded to the closed bedroom door while her hostage poured coffee beans into a grinder, found a brown paper filter for a drip glass pot.

The grinder whined for thirty seconds. Anyone would have known better than to try to speak above that noise. Faye watched Merle's face brew answers for thirty seconds.

Merle shook the ground coffee into the filter-lined, cone-shaped dripper on top of the empty glass coffeepot and thus logically kept her eyes on what she was doing as she answered Faye: 'You told me to see if I had clothes for him.'

Merle watched herself fill a white teakettle with water from the steel sink faucet.

'What else did you see?' asked the woman with the gun.

Merle swung the teakettle from the shut-off sink to the stove, set the white kettle on a black burner, turned its stove knob to birth a *whump* of blue flame.

Merle met the younger woman's eyes. 'What do you want to ask?'

'I heard him cry out in there. Twice.'

'And yet you didn't come running to save your partner.' The older woman's shrug raised her lips in a smile. 'Twice, huh. Maybe he's having a good day.'

'*Twice* is two truths that you better remember,' said Faye. 'His day will be a hell of a long way from good. And your day is going to be no better than his.'

'Or yours.'

'We're in this together,' said Faye.

'Can we sit while the water boils? You look almost as bad as I feel.'

Faye let the older woman choose her chair in the living room. Sat on the couch where she could watch the nervous archivist, the apartment entrance, and that white, *still closed* bedroom door.

The woman old enough to be Faye's mother said: 'Did you get any sleep?'

'Enough,' lied Faye.

Damp blond-and-gray hair nodded toward the closed bedroom door. 'He got six hours. He could use six days.'

'Couldn't we all.'

Faye said: 'When I was a kid, they told me it took six days to make this world.'

'Do you have that kind of faith?'

'I want that kind of hope.'

'Hope and perseverance and doing exactly what you're supposed to do when you're supposed to do it is our - *your* - best chance to make it in this world.'

'And you're in charge of *supposed to*.'

Faye nodded.

'I wouldn't want your job.'

Let's hope not, thought Faye.

'I knew a woman cop - police officer. We were friends for a few years. She was mostly plainclothes on the Capitol Hill police force - Congress's force, security guards mostly, one of the *what*, twenty-some kinds of badges like yours out there in this city. We used to go out for dinner sometimes. Drinks. Check in with each other.'

'Who is she?'

'For nine years she's been Mrs. Her Boss Finally Retired And Divorced and they moved to Ohio where he's from.'

'Does she still check on you?'

'Nobody checks on me.' A sad smile signaled some greater truth in the older woman's words. 'Look, I'm scared and nervous and trying to get to know you and this thing . . . It's all up to you.'

'Yeah, but it's all about him.'

'What about him?' said the woman who'd emerged from that bedroom.

'You can probably tell me as much about the man as I can tell you,' said Faye. Kept her tone neutral when she added: 'More.'

The teakettle whistled.

'What I can tell you won't matter to what you gotta do,' said Merle, her yoga grace overriding her years and fears and unfolding her from her chair to walk into the kitchen, turn the fire out under the white teakettle.

Bullshit, thought Faye: *You've built a bond with him and you're banking on it.*

Her mind's eye blinked. *I hope some of fucking him was for real.*

She knew Condor hoped so, too, even knowing what they all knew.

Merle poured steaming water over the coffee beans in the cone atop the glass pot.

Water trickling over ground coffee seemed to cue the older woman. She whirled, stared at Faye standing there wearing a ballistic vest and sidearm, said: 'Does your mother know what you do?'

'Does yours?' said Faye.

414

'Never did.' Merle sighed. 'And now I'm never going to get that chance.'

She blinked. Asked Faye: 'How crazy is he?'

'Too much,' answered Faye.

'Or not enough.' The aroma of brewing coffee filled the apartment. 'He thinks this is all happening because he was starting to lose the crazy that makes him forget.'

'Maybe, but that's the kind of intel development that only he would know.'

'Or maybe somebody inferred the possibility,' said Merle. 'And sometimes, the possibility of what might happen is enough to motivate somebody to act, strike first.'

'I thought you were a mild-mannered librarian,' said Faye as she watched the woman in the kitchen take one, take two, take three cups from the cabinet.

'I watch a lot of movies,' said Merle. 'And I worked for a movie called Congress.'

'They need a better script.'

The women shared a smile.

'Speaking of work,' said Faye. 'What about your job?'

Merle looked at the practical watch on her wrist. 'I can call in sick or - *No*.'

'*No?*'

'Better,' said the older woman who'd survived decades in Washington, D.C. 'I can call my boss and say I want to save my sick days but take some time off now, and offer to let him count it as me being in that whole "sequester" budget-cutting mess the boys and girls in Congress forced on us. Him furloughing me for a few days will give him an out when the orders come down from our budget director, and they're gonna come, we're all just waiting to see if the cuts are going to make us personally bleed. I get credit for taking one for the team and nobody will come asking or looking for me.'

She shrugged. 'As if they would anyway.'

Merle lifted the cone filled with dripped-through ground beans off the glass pot now filled with brown liquid she poured into two cups before setting down that pot of scalding brew she could have thrown at Faye's eyes, asked: 'Milk? Sugar?'

'Black,' answered Faye.

'Straight,' said Merle as she passed the cup to her captor. She opened the refrigerator, topped off her own cup from a carton of milk she left on the counter.

Merle took a sip of her coffee, held the innocent cup in both her hands, said: 'What else can I do to help?'

'So now you're on our team?'

'Looks like you two brought back the draft.'

'And you trust us? Believe us?'

'You mean how do I know you are who you say you are?' Merle shrugged. 'How do you know anybody is who they say they are?'

She shook her head. 'We lie to ourselves about who we see, we lie to ourselves about who we are. Then we buy our own lies and try to spend them as our lives.'

Merle gave Faye a smile both of them knew came from irony not amusement, said: 'Guns are the ultimate reality check. You've got them, not me. But even without them, the odds of you two both being this particular crazy add up to unlikely, so who you are is probably who you say you are. Mostly.'

'You play the odds?' asked Faye.

'I play what I get,' answered Merle. 'Now what else can I do?'

'Let's talk about that after he joins us.' Faye nodded to the closed bedroom door.

The older woman with damp gray-blond hair smiled as she raised the cup of milk-colored coffee and before she sipped from it said: 'Are you sure he's coming out?'

21

IF I COULD HIDE, 'NEATH THE WINGS
- John Stewart, 'Daydream Believer'

Close your eyes.

Lie on this bed.

Pretend you belong here.

That you deserve this.

That no one wants to kill you.

Alone & naked & flat on his back, Condor felt soft sheets on the mussed bed where he'd collapsed, his ankles dangling above the floor that led out of this room, this wonderful room smelling of sea and musk, out to the rest of the apartment where she'd gone, where Faye and the guns were, and from there down the green hall to the elevator or stairs, a street of residential Washington, roads that led to the monuments and Capitol and White House and Complex Zed and a mortuary in suburban Virginia with a crematorium that created ashes no one would ever scatter in some garden of the known dead.

Stay here in this sunlit bedroom.

Afterward, both of them naked under the sheets, his head on her pillow, his heart her pillow, a cloud of the lilac shampoo scent from her gray-blond hair floating with the musk of some past perfume and the scent, that scent, that warm sea scent.

Merle'd said: 'Was it like you imagined?'

'Better. I was too worried about getting shot to be too nervous.'

'Funny, I was worried about getting shot, too.'

He felt her smile and she said: '*Bang*.'

The bed trembled with their soft chuckle.

Merle whispered: 'What else should I be worried about?'

'Getting shot tops the list. Then everything else until it's all back to normal.'

'Maybe I'm worried about that, too.' He felt her fingers move on his chest. 'Maybe it's lucky that my normal changed.'

She whispered: 'Should I be worried about you?'

'Getting shot?'

'You know what I mean,' she said.

He didn't, wondered, said: 'Whoever I am, it's too late to change.'

Condor turned on his side so she could see his face even if he knew *she knew* better than to trust his expression, said: 'But none of me wants you hurt. Hurt any way.'

Her eyes dropped from his. Her lips softly kissed his bare chest.

She didn't look up, said: 'What should I do?'

'Grasp your true reality,' said Condor. 'Course, that doesn't mean you can do anything about it, but then at least you've got a chance at taking your shot.'

'Are you saying it all depends on your perspective?'

'Bullets don't care about your perspective. They only care where you stand.'

He felt the mattress rise and fall with his four breaths.

She said: 'So we better stand up.'

Merle swung away from him, a swirl of long gray-blond hair and round flesh and bare feet kissing the floor, her nude spine to him, the yoga-conditioned swell of her hips curving before his eyes and then her hand reached back.

'Come on,' she said. 'We need a shower.'

She put Condor under the nozzle spraying hot water into the white porcelain shower-tub, stepped in with him, closed the shower curtain - a gray plastic sheet colored by artwork, a translucent reproduced painting of nineteenth-century Parisians from a moneyed class walking in the park where everything seemed safely controlled.

He soaped and shampooed so as not to bump her, white suds of lather washing down her water-slick chest, sliding over her low-slung full breasts, her slight paunch that age won from exercise, down her loins, her legs that were just the right length of long. He stepped back to let water spray her face, rinse away the lather and scents of yesterday.

Then she stood as far away from him in the shower-tub as the porcelain and walls and plastic shower curtain allowed. Water beat down him, propelled drops flying around his blocking bulk to hit the edges of her naked front as her blue eyes pushed him.

She said: 'I know one thing you're worried about.'

Condor felt his breath deepen, his pulse race.

'*Yes*,' she said: 'You made me have to be here with you.'

Oh so slowly took one barefooted step on the wet porcelain tub toward him, took another until only a breath separated their naked fronts as water beat down.

Merle said: 'But I choose to be here like this.'

She wrapped her arms around him and held her bare flesh to his.

How many breaths they'd stayed there, he didn't know, didn't count, didn't think.

Then her hands moved behind him, faucets cranked off and the spray of the water fell to nothing but drips from the showerhead, then silence.

Metal loops screeched on the shower rod as she jerked open the plastic art curtain.

'I'll get us towels.'

She left him standing there, naked and wet in her white tub.

Pulled three towels off bathroom shelves. Wrapped her hair up in one so the towel became a turban. Wrapped a second towel around her chest so the downy soft white cloth covered her from the top of her breasts to mid-thigh. Tossed the third towel to him and smiled as he surprised himself and caught it.

'We need to do laundry.' She walked back to the bedroom.

Condor stepped from the tub, drying off as he hurried to be with her.

Found her in the bedroom, stacking his clothes on the chair, a pile on the nearby table from his black jeans pockets of the money and stray receipts and his handkerchief.

Merle rambled: 'I don't know about your thermal underwear, but I'll wash them, too. Supposed to be like a real April spring for the next couple days. I don't have men's shirts, but your blue shirt should wash out okay enough, brown stains on the collar, weird, but we'll see. I'm not much for ironing, but if it's too wrinkled, there's a ratty black sweater in the Lost & Found box that might fit you or over it and . . .'

She realized he was standing there.

Staring at her.

Or at least . . . toward her.

'What?' she said. Smiled.

Frowned: 'Vin? Are you . . . here? Are you okay?'

'You don't have to do my laundry. Our laundry. You're not . . .'

'I'm not going to make it if they can smell you coming,' she said.

'Whoever they are,' he told her.

'That's your end.'

She turned from the laundry pile in the chair and faced Condor. Unwound the towel turban, rubbed her gray-blond wet hair dry, squeezed its long locks with the towel she then dropped onto the laundry pile.

Merle closed her eyes. Shook her head from side to side, her long wet locks whipping out this way & that way flinging water drops from her hair like commanded rain. Her spinning loosed the towel around her body so it fell, a revelation of swaying breasts and belly and water-wet lap. She caught the towel with her right hand. Stopped shaking her head. Her eyes opened and saw her nakedness fill his stare.

As he stood there.

Towel over his shoulder.

By the edge of the bed *where*.

Her smile came long and slow and sweet as she saw what she saw of him.

'Well,' she said. 'That's a surprise.'

can't talk can't move can't think can I can I . . .

She let the towel she held fall to the floor. Shook her head. Brushed damp hair off her face and over her shoulders to hang down her naked back as she smiled at him. As she stepped across the room toward him, saying: 'But we've already showered.'

Her arms circled his neck like snakes.

The wet warmth of her flesh pressed to him.

The crown of her damp head came to his chin and he kissed her there, smelled her blond-gray lilac shampoo tangle as his hands trembled and ached to move from his bare sides, to touch her. He kissed the side of her head, tried to turn her lips up to his with the gentle push of his cheek but her face burrowed against his chest.

She whispered: 'We don't have time.'

Then turned her face up to their kiss.

And his hands cupped the round surrender of her hips as he pulled her closer.

Her arms tightened around his neck as his hands slid up her sides and filled with the stiffening weight of her breasts.

She broke their kiss, nuzzled his chest, pressed her lips to his neck. Her hands cupped his hips as she kissed his heart, as she bent into him, her own hips brushed the edge of the bed and she said: 'Make time.'

Kissing him, pulling him closer as she sat on the bed and he stood there, saw her, felt and saw what she did, what she was doing and oh, *oh* when that moment came he could not kill his scream.

Again afterward, she lay with him on the bed, but only for a few moments. Left him there for the bathroom. He heard her brushing her teeth. She came back, crawled onto the bed, said: 'Use my razor on the edge of the tub. And your toothbrush.'

Smiled. 'When you're ready.'

She dressed in a blur, wore a black bra and matching panties under her loose jeans and blue shirt. Toweled her hair again though it still hung damp. Picked the laundry out of the chair. Told him: 'I'm going to make coffee.'

'Knock before you touch the doorknob.'

'But it's my apartment.'

'Not anymore.'

Merle said: 'What's a girl gotta do to have her own life?'

But smiled.

Shifted the laundry in her arms and knocked on her own bedroom door.

Waited, knocked again.

Through that closed door, Merle and Condor heard Faye say: *'Just a minute.'*

Less than a minute, judged Condor, then Faye called out: *'Okay.'*

Merle opened the door, stepped outside the bedroom and closed the door behind her exit all without Condor seeing his de facto mission partner.

The blue disposable razor was well past its prime as he scraped his soaped face smooth in the bathroom sink's mirror. Her toothpaste gave his mouth a minty-fresh taste.

He walked into the bedroom looking for the lost & found scavenged clothes -

Felt himself falling, plopping his butt on the bed, collapsing flat on his back with his eyes full of the solid ceiling pressing down on where he lay.

Stay here. John Stewart's song. Calculations of what he had to do and couldn't do. Dreams of staying *right here, right now* then *maybe . . .*

'Maybes drive you mad.'

He didn't turn his eyes from the ceiling to see the *who* or *what* of that ghost.

Said: 'Too late, I'm there now.'

'Make time.'

Those words, thought Condor: *She's not dead. She's just in the other room.*

'Are you sure?'

'I'm sure I want what I now know I can have.'

'Grasp your true reality.'

'Fuck you,' Condor told the parroting ghost.

But without conviction.

And the ghost knew that.

I can't let her get killed.

Killed too, he added before the ghosts could get to him.

Merle's smile. The curving open of her lips. The perfect words she found. What he thought she knew. The way she let him hold her. How she'd held him back. That was enough, or almost enough, or at least far better than he had a right to expect. *Is she my last her?* He let that thought go as . . . unworthy.

Get Merle to her new normal, safe, alive.

Everything else . . .

'You already know everything else.'

But *he* said that. Not some ghost.

Condor sat up, naked, his feet flat on the floor and his mind saved from illusions that he could hide.

He said out loud: 'Are you satisfied now?'

Got no answer.

No answer from any ghosts.

Odd.

Aromas of coffee beckoned him.

He got off the bed. Dressed. Walked to the door he had.

22

STUFF HAPPENS
- U.S. Secretary of Defense Donald Rumsfeld

The bedroom door opened.

Faye blinked when she saw who stepped out to join her and Merle in the kitchen.

Said: 'You look . . .'

'Nowhere near as good as any of us want.'

The man whose life Faye protected with her own wore gray sweatpants that were too small and a black college sweatshirt that was too big, bare feet, and a wry smile.

'Don't worry,' he said, 'I fake it better after coffee. Besides, it's barely nine A.M.'

Merle said: 'If you want me to make that call, this is when it should happen.'

Faye chose the landline for Merle's call, put the exchange between the gray-blonde archivist and her Library of Congress boss on speaker. Watched Condor *get it* as the telephone transaction played out like Merle'd predicted.

Like she'd promised.

'So we got cover,' said Condor.

'We've maybe got a roof,' answered Faye.

Condor smiled at the woman he'd helped Faye hijack.

Or did I help him get her?

He asked Merle: 'Do you get the paper?'

Faye said: 'We'll go online for - '

'Old school,' said Condor: 'We don't want to leave the newspaper out to raise questions.'

'I get *The Post*,' said Merle. 'Off the stack they deliver downstairs in the lobby.'

Condor looked at Faye.

She reached behind her back. Passed the .45 to him. Grabbed her coat to cover the gun on her hip and obscure her body armor, took what Merle said were her apartment keys and left the two of them alone.

Low risk, right?

Leaving them alone. Armed. Phones.

The proper option for partners. Giving Condor his best chance *in case*.

Faye eased down five flights of stairs. Opened the LOBBY door a crack.

Saw no one, nothing amiss.

No one shot her as she stepped into the apartment building's front entryway.

No corridor security cameras caught her lifting a newspaper off a rack across from the elevator she marched to, tapping the call button and not showing the relief she felt when the doors jumped open and gave her an empty cage to ride. She pushed the button for the floor above Merle's, got out, walked down the fire stairs and knocked on 513's door, her right hand empty by her side.

Condor let her in, took the newspaper from her as she relocked the door.

He held up the newspaper: 'My bet is a full-block blackout.'

'No,' said Faye. 'Too much street action. Veil.'

Condor shrugged. 'With spin.'

From her living room chair, Merle said: 'What are you two talking about?'

'All the news that's fit to print,' said Condor, riffing off the motto of *The Washington Post*'s then last remaining serious rival as a dead-trees newspaper.

Page one of *The Post*'s Metro section.

A boxed story the size of Faye's hand, probably shoved into print at the last possible second the night before: A drug deal gone bad on a subway platform left one innocent bystander stray-bullet dead, woman, identity withheld pending notification of next of kin, one street thug killed by police, one undercover officer shot in serious condition, one cop with minor injuries, no delays expected in morning rush-hour traffic.

'The bodies don't add up,' said Condor.

'Depends on who sees what to count,' said Faye.

'The Red Line,' said Condor. 'Janitors commandeer the next train for covert cleanup and removal.'

'This cost,' said Faye.

'The price on our heads keeps going up,' said Condor.

Faye used their hostess's laptop. Found nothing about the D.C. Metro gunfight on the *New York Times* website. Read online editions of all Washington news outlets, checked local TV and radio stations' website, many of which carried variations on the original *Post* story or 'updates' that implied progress but offered no new details, though a couple of sites had cell-phone photos of ambulance and cop cars parked at the subway entrance, their emergency lights spinning red & blue blasts into the night. She found a neighborhood Listserv report about 'vandals' racing their bikes through a restaurant 'breaking a lot of plates.' The Listserv posted an eleven-second cell-phone video of clattering crockery & unintelligible shouts, showed the back of a man in a red jacket wobbling his bike toward the front of a cafe past stunned diners. One Listserv comment 'linked' this 'hooliganism' to an increase in graffiti spray-painted on neighborhood walls, while another noted that 'incident shows America must have evolved because this not racial 'cause one biker /white one / blk,' then the online discussion veered into rants about restaurants attracting rats.

'So nobody knows what's going on,' said Merle.

'Including us,' said Condor.

'Knowledge comes in levels,' said Faye.

'Next comes a data blizzard,' said Condor. 'A shotgun blast of controlled misdirections, all "factual," all riding a big secret in plain sight.'

'So what do we do now?' said Merle.

Faye looked at her, looked at Condor.

Condor looked at Faye, looked at Merle, looked back to Faye.

Shrugged.

Merle said: 'No.'

23

*TOO MUCH CUNNING STRATEGY . . . AND
STRANGE THINGS START TO HAPPEN*
- *Tao Te Ching / The Tao of Power*, trans. by R. L. Wing

'I'm not going to let you two decide *what's next* without me,'
said Merle.

Smart, thought Condor. *Bold*. He told himself to cloak the
pride in her he felt.

Faye said: 'We don't want to get into an issue of what choice
you have.'

'We're there,' countered Merle. 'We always are. Right here,
right now, I'm either your prisoner or something more.'

'Like what?' said Faye.

'I don't think this has a name. I'm a woman you hijacked
who wants out of your trouble. I'll do what I gotta do. You
want me as part of your solution, not your problem.'

'You could be a one-bullet problem.'

Condor tensed.

Merle said: 'We're all a one-bullet problem.'

The Capitol Hill worker put her empty coffee cup on the
glass table. Told the spies in her living room: 'You don't
know who your opponents are, or what's at the core of
them wanting you . . . like dead. And now what happens to
you, happens to me.'

Acceptance and challenge shaped Merle's smile, but *she
calls me Vin* wished he knew all that the curve of her lips

contained as she added: 'I'm the only ally you know you've got.'

'*Ally* is a strong word for a draftee,' said Faye.

'Whatever,' said Merle. 'You've got to figure out how to get us safe, like into some kind of witness protection program.'

Faye and Condor laughed.

'Been there,' he said. 'Got me here.'

'So find a better program,' snapped Merle. 'You - *we* can't just wait on whatever it is your *they* do next. Not if they're as powerful as you say, as they seem.'

Condor said: 'You're trying to take us somewhere.'

'You've found an agenda,' said Faye.

'We've all got agendas so what the fuck difference does that make,' said Merle. 'What I, what *we* gotta do is figure the best way to stay alive. Politics is about what you do and Washington works on who you can convince to help you.'

Merle put her eyes on Condor as she said: 'I got a onetime I've never played with a Senator. Call it a favor, call it quid pro quo for what he'll be afraid I could do if he says *no*, call it his guilt,*whatever*: I've got one *ask*. He's got power. Do the math.'

'You'd do that?' said Condor.

'It's the choice I've got.'

'Senators are button-pushers, not *get you home alive* guys.'

'He can make calls, get - '

Faye said: 'Let's say he only calls the right guy. Whoever he calls has to figure out the politics and law of what they can do and what they will do. Even if he jumps when you snap your fingers, he's gotta politic others into getting airborne with him.'

Condor said: 'His power is in the suites, not the streets.'

'But keep him in mind for when we're inside,' Faye told the older woman.

'Inside where?'

'Inside our system with a shitload of angels or at least neutral gunners so we can get the good guys to move us off the bullseye and hunt what's really going on.'

'You got a better way than me to do that?' Merle asked Faye.

Condor looked at his partner, his fellow pro, the government spook who said she wanted to save, the young woman with a Glock on her hip.

Saw Faye's face tremble with her silent scream *YES*.

24

WHEELS TURNIN' ROUND AND ROUND
- Steely Dan, 'Do It Again'

Faye hunkered down in the backseat of a car parked a block beyond Merle's apartment building. Cool air flowed over Faye from the curbside front window she'd punched out as quietly as possible seventeen minutes after they'd sent Merle on a run.

Merle on her own. Solo. In her car. Out of their control.

Time elapsed since Merle's launch: two hours, forty-three minutes, and a quarter-circle sweep of the second hand around the watch dial on Faye's wrist.

Time of day in D.C.'s real world: 11:23 A.M. on an ordinary April Thursday.

Crisp blue sky. Smells of spring green. Parking spaces along the curbs of this residential neighborhood materialized when its luckier residents went to work. Faye'd spotted uncrushed brown leaves banked at both undersides of this car's tires, its windshield dusted with green powder pollen, figured the vehicle belonged to someone who commuted via more economical public transportation where no delays were expected from last night's *incident* on the Red Line.

She's got seventeen minutes left before we pull the trigger, thought Faye.

They'd kept Merle's cell phone when they launched her.

'But what if something goes wrong?' she'd asked.

Condor'd said: 'It's already wrong. This is your shot at making it right.'

'No,' said Merle, 'what I mean is - '

'We know what you meant,' said Faye. 'Stick to the plan.'

'Stick to what should happen, what we need to happen,' added Condor.

Merle stared at both of them, then focused on him, said: 'I'll do my best.'

They gave her a thousand dollars in cash.

Faye'd expected the hug and kiss she watched Merle give Condor. Was surprised when the older woman wrapped her arms around her until Faye hugged her back.

'See you,' said Merle.

She left the apartment, the door closing behind her with a *click*.

One heartbeat.

Two.

Faye slid Merle's laptop into the backpack purse, dropped in Merle's cell phone along with batteries from the landline phones: that number still worked, took messages, but without the batteries no one could use the twenty-century-style communicators to make a call, connect with 911, with anyone who would listen to anything Merle had to say.

Condor wore his black leather jacket, black jeans and wrinkled blue shirt. Faye saw his thermal underwear top under the blue shirt, black sneaker-like shoes tied with the hard-to-slip knots favored by mountain climbers and Special Ops teams. The .45 rode holstered on the right side of his belt along with a clip-on spring knife while the belt's left side held three stacked & packed spare magazines in a pouch. As long as he kept the jacket unzipped, he didn't *print* - show the outline of *concealed weapon*.

Faye'd strapped on her Glock and two spare magazines. *You had to shoot the gunners at the subway. You had to kill them.* Faye had two of Delta Force's new palm-sized non-public flash-bang grenades in her backpack, a silencer for her pistol, a sleek black flashlight, a cigar-sized aluminum tube containing lock picks and tension bars. She left the bullet-heavy speed loader for the lost .38 revolver on the glass coffee table.

They went out to the world.

Hunkered down in the broken-into car, Faye checked her watch: fifteen minutes left.

She stared over the car's front seat, past the sidewalk leading to Merle's building, uphill past the intersection to trees on a playground where chained swings hung empty and still. Condor hid in those trees. He'd have some phony cover alibi in case a nanny showed up with young charges and spotted an older man who could be accused of creepy loitering. But so far this morning, Faye'd seen no children on the sidewalks. Maybe the swings and playground were relics of what had been or totems to what could be.

Don't think about that. They're just empty swings.

Her watch said fourteen minutes to go.

Her eyes flicked to the rearview mirror she'd adjusted to capture the view behind the parked car - oncoming traffic plus a glimpse of anyone on the sidewalks who wasn't sneaking forward in a combat crouch and shielded by the parked cars. The passenger side mirror helped her surveillance of that sidewalk. As for across the street, even if she went beyond using the driver's side mirror and turned to look, what she saw was parked cars.

You never have perfect optics.

From his hide on the hill's playground, Condor could cover traffic coming the other way or turning onto this road from either direction on the intersecting street.

Eleven minutes to go.

Ten.

Nine minutes and a red Ford parked in front of the apartment building with a flash of brake lights in the midday air. The driver's door opened. Out climbed Merle.

Alone.

Acting normal. Acting as if she always got out of her car like a refugee. Looking back the way she'd come, then looking the other way down the street toward where she didn't know Faye was hiding, so *not* acting like she was expecting someone. *Good.*

Why two sacks in her hands?

Merle walked from her parked car, followed the sidewalk to her apartment building. Ungraceful gait: *Nerves, natural, that's natural.* Entered the front door.

The elevator ride to her fifth floor will take Merle two minutes. Faye scanned the streets, sidewalks, hunting for anyone who'd followed Merle.

She'll find her apartment empty. Find us gone. And do what?

Give her seven more minutes. To see if she stays. To see if she runs outside, flees, tries to signal someone. To see if some cover team she'd summoned had given her a cell phone and would come charging when she called to report *targets lost.*

Give her seven minutes alone in her home.

That was Faye's plan with Condor.

He couldn't wait.

Or told time differently.

Two minutes early, Faye saw him leave the playground, growing bigger and more identifiable with each step he took toward the apartment building. A rebel but still a pro, not looking in Faye's direction - and not *not* looking her way.

No cars roared out of the high-noon sun to drop a snatch team on him.

No bullet cut Condor down as he entered Merle's building.

Give him five minutes.

When she'd waited and watched and no Op team appeared, Faye eased out of the car she'd vandalized, joined Condor and Merle in the apartment.

The older woman glared at Faye: 'You didn't trust me.'

'We don't trust our situation,' said Faye.

'Like I told you,' added Condor, 'you could have been grabbed - '

'Or called someone *just* to betray you,' snapped Merle. 'That's what you think.'

'That's how we have to think,' said Faye.

Condor said: 'It's all about the smart move. That was the smart move for us.'

'Guess I should have thought of a smart move for me,' said Merle. 'For us.'

'Sure,' said Faye. 'And you - '

'Got lunch.' Merle lifted one of the sacks on the kitchen counter.

Faye focused on the four disposable phones from the other sack.

'I got more cash, too,' said Merle. 'From my ATM.'

Faye frowned. 'That's - '

'Not a risk until she's IDed as with us,' said Condor. 'Smart. Now or never.'

'*Yeah!*' Merle told Faye with a defiant look.

Fay programmed the three expensive phones' CONTACTS with initials: C, F, M.

'Do you want to see the receipts?' asked Merle. 'Like you said, I bought them as separate cash transactions. Got the cheap phone in another store. Wore my baseball cap and sunglasses. You can check the receipts against your change. I paid for lunch.'

'You were worried about us doing an audit?' said Faye.

Merle smiled. Met Faye's probing eyes. Said: 'Be prepared.'

They ate carryout plates of deli bar food from an upscale grocery store.

Faye knew the cold noodles she ate were sesame, knew the broccoli still had its crunch. Watched the older couple share bites off each other's plate. Faye stuffed lunch trash and the cell phones' wrappings into a sack, carried it, her backpack purse and the credit card she sneaked out of Merle's purse to the bedroom, said: 'I'm going to check our gear and trash for the burn bag, grab a shower.'

'I'm on watch,' said Condor.

Then like he and Merle expected, Faye shut herself behind that white door.

Took Faye eleven minutes to log on to the website she'd found while sitting Charlie Sugar - counter-surveillance - in the burgled car outside the apartment building, use the credit card stolen from Merle, do what she did and hope that it worked. She crammed trash into the sack, forced herself to take a real shower, and for a moment, *for just a few moments* as the hot water beat down on her face, freed sobs of tears to wash her cheeks, ease the pressure in her spine, the weight gripping her heart.

Composed herself, her gear, her backpack, rejoined her comrades.

She sent Merle into the bedroom to pack an overnight bag.

When the older woman was out of sight, put the credit card back in Merle's purse.

Condor gave Faye a frown. Said nothing.

A rebel but a pro.

The three of them walked out of the apartment seven minutes later.

An ordinary April Thursday, 2:17 P.M.

Beautiful Rock Creek Parkway curves through Washington, D.C., alongside the Potomac River from the Navy Yard with its former espionage centers, past memorial gardens for FDR and the broken souls of the Depression who resurrected themselves through the horrors & heroism of WWII, around marble monuments for murder victims Martin Luther King and Abraham Lincoln, flows a rifle shot from the Vietnam Memorial's mirror black wall of names and statues of American soldiers from the Korean War who march through the riverside trees like ghosts. The Parkway passes under the multiauditorium albino complex named after one of our assassinated presidents and past what was an apartment/hotel/office complex called Watergate and the rehabbed former hotel where button men of that scandal staged one of their covert operations. As it flows toward Maryland suburbs, the Parkway passes Georgetown streets haunted by Rose Men, then comes the zoo where at dawn you can hear lions roar while off to the right rises the now gentrified neighborhood of Mt. Pleasant where brown-skinned Latinos rioted against mostly black-skinned D.C. cops in the last days of the twentieth century. The Parkway then widens from a tree-lined road to an urban canyon, a green valley with paths for bikers and joggers, tabled picnic sites and grassy stretches for volleyball games, shadowed glades that cloak dump sites for homicide victims both functionally famous and forever forgotten. Before the Parkway crosses the District line, roads lead out of its valley to neighborhoods of million-dollar homes, embassies surrounded by black steel fences and invisible electronic curtains, a public golf course nestled in the forest between the Parkway and Sixteenth Street that creates a straight drive south to the White House and north to Maryland past the legendary tree-lined grounds of Walter Reed Army Medical Center that on this day was slated to end its hundred-year reign as America's most famous military hospital for 'commercial redevelopment' Faye believed was prompted not so much by facility obsolescence or tax-saving economics as it was to move wounded warriors out of the city so urban-dwelling policymakers need no longer routinely see wheelchair-captured and amputee and burn victim veterans of their decisions wandering the glorious capital city streets.

Merle drove her red Ford north on Rock Creek Parkway.

Condor rode shotgun.

Faye lay across the backseat.

A quick glance profiled this car as two aging, innocent civilians out for a drive.

The red Ford turned off the Parkway and onto the golf course road.

Faye heard Condor call '*Clear!*' and felt Merle brake the car to a crawl.

The red Ford was almost stopped when Faye leapt out of the backseat.

The Ford sped up, drove away, left her alone on the road.

Two minutes later, she'd walked out of the Parkway at the intersection of the golf course road and Sixteenth Street. She turned right, put the 209-meters-away specter of Walter Reed and its security cameras behind her, walked toward the 50-blocks-distant White House past blocks of apartment buildings where *maybe* no fish-eye lens recorded her passing. Two hundred paces that direction and she jaywalked across the busy divided city street, walked back the way she'd come - but now on the other side of the road, headed north for any cell tower tracking analysis.

She used the cheap disposable cell phone. Kept walking as she dialed the cell phone number she'd memorized less than forty-eight hours before.

Second buzz and her call got answered with unresponsive silence.

Into her phone as she walked, Faye said: 'Say it ain't you, Sami.'

'Where are you?' said his voice. 'Are you okay? What are you - '

'Why'd you sic a wet team on me, Sami?'

'Not our people! They beat us there. Do you have Condor? Are you - '

'Who were they?'

'Unknown.'

'Bullshit! You're in the belly of the beast - *you are* the beast. They were trained, equipped, targeted and briefed pros and *the fuck* you don't know!'

'Never seen anything like it. One guy, sure, maybe two. But we've got four bodies we can't find in the system. Any system, including NATO and Interpol. No prints. No facial recognition. No forensics. No intercepted chatter about MIAs. Sterile gear, no consistency. All we got are ghosts.'

'What's going on, Sami?'

'You tell me and we'll both know, kid. It's all we can do here to keep the world from flying apart, the cover from exploding.'

In the street, somewhere far off to her right, Faye heard a distant police siren wail.

Nothing, it's nothing, routine, too soon to be connected and targeted to me.

And one siren in Washington's *D*istrict of *C*rime wouldn't be enough to give any listeners on Sami's call a quick bead on her.

'There's at least two more opposition gunners out there, Sami.'

'How do you know?'

'How do you *not* know?'

'Condor: is he okay, is he functional, what's his state of mind, where - '

'And here I thought you cared about me.'

'We care about the same things, Faye. You know that. Know me.'

She didn't respond.

Sami said: 'Think, Faye. I told you something was off, wrong, screwy. That's why I sent you out there on your own. And I was right!'

'Congratulations.'

'How are we going to - '

'What "*we*," Sami? It was just you and me and then *we* included that wet team.'

'I don't know how we got compromised. I don't know that we were. Maybe the opposition got lucky. Maybe you got . . .'

'Give me something I don't know, Sami. ABC: All Bullshit Considered.'

'Whoever they are, why-ever they are . . . I got the tingles, the creeps that I can't promise you I'm not compromised in ways I can't see. So you tell me: what do we do?'

'I'm coming in.'

'Yes! Where? How? With Condor, right? What should I - '

Faye hung up. Pulled the battery from that phone, tossed its parts into a trash can, crossed the street, walked back down the road to the golf course and Parkway.

The red Ford rolled back onto that same road when she was twenty steps into the trees, slowed to let her climb in, then sped off.

'Got nothing but denials,' she told Condor as she lay on the backseat. 'He's lying or telling the truth, maybe compromised, maybe not, but at least he and whoever he trusts now have to assume I - *we* - are coming in. They'll swarm the streets, *sure*, track the call to that neighborhood, but they'll concentrate on the two locations I'm most likely to exploit: Complex Zed and CIA HQ at Langley. The good guys will make perimeters to get us inside, the bad guys will stake those sites out to snipe us when we show.'

Merle whispered: '*We* means . . .'

'I don't think they know about you.'

'So I could just . . .'

Faye and Condor finished her thought with their silence.

'I can just drive,' said Merle. 'Where you tell me to.'

They found an underground parking garage with rates by the hour, day or month two blocks from the target. Faye paid a vacant-eyed attendant for three days in advance.

The underground concrete cavern echoed with the closing of the car doors from the red Ford they parked in its designated yellow-striped slot. They stood in flickering artificial light. Smelled burnt gas, oil, cold metal from a dozen other vehicles crouched on this level. Shadows obscured the distant cement walls.

'Never liked these places,' whispered Merle.

Faye said: 'At least you can't get spotted by drones.'

'Unless they've already cross-haired the building above us,' said Condor. 'Rubble buries anything.'

'You're such cheerful people,' said Merle.

The best Op formation called for Merle walking on the street side of the sidewalk, Faye between her and Condor, the collar turned up on his black leather jacket, not enough to obscure his face for later identification via any security camera they passed, but odds were, no lens in any of the storefronts or flat faces of the modern buildings they passed on this classy Washington street had cameras linked to the NSA grid.

Two blocks. They had to cover two blocks and not get spotted, caught, shot.

Mid-afternoon foot traffic was light, but they weren't alone enough to stand out. They reached their target address and caught a break: no security guard was on day duty at the building's front desk, no one was lurking in the lobby, no postman spotted them.

'The mailman,' said Condor.

'What?' said Merle.

'Never mind,' he said.

Faye herded them into the elevator, punched the floor button.

'Tool up,' she told Condor.

Merle's eyes widened as the man she'd embraced filled his hand with the .45.

Condor kept the pistol pressed low along his right leg.

Faye heard the *click* as he thumbed off the safety.

The elevator stopped.

Those cage doors slid open.

Faye rolled out first and fast, checked both ways as Condor whirled behind her, his eyes probing the opposite direction as hers until she whispered: 'Clear!'

Merle nervously stepped off the elevator.

'Stay between us,' Faye told her as they hurried down a corridor of closed doors.

Stay closed stay closed stay closed!

At the target door, Condor gestured for Merle to stand against the opposite wall of the corridor, rooted himself near the target portal, held his gun in front of him, ready to whirl whichever way they'd need to send death.

Faye worked on the lock with her picks and tension bar for thirty seconds before the first *click*. The second lock took half that time, then she pushed the door open, stepped in, whispered for the others, Merle coming in fast and Condor bringing up rear guard. Faye eased the door shut, had to disturb the corridor's silence with the relocking *click*.

But they were in.

Merle whispered: 'That was fast.'

Faye said: 'I've done this before.'

25

PUT YOURSELF
- Citizen Cope, 'A Bullet and a Target'

Condor aimed his .45 at the blond man's face, said: 'You're not who I expected.'

Blue eyes blinked behind the blond man's glasses as he stood there in his own apartment, his eyes locked on the gun held by a stranger who'd surprised him, pushed the door closed behind his after-work entrance and zeroed him with what the suit & tie blond man would forever after think of as *'the biggest black hole in the fucking universe.'*

Condor saw the blond man blink again, then say: 'I didn't expect you either.'

Across the room, Faye said: 'You're both the right guy.'

From off to his right, Condor heard Merle whisper: *'Don't shoot him.'*

'Whoever you are, lady,' said the blond man. 'I'm with you.'

Then he told Faye: 'Actually, I came for you.'

And Condor grinned.

'Chris Harvie,' said Faye, 'meet . . . Call him Condor. And this is Merle.'

'Could he . . . I don't know, lower the gun now?'

Yeah, he's cool.

Condor holstered the .45 and claimed the younger, taller man's hand for a shake.

Why is Faye hanging back? Like she's . . . Embarrassed. Ashamed. Scared.

'Just like you said in your text,' Chris told the green-eyed Glock-packing woman who trembled near him. 'I came straight home after work.'

'Told no one?' whispered Faye.

He shook his head *no*.

And she ran to him, into his arms, buried her face against his chest and said so everyone in their known universe could hear: 'I'm sorry!'

Chris kissed the top of her head, then again, said: 'Whatever, it's okay.'

He'd previously only glimpsed the Faye who now stood back and stared at him, said: 'No it's not.'

I've been you, thought Condor.

The four of them sat on secondhand recycled office chairs in front of the wall made by Chris's sophisticated and expensive sound & cyber system.

Faye said: 'I'm sorry, but this best choice puts you at terrible risk, your life, your career - I'm serious!'

'The big gun convinced me of that,' said Chris.

'We can't laugh about this!' argued Faye, fighting a smile.

'We have to laugh about this.'

Faye said: 'You're a lawyer and there are laws and security codes we're probably breaking on top of all that, but . . . you have to know enough to know *why*.'

Then she revealed a framework of truth, disclosing Condor just enough, justifying and exonerating Merle, taking the blame and the blood all on her.

'And now we need you,' she told Chris.

Condor interrupted: 'Tomorrow, it's got to be tomorrow.'

'What - ' Chris held up a hand against both Faye and the man called Condor.

Who he frowned at, asked: 'What did you mean, I'm not who you expected? This is my apartment, my home, she's my . . . my *I'm hers.*'

Condor said: 'The way she talked, I thought you'd be taller.'

A smile twitched Chris's lips, he blushed, stared at the floor.

Faye's eyes searched that plane, too.

Let them have the moment.

Let it touch you.

Chris looked up, his motion pulling all others' eyes to him as he said: 'I get it. Look, I don't do what I do because it's a job, and I didn't take this job to punch my ticket to some "*better*" gig, and if I'm not here to matter, I don't belong here at all.'

Faye said: 'I . . . *You know.*'

'Yeah,' said Chris, '*I know.* But now what matters is this . . . *thing* we're in.'

He looked at Condor, said: 'Besides the obvious cosmic reality, why does what we do next have to be tomorrow?'

'Because it's Friday,' answered Condor.

Faye told the blond man who'd loosed the tie around his neck *why, what, how.*

'Yeah,' said Chris, 'it's gotta be tomorrow.'

Merle said: 'What about tonight?'

Tonight was frozen pizzas, a refrigerator six-pack of cold microbrewery beer, speculation and nervous silences, things said and not said, glances, eyes full of questions and words full of hope. They used Chris's computer to map out their moves, Google Street View and satellite images to scan what they'd see in the future.

As the small one-bedroom apartment filled with the aromas of baking pizza crust and simmering tomato sauce, cheese bubbling and coins of pepperoni and sausage curling their circles in toward their centers, Condor inventoried this other place where he didn't want to die.

A particular bachelor's home. 'Particular,' *yes*, as in *this one*, but 'particular' *more* in what was chosen and cherished.

Almost like me.

Or who you could have been *if*.

A wall of electronics. Great speakers, a dollar-devouring computer and music system, racks of CDs arranged in categories of subtle distinction. A few photos of a mom, a dad, a brother and two sisters, one older, one younger. Among the framed photos on the walls hung original art by a creator with a flair for purple and red crayons and dinosaurs, a display that screamed *nephew* to Condor. One frame held the iconic *New Yorker* magazine cover after 9/11, an all-black skyline enveloping even blacker silhouettes of twin towers. Another frame showed a rare indigo night aerial shot of the glowing U.S. Capitol dome that Condor and Chris saw from the sidewalks of every ordinary workday. Stacks of books lined walls, a couple volumes of Camus, law tomes and histories, novels. Titles Condor spotted included Dos Passos's *USA* trilogy, *East of Eden, Neuromancer, The Nature of the Game, Crimegate*. The TV was small, a few DVDs stacked beside it. A cable hookup. The quick search & secure stalk through the apartment he'd done with Faye after she broke them in had shown Condor the lone bedroom, a closet with half a dozen suits plus sports jackets, ties, plastic bagged from the dry cleaner's, shirts and lots of running shoes - '*Ultimate*,' Faye'd whispered, a comment he didn't understand but let pass as strategically irrelevant. Their good luck meant frozen pizzas in the otherwise bleakly sparse refrigerator unit.

You could live like this.

Almost.

But the madness you bring with you would crash this sophisticated order.

Condor looked across the five remaining slices of pizza to the floor space where Chris sat beside Faye, asked him: 'Has anybody been watching you?'

'Ah . . . No.'

'No odd looks at work? Strangers suddenly around? Familiar faces appearing when you didn't expect them?'

'You mean other than you?' Chris shook his head. 'Nobody's watching me.'

'Somebody's always watching you. What matters is who's looking and why and what do they see.'

'Chris,' said Faye, 'if we - if *I* wasn't here, is this how it would be?'

'You mean am I maintaining a normal profile and not breaking my known patterns in a way that would alert whoever is crazy enough to care?'

'I care,' said Condor.

Chris cocked his head and with an exaggerated expression of affirmation, said: 'Exactly. But no, this - what's happening on the floor of my apartment on a Thursday evening, pizza with friends, not my usual after work, not a bite out or a game or a . . .'

He smiled at Faye. 'But I've been spending more time like this lately. Waiting.'

Condor said: 'What's different between now and like then?'

'Noise,' said Chris. 'NPR, music or even a game. Something would be on.'

'Make that happen,' said Condor.

Chris's quick keying of commands into the sound system created a random playlist of songs heavy on alternative country/folk/rock songwriters shotgunned with jazz like Miles Davis and once fabulously famous but now tastefully forgotten moments of music.

Was one of those pop songs, a studio syncopation of electric guitars and violins and commercially soulful male voices wailing words that triggered memories in anyone who'd heard this tune more than thrice, a song with juvenile lyrics that meant nothing akin or ironic to this moment, nowhere near a *clong*, just a catchy three-minute musical chorus in rock 'n' roll slow-beat time.

Condor -

- old man grunting, straining, but quickly -

- got to his feet, his hand reaching down and finding Merle's instinctively reaching-up hand to be grasped.

'Dance with me,' he said.

Unfolding, yoga graceful, wide eyes scanning him, saying: '*What?*'

'This is the chance we get. Dance with me.'

Wet filled her blue eyes but she had no strength to resist him taking her in his arms, holding her right hand with his heart-side grasp, his gun hand pressed on her blouse, on her bra strap, on her spine as he swayed them into *step-step-slide, step-step-slide* and the music played and she pressed her face against his blue shirt to dot it with her tears, as he felt the push of her breasts, the smell of her gray-blond hair and *this moment*, this moment of dancing to cheesy music he would never have picked, music that meant only this dance, this dance in an apartment where a couple who could be their children sat on the floor with beer bottles and bad pizza and watched them sway through time.

'I was afraid you wouldn't come back,' he whispered so only she could hear.

Her head shook *no* against his chest.

'We're here,' he said.

'I'm trying,' she whispered. 'My best. My best.'

She held him and she danced and they danced.

The song ended. Songs do.

He stopped, she stopped, they stopped, stood in a home that wasn't theirs.

Condor saw Faye sitting on the floor, fighting sinking into slumber.

Said: 'Now there's something we need to risk.'

'What?' whispered Merle standing *oh so close* to him.

'School,' said Condor as he watched Faye stir herself back to the killing edge.

Chris echoed Merle: 'What?'

'You never know what you'll need to know,' said Condor.

So for thirty-seven minutes, he and Faye risked not being on a National Rifle Association (NRA) - Occupational Safety and Health Administration (OSHA)–approved range, and first with Condor's .45, then with Faye's Glock, made Chris and Merle practice aiming, firing, chambering rounds and (on Condor's pistol) learning the safety to click off. Spies made citizens learn how to load ammunition magazines even though almost no scenario envisioned that necessity, but the exercise helped demystify weapons neither Merle nor Chris knew before that night. They learned the three-point aim, breathe & squeeze, the Weaver stance, the OSS pioneered from-the-belt quick-fire move. Though such things are not advisable for long-term weapons preservation, long term for this crew projected as high noon tomorrow, so Chris and Merle practiced dry firing the pistols. *Click! Click!*

After Condor and Faye reholstered their fully operational pistols, Condor again led them all through tomorrow's best-case choreography.

Then made Chris and Merle talk through the plan backwards.

Condor quizzed them on *what-if*s he answered as soon as their faces showed him they understood the scenario he'd spelled out.

He saw Faye's concentration fade.

Lied and said: 'We're ready.'

Chris and Merle cleared a space on the main room's floor for a self-inflating air mattress left over from his sister and brother-in-law's visit. Merle used extra sheets, a fuzzy blue oversized blanket and two pillows to make a bed for her and Condor.

The apartment's one bathroom was in the hall.

Chris used the bathroom first, then Faye.

Faye motioned for Merle to take her turn. The older woman did.

Condor nodded toward the bedroom where Chris waited. Told Faye: 'You've done all you can do. Get what you can in there.'

The bedroom door closed behind her.

Merle came out of the bathroom, walked past Condor with a tired, tearful smile. He heard her undressing, getting onto the bed held by this floor.

Behind the closed door of the bathroom, Condor used the toilet.

Washed his hands, brushed his teeth, rinsed his mouth and spit.

Counted out the night-time pills he chose to take - his heart, his bladder, his pains, his edgy insomnia - swallowed them with water from the sink faucet he cupped in his hand. Noted that no one living or dead was in the bathroom with him, that he was alone.

Condor stared at the man in the mirror.

Said: 'There you are.'

26

THE ESSENCE OF LOVE IS BETRAYAL
- Chris Harvie

Not here, not now, thought Faye as she entered Chris Harvie's bedroom.

But she knew that was a futile lie.

And as that door closed behind her, as *he* closed the exit behind *them*, Faye scanned this room lit by a lamp on the scarred wooden table holding the book he was reading, checked to be sure the shade was pulled down over the waiting-to-shatter glass window between her and the street-lit killing night.

She turned toward his comforting reach, said: 'I'm sorry!'

He cupped her face, smiled at her tears: 'What else could you do?'

'Not have gotten involved with you. At all. In the first place.'

'In the first place, I love you. After that, it's just how our luck got us here.'

She slid into his arms, whispered as loudly as she dared: 'I love you.'

'I know.' He kissed her forehead, her wet cheeks, her dry lips.

'Come on, get in bed, go to sleep,' he said. 'You're dead on your fee -

'Bad choice of metaphors,' he blurted.

'Wrong,' she said. 'Dead on.'

Faye pulled the blue blouse out of her black pants, flew her hands up its line of white buttons until they were all undone.

Opened the blouse. Touched the puckered white scar slashed up from her groin across her taut white stomach.

'You deserve to know how you got here,' she told Chris. Her fingertips brushed the scar lined on her stomach like a lonesome road: 'You deserve to know about this.'

Tell him.

Paris. Call it last year. And you're doing everything right.

The Seine, stone bridges across its rolling gray ribbon between beautiful walls of apartments rising over streets that traffic in the best that humans can be. Museums. Sidewalk cafes. All the women are beautiful because they've found one thing in how they look to believe in as *magnifique*. All the men are taut with the intensity of caring. No one looks stupid except for an occasional tourist who brought his mirrors to the city of lights instead of his sunglasses. He's not like most of the millions of lucky souls who visit this *cosmopolis* where crosses of salvation rise in the same stone castle that's home to flesh-eating gargoyles. Marching past street stalls of North African leather goods comes a well-suited woman carrying a Hermès briefcase and closing a billion-euros financial package with curt orders into her cell phone. Profitable movie theaters play François Truffaut and John Ford movies older than 90 percent of their patrons. And though you can buy heroin at the plaza called Stalingrad, the retail market point for multinational cartels & syndicates, Parisian dealers never guarantee happiness.

But your Paris is narrow broken pavement streets, cramped apartment buildings violating housing codes in hundreds of *who cares* ways, smells of cooking goat and North African staples, water, *Mon Dieu* you'd kill for a glass of water and you could, *you can*, you're packing a Glock in a holster taped handle-down to your smooth stomach under the Moroccan blouse above the black slacks and flat shoes for running or kicking. Nobody you pass on the narrow sidewalks looks at anybody, or else it's some man who glares X-ray vision at everyone. You wear brown contact lenses because green eyes are a reveal. Thank God you're not pretty, so nobody's going to go out of their way to notice you except for people who hate the headscarf wrapped around your face and covering your dyed hair that passes for the Algerian-French blend you and your ID papers claim.

Six weeks' language prep at Langley sandpapering your textbook French.

Seventeen days of Immersion Familiarization with an NOC team in Algiers.

Boats, trains, buses and walking to a Paris address you only knew from videos.

Your Op name is Djamila.

The real Djamila has been Tagged & Targeted in another Op from some other CIA crew, or maybe they were Pentagon. The Agency scooped her up during a 'family' trip to Yemen, found the explosives in her battered suitcase.

The al Qaeda affiliate barely trusted any woman, so her explosives' customized detonator with perhaps traceable components, that clue-carrying detonator, went to Paris by UATT (Unknown At This Time) - pronounced *'you-at'* - means & methods.

The bad guys are obsessed with Op Security. Got great tradecraft.

Took four weeks, but our best wringers sweated enough lies and evasions and slips from Djamila to piece together much of what she knew, then bluffed her out of what she had left by letting her think we had it all anyway, but would turn her over to Malaysians or Israelis or somebody who scared her more than we did if she didn't tell us everything and if it didn't match what she thought we already knew.

Wonder whatever happened to Djamila.

But you can't think about that.

Not in your Op.

Not when she reveals the target is America in Paris.

Not when you're doing everything right.

Your Op plan is classic: You become Djamila. Cool it in Paris until she gets a mobile phone call to a rendezvous. A Montprix - a French franchise store. In the cosmetics aisle. You meet a man named Neuf - that's right: Nine, a number that implies a sizable Op cell, and that's an intel bonus or it's batshit, depending on how you play it, but so far you're doing everything right. Textbook. Streetwise.

Neuf's never seen Djamila. You only know he's got a scar on his wrist that can't be seen from street-pole surveillance cameras. He gives her - *you* - the attack's *when*:

Tomorrow.

Remember, you're in an NOC Op. No notice to the Agency Chief of Station in the embassy, no liaison to the DGSE (*Direction Générale de la Sécurité Extérieure*) or DCRI (*Direction Centrale du Renseignement Intérieur*), or to DRM (*Direction du Renseignement Militaire*) or DPSD (*Direction de la Protection et de la Sécurité de la Défense*), or even to their off-the-books group - *won't tell you that name*. You and your team are alone. All you know is the target is American or maybe NATO with a long shot of it being French, because chatter NSA monitored off suspects sweated out of the real Djamila indicate that the bad guys think they have some inside track about French intel and security moves and are about to make the French pissed off at their allies.

The analytical conclusion that the bad guys want to divide and conquer us with some America-targeted bomb attack in Paris with even a hint of our allies being compromised or penetrated made Langley nervous with its complexity. So they made Sami run this Op simple: totally in the black, no allies' involvement.

In that Paris drugstore aisle. Cheesy French music playing over the loudspeaker, Neuf says tomorrow he'll be 'another person,' which you figure means in disguise. The plan is for you *Djamila* to go to a safe house and deliver the explosives for him to check - which is why the Op couldn't switch phony material for real explosives. We knew they'd check, and if they found bogus bomb material, they'd go in the wind and come back at us some way we didn't have penetrated.

After he checks your delivery, only then will he phone someone called Sept - Seven - to bring the trigger device. They'll make the bomb operational. And off the three of you will go to the then-disclosed target. You're supposed to provide cover surveillance and film the whole thing with your cell phone, then wait to get the right call to email it to the number you'll be given and maybe from there to YouTube.

What Neuf doesn't know is you're wired and geo-tracked and hooked in to a Black Ops cover team which, when you confirm the target, will charge while you shoot the guy holding the bomb - disable preferred, but do what you gotta do. Even if that means you taking on both Sept and Neuf, the cover team rescuers are close.

But they've got to hang back. The bad guys are Op savvy. Ready to rabbit. So it's up to you to wait until your team can grab the optimal *get* of the bomb, the trigger and Op soldiers.

And so far, you're doing everything right.

Come rendezvous, you know Uncle Sam has your back, though from a distance.

Neuf shows, wears a suit and tie, clean shaven. He's carrying the gym bag favored by stockbrokers, plus an attaché case - either one of them good for the bomb. He walks you to an apartment in the 18th arrondissement, bare white walls, no furniture.

And while you're waiting, he says when he gets to paradise, he hopes you'll be one of the blessed virgins waiting for him.

I mean, what can you, what can Djamila, what can anybody say to that? The bomber on his way to martyrdom has a crush on you.

You should have paid attention to the timing of his dream.

Sept shows up. A big guy, Western-looking. Like Neuf, he's suit & tie city.

But you wait. You tell yourself you gotta wait. No way could the cover team advance to a close and quick-enough breach of the apartment for a clean takedown. Get out in the street, after Neuf reveals the target, then speak the Go Code.

Neuf marries your explosives to the timer Sept brought. The bomb's in the attaché case. Neuf needs five seconds to unsnap the catches, open it, flip the bomb trigger. Plenty of time to shoot him first, shoot Sept if the Black Ops boys haven't dropped him because *first* you'll give the Go and they'll be running. You can grab the case. No explosion that will kill you, too. No intel scandal. The good guys win again.

What could go wrong when you're doing everything right?

You mutter something about sixty seconds, not the Go Code, but your throat mike broadcasts it as a 'get ready,' and knowing how your cover team works, you figure they'll be moving closer, ready -

Neuf shoves the attaché case into Sept's arms, whirls toward you -

Knife! Where'd he get that fucking knife stabbing -

He's multitasking. Making his virgin reward *and* obeying orders you'd never expected. Djamila was supposed to die in this apartment. She was an easy sacrifice for security, an expendable liability. Make her transport what you want into place. If she's caught, she's expendable, no great loss. If she completes her mission, then terminate her. Don't call it betraying her, call it Op security or serving the greater cause.

But Djamila's not Djamila, it's you.

Training. Hours of practice. One night in Buenos Aires. You grab the lunging knife wrist and jerk, palm heel smash Neuf's elbow. You hear the knife hit the floor.

Neuf gets off a punch, knocks enough wind out of you so all the throat mike transmits is a grunt. You finger slash Neuf's eyes, nail a snap kick into his hip . . .

Behind you, Sept punches for your spine. But he was smart enough to set down the bomb before swinging into a fight, and that *smart* delay gives you time to whirl, turn his off-balance strike through a hip throw and crash him to the floor.

Where he scoops up the knife, bounces up with a stab that cuts you . . .

Cuts me . . .

Cuts you groin to guts. Like a rip in time. You fall back. Grabbing your gushing blood, grabbing your gun, years of training and BAM! BAM!

Sept flips ass over teakettle, drops the knife.

Neuf grabs the attaché case, runs out the door. You shoot. Hit the wall.

Burning fire in your guts as you swing your Glock to zero Sept who's flopping around on the floor and he screams at you.

Screams at you *in English*, in *British*: 'Fockin' bitch!'

Both of you lie on the floor in that unfurnished Paris apartment. You realize he's some kind of London spook, SAS it turns out, all set to take down Neuf's Op they penetrated from their end. But now the man with the bomb has run out the door. Later we learn from two cell guys SAS sweeps up, Neuf's headed for a nearby apartment building where CIA has a NOC Op you and your team know nothing about. That secret CIA base being blown up would not only piss the French off because we made a target for killers in Paris, but we put spooks on their soil without telling them. Plus people will get slaughtered, damaged, public mess.

As the gun slides from your hands - BOOM!

Your cover team closed in on Neuf, but he's on the sidewalk, narrow street, running with his hand on the bomb in the case and when he spots *gonna get me . . .*

BOOM! He's a martyr. BOOM! A garbage truck and two parked cars. BOOM! Fragment wounds on three cover team gunners. BOOM! A seventy-three-year-old Parisian woman in a black coat, walking her yippy little dog . . . *Boom*.

Yeah, could have been a whole lot worse. Could have been so much better. One dead and your backups have wounded and you're lying in a puddle of your own blood hearing those classic French sirens *Wee-ooo! Wee-ooo!*

Then you black out.

And so now I'm officially a traitor. Told secrets to an unauthorized person.

Faye sat beside Chris on his bed.

Said: 'I didn't die. Everybody's pissed off. The press cover story stinks. The French, the British, execs all over the CIA looking to point the finger of blame. The Agency had to - Sami had to - go up and tell the Hill a version of the truth, get lucky and get some kind of pass for fucking up. I earned some blame for not tumbling to *what was what* sooner, for shooting a British agent, for not dropping Neuf and the bomb. The French deny they were compromised by the bad guys and all we got saying otherwise is chatter we don't want to disclose how we got. But Sami pled my case. I got to start working my way back to being on the inside, being the *who who matters, who knows, who does*. Sami opened the door on the soundproof glass room inside your Committee offices and I walked out and got a cup of coffee.'

'And me,' said Chris.

'And you. You trusted me. Freed dreams. Let me fall for you. Let me believe. And now I've betrayed you. Put you here. And I'm sorry, I'm so sorry!'

'This is where I live.' Chris wiped a tear off her cheek as they sat on the bed. He grinned. 'You know how hard it is to find a great apartment in this town?'

Call it an upside-down grin and she leaned into him.

Faye said: 'I got an innocent civilian killed in Paris. I can't do that again. I can't do that here. I can't, *I will not* do that to you.'

'You forget,' said Chris. 'I'm no civilian and I'm not innocent.'

'Liar,' she whispered with all the love in her heart.

Let go, just let go.

'I got your message from the mirror in the Tune Inn,' Chris told the spy in his arms. 'The woman who found it called me from the bathroom. She read it to me three times. Didn't ask a single question. Promised to wash it off before she walked back out to the bar. Didn't let me thank her - thanked me for letting her be part of us, our story. For letting her believe someday she'd write on a bathroom mirror with her lipstick. She told me I was so lucky. I told her yes, I am.'

As he laid Faye down to sleep, Chris switched off the bedroom light.

27

BETTER ROADS
- Lipstick graffiti on a bathroom mirror

You're driving the car.

Spring morning. Friday. Washington, D.C.

A cocked & locked .45 as heavy as a heart attack rides in the inside left pocket of your unzipped black leather jacket for a *while-driving* grab.

City streets. Rush hour. Gliding with the flow of Metro buses and dark SUVs. Minivans, family sedans. Taxis. Kamikaze bicyclists wear swooping plastic helmets and cubicle clothes. Through your open windows come car honks, street shouts, amped-up music. You smell exhaust, city pavement, the sweat of fear.

Merle rides behind you. Her hands are empty. Nothing under her jacket but hope. Says she can work as left spotter. She's not schooled in what to see.

In the backseat next to Merle, Faye rides shotgun/right-side spotter. Holds her Glock, has the optimal post to shoot any shark cars.

Chris Harvie sits on the front passenger cushion of this vehicle he owns. He knows the way. Might be the face that needs to smile at some man with a badge & gun.

Call it a one-point-seven-mile drive from where the car is parked in the underground garage of an apartment building rising out of streets once walked by Duke Ellington.

Call it a nineteen-minute trip.

You're gripping the black padded steering wheel.

The traffic light ahead turns RED.

'Watch your zones!' Faye, *tense.*

Standing on the corner beyond your driver's side window:

Faded black baseball cap atop snowy hair. Scraggly white beard. Filthy green hoodie, worn blue jeans. Crinkled crimson skin, vacant blue eyes, dirty hands that hold a white sign black-marker scrawled: HOMELESS

Condor knew the man on the corner was really there.

Thought: *Nobody's hunting him.*

Earlier that morning.

Chris's apartment.

Gearing up, and Faye says: 'We don't *think* they know about this *us*. Don't *think* they've figured our play. The good guys are expecting Condor and me to make a move. We don't know the bad guys. Their only agenda we care about is they want us dead.'

Merle said: 'You mean you and Vin?'

'Who's Vin?' said Chris.

'Now I'm me,' said Condor.

Chris *got it*, asked Condor: 'Any words of wisdom?'

'Everybody needs a way to die,' said Condor.

'You're a horrible leader,' said the man who worked for the U.S. Senate.

Condor said: 'We also all need a way to live.

'And this,' said Condor, his smile cupping them all, 'this is our best shot.'

Faye said: 'Let's go.'

'Wait!' Merle blushed. 'Sorry, I . . . I need to use the bathroom again.'

Nerves.

Five minutes later they're all riding down in the cage of Chris's elevator.

A slammed door boomed through the concrete cavern of his underground garage.

Roofs of parked cars. Empty parking slots. Flickering fluorescent lights wave shadows on concrete walls. Oil stains. Invisible rancid garbage.

Call the slamming door *nothing*. Call it *normal*. Get in the car's assigned seats, boom your doors shut. Lock them. Your job is to grind the engine into life, *GO*.

Now in traffic on the street, the overhead signal light flashes GREEN.

Drive Massachusetts Avenue east to Capitol Hill.

Check your mirrors. No cars change lanes with you. No smoke-glassed SUVs surge into your wake. No motorcycles zip alongside for a *confirm* look. Or a quick shot.

Mass Ave led to North Capitol Street, curved around the front of the giant Union Station center for trains and subways, Metro buses, double-decker tourist movers.

But Condor turned their car right onto North Capitol, past an Irish pub that caters to Congressional staffers, lobbyists, policy wonks and other white-collar workers who fill the flat-faced, mirror-windowed, multiple-storied office buildings rising off to the right of this moving car. Half a football field later, he turned left on Third Street . . .

Cranked a quick right turn through the unguarded vehicle entrance for a man-high black chain-link fence:

LOT 11
SAA AUTHORIZED PERMITS ONLY
U.S. Senate Sergeant At Arms
Unauthorized Vehicles Will Be Towed

As Condor followed Chris's directions to an empty parking slot, Faye said: 'Congress has its own army-sized police force. Why no cops on this gate?'

Chris shrugged. 'This is a staff lot. Mostly, the police guard the buildings.'

'And the Members of Congress,' said Merle in the backseat. 'The Senators.'

In the parking slot, front bumper almost kissing the black chain metal fence, Condor said: 'Windows up. Look normal.'

All four of them got out of Chris's car.

Across the parking lot by the open pedestrian gate stood a second wood kiosk - empty, no white-shirted cop or even a civilian political appointee with a steady if mind-numbing job checking IDs. Near that gate was a steel-boxed phone topped by a blue light. Bold blue letters down the side of the phone box read: EMERGENCY.

'Cameras?' said Faye.

Chris casually looked around. 'Probably.'

'Officially,' said Faye, 'BOSS [Biometric Optical Surveillance System] won't be on line for two more years, but we all know what *officially* means. Even without BOSS zapping real-time facial recognition scan results into the grid, if they know we're coming here and are up on or hacked this zone's cameras . . . They'll spot us first.'

'Then they're already on us,' said Condor. 'We are who we are.'

'A three-minute walk?' Faye asked Chris as they stood by his parked car.

'At most. You saw the map, the Google Street View.'

'The real terrain always surprises you,' said Faye.

Condor said: 'Let's go.'

They stepped into the formation they planned at dawn.

Chris took *point*. Wore a suit, his Senate Staff ID dangling around his neck.

Faye walked two paces behind and to Chris's right: *forward fire position*.

Unarmed Merle walked behind the younger woman, and to her left.

Condor took *drag*, hands dangling alongside his unzipped black leather jacket. Two spare ammo magazines filled the back left pocket of his black jeans, their empty pouch and the .45's holster clipped to Faye's crowded belt under her black coat.

Don't let my pistol pop out of my belt.

Plan is, slip the .45 and ammo to badge-packing Faye before the metal detectors.

Don't let me need my gun until then.

'Two choices for our on-foot,' Chris explained that morning when they were still safely in his apartment studying his computer screen. 'Well, two *logical* choices.

'Out of Lot Eleven's pedestrian entrance on the diagonal Louisiana Avenue, maybe twenty steps to D Street. Go left two blocks. Right a short block. Walk up the white marble steps and we're at the Russell Senate Office Building. Most everybody takes that route.

'Or, detour through the park alongside D Street. From where we come out of Lot Eleven, cut through the park on crisscross diagonal sidewalks. Could be other pedestrians. Tourists. Union Station commuters. Staffers. Joggers. Bikers. Now and then you see a homeless person sleeping or slouched in the grass.'

'Security cameras?' asked Faye.

'I doubt it. No place in the park to mount them, no pre–9/11 existing poles or structures. Every inch of land up there is historic preservation.' He shrugged. 'D Street is wide. Major sidewalks. Quicker, straight shot. You can scope out the cars driving past. See the first police checkpoint two-plus blocks away. See somebody coming.'

'We're four somebodies,' said Faye. 'We'll stand out. Easier to spot, ID.'

'Okay,' said Chris, 'one block through the park, zigzag sidewalks, then we gotta step out to D Street, but by then, we'll be right under the eyes of the police checkpoint.'

'A walk in the park,' said Merle. 'To Hart's main entrance, right?'

'Yeah, the staff and public entrance,' said Chris that morning in his apartment as he finished his cup of coffee. 'We should time it so we get there after rush hour's long lines at the security check, white-shirted cops and metal detector arches. Sometimes they have a dog. We should show up between nine twenty and nine thirty.'

Now it's nine fifteen on a beautiful spring Friday morning.

Carillon bells chimed atop the one-hundred-foot tall, thirty-foot wide white cement Robert A. Taft Memorial a few blocks from where they stood in the parking lot.

'Who's he?' said Condor after Chris named the source of the bells.

'Who cares?' said Faye.

They marched out of Lot Eleven to cut through a manicured urban oasis. A circular garden filled the center of that park with spring flowers and holly bushes whose emerald leaves cut like razors. Bushes and trees flanked their path, tunnel walls of intermittent foliage that dappled all views of Condor and Faye and Merle and Chris marching on that tan sidewalk toward the known necessity of a head shot.

Condor walked *drag*, the cowboy term for the last rider behind the herd.

Who says post–9/11 America has forgotten its heritage.

Merle marched two paces ahead of him. He knew the tactical folly of watching the rolling sway of round hips in her blue jeans, but *damn*. Walking ahead and off to Merle's left, out of line to increase the odds that one bullet won't drop two members of the patrol, came Faye in her black coat under her backpack purse, scanning the vacant path they're following, the path that runs past where Chris walks point.

Not as good as those Marines in the 'Stan, but they get the idea, thought Condor.

A bicyclist whipped around the cement circle surrounding the garden in the center of the park. Pedaled toward them on a ten-speed steed. Even at forty meters, thirty-nine, thirty-eight, Condor noticed the biker's a man, not wearing a safety helmet, has only the hood of his black sweatshirt pulled over his bent-down skull.

Call it thirty-two meters and like a show-off seventh grader, the whizzing-closer biker . . . sits up to ride with no hands.

Condor and Faye heard cinema archivist Merle who walked between them mutter: *'I've seen this movie.'*

See the biker sitting tall twenty-nine meters & closing, riding with no hands - his hands coming together out in front of him holding -

'Gun!' yelled Condor.

Faye'd been looking back to Merle, whirled forward to face -

Great shot.

Black hoodie male, *no-hands*, balancing on a bike. Sitting tall. Racing twenty-seven, twenty-six meters toward Primary Threat/Priority 2 Target who's broken her expected motion to look away/whirl back and it's a silencer-handicapped 9 mm pistol two-handed shot, *propelled shooter* to *evading target* profiled as wearing a ballistic vest, a *phutt*-whine.

The bullet ripped across the right side of Faye's skull.

Her cry turned Chris around to see her staggering as double-tap follow-on rounds punched into her chest, her ballistic vest.

Chris charged their attacker: *'No!'*

The biker snapped a *phutt* shot that whined a bullet past Condor's right ear, then that black hoodie gunman needed to zero the suit & tie charging his bike.

Phutt! Phutt! Phutt! Silenced slugs punched red holes in Chris's center mass.

He crumpled on the sidewalk to become an island birthing its own maroon lake.

Biker one-hand grabbed his handlebars as he flew past the fallen man. The first target he shot is staggering. He scans to acquire Priority 1 Target, a guy in a black leather jacket who's crashed through a bush, off the path but not hidden and certainly not bulletproofed by foliage and -

Merle shoved the biker blowing past her.

Forward momentum plus inertia plus trained athleticism. They're not enough. The black hoodie killer somersaults over the handlebars of the bike as it flips into the air. He breaks his fall with a forward judo roll, but the sidewalk knocks the gun from his hand as he crashes into a bush opposite the foliage wall where Condor dived.

Faye staggers to a shaky combat crouch, claws her Glock into her right fist -

Spots Chris in a scarlet lake.

Condor's on his feet, .45 in fist, booms a shot toward a black shape scurrying on the ground beyond two mulched bushes.

Faye blasts a round toward their attacker, her shot even more wild than Condor's. As Merle runs into their field of fire.

Condor swung the black barrel of his .45 from Merle to *where's the black hoodie biker*? Condor glanced left, behind him: Faye's wobbling toward where Chris is . . .

Is dead.

No doubt.

Faye's got a crimson smear matting the hair on the right side of her head, dazed eyes, she's trying to aim, shoot. *She'll kill us with wild fire!*

Condor pulled Merle behind him as he kept his gun zeroed to the last place he'd seen the assassin biker.

No other fire! No other shooters! Where are they? Where are they?

'Grab Faye!' he yelled to Merle.

Merle yanks Faye away from the sticky red lake surrounding Chris.

Condor backpedals across the park, pulls the two women with him.

Faye lunges toward where the killer should be. Fires two blasts from her Glock, bullets crashing through brush, the booms echoing off the marble of Union Station blocks behind them, the sound fading against the marble buildings of Congress.

Condor thrust the .45 in his belt, grabbed the Glock from Faye, and with Merle muscled and ran the sobbing, blood-matted-haired younger woman from the park.

Nobody's shooting at us! Still nobody shooting at us!

Sirens cut the air.

Their shoes scraped the pavement of Lot Eleven: Chris's car. Condor has the keys. Wet boys should be right behind them, a combat team in *move-shelter-shoot* attack mode. Condor shoved Merle and Faye into the backseat of Chris's car, dove behind the steering wheel, keyed the engine to life.

Any second! The bad guys will start shooting from behind us any second!

He slammed the gearshift into REVERSE, punched the gas/stomped on the brake. The car shot backwards out of the yellow-striped parking spot - squealed shuddered stopped. Condor jerked the gearshift to DRIVE, smashed his foot on the accelerator.

The car rocketed back into its parking spot.

Crashed through the black chain-link fence.

Flew out of Lot Eleven. Tires bounce on the sidewalk, steel scrapes concrete, the car lurches into the road. Cars coming at it from both sides hit their horns and brakes.

Condor and his surviving crew careened toward downtown D.C., their engine-clattering getaway car spewing hot metal & oil-stench black fumes.

28

NO MORE FOREVER
- Chief Joseph

... head my head dead, he's dead why not me, him not him, head ...

Faye's right hand blurred into focus as it dropped from her head and like an echo came her realization: *'Blood on my hand.'*

Waking from nowhere, Faye felt herself thrown with inertia -

Caught, held, stopped, cradled in the arms of *woman, some woman* Merle.

Backseat, thought Faye. We're sitting, *riding* in the backseat of a car.

And ...

Burning bright sunlight glaring blue and white flashes in all the windows.

And ...

Sound, no sound, why is there no sound?

Condor is driving.

Like a bat out of hell, went through her mind, then: *Not bat, he's Condor.*

A swerving right-hand turn sucked Faye into a whirlpool of sound: *Car horns/shouts/crying tires/whooshing wind past the open windows*, and hot, sweating ...

'Shot him,' Faye heard herself mutter. 'They shot him.'

'Faye!' Condor yelled as he cranked the car around a corner. 'Can you focus?'

Merle loosened her grip around the wounded woman. Said: 'Are you okay?'

'They shot me in the head,' whispered Faye.

She stared at her blood-smeared palm.

Merle kept her from touching her throbbing/burning skull.

'You're okay,' Merle lied. 'The bullet just cut along the side of . . . Gash in your hair, blood yeah, but . . . It didn't break the bone, go in your head!'

Condor yelled from the driver's seat: 'Concussion!'

Merle locked her gaze on Faye's green eyes with their mushrooming black pupils.

'Yeah,' said the older woman who had gray-blond hair that wasn't matted with her own fucking red gore. 'Maybe.'

Engine valves clattered. The hurtling car jerked, spasmed.

Faye said: 'Stinks, oil, what's burning, what's . . .'

The car felt like a fighter plane, veered out, traffic 'n' *Condor's swerved the car into empty space at curb, but . . .*

Bus stop. We're parked in a bus stop.

Car door opened as Condor disappeared between her eyes and the windshield.

Faye said: 'Chris is dead.'

The curbside door beside her flew open.

Condor helped Merle guide Faye from the backseat to the sidewalk. 'Yeah, he's dead. We will be, too, if we don't move. You've gotta move, Faye. Come on!'

But no.

Faye felt herself zoom back as if she could see them standing on that sidewalk:

Condor in his black leather jacket, fretting beside her like a trapped raptor.

Merle looking older, terrified.

And her, *me*, a smear of dark red goo matte on my cracked head.

We're in Chinatown.

A grand three-pagodas-topped arch rose over the city street, a faux portal with fake gilt and green friezes of gold-painted calligraphy that could mean anything or nothing. Past the arch, Faye spotted a mammoth red-brick church with a rusted spire stabbing heaven. This early in the morning, this early in spring, this early in tourist season, vendors had yet to crowd the sidewalks in front of Asian restaurants and stores where you could buy plastic Buddhas (standing laughing or *zazen* somber), satin jackets emblazoned with dragons, black *gung fu* slippers, electronic gizmos for every credit card, herbs & spices and bins of red, white & blue souvenirs, postcards for if you still believed in Ben Franklin's snail mail, umbrellas - whatever the shopkeepers could make your heart desire.

'Come on!' said Condor.

But he left it for Merle to take Faye's arm, to help the wounded woman.

Keeping his hands open and dangling by his sides for *gun*, realized Faye.

'Shooters!' muttered Faye as they made her stumble along H Street's sidewalk.

She pawed her belt where . . . *No gun! Where's my gun!*

'Wet boys, the Oppos, where are they, where . . . where . . .'

'They're out here.' Condor led the way across H Street, down toward the massive indoor amphitheater for Bruce Springsteen concerts and hockey games. 'Gotta be.'

She saw him scanning the air above other sidewalk shufflers.

What, what's he looking for? What - Cameras, closed-circuit surveillance.

Who's in that closed circuit?

Condor stepped into the doorway of an abandoned store with white-washed windows bearing a sign: COMING SOON!

But what, thought Faye as Condor pulled her into the doorway that was the size of a coffin standing on its end: *What soon comes?*

'Turn your bloody side away from the street,' he said. 'Act like you're crying.'

Faye heard him tell Merle: 'That drugstore. Get baby wipes, disinfectant ones. And there, the store next door, whichever, buy a hoodie sweatshirt for her - a big on her!'

All Faye could do was stand in that coffin-sized doorway. *Head throbbing, oh God fire on the right side of my brain!*

Breathe. In. Out. Say: 'Why haven't they killed us yet?'

'I don't know,' said Condor.

The only time Faye knew was *now*, but there must have been more, because now Merle was here carrying store sacks that had not been before. Faye felt stinging dabs on the right side of her head, pats and *Oww!* pulls of her hair, smelled . . . *Lemons*, the wipes Merle's using smell of lemons and alcohol and . . . and . . .

'Watch out!' Condor pulled Merle away from the woman hidden in the doorway.

Faye jackknifed forward, vomited.

Staggered - stabilized standing in her own shoes by Merle's grip.

Another swirl of nausea, then Faye felt lighter, clearer.

Felt Merle wiping her face, her lips, a swab inside her mouth. The flutter of a wipe falling into the vomit-smelling concrete doorway *fuck littering*. Faye heard Condor tell the older woman: '*Stand beside me facing out, screen us, watch for scanners or shooters.*' Faye felt him take off her backpack. Make sure the pockets of her black coat were empty. He eased that wrap off her. Tossed the coat over the puddle of what had been in her guts. Condor took the holster and ammo pouch for his .45 off her belt.

Then, *oh then*, that weight she'd carried for years rode holstered on her right hip. Energy flowed into her arms, her hands flexed. She helped more than hindered as Condor slid her into the soft sleeves of something, reached around to pull up a zipper, his hand brushing her breasts *Chris kisses no No NO* and then hands on her shoulders turned her around to face the street, see Condor's face, *blink*, and she's *here, now*.

Merle washed Faye's face with lemon wipes, tossed them into the rancid doorway, white squares fluttering down to another lifetime's black coat.

She gave a bottle of water to Faye.

Faye filled her mouth, swished it around, spit out what was to the sidewalk.

'*Eww!*' Two teenage girls pranced past toward the rest of their lives.

'Okay,' said Faye. She started to nod *yes*, but that hurt far too much.

Condor covered her wounded head with the hood on the sweatshirt she now wore.

Pink. I'm wearing a candy-pink hoodie.

Condor slid his aviator mirror-lensed sunglasses over Faye's eyes.

Waved down a taxi and beckoned for Merle to climb in, help as he guided Faye in. His eyes scanned the street and he jumped in the taxi, told the cabby: 'Go!'

Rolling, the taxi's driving us through downtown D.C.

Condor told the taxi driver to take them to the National Zoo.

Faye whispered: 'We're going to see the animals.'

No one in the cab knew if that was a question or a statement.

Didn't matter. After five minutes of Condor checking mirrors and side streets as the taxi drove, just past the hotel where a well-off white boy who'd failed as a Nazi and a rock musician tried - *and failed* - to murder President Ronald Reagan in order to impress a movie star, Condor said: 'Pull over. Beautiful day, we'll walk from here.'

The three of them stood on the curb near the first communist Chinese embassy.

Condor waited until he knew they'd vanished from the driving-off taxi's mirrors.

'Come on,' he said. 'We gotta get over the bridge.'

Head-throbbing, but clearly, I can see clearly through his sunglasses.

Faye said: 'You've got to be fucking kidding me. I've been . . . he's dead and . . .'

'*We're,*' he said. 'Focus on that: *we are.* All the blood and shit, but *we still are.*

'And now, we are getting our asses across that bridge.'

'Paris's great bridges,' muttered part of Faye not yet back under her control.

But this was not Paris.

This was Washington, D.C.

Call it the Connecticut Avenue Bridge. Call it the William Howard Taft Bridge. *Who was he to the man whose name Chris taught us for the Capitol Hill tower with ringing bells?* Call it a long-ass way Faye wasn't sure she could walk.

Merle whispered: 'What if they can see us?'

Maybe they could, but Faye could only shuffle one step in front of where she'd been, follow the sidewalk of this billion-mile-long bridge through the heart of Washington, D.C. Far on the other side, she saw two-story stores and cafes near the Woodley–National Zoo subway stop, knew she couldn't actually see the colorful high wall mural portrait of a white-blond wondrous Marilyn Monroe - *M.M., Merle is M.M., too, but gray-blond and Condor's something and holding my arm.*

Giant bronze statues of lions guard each corner of that bridge.

Faye glanced up at the lion they walked past: 'He's got his eyes closed.'

Halfway across this stone bridge supported by concrete arches a hundred feet above the treetops of Rock Creek Parkway, Faye looked over the corroded green railing -

Swooned with vertigo, swayed inside Merle's grip, closed her eyes behind Condor's sunglasses until the universe stopped spinning.

Let herself look.

Traffic whizzed past on the other side of the railing, its *whoosh* as unbalancing as looking down to the treetops and the long fall.

Faye glanced up to the blue sky.

Green lampposts topped by green metal eagles, their wings spread wide.

But they can never fly away.

There! The other side of the bridge, we made it, we're . . . Still in killers' gun sights.

What a sight we make.

A sliver-haired, craggy man wearing a backpack purse over a black leather jacket.

A gray-blond *used to be a beauty* who could still move but had nowhere to go.

A slumping shuffling loser *bitch* hiding inside a candy-pink hoodie and aviator sunglasses with matted hair and stinking of vomit.

Condor led them away from the street corner with its subway entrance and outdoor cafe tables, down the slope of Calvert Street toward the access road for Rock Creek Parkway. Farther in that direction loomed the sprawling complex of a hotel that catered to conventions and tour groups and expense accounts and neighborhood residents who in the coming summer would scam their way in to use the outdoor pool. He led Faye and Merle to a grassy apron between the Parkway entrance/exit road and the hotel's fence of metal bars. Led them to shadows on the grassy slope made by three close-together trees. Led them to the other side of those tall living sentinels where they could sit, collapse, not so easily be seen.

Merle passed the last water bottle she'd bought in Chinatown.

Condor took a swig. Held the bottle to Faye: 'Replenish.'

She drank half of what was left, saved the rest for Merle.

Who took three swallows and clearly yearned for more as she screwed the cap back on the water bottle, saving some *just in case*.

Condor said: 'Why was there only one shooter?'

'What the fuck!' exclaimed Merle. *'How many does it take!'*

Faye said: 'Sami has an army.'

'And our Uncle Sam sure does.'

'If it's not any uncle Sami,' said Faye, 'then who?'

'Maybe it is us,' said Condor, 'and maybe it isn't.'

More *all back* every second, Faye said: 'What the fuck are you talking about?'

Condor whispered: *'The Vs.'*

29

A WALK IN THE PARK
- The 1972 across the street from the White House presidential aides' huddle on covert ops, including the (*unsuccessful*) murder of muckraker journalist
Jack Anderson

What a rush.

The clarity of a blue sky spring morning.

Sitting on a grassy knoll.

'What are you talking about?' Faye said to Condor.

Merle glared at them: '*Who are you people?* She's been shot, Chris is dead, we're . . . You almost got us killed! I did everything I could and it didn't work. Now we're worse off and he's dead, and I can't . . .'

Her rant ran out, she took a breath, whispered: 'Who are we?'

'No,' said Faye, looking right at him, right at Condor: 'Who are Vs?'

They sat there on a city park–smelling grassy knoll that April morning, Condor and two women he'd never even talked to the week before.

And he asked: '*What would you do?*

'New York City is two towers of smoke. The Pentagon's wall is crashed in. Corpses cover a field in Pennsylvania. And except for a few novelists and one ex-spook living outside the Beltway, all our tomorrow people, the ones who are supposed to be looking ahead and seeing what's coming, their eyes didn't see or their mouths went unheard or their hands couldn't stop the horror.

'So a lot got done that we now can hardly believe. Forget about torture, renditions, secret prisons, us invading a country that had nothing to do with 9/11. That's old news and this is about what's new.

'How would you create a new spy service? We created Homeland Security and the Director of National Intelligence and got puzzle boxes on top of puzzle boxes.'

Faye pressed: 'The Vs?'

'Vapors. It's all vapors. No name, no headquarters, no gear, no IDs, no website or email address, no data chains, no flow chart because there is no organization, no budget, no mention nowhere. No box. No credit. No blame. No existence, no personnel. Maybe seven policy czars know about it, maybe by now V is all automated.

'Because it's vapors. Software. The logical transitional constellation of a quintillion data points. Dark web. Deep web. Hidden web. Vapors running through it all. A regular agency good guy enters a bad guy on a "threat ladder" or watch lists. Threat identified. The software starts to work on him, or the group, or the money-laundering bank, or . . . whatever, whoever, he's targeted in the machine.'

Merle said: 'Machines don't shoot people.'

'That's rather definitional. Armies and librarians are all part of some machine that sends pension credits and drones with missiles.

'The software computes that a guy named Seba Pezzani is a growing threat, but he isn't fitting into a doable profile for our *"real world"* spy or security agencies. So a plane ticket vanishes from some billion-dollar federal contract. An ATM activates. A pistol gets delivered from an Air Force base to a cafe in Rome and an action unit V with whatever credentials or authority and knowledge he needs. Who knows where our orders come from, who's really in charge, how all our needs actually got created. It's not *"need to know,"* it's knowing *only* what *seems* to be needed.

'The V uses people and systems to get things done and they never realize it. Soldiers or cops or office managers or guys on the street never know who put them there. They do the job they're supposed to do. No extra pay, no full knowledge, no big picture the V doesn't control. The best puppets don't know they have strings.

'Maybe a Level-One Action Operative knows he's a V, but he never knows the whole system. Maybe he thinks he's detached from Delta for sanctioned Special Ops. Maybe he's an ex–Navy SEAL who works as a personal trainer at a Missouri YMCA until he gets a text. A CIA brick agent whose Case Officer isn't really in charge of her. A retired FBI agent, a homicide cop who gets an extra thousand bucks a month from a CIA black account that records as part of the regular bribe to a Mexican general and it's all covered by IRS's computers, though Level-One Vs don't do this for the money. They believe.

'And what gets done, gets done. Only extreme cases. Only high necessities.'

'Targeted killings,' said Faye. 'Illegal assassinations. Other . . . neutralizations. Like throwing troublesome people into insane asylums, frame jobs.'

'Beautiful system,' said Condor. 'An evolution from how the Intelligence Support Activity got its start, though the V will never become a Pentagon office.'

Merle said: 'It would never work.'

'Facebook knows what ads to show you. Marketers profile what you'll want. Facial recognition systems plus behavior analysis, reconfiguring police reports and maintenance schedules on an airliner . . . *You get it*: if you link the vapors, you can see what needs to be done and you can do . . . amazing things. Not often, but when you do, nobody knows it was you, nobody knows it *was* done. You rewrite the record as you change it. Reality becomes what the data says it is.'

'Case officer,' said Faye. 'The Green Light. The decider. There has to be - '

'A dead man's switch? A heart amidst the brains of the machines? The human touch?' Condor nodded. 'There wouldn't *have* to be, but we still made one. But just one. One human entity as a fail-safe Level-Zero *control* with full knowledge programmed and final-say. Paychecks not on any audit. A quiet life with an intuitive desktop in an ordinary house in an American hometown. It's the twenty-first-century model. You work from home. The neighbor everybody waves to and nobody knows.'

'Who did this?' whispered Merle.

Condor said: 'I think it was me.'

The woman he . . . he . . . call it *whatever*, Merle stared at him.

The woman warrior who sacrificed her life for his stared at him.

'Street years,' he said, 'the week before 9/11 and I was ready to walk away, not old, but there're only so many scars you can carry. Then *boom*. And as I recovered from . . . from one rough Op, I had a great idea, a reputation and clout, some access to a place where everybody wanted answers.'

'But you went crazy,' said Faye.

'Well . . . *yeah*,' said Condor. 'The sheer rush of it, the knowing of what you could do and had to do and *did*.'

'So why do they want you dead now?' asked Faye. 'Jesus, back on Tuesday, they would have settled for you getting locked back up forever as a crazy murderer.'

Condor shrugged. 'Maybe somebody's pulling the plug on the whole system.'

'Or the whole system is trying to be sure nobody pulls the plug on it,' said Faye. 'And you, fighting their *forget-it* meds . . . Your data metric would register high risk.

'But,' she said, asking the investigator's ultimate question: 'How do you know?'

'The lone shooter on a bike,' said Condor. 'Like a *clong* only no music. Seeing him made me *realize*. Realize it wasn't Sami or Uncle Sam Ops. Because they only sent one shooter. Had to be a system short on personnel. A small Op, small team -

'And *that* flashed me on remembering the V. We dropped four out of six at the subway. No replacements, especially if the V is getting shut down. All that fit with my cover team having made the first move. The V originally brought in every *street meat* unit they had for my neutralization. Pre-position every Level-One Action V to be ready, to be ahead of you and Sami and the real guys, to be in them but not of them.'

Faye said: 'The Homeland Security guy who showed up at your house, the guy I almost shot! He was the gunner on the subway platform who got away! *The biker!*'

'Got your partner working on orders V created, killed him, waited. Knew I'd be home from work. Knew you or a team would come. I'd get taken out by the good guys.'

'But this morning,' said Faye. 'How did they know our play this morning? We're off all grids, no data for them to hijack, but even with only one guy - '

'Probably two guys,' said Condor. 'Six at the subway attack, two left. A spotter somewhere, plus the shooter on the bike. But somehow knowing we were coming, knowing Chris was taking us to the Senate Intelligence Committee offices where there'd be too many plugged-in people to hijack or control so then we couldn't be hit and we'd have gotten to Sami safe. And maybe figured all this out.'

'Two guys,' said Faye. 'How?'

Merle whispered: *'Me.'*

Faye and Condor choroused: 'What?'

'Oh God, I'm sorry! *Me me me!'*

Merle said: 'You people with your guns and your secrets, your claims that what I know isn't the real world, wasn't my world. Not after you came. Even if I . . . even if we . . .

'I'm smart. Savvy. In politics, in life, always cover your ass. I believed you, wanted to be with you, but I bought myself a protection policy. An outside alliance. You had me buy *four* phones, I went to my ATM and got money and bought *five*.

'I played my one *ask*,' she said. 'The smart thing to do, not just meekly obey my way into some shit storm. I did what would have worked and would have made our chances better and maybe covered me if you . . . If I got dumped or duped or set up.'

Condor said: 'You called him.'

'Who?' said Faye.

'The Senator who owes me,' said Merle. 'Called him yesterday. Told him to be ready, that he was going to help me with a whistleblower from the CIA, a guy I met at the Library of Congress, that maybe this would make the Senator a hero but if it didn't, it would cover his ass.'

'And you said - '

'And I said *Condor*. I spoke the word. I should have guessed what he must have done. He covered *his* ass. Probably made a call, generated a query, created a *Condor* data link so that by last night . . . Your V trolling the grid knew he was linked.'

'They just didn't know how,' said Condor.

'Just before we left Chris's apartment this morning, I went to the bathroom, cell phone hidden in my panties . . . Sent the Senator a text. Told him hell or high water, hearings or constituent or fund-raiser meetings be damned, he had to show up at nine fifteen at the main entrance to Hart and wait to escort me and mine to the Intelligence Committee offices. Safety in numbers, right? Especially when one number is a U.S. Senator. That's what was so smart. Hiding behind him.'

'Your phone!' Condor told Merle. 'They were tracking that as soon as you texted the Senator. GPS knew where we were, the parking lot, knew we were coming on foot. One spotter on a laptop relaying data, the other . . . How he got a bike . . .'

Merle flowed to her feet before Condor or Faye could stop her.

'Oh God, they're on us now!' said Merle.

'The phone! Get it out, pull it - '

'No,' she said.

'No,' she whispered.

Her eyes focused far away as Merle said, 'Me being smart got Chris killed. Me being smart might let you stay alive.'

Merle's cheeks glistened.

Condor stepped to comfort her, took his hands in hers, she cupped his face -

Merle kneed him in the groin.

Condor collapsed to his knees on the grassy knoll.

Blinding pain gagging gasping . . .

Hearing Merle: 'I wish I could be who you want me to be!'

His eyes opened to a teary blur of Faye in a pink hoodie struggling to stand.

As up the slope from the grassy knoll ran Merle, up to the busy D.C. street . . .

Gone.

She's gone.

'Come on.' Faye pulled Condor to his feet, the wounded helping the lame. 'You can't catch her. She did what she did. Now she's trying to make up for it. She knows they're on the phone she's got, they'll track her, so she's running until . . .'

Faye caught her breath. 'She got Chris killed. And she bought us our *until.*'

She and Condor pulled the batteries of the cell phones Merle'd bought them, tossed the debris into the woods. Late-morning sun warmed them as they shuffled off a grassy knoll, the wounded leaning on the old & lame.

'I want to shoot her,' confessed Faye as each step made her lean more on him.

'I want to shoot me,' said Condor as a greater ache replaced the one in his groin.

They kept their guns holstered out of sight as Condor helped Faye toward the hotel's taxi & shuttle bus–crowded horseshoe driveway. He adjusted the pink hoodie to cover the mess on her head, didn't need to tell her to keep her face down because she could barely hold it up, barely keep walking beside him.

Nervous families everywhere, thought Condor as he shuffled toward the hotel's sliding glass doors, a female form in a pink hoodie wrapped in his left arm, his right hand pressed against his black leather jacket. *Dads. Moms*.

Half a dozen suits & ties fretted in the airplane-ride-dressed crowd of . . . *More than tourists*. Condor dodged an overstacked luggage cart, pushed through loud families.

College kids, he thought, then, *No: soon-to-be college kids*.

School visits. Lots of universities, colleges in D.C. Everybody should see Washington. Bring the whole family, make a vacation of it and *no*, we won't embarrass you, we deserve to see the place we'll mortgage our future to so you can learn how the world works and get a recognized passport to a tomorrow of paychecks and promises.

Someone's nine-year-old little brother in blue jeans and booger stains dashed through the crowd. A school-colors lanyard & plastic name-tagged ID flew off the boy, but he never looked back. Never saw Condor rescue the ID from being trampled by shoes hurrying across the vast hotel front lobby floor.

The lanyard's name tag read: VISITOR.

Aren't we all.

Deep in the lobby lounged couches and padded chairs, end tables to hold cocktails from the hotel bar. As eleven A.M. checkout ticked closer, most chairs were filled by suitcase-guarding spouses or (*less often*) solo high-schoolers thinking that back home wasn't so bad after all. Last-minute discards cluttered the end tables - brochures, visitor packets, other relics from the era of dead trees.

An older woman used a black cane to leverage herself from a lobby chair.

Condor lowered Faye into that vacated seat. Adjusted her slump so the hood covered most of her pained face. He shrugged out of her backpack purse he'd been wearing since Chinatown, set the clunking backpack in Faye's lap.

Whispered: 'Don't let people see your face. Try to look young.'

The lanyard draped around his neck.

I am who I say I am.

He floated here. He floated there. Cruised through the crowd. Past the lobby cart with the barista selling chocolate and coffee confections, pastries. Past the front desk where black-suited clerks dealt with a crush of airport-bound guests.

A packet from the same university as his VISITOR name tag drifted to his hands.

Elevator doors slid open. Out hurried a haggard dad with a sullen ten-year-old daughter whose hand was grabbed by a mom with an unmistakable *had it up to here* look. A nearby college-age daughter slouched in another world even though she could have reached out and touched the woman who gave birth to her. Mom yelled at the man who'd given these two daughters to her: 'Come on, the Stevenses are parked out front to drive us to the airport!'

Already four steps behind his fleeing family, the father slapped an electronic key card on an unmanned counter with a slot on its front wall that read: KEY DEPOSIT. His face showed *good enough* as he hurried out of the hotel after his family.

No one saw Condor palm the key card off the counter.

The clock above the crowded front desk read 10:57.

No one destined for the Stevenses' airport ride came back through the hotel's sliding glass doors. Out there, in the horseshoe driveway, amidst the thinning herd of taxis and shuttle buses, Condor saw no anxiously parked & packed private vehicle.

A confident woman in her mid-thirties wearing a black-skirted business suit settled at the concierge's desk across the lobby, clicked on the desktop computer.

Condor and a posh woman clutching an iPhone reached the concierge's desk at the same time, but with a grandiose sweep of his arm, he signaled Ms. iPhone to go first.

Of course she said: 'Thank you.'

Sat down and started talking to the concierge, who met her words with a smile and only a fraction-of-a-second look at the silver-haired gentleman who'd kindly stepped aside and now waited with his hands crossed over his black leather jacket and a look that said he appreciated the concierge's appreciation.

At 11:04, the posh woman climbed into a taxi outside in the hotel's horseshoe driveway and the nice gentleman who'd waited took the seat across from the concierge.

Any hospitality professional could see he looked terrible.

The man wearing the lanyard used by parents visiting a D.C. university set the packet they'd given him on the desk, sighed. 'I'm sorry, we didn't expect this trouble.'

'What can I do to help, sir?'

'Got a time machine for guests? Or maybe a daughter exchange - bad joke, I love her, we wouldn't trade her for the world, but . . . They all say this is the difficult year.'

The concierge's polite smile offered encouragement. Understanding.

'And I know, it's late, but the crowd at the front desk, and I didn't spot you here until . . .' *Now let her off the hook.* '. . . until that woman needed to go first, and yesterday, orientation, how were we to know? Sure, why not let the older girl spend the night with her new roommate and her parents, and this morning she's here waiting for us in the lobby like she was supposed to, but - *Don't look, but over there? In the pink hoodie?*'

The flick of the concierge's eyes confirmed: pink hoodie, female, slumped in a chair trying not to be seen, not to be here. Verified data.

'We come down to go with the Stevenses to their place in Virginia before we catch the plane out of Dulles tomorrow and *Oh shit*, she's sitting there trying to hide the scabbiest, yuckiest bloodiest bruise on her head, saying she won't go with the Stevenses, won't go to school here, just wants to go home, and *no* she won't talk to her mother and the little one's got . . . let's just call it "a condition," needs her mom to go with her, not be the one to stay here with Callie and get to the bottom of *what's going on*.'

The concierge gave him a lipstick frown: 'Sir, does your daughter need medical attention?'

'No, I was a medic - No way could you have even been alive during Vietnam. Bottom line, we split things up, my wife and I, so I didn't pay attention if she pre-checked out or at the desk, but here's the thing: Deb and my wife are going with the Stevenses, I'm going to stay here and let Callie come around to telling me what the hell's going on, and tomorrow we'll meet up at Dulles, but . . .'

The silver-haired father passed his key card to the concierge. A hard piece of evidence, of reality, of truth.

'The waiting to get to you made me miss the check-out time, automatic or whatever my wife did at the front desk, but here's my key.'

The concierge swiped the volunteered electronic key card through the reader slot on her desk, said: 'Yes, Mr Cordingley, we show an automatic checkout.'

'You're right, and that's the problem. I've got a teenage girl trying not to burst out crying at any moment, answers to get before we get on the plane home tomorrow, and I needed to roll our checkout to then before eleven, but you weren't here until now and the wait . . .'

'You want to extend your reservation?'

'You're right, please, just like it is, or if we need to take another room . . .'

They did, smaller room, twin beds, 729 West, on the same credit card?

Of course.

The quiet of a hotel room.

Condor lay on one freshly made bed.

Faye lay on the other bed.

She started to cry.

Me, too.

Gone, then *whoosh*: back. Maybe he slept, maybe he didn't. Afternoon light filled the hotel room windows. His watch shows four o'clock.

And he heard Faye say: 'Wait.'

Condor sat on his bed to face her sitting up, feet on the floor to face him.

She said: 'You've got the backpack, the laptop computer from Merle?'

He got the laptop, handed it to her.

'Confession,' she said. 'When I was alone, I downloaded a "Protect Your Kids" program. Cost Merle's credit card a couple hundred dollars. I programmed our disposable phones with a GPS tracker parents buy to snoop on their teenagers, set up the system in this laptop. A full analysis of her phone at the Agency would spot it, but it's designed to hide itself from savvy teenagers, so . . .'

'So the Vs tracked her secret phone she hid from us, *but* because of what you hid from me and Merle, you and I can secretly track her other phone?'

Faye shrugged.

'Can it back trace? Can the V - '

'Maybe,' said Faye. 'But only if somebody's looking to do that.'

'And if they've . . . got Merle, clearly it's a throwaway burner, they'll pull our pre-programmed numbers but we ditched those phones, no batteries, no signals, so . . .'

Three minutes and they were staring at the laptop screen's street map of a neighborhood just outside the Beltway in the urban sprawl that is America's capital.

A blue dot pulsed on the screen's map. The address displayed.

'She's there,' whispered Condor.

'The *phone* is there.' Faye worked the laptop. 'Been there since 2:07. Before that - look, the map tracks her route, one stop near here at . . .'

'The zoo,' said Condor. 'She ran to the zoo. Found someplace to sit, the bear pit, watched animals until . . . They came and got her. They didn't just kill her there, or - '

He grabbed the laptop. Clicked onto the *Washington Post* website.

'Senate aide shot on Capitol Hill. Car stolen.' He read the story by reporter Claudia Sandlin, a half-dozen paragraphs, Congressional police force, FBI, suspects including a woman, stolen car found oil pan burned-out in downtown D.C. Unknown if a strong-arm theft of a bicycle from a commuting EPA worker who was knocked unconscious six blocks away earlier in the morning was related.

Condor whispered: 'They've lost control.'

'Who?'

'Everybody. Sami and the Agency and the V. Too much, too fast, too public.'

He clicked to fill the laptop screen with the map and its pulsing blue dot.

Tell Faye the truth.

'This much chaos,' he said, 'the V's down this much . . . Good chance we could Panic Line or other way go in, get to Sami, an official if . . . banged-up exfiltration. Get in alive and give it all up to the good guys, to the system, to what's supposed to work.'

She stared at him with her green eyes where the pupils now looked normal.

But she's not seeing me.

The blue dot pulsed.

Condor said: 'They either killed her or got her, but they got her phone. Either way, that's where I'm going.'

'If we go in to the Agency - '

'What will be their priority?' said Condor. 'Whoever they are. Whoever we can trust. Sami? The V still running on a hijacked official record? The moment we show up, we get logged in by somebody, and you know some innocent rule-follower will do that, then that blue dot . . . Then there's only one smart option for the V with that blue dot.'

He picked his .45 off the bed. Looked around for his black leather jacket.

'It's about more than Merle's blue dot,' he said. 'She'd be enough, but . . . *Truth*?'

Faye nodded.

'If I go in without finishing this, I'm just part of the program,' said Condor.

'You're only one beat-up old man.' She wobbled to her feet. 'Odds are, two of them minimum. And they're good. They could probably put us down in their sleep. You know that, I can see it in your face. Hell, even if I was at my best . . .'

'You've got a concussion.'

'Pro football players get back in the game with concussions.'

'They die young.'

'It's not about dying anymore. This is about what I've got to live with.'

She took a step -

Fell back to sitting on the bed, bumped into Condor, knocked him to his bed.

They stared at what they couldn't avoid seeing.

She said: 'You can't take them on without me, and I can't make it. Not now.'

The blue dot pulsed.

Faye said: 'Whatever the worst of it is for Merle, it's already happening or happened or never gonna happen because they're holding her, maybe no extreme measures or . . . monster mayhem. Even if we could walk out that door now, quickest we could get there is forty minutes. Like this. Like who we are now. No prep, no Google Street View recons, no nothing but two fucked-up, off-the-rez guns. You like those odds?'

Don't tell her that she's right.

She said: 'If it's only a phone waiting for us, something some citizen found, if we go now, we'll get dropped like this and odds are, only our going down to show for it.'

'When?' he said.

'When we see what more chaos breaks loose. When we see more whatever *they* do. When we got a chance. When you and I are who the fuck we can be.'

'When?' he repeated.

'You know when,' she said.

And when they'd showered, when they'd room serviced and when she'd eaten without throwing up, when they'd watched & read news and when they'd computer reconned and strategized and when he'd gone out & come back, when he'd shared pills to fight pain & coax sleep and when they lay under the covers of their separate beds, when the turned-off laptop was set on the shelf near the black-screen TV . . .

What he knew, what he felt, what he saw and heard in his waking and his dreams and his nightmares was a blue dot pulsing like a lone human heart.

30

EVERYBODY NEEDS A WAY TO DIE
- Condor

Saturday-morning suburbia and Faye sits in a stolen car - fuck it, fuck them.

Fuck me.

Outside the windshield is a cul-de-sac. Seven low brick houses spun out around a traffic circle, a road spoke leading downhill to the dead-end street that got you here, *now*, eleven A.M., checkout time back at the hotel for lies you left at dawn, *sayonara suckers*.

Call here Silver Spring, Merry-land, just a kiss outside the Beltway but still *Death City*, America, a suburban human terrain of wage earners. The lucky households are home to two of them. Too many households get too few or too tiny paychecks in this neighborhood where *getting by* is a step above *getting gone*.

Lots of April-green trees.

A wall of trees, then a high wooden fence on the Target Zone's rear perimeter, a couple low bushes, sidewalk leading to the front porch, black steel railings, five painted-red concrete steps, then the aluminum storm door with its top-half window and behind it, a solid white door. Could just be wood, could be reinforced metal, but if so, call that a landlord's paranoia because V doesn't profile with permanently secured safe houses.

Call the TZ a Crash House.

No fucking shit.

Got a back door, but getting to it means vaulting the backyard fence. *No way* can Condor get over that wooden wall in great shape & good speed for a breach.

All the windows are rolled down on Faye's stolen car crouched at a curb outside the cul-de-sac circle where two of the six non-target houses still have cars parked near them instead of cars gone grocery shopping or to kids' soccer games or whatever real people with real families do on cool green April Saturday mornings. Gray-black clouds roll over the cul-de-sac, but when did a little rain kill anybody, whereas some days staying inside means you're home when trouble comes calling, even if trouble only means to hit the house next door, those guys who you never knew, who just moved in.

How many guys?

Two guys, got to be no more, maybe less.

Plus one.

Please: plus one.

And *please*: Don't let rain wash these streets. Not yet.

House windows blocked by drawn white shades. White door. Five red steps.

Her rolled-down windows brought sounds Faye strained to hear, the scent of lilacs. She slouched behind the steering wheel, eyes staked out scanning, not locked on the TZ where *nothing* moved, where nobody could be home. Her gaze dropped to the front seat, a laptop screen and the steady pulsing of a blue dot, the words: RANGE 232 FEET.

And that address.

That house.

The TZ.

Her left thigh pressed down on the Glock .40 on the seat between her legs.

Come on, Condor! They'll make me if I keep posting here!

He'd left her alone in the hotel room for ninety-seven minutes last night.

Left her propped up in a chair with the Glock first-aid-kit white-taped in her hand in case she fell asleep or the concussion inspired a seizure at the wrong moment, the door getting kicked in while she's flopping around with no gun.

Took three taxis, two stops, he said.

Fuck cruising cover teams: We own these streets. Or die trying.

Code-knocked on the hotel room door, followed up with his *'It's you.'*

Showed her what was in the store sacks.

Look what we've got now, he'd said. Look what we can do now.

Now, motherfucker! thought Faye as she sat in the stolen car. *Now.*

An engine whined behind her on this suburban street to the cul-de-sac.

Faye scrunched beneath the stolen car's dashboard.

Thumping behind her came from the duct-taped man locked in this car's trunk.

Collateral damage. Civilian casualties. The blood of innocents.

Nothing's ever easy. Nothing's ever free. Nobody is a saint. We're all sinners.

We're all the duct-taped man locked in the trunk of a stolen car.

Still . . . *Sorry.*

A whining engine wave rolled like a wall over the stolen car. Faye saw a blur of brown metal, then it was gone and the screaming engine noise flowed with it.

Ease up. Just enough. Eyes above the dashboard, watch the cul-de-sac.

You've seen a thousand such brown delivery vans in the streets of America, of Europe, of China and India, too. A global delivery service beyond any one government system.

Street meat sent via cyber. You want it, you pay, brown brings it to your door.

The oversized step van everybody knew whined to a stop in front of a house across the cul-de-sac from TZ, one of the homes with no cars parked nearby.

The brown van's engine cut off.

No! What if it doesn't start again? What if it can't move?

Don't worry, Faye told herself. *The driver's a professional.*

The brown van's driver stepped to the pavement of the cul-de-sac. Even from half a block away, Faye recognized the driver's expected brown uniform pants & shirt. She saw his bald head, cue-ball bald and pink, and that's what you noticed, plus he wore those dorky flip-up sunglasses clipped to black horn-rimmed hipster eyewear. And even at this distance with her eyes behind Condor's aviator sunglasses, Faye's attention got diverted by a weird black smear on the left side of the driver's neck but she couldn't identify it as what it was, a spider web tattoo.

The brown-clad driver rattled open the van's rear cargo door. She couldn't see what was in the back of the van where a SWAT team could have huddled, but houses in the cul-de-sac could. The driver pulled a padded shipping envelope from a respectable load of shipping bags, packages, and boxes. He hurried up the sidewalk to the house he'd parked in front of, pushed what looked to be a doorbell.

Waited no more than five seconds before he knocked on then unlatched the aluminum storm door, put the padded envelope on the narrow ledge between the two front doors and scurried to his waiting brown van, no time to waste.

The brown van roared its engine to life. Gears ground.

The brown step van pulled away from that delivery address.

Circled along the top of the cul-de-sac.

Drove just past Faye's visual lock on the TZ.

Fucking stopped.

Again the van's engine died.

The bald spider-webbed driver hopped out of the van.

Rattled open the rear cargo hold. Got a brown-paper-wrapped box the size of an attaché case. Gripped one box edge in his left hand as he hurried . . .

Up the sidewalk to the TZ. Up the five red cement steps. Up to the aluminum outer door. Pushed the doorbell. Again, no more than five seconds and he's knocking on the aluminum storm door, opening it wide, bending over to position the heavy box on its narrow edge, but when he eased the aluminum door closed, it wouldn't shut all the way, gaped open enough for a curious citizen or a cruising cop to notice. The bald driver didn't care, hurried back to his van, fired up the engine, drove out of the cul-de-sac, turned left and cruised past where Faye huddled behind the steering wheel of a stolen car.

The van engine whined back the way it came, out of sight of where it had been.

Faye kept her eyes locked on the TZ with the gaping-open aluminum door.

Saturday morning in a quiet suburban neighborhood.

Back on Wednesday - *Jesus, was it only Wednesday, three days ago?* - at Complex Zed, when Sami sent her out, turned her loose, and she'd gone to the EDD, the Equipment Disbursement Detail, got Santa to give her cash and credit cards, give her ammo for her own gun and the ballistic vest she wore now, the .38 and .45 Condor used.

And Santa'd said: 'You going to war, Agent?'

Faye'd lied and told him: 'I know what I'm doing.'

Wish I could go back, say something different.

Tell Santa: 'Not going to war, going to finish one.'

Now on a suburban Saturday morning, the backpack purse Santa'd helped her fill lay crumpled and flat on the backseat of the stolen car. One of Santa's two Delta Force compact flash-bang grenades was *gently* duct taped to the left side of the bulletproof ballistic vest she wore under her fucking pink hoodie.

Eyes on TZ.

The door - *the white door*, last door before in there - that door slowly opened.

Let her see a compact man, short brown hair, beard like Spec Ops, unbuttoned shirt. The man in TZ's now open entryway stood on the other side of the outer aluminum door propped open by a delivered package, scanning for shooters.

Saw nobody.

He picked up the brown van–delivered package.

White light BANG! as the Delta Force grenade IED duct taped to the bottom of the delivered box blew the bearded man backwards into the house.

Faye swung up behind the stolen car's steering wheel, keyed its engine to life and stomped on the gas, careened a hard right turn into the cul-de-sac braking to a stop in front of the TZ, jumping out of the car with a Glock .40 in her right hand, her left hand slapping a store-bought, magnetized emergency spinning light that spun red flashes of officialdom from the top of the stolen car that might - *might* - convince civilians in the cul-de-sac that there was no need to call 911 after that big boom and flash at the house where the *could-be-a-cop-car* car now parked, with a woman wearing a pink hoodie charging the glass-broken, aluminum-buckled outer door.

A bald man now wearing black jeans and a black leather jacket ran toward the stolen car with the spinning red light.

Faye cleared the five red concrete steps in two strides, shoved the buckled aluminum door aside, snapped her Glock up to zero -

Man on the empty living room floor! Uncurling from fetal position! Beard, brown hair, gasping, face burned making noise he can't hear and -

Gun, he's got a gun, fumbling a pistol with a silencer, hands turning it!

The blind, deaf, and burned man was a warrior who knew his weapon.

Knew how to push its silencer-sausaged barrel into his mouth, jab the cold black bore toward the top of his skull - *Phutt!*

Crimson gore sprayed the white wall by the kitchen door.

The man with the gun in his mouth lay crumpled like a gone-to-sleep child.

What lie did you buy?

What truth couldn't you face?

No time, gun up, Faye zeroed the hall to the right of the empty living room:

Two open doorways on the hall, right side. Probably bedrooms.

End of the hall, open door, medicine cabinet above a sink: bathroom.

Left side of the hall, open door, a glimpse of . . . washer spigots, dryer plug-in, machines gone. Laundry room, storage closet.

Condor, beside her, bald head from the electric clippers and razors he'd bought at the late-night drugstore, the same family emporium with a children's aisle full of close-outs from last Halloween, temporary tattoos made from and washed off by water like the rain that mercifully hadn't yet fallen today to smear the ink on his neck, the eye-trapping spider web. He had his .45 combat focused, obeyed her gesture to clear the kitchen.

As he moved to his fire zone, she eased down the hall toward the open bathroom.

The hallway seen over the barrel of her Glock:

First bedroom door.

Edge forward along the wall.

Faye dropped to her hands and knees -

Whirled/rolled flat on her back & stomach past the first open bedroom door, facing & gun aiming *in*, watching a spinning topsy-turvy turning view of . . .

Sleeping bag * open suitcase * dirty clothes * water bottle * closet open empty -

Nobody.

She pulled her legs under her as she sat with her back pressed against the wall, the second bedroom door open and to her right, better view of the laundry room *empty*, see most of the interior of the end of the hall bathroom *empty*, second bedroom *Gotta be!*

One grenade left *fuck it* lob it in the bedroom *close eyes cover ears open mouth* -

White light/BANG!

Faye's world burned and bonged for maybe fifteen seconds before she could see and stagger to her feet, combat charge into the room she'd blasted.

The man pushing himself to sitting against the empty white wall was a mess: scrapes on his goatee/scraggly-bearded face, Band-Aid on his forehead below short-cropped dirty brass hair. He wore a white scooped-neck T-shirt, gray sweatpants, and bare feet. A non-hospital-applied long white bandage striped from his left collarbone down his sinewy muscled chest to well below his heart, like it covered a furrow from, say, a .45 bullet. He had a black eye, puffy lips that must have drawn stares when he stalked through the zoo the day before, but he'd made it then, and he made it to sitting up now, but his gun, some kind of prototype black automatic pistol with a silencer, his pistol he'd been a star with yesterday, that gun lay blown across the room.

Faye guessed his still-dazed eyes came from field-kit pain-fighting morphine.

He'd been the executioner who crucified her asshole partner with knives.

He'd been the *protocol* Homeland Security agent outside Condor's house.

He'd been the Monkey Man on the subway platform before Condor's shots dropped him into a rushing-out train.

He was the biker.

He pushed his bare heels on the carpeted floor - not to get away, but to sit straighter against the white wall.

As he stared into the bore of Faye's gun.

She let her vision expand to take in where he'd been living. Sleeping bag on the floor, camping lamp and other gear, a cheap suitcase with his clothes, two high-quality black cloth material bags she instinctively knew were full of combat gear.

A paperback book lay on the floor beside his camping pillow. Some novel.

The Vs squatting in this house were out-of-towners. Brought in from the black.

The battered V stared at the woman beyond the gun zeroed on his life.

Said: 'So . . . *Hey.*'

'*Hey*,' said Faye.

Black gun barrel pointed straight at the man sitting against the white wall.

Who told her: 'Your turn.'

Faye didn't see her Glock flash or hear the roar as she shot him in the head.

Then: *There he is, shooting nobody no more with his bloody three eyes.*

She combat swept the empty kitchen where the only documents were eviction notices this team had torn off the white door when they moved in to squat.

Eased down the basement stairs.

Condor sat on the basement floor beside a support beam for the ceiling. Once upon a time, the basement's other room had been a home office, wired for computers and a big-screen TV, but now that carpeted room was empty, as was its adjoining bathroom. Out here, where Condor sat, was only *empty basement* with a clear plastic drop cloth unfolded over the home-owner-installed floor tiles. On that plastic drop cloth sat Condor.

With Merle.

She was naked. Slumped with her spine against the support beam, arms limp at her sides, wrists stuck to strips of white tape. Condor'd cut her free from the beam. Her cheeks were red from ripped-away white tape stuck over her mouth. Blond-gray hair hung matted and tangled to her slumped bare shoulders. Faye smelled that Merle sat in her own waste. Condor'd been whispering to Merle as Faye followed her gun down the stairs to the basement, but by the time she joined them, he'd stopped. Merle's eyes were open but whatever she was seeing wasn't there.

'Did they drug her or . . .' Faye found no more words.

'Doesn't matter,' whispered the suddenly old-looking man. 'She's gone.'

Faye heard him strangle a sigh, or maybe it was a sob.

He told her: 'Maybe Maine. The hospital. Maybe she'll come back there.'

Then . . .

Oh then!

. . . he softly so softly pressed his lips to her forehead.

Clumped back up the stairs, the .45 dangling limp and impotent in his hand.

They found Merle's phone on the kitchen counter.

Faye never knew what made her open the refrigerator door.

But she did.

The only thing she found in that cool-air refrigerator waited on its top shelf:

A clear glass jar where two eyeballs floated in pink lemonade-like liquid.

She felt Condor come stand behind her.

He said: 'Your partner. What they took to frame me after they crucified him.'

Faye whispered: 'Who are these people?'

Condor reached around her, closed the refrigerator, said: 'They're us.'

When she looked at him, he added: 'Only let's hope we're better and luckier.'

'This isn't who I wanted to be,' said Faye.

'Me either. But here we are.'

Faye said: 'We've got to decide - '

Condor dropped to his hands and knees beside the suicide corpse, sniffed the curled-up body like . . . *Like a werewolf*, thought Faye. *Or a . . . vulture*.

'Smells like gasoline.'

He spotted the bulge in the dead man's front pocket, pulled out an iPhone.

'There's a GPS in it, right?' he asked the younger woman.

She showed him how to access the GPS and its search request. She went to the bedroom, to the other KIA enemy, got the cell phone from beside his bed and didn't look at him, at what she'd done, no she didn't. *Deserved is deserved and dead, Chris is dead.*

Faye got back to the living room as Condor headed toward the front door, car keys he'd scooped off the counter in one hand, the suicide man's iPhone in the other.

Is his .45 in the holster under his black leather jacket?

Siren: coming closer.

Neighbors.

Not such an ordinary suburban Saturday.

'Wait!' said Faye as Condor walked outside, as she chased after him.

He stood on the red concrete front porch. Pointed the car key's fob at the parked vehicles other than the stolen car he'd scouted the night before then gotten the tools for at the drugstore and broken into with Faye at dawn three peaceful neighborhood blocks away from the hotel. Condor pushed the LOCATE button on the fob.

Lights flashed on a new-model Japanese-designed car built in Tennessee to politically appease Americans. Faye heard its driver's door unlock with a *clunk*.

Faye asked Condor: 'What about the delivery van driver we hijacked and taped up and stuck in the trunk of the car we stole?'

Bald Condor said: 'Let him breathe.'

Then he roared away in the car that had been the killers', the Vs'.

Siren: maybe five blocks away.

Faye held the HOMELAND SECURITY ID folder out and open in her left hand.

Used her right thumb to work the cell phone from the man she killed, *I killed him, I killed him*, call the number she knew.

After two buzzes - he's checking caller ID, launching trace - Sami answered.

Faye said: 'Guess who.'

A police car topped by a spinning red light sirened into the cul-de-sac.

31

GONNA TAKE SOMEONE APART
- Richard Thompson, 'I Feel So Good'

You're driving a stolen car where it's supposed to go.

A robot woman talking out of a cell phone tells you so.

'In fifty feet . . . turn right.'

Of the last seven locations this phone had mapped, five had been gas stations near on/off ramps for the Beltway.

The sixth address belonged to the Crash House where Condor'd stolen this car.

Where Merle.

Location seven had to be it.

Familiar streets.

He wasn't sure if he remembered where he was, and if so from *when*, or if he'd just driven so many American suburbs that the streets now all looked the same. Certainly nothing outside the windows of his car showed a geographic or cultural individuality, an unmistakable identity, an easy clue that this 'town' claimed its turf alongside quick highways to CIA headquarters and the Pentagon. To the National Security Agency, FBI headquarters, Complex Zed.

Once upon a time, these streets hosted a satellite veterans' hospital for Walter Reed - rumor had it, the psych ward - but that facility had been shut down, as had the 1950-something faux castle complex where two buildings were still surrounded by a gray cement wall complete with parapets to look like a local hustler's version of what in that *way back when* had been a brand-new futuristic dollar magnet called Disneyland.

A railroad track slid by Condor's view outside the driver's window, steel rails that made him think he heard a lonesome whistle blow.

You're done with hallucinations.

Stuck in this *real*.

With the graveyard the robot woman guided him past.

Gardens of the dead are everywhere.

The stolen car he drove smelled like gas inside its passengers' compartment.

Figure that one out.

He drove past old houses, some sagging, some rehabbed by the latest hopeful generation of Moms & Dads with kids, so there was a playground, another set of empty swings. Front porches, a seedy apartment complex from some pale lime stucco-walled former motel. Lawns led back from the street. Lots of space between the houses. Hard to hear what was happening next door.

'Arriving at destination . . . On left, one hundred feet.'

He parked the car at the curb across the street and half a block from *destination*.

Looked like a horror-movie country house this capital city grew up around and forgot. Two stories, probably three bedrooms upstairs, downstairs dining room, study, front parlor maybe, kitchen, bath. Probably a basement for a furnace. Or whatever.

Almost looked like a real home.

Until you settled it in your eyes *just so*.

Saw the black iron fence around the double-lot property was more than hip-high to discourage hoppers without encouraging stares. Saw that though the house's white peeling paint looked like it could use another coat, there was a sheen over the whole structure, a reflective lacquer you couldn't buy in any hardware store. And the first-floor windows: tinted isn't the right word, for though they shone a quiet blue in both sunshine and moon glow, those windows let in light but not sight, let out vision but not voltage. Their glass was thick, far beyond the muscle of any rock-throwing neighborhood hooligan. The two doors over the front portal looked no more formidable than the doors you drive past in any crime-conscious American neighborhood, but looks . . .

Well, looks are as looks see.

What else Condor saw from the parked stolen car let him know the robot woman hadn't erred in bringing him here. A shed twice the size of that brown van from this morning rose a prudent distance from the house. Though no thick black wires connected the shed to the house, Condor knew the windowless and lightning-grounded shed held an emergency generator and sat on a vast underground fuel tank, just like he knew the glass rectangles on the house's roof that he could barely see through strategically planted trees, those glass panels were solar converters, *just in case* or even *just because*. And there was no mistaking one - *no*: three satellite dishes amidst the gables pointing up from the top-story windows where bedrooms awaited sweet surrenders of *yes, yes, yes*.

A nine-year-old dented tan American sedan sat in the pebbled driveway.

The car looked like it seldom saw any extended roads.

Why leave when you're already there.

Here: Tier Zero.

Like a movie director, Condor whispered: 'And . . . *action*.'

Opened the stolen car's door and climbed out to the street.

Knew security cameras watched him walk toward the house.

Worried not so much: he could have been made dead when he drove up.

Bet every badge & Black Ops gun is now dispatched to stay away from here.

Still, after he unlatched the black iron fence gate and crunched over the pebbled path to the front porch, he filled his hand with the .45.

If you're not bringing flowers . . .

His left fingers brushed the handle on the aluminum storm door.

No blast of electricity.

No trapdoor sprang open under his shoes to swallow him into the long fall.

No sound of an alarm.

The aluminum door creaked when he opened it. He wrapped his gun-free left hand around the inner door's brass knob . . . *that turned*, opened the door.

A whiff of gasoline came out to the front porch.

Then - as fast & smoothly as a battered sixty-something shaved-bald man could - Condor charged into the house, into the long front hall, his back slamming the inner door shut, his .45 swooping left, right, aiming up the empty stairs leading to the second floor.

Hooks on the hall wall held a rain slicker, a parka retired by increasingly mild and snow-less winters, a faded brown (*not candy-pink*) hoodie and a New York designer hip-length brown coat of quality leather.

Some security camera's showing you crouched here, black leather jacket, gun.

Against one hall wall stood two red plastic five-gallon jugs labeled GASOLINE.

Combat stalk down the hall.

Scan your target environment over the barrel of your .45.

Brown hardwood floors, scuffed but kept dust free by an undercover janitorial crew from the NSA's complex at not-far-away Fort Meade who had no idea why they climbed into phony 'Maid Machine' vans to drive nearly to D.C. and clean a private house. But they knew the penalty for talking about this job fell under provisions of the Espionage Act of 1917 with a *maybe they'd skip the trial* penalty of death.

The walls were painted a soothing shade of ivory.

Dead ahead, at the end of the ten-steps hallway and before stairs to the second floor, the walls opened up, ceiling arches that in a regular house would reveal, *say*, a formal dining room off to the right, while off to the left would be the sitting room, the living room, the family room: call it what you will, what it was here wasn't that.

Condor kept his back against the hall wall as he eased toward the open rooms.

What he saw in that room to his right: a twentieth-century whiteboard wiped clean, file cabinets, stacks of computer disks, CPUs or internet servers.

Two Vietnam-era five-gallon metal gas cans squatted near those cyber slaves.

Condor cradled his heavy gun in the two-handed grip, elbows bent so the .45 that had served America for more than a hundred years pointed toward the ceiling. The cold black barrel rose past the centerline of his face, his eyes looked over the steel shaft's hole, the scent of gun oil & fired bullets, the hard tang of metal close enough for his lips to kiss as he double-gripped the thick butt and his finger curled on the curved trigger.

Now or never.

He leapt into what could have been a living room - zeroed the .45.

At her.

She sat cupped in the C-curve of a touchscreen desk.

That flat C-shaped desk surface tilted up to face her eyes and hands with vermilion fingernails, short for keyboarding. When, *like now*, the desktop's touchscreen was in sleep mode, rather than go dark, the desktop became translucent, so Condor could see her mostly bare desk held a double-edged dagger.

A letter opener on a desk without a single scrap of paper.

Her hair looked like rusted steel streaked with silver wires and curved on each side of her face but . . . but like it often wasn't brushed, not like today when it was glorious and red. Her skin was pale white. Call the dark blue outfit she wore a business dress, open at her neck, trim tailored waist, a comfortable skirt that knew how to cling and ride above her knees to reveal slim black-stockings-sheathed legs. From the room's open arched doorway where he stood aiming his gun at her, Condor couldn't tell if she still had freckles, though time would never have let her lose the laugh wrinkles on her face, high cheekbones, clean jaw, burning blue eyes. Her thin smile was a fresh lipstick slash of midnight crimson.

She dressed up for this.

For you.

Every great strategy begins with a diversion.

Her voice was a strong tenor.

'*You could have been a rock 'n' roll star,*' he'd once told her. She'd smiled.

Here and now, the words from her smile said: 'You always wanted a big gun.'

'I've got what I've got.'

'I hope that's enough.'

Nothing on her desk but the dagger that's at least six inches from her hand. Scan the room, the walls: shelves, books displayed like antiques, objets d'art or were they mementos, *both, whatever*, guns: no visible guns.

Gas cans near that wall of wispy blue windows.

She said: 'So this is how you look when you're old. I thought you'd keep your hair.'

'Some things gotta go.'

'Some things come back.'

Swing left, swing right, swing full circle and the world swirls past your gun sights and then it's back to her, on her. She hasn't moved. Looks right at you.

Says: 'It's just you and me, kid.'

'Nobody's a kid anymore.'

'Have you gone and gotten all responsible on me? All adult? All . . . sane?'

'More than I was before.'

'Is that going to be a problem?'

'You think so,' said Condor. 'That's why you tried to kill me.'

'Be fair: the Op was to put you back someplace where you'd be safe and taken care of and not stressed. The killing you only came after you fucked up the program.

'In all fairness,' she continued, 'haven't you ever made a mistake?'

Condor stared at her.

Lowered the .45 from a dead-center aim.

Holstered his weapon.

Felt his heart slamming against his ribs.

She said: 'So you didn't come here to kill me.'

'I didn't come here to die.'

'Why did you come here?'

He took one breath, took two before he said: 'You knew I was coming.'

'Your data lit up cyberspace.'

'You knew I was coming *before*,' he said. 'So you topped out my target index.'

'You showing up here like this, guess I was right.'

'Self-fulfilling prophecy.'

'If you can't fulfill yourself, who'll do it for you?'

Condor frowned. 'What I can't figure is, are you full of shit, stoned on power or did you go crazy, too, or did the program just swallow you into what it can do?'

'What do you care?'

'Once upon a time,' he said.

'Once upon a time,' she said.

'Confession,' she said. 'You looked good in the surveillance footage. I don't mind bald, but I like you the way you really are.'

She gave him a crimson frown. 'The woman Merle: is she my replacement?'

'She was never a *promoted colleague*. A *conflict*. A *co-whatever* all we were.'

'Just a co-conspirator. A collaborator.'

'She's a person who cared - '

' - and couldn't get out of the way of Condor. Is she dead? I haven't looked.'

'There's nothing there for you to see.'

'How about for you?' Oh, that smile that knows you well. *Knew* you well.

Condor drifted to his left - her right, she's right-handed, the dagger or whatever weapon, she'll prefer to use her right hand that's lying flat and empty on the desktop.

'Why didn't you run?' he said. 'Ten strokes on a keyboard and you could have vanished into some wealthy widow sunbathing on the shores of a luxury sea.'

'Why go be somewhere when right here I can be everywhere?'

'Time and space are more than an illusion.'

'Depends on your data.

'Besides,' she said, 'maybe I was waiting for you.'

'Why?'

'Everybody needs somebody to talk to. Life is call and response.'

'And that's what you want from me. Now?'

'I want what I can get. One way or the other, you're going to give it to me.'

'What about . . .' He nodded at her desktop portal to the world.

'Whatever I - *we* - get will be a change they can be made fine with.'

'Are people getting nervous? Squeamish about the V? Is that why I suddenly became an imminent threat, because me in that mix *getting sane* . . . ?'

'People are always nervous. That's why they've got me. And you.'

'Together.'

'Again.' She shrugged. 'Control was always too complex a job for just one person. We made it work. A new *us* could be fun. And of course, vital.'

'What about all the cans of gas?'

'I'm a careful girl.'

'And if you can't be control, well then . . .'

'Why wish that on anybody else?'

'Except me.'

She smiled. 'Or us.'

'Or maybe just us *for a while*. Keeping your options open. Ready to reboot.'

'My life is purpose, is about what's crucial, what needs to be done.'

'Having that agent crucified on my - '

'He was worse than an incompetent asshole and a drunk. He was selling *sources & methods* intel to a private contractor. Fool thought he was just cashing in on what the private sector was going to get in five years anyhow. Such a terrible agent he didn't realize his buyers were fronts leading back to a terrorist group.'

'So you terminate him and use that to frame me, two birds with one crucifixion. But what about killing that guy Chris? Merle and crashing everything into Faye?'

'They're more than just names.'

'Yeah,' said Condor. 'They're people.'

'They're data points of cause and effect. Maybe threat matrix computations and outcomes got a little out of control, but whose fault is that?'

'Whoever made them into *ones* or *zeroes* choices.' Condor shook his head. 'Not me.'

'Really? Or were they consequences of something you created, something you did?'

'You took over.'

'When you malfunctioned, I was there. You put me there. Here.

'And what I do,' she said, 'what the V does, what you did, you know it's true: if we don't do it, we'll get it done to us. We stop the worst there is before it becomes real.'

She's shifting in her chair, keeping her eyes on you as you move around her desk.

Like a child, she said: 'I finally like doing that thing you liked me to do.'

Gas cans, guns, dagger, hidden buttons: what weapon?

'And now you're here,' she said. 'But instead of being the *what-if* whacko we both know you are, you're acting like the data indicated and predicted you might. Only this time, looks like you really might have a chance to destroy and deactivate like you failed to last time, back when you went crazy. Are you crazy now?'

'Who knows,' he said. 'How about you?'

'Who cares,' she told him. Sighed. 'I am lonely.

'But you know about that, too,' she said. 'That was why you recruited me.'

'No,' he argued. 'You were the best of the Girl Scouts. The best of all those women CIA analysts who got Bin Laden after you came to work with me.'

'Maybe,' she allowed. Nylons crackled as she crossed her legs, their black-sheathed slimness slipping out from her skirt *oh God she's wearing the black garter belt* and she said: 'It was so . . . touching how hard you worked to not let my legs matter.'

You're around the end of the desk now. Close enough to lunge. Grab her. Standing to her right side. Her eyes are pointed in front of her, but what she's watching, who she's seeing, is you.

The dagger lay on her plexiglass desktop. He let his fingers float out. Stroke the length of the shiny blade. Her hand resting beside the dagger trembled.

Perfume, she smells of opening flowers and magazine dreams.

'What about now?' he said, walking behind her chair.

Now you're behind her, the smell of her hair, dark roots she has to dye, *what good spy doesn't*, a thin gold strand lies on the V of soft white flesh below her bare throat, the necklace hangs down to where he can't see but you know it holds the amulet given her by a woman trapped & broken in a Darfur refugee camp.

She'd refused to cry when she told you that tale.

We are held together by the songs of our times.

'Now you're here,' she told the man looming behind her.

She didn't look. Let him be where he was like it didn't matter, like that was good.

Condor raked his fingers along the back of the tall black leather chair she sat in at her curved touchscreen desk that was years from being seen by the citizens of the country who'd paid for it. He felt the leather give under his fingers' scratch, wondered if she felt their pressure cross her back, kneading her flesh near her bra strap. If she wore a bra.

Then he was on her heart side.

She glanced up, blue eyes and a soft smile invitation.

Saw him looking at the technological marvel of her desktop.

Knew he was talking about the touchscreen that made minding the universe so simple a sixth grader could do it: 'Seems like we're always one upgrade behind.'

'Think how I feel,' she said.

And he did.

'After all,' she said, 'I've been around a little longer than you.'

She turned her lean V face toward the man bent over her desk. Slowly - oh so slowly - raised her left hand to brush away the red hair falling across her sky eyes.

Said: 'Being older is more interesting. I'm glad you never minded.'

He raised his gun-empty right hand. Held it palm out toward the inclined desktop screen. Said: 'Like this?'

He felt the *chi* in her change even as the screen in front of his right palm lit up from the heat of a human. Tension flowed from her as she stretched her head toward heaven to better see over his hand with its remembered stroke of her flesh.

Condor karate-chopped her throat.

Her crimson head bounced off the black leather executive chair.

Grab her skull and chin whirl & twist!

He heard the snap of her spine and let go, *let go*, staggered away from the chair.

And what he'd done. What he hadn't delegated. Done not because it was part of a program. What he had the honest humanity, the guts to choose.

What worked better?

Who but you?

Condor staggered backwards. Hit the wall with his hips, the holstered .45 clunked. His left leg bumped something that vibrated: a five-gallon can of gas.

All over the house. Ferried here in the car he'd parked outside by a warrior, some nameless *wannabe hero*. What was left of dead dinosaurs now waited in war-surplus metal gas cans and ultra-new red plastic jugs to be spilled and sloshed and dumped on this fusion of the smartest we can be.

A roaring fireball of orange flames and black smoke movie in his mind.

Somehow the .45 ended up in his hand.

He lifted it up to consider.

Heard: *Who's left to shoot?*

32

INTO THE VACUUM OF HIS EYES
- Bob Dylan, 'Like a Rolling Stone'

Faye sat on an American front porch.

She wore a pink hoodie though her sore, scabbed head was bare to the sinking sun.

Gone was the ballistic vest she'd worn for most of the last three days.

Stone-faced handlers had it now. They'd shown up seventeen minutes after cops who'd been radioed to obey *Agent On Scene* and stay out of the 911 *dispatched to residence*. Later, inside that house, a sweatsuit medic dressed her wound. Faye didn't bother to wait until he was gone before pulling the white bandage off, he didn't bother to tell her *no*. An innocent-looking moving van showed up, let neighbors watching from their front porches and windows see its crew dolly out a refrigerator box, a washer/dryer box.

Merle . . .

They took Merle out in a horizontal box labeled *mattress*.

Opened that cardboard as soon as they'd lifted it to hidden deep in the van.

Sure they did.

Faye didn't see the movers get rid of the glass jar of eyeballs in the refrigerator. She didn't want to know about that. She didn't want to be part of that.

But I do. And I am.

Faye listened while a bone-tired woman from Sami's team worked out the cover story to dribble to this cul-de-sac's *looky-loos* and *street ears* and *tattle tongues* and *cell phone snappers*. Faye became *pink hoodie woman* became *real estate agent* shown up to prep for movers, found *squatters*, maybe a meth head cooking, saw a flash of something as the squatters boomed out the back door, over the fence, *gone* who knows where, cops checked the woods. How much of that the neighbors got & bought didn't matter, there was nothing over police scanners to attract an actual journalist who could publish a story.

Faye told the handlers *no* when they asked for her weapon.

Told them *no* when they asked *what happened*.

Told them *no* when they said *okay, time to leave*.

No one told her refusals *no*.

And the 911 cops left.

And the moving van left.

And the stone-faced handlers left.

All except for the bone-tired woman who worked for Sami plus two janitors in blue jeans and T-shirts and medical masks who'd be a long time washing white walls with their sponges and buckets of water & bleach. Well, one janitor was washing walls. The other one seemed only to be watching the bone-tired woman watch Faye.

We've all got a duty.

Faye said: 'I'll wait outside.'

Walked out to April's cool afternoon air, sat on the top stoop of the red concrete front porch like a pink hoodie teenager yearning for that better place to go.

She knew a bone-tired woman or a blue-jeaned janitor watched her from inside the house.

Faye watched the neighbors quit their vigils for what waited inside their homes, TV or computer screens or someone who loved you and you loved.

She watched the shadows of trees and utility poles lengthen across the gray pavement of the suburban cul-de-sac.

They took the car we stole.

And the man duct-taped in the trunk. No doubt he went someplace where it was worth his while never to have a story to tell, including to his bosses.

Someone came home across the cul-de-sac, frowned at a box he found left by a delivery service, but there was no brown van parked anywhere near he could take it to.

Evening's chill reached through the long sunlight of this Saturday afternoon.

Would be rough to sleep outside in a cemetery tonight.

The car driving into the cul-de-sac could have been anybody's mobility machine.

Silver paint, four or five years old, nothing special for a steady paycheck. Faye didn't bother scanning the license plates after the windshield showed her who sat behind the steering wheel, who was alone in that steel and glass. The silver car drove around the cul-de-sac, cranked hard left - braked to a stop facing the center of the cul-de-sac. If the car had a standard transmission, the driver was smooth: white backup lights joined the red brake lights without grinding gears. The car parked with its rear tires touching the curb in front of the house with five red cement steps where Faye sat wearing a pink hoodie.

The older man who drove the car got out and walked toward her.

Faye felt whoever was behind her in the house draw away from the windows, from being able to hear a thing said outside on the front porch. She waited until the man from the silver car reached the bottom of the steps.

Then said: 'What took you so long?'

'We're here now.' Sami gave her a sad smile. 'How are you, Faye?'

'Fan-*fucking*-tastic.'

'Your Chris was a good man. Better. There are no words for our kind of sorry.'

'*Our kind of sorry?* Is that all you've got? What took you so long to get here?'

'Twenty steps from the launch car, my cell phone goes crazy. Calls I gotta take. Then a place I gotta be.' He shrugged. 'Few places, actually.'

Faye said: 'Where's Condor?'

'That's what this is about,' said Sami.

He wore a shopping-mall tan Windbreaker plausibly unzipped to the cooling air. His shirt and khakis could have come to him via the internet and a brown van. Faye knew that under that banal Windbreaker, there'd be a belt and a holster on that belt for a pistol, *fuck it, fuck him.* He stood there, aged as more than an older brother, less than father, gray-flecked curly short hair, teenage-fled Lebanon fostered in Detroit raised by the Marine Corps. There'd be a gun in an ankle holster, too. Sincerity in his soft sad smile that could cut to your core. And might.

Sami said: 'Who's Condor?'

'Don't fuck with me.'

'Never,' he said. 'But I've got to give you a choice.'

'Is he dead?'

'Let's say there is or was someone by that identifier. It's been used so much that both *yes* and *no* to your question are true.'

'*What the* . . . To cover your ass or . . . or who knows why, you could do a maximum-cover drop on Condor, fog who he really was and what he really meant until all that was more like some novel or movie than real. But why bother, even if it's to keep cover on the scandal, "*runaway rogue spy whatever*," call it V, but . . .'

Faye blinked.

Sami came back into focus.

'You're the verifier,' she said. 'That's why it's you here instead of him. So I would believe. So I would . . .

'He's gone back in,' whispered Faye. 'He took out the V and the community took him back in.'

'Close,' said Sami.

'There is no close,' said Faye. 'He beat *them* or *it* - '

'*Her*,' interrupted Sami.

Faye felt her jaw drop.

Didn't stop: 'He either took out the V and *her* or they took him out. And if you're here, he won, but is he fucking alive?'

'*Yeah.*'

Sunset bled the sky a redder pink than the wrap she wore.

'What's important for you to realize,' said Sami, 'what matters for you, is that he's alive, and the person who recklessly green-lit the man you loved and risked, that person, that woman . . . *Dead.*'

'So I owe him one.'

'Good to hear you say that,' said Sami.

Faye's stomach went cold.

'You owe yourself, too,' he told her.

The woman in the pink hoodie sitting on an American porch listened to the man who'd come there to . . . *To what?*

'The V,' said Sami. 'Not one entry in our whole Intelligence Community. Yet it's everywhere - and that's saying something. Our IC budget is fifty billion a year.

'That could change.' He shrugged. 'Go down some, these things have a cycle. Are keyed to wars, crises. Or us getting caught wild in the streets like . . . Poor Chris.'

'Whatever you're doing,' said Faye, 'don't use him. You owe me that much.'

Recognition slid along their stare.

'We were talking about cycles,' said Sami. 'The V predicted it, which surprised the hell out of newspaper names I had to meet with instead of responding to your call. All it takes is a triggering event to send a cycle one way or the other. Condor could have been a trigger for the system having to deal with the V and what it is.'

'What it does - *did*,' said Faye. 'All illegal.'

'Illegal is a term of law decided by courts and presidential signatures,' said Sami.

'You've got to be fucking kidding me with that.'

'What, your "*moral authority*"? That seldom triumphs in a Beirut back alley.'

'Targeting Condor and Chris was not a Beirut alley, that was the V not wanting to be accountable for how and why they whack people.'

'High value, high risk, high impact, hostile targets.'

'Everyone qualifies as that kind of homicide to somebody, sometime,' said Faye. 'There are laws, due process.'

'Exactly,' said Sami. 'What the processes do.

'One of the triggers in the cycles, maybe tomorrow, maybe the next day, some scandal or leak will blow a window into the IC, say NSA sucking up every email, every phone call, every website and traffic. Maybe there'll be a public uproar, though I think not so much. The public - that great *whoever* - they already think all this is happening, but they just don't think it's happening to them, so *who cares, what can you do*? And the V is just the logical progression, merging software and necessity and probabilities.'

'Data isn't truth,' said Faye.

'Right, but we're damned to knowing only data and damned to having to do something about it. Or have something about it done to us. The V, when has such a wondrous capability ever been discarded? Only practical, smart, to recognize that.'

'You want to be Big Brother, Sami?'

'There is no Big Brother, only Big Us.

'And in that us, there's *u* and the *s*, and the *s* can mean *the system* or it can mean *the shit* not necessarily of how you get to live, but certainly of whether you get a chance to be somebody who is more than just counted, to be somebody who does the counting.

'Being just *u* sucks, my friend, my comrade in arms, my colleague. But being *u* connected to the *s*, being *us* . . . That's a life where you can do something worth doing.'

'The V,' whispered Faye. 'Condor didn't beat it, didn't destroy it.'

'He is it,' said Sami. 'Now. But only partially.'

'Yeah,' said Faye, 'he's got you.'

'You don't get it yet.' Sami put one foot on the bottom red cement step and held on to the porch's black steel railing so he could lean closer and confide to Faye.

'The V didn't get out of hand,' he told her, 'the V got into the wrong hands, and that's been corrected. All the people who know what we know recognize that human error shouldn't cause us to ignore inevitable capability.'

'There's always human error, Sami. Unless you turn it all over to the machines.'

'What are we, nuts?'

He pushed his hand against her glare. 'Don't give me yet another singularity scenario. What it comes down to is who's the heart and mind of *us*, of control. Someone should have that job who knows just how horribly wrong the whole thing can go.'

'Condor,' she whispered.

'And you,' said Sami.

Call it sundown in a suburban Saturday cul-de-sac.

'What do you mean: *me*?'

'Who better to be the V than you who knows how bad it can be?'

'Condor . . . And you . . . ?'

'And you. Three of us. A triangle. The strongest shape.'

'That's a sphere,' said Faye.

'Fuck your metaphors and mind games,' said Sami. 'You know the system is there. You know it went wrong. You know it's never going to be scrapped. Forget the more than two hundred Top Secret offensive cyber-operations we do a year, things like worms turned loose in a rogue nation's nuclear bomb programs, TAOs, Tailored Access Programs like the Chinese hit us with all the time. The V is progression beyond that. We're going to be fighting whole wars like this. Living whole lives like this. We're all wired in together. Pretty soon it'll be more about *the wire* than it is about *the we*. Doesn't matter if you think that's not so smart. We're so smart we fight wars over burning gas made from dinosaurs that couldn't adapt and those ignitions cause pollution that's making the polar ice cap melt so chunks float off and you can watch it all happen with your cell phone, watch the chunk coming.

'You got a chance to do something right now,' said Sami. 'You can be part of the process so guys like Chris won't get shot. You can shape power or ...'

'*Or what*, Sami?' The Glock weighed on her belt. 'Or be deleted?'

'Never happen. Not on my watch. Not on Condor's.

'You're a hero, Faye. But you can't do shit about stopping the V or your biggest fans Condor and me. Who you going to tell, who's going to believe you, who's going to let you get away with being a traitor? You can go back to the Agency. Get any posting you want in the real world. You'll be a star without us. You can take their combat buyout, go build sand castles on the shore. Get a lucky not-Chris, get some kids, get old and gray and never know where you might have gone or the good you might have done.'

'Or?'

'Or find out.' Sami smiled. 'We want you and need you to be you with us.'

'Why are you doing this?'

'I know some of the streets in this night and what should be done.'

'Why him? Why Condor?'

'I think he discovered he's always been this kind of crazy.'

Sami stood back and settled in his shoes, said: 'But it's up to you. Isn't that great? That's what all our fighting and dying is for, so it can be up to you.'

Feels like something is skimming the air above me, watching me.

The man who'd been sent to save her, get her, walked back and got in his silver car that was parked pointed out of this suburban cul-de-sac. Faye heard him key the engine, heard it rumble, purr. And in the gray light, she saw him lean across that car's front seat.

Heard the clunk, saw the slow swing of gaping metal create a choice for her.

A waiting engine rumbled in that gray light.

As she stared at the car's empty front passenger *shotgun seat*.

At that car's open door.

RAVE ON

Wonderful artists & colleagues & inspirations, plus loyal fans & friends & trusting sources helped Condor *fly.* THANKS *to all of you, especially:*

Jack Anderson, Rick Applegate, James Bamford, Richard Bechtel, David Black, Hind Boutaljante, Jackson Browne, Buffalo Springfield, L.C., Michael Carlisle, Tracy Chapman, Tina Chen, Stephen Coonts, Citizen Cope, Dino De Laurentiis, Nelson DeMille, Sally Denton, Sally Dillow, Tom Doherty, The Doors, Faye Dunaway, Bob Dylan, Jean Esch, Bob Gleason, Bonnie Goldstein, H.G., Nathan Grady, Rachel Grady, John Grisham, Francois Guerif, Julien Guerif, Jeanne Guyon, Jeff Herrod, Seymour Hersh, John Lee Hooker, Richard Hugo, Stephen Hunter, The Kingston Trio, Starling Lawrence, LM, Ron Mardigian, Mark Mazzetti, Maile Meloy, Lee Metcalf, *The New York Times*, Roy Orbison, Jp, George Pelecanos, Otto Penzler, Seba Pezzani, Walter Pincus, Sydney Pollack, Kelly Quinn, David Rayfiel, Robert Redford, *Rivages Noir*, Cliff Robertson, S J Rozan, Derya Samadi, Roberto Santachiara, Lorenzo Semple, Jr., Yvonne Seng, David Hale Smith, Bruce Springsteen, Steely Dan, Jeff Stein, Buffy Ford Stewart, John Stewart, Roger Strull, Max von Sydow, Simon Tassano, Richard Thompson, Shirley Twillman, Paul Vineyard, BW, Jess Walter, *The Washington Post*, Tim Weiner, Les Whitten, David Wood, Bill Wood, The Yardbirds, Jesse Colin Young, Warren Zevon, and Anlan Zhang.

This double edition published in 2018 by
No Exit Press, PO Box 394, Harpenden,
Herts, AL5 1XJ, UK
noexit.co.uk

SIX DAYS OF THE CONDOR
© James Grady 1974, 2007
LAST DAYS OF THE CONDOR
© James Grady 2015
OUR CONDOR SKY
© James Grady 2018

A CIP catalogue record for this book is available from the British Library.

ISBN 978-0-85730-264-9 (double edition)

2 4 6 8 10 9 7 5 3 1

Typeset by Avocet Typeset, Somerton, Somerset
in 13.5pt Bembo
Printed and bound in Denmark by Nørhaven, Viborg

For more information about Crime Fiction go to @crimetimeuk

NO EXIT PRESS
UNCOVERING THE BEST CRIME

'A very smart, independent publisher delivering the finest literary crime fiction' – *Big Issue*

MEET NO EXIT PRESS, the independent publisher bringing you the best in crime and noir fiction. From classic detective novels, to page-turning spy thrillers and singular writing that just grabs the attention. Our books are carefully crafted by some of the world's finest writers and delivered to you by a small, but mighty, team.

In our 30 years of business, we have published award-winning fiction and non-fiction including the work of a Pulitzer Prize winner, the British Crime Book of the Year, numerous CWA Dagger Awards, a British million copy bestselling author, the winner of the Canadian Governor General's Award for Fiction and the Scotiabank Giller Prize, to name but a few. We are the home of many crime and noir legends from the USA whose work includes iconic film adaptations and TV sensations. We pride ourselves in uncovering the most exciting new or undiscovered talents. New and not so new – you know who you are!!

We are a proactive team committed to delivering the very best, both for our authors and our readers.

Want to join the conversation and find out more about what we do?

Catch us on social media or sign up to our newsletter for all the latest news from No Exit Press HQ.

f fb.me/noexitpress 🐦 @noexitpress
noexit.co.uk/newsletter